The Sins of Our Fathers

Also by Åsa Larsson in English

The Savage Altar
The Blood Spilt
The Black Path
The Second Deadly Sin
Until Thy Wrath be Past

Åsa Larsson

THE SINS OF OUR FATHERS

Translated from the Swedish by
Frank Perry

MACLEHOSE PRESS
QUERCUS · LONDON

First published as *Fädernas Missgärningar* by Albert Bonniers Förlag in Stockholm, Sweden
First published in Great Britain in 2023 by

MacLehose Press
An imprint of Quercus Editions Limited
Carmelite House
50 Victoria Embankment
London EC4Y 0DZ

An Hachette UK company

ISBN (HB) 978 0 85705 174 5
ISBN (TPB) 978 0 85705 175 2
ISBN (Ebook) 978 0 85738 999 2

10 9 8 7 6 5 4 3 2 1

Designed and typeset in Minion by CC Book Production
Printed and bound in Great Britain by Clays Ltd, Elcograf S.p.A.

The Sins of Our Fathers

TUESDAY 26TH APRIL

Living became a bit easier once Ragnhild Pekkari had made up her mind to die.

She had a plan. To ski across the crust the night frost left on the snow, a two-hour trip unless you broke through it. When she got to the spot, a *jokk* across which a snow bridge would always form, she would light a fire and enjoy one last cup of coffee. Afterwards she would melt snow and pour it into her rucksack to make it heavy and wet and to push any air out. Then she would ski onto the snow bridge. There would be open water flowing beneath. If all went to plan the bridge would collapse. If not, she would push herself over the edge with a quick thrust of her ski poles.

It would happen incredibly quickly. No chance to change your mind, not with skis on and a sodden rucksack that refused to float.

And then it would finally be over.

She had made an appointment with death. And meet it she would – on the very day she had chosen – but not in the way she had imagined.

Once the appointment had been made, the worst of the weight was lifted. Her being grew tall like the birches in the woods. The winter snow had hunched them into frozen arches. Now that winter was giving way to the mildness of spring they were straightening up, shifting from grey to violet, the liturgical colour of penance.

She had begun her retirement in June the previous year. The head of the clinic gave an obviously unprepared speech, getting the number of years she had been employed there wrong, even though it would have been so simple to check. That little shit. He was the kind of doctor who felt threatened by her height. His right hand, Elisabeth from the management team, had shopped for the present: a bottle opener in the shape of a silvery dolphin. That was it, after all those years. Elisabeth had been working in admin for more than twenty years and was completely out of touch with what the other nurses actually did on the wards. She was firmly on the side of management and kept piling on the pressure with additional duties and mean-spirited schedules. And then, to top it all off, a silver dolphin. Ragnhild managed to squeeze out an insincere thank you, which made her feel like going home and cleaning out her mouth with wire wool.

The entire farewell do, with its cheap paper serviettes and shop-bought cake, was enough to make her sick. Some of the doctors had come into the break room and then left. Ragnhild had exchanged looks with the other nurses: odd the doctors never came when paged if a patient was ill but would always move faster than light towards anything sweet. "What are we celebrating?", one of the junior doctors had asked with his mouth full.

When her last shift was over, there was a round of hugs with her colleagues. She stood for a while in front of the locker that had been hers for almost thirty years, shut it for the very last time and left the hospital with a sense of unreality and that bloody dolphin in a bag.

After that, summer had gone by as usual; it had just felt like a really long holiday. Autumn arrived, and she established new routines. She signed up for an advanced course in weaving together with a retired former colleague. She exercised every day, went to the gym or hiking in the woods. She read books, of course, almost one a day.

The first half of winter passed. She knew that they were short-staffed at work, but no-one called her to fill in. Elisabeth hated her and clearly did not want her back.

She spent Christmas on her own. It was astonishingly lonely. She had always worked the major holidays before.

A memory from childhood came to her at the beginning of March, one Monday as she was on her way back from the shop, bags in hand.

She can't have been that old, six maybe. She had gone out on the ice with one of her uncles who was chucking an old boat engine through a hole he had sawn out in the surface. Her aunt had been rinsing the sheets there that very day, so he was taking the opportunity to get rid of a load of junk. Pushing old fridges and so on out onto the ice was not unusual at the time. They would sink to the bottom once the ice had melted. But since there was a hole there anyway, you could chuck stuff in before it froze over. She had stood at the edge of the hole. Her uncle had not warned her to keep away. She watched the heavy engine splash into the water and sink slowly, almost drifting, until it reached the bottom with a soft thud.

She was remembering the dizzy feeling when she looked into the depths. The danger of standing that close, the slow hypnotic downward dance of the engine in the sunbeams. It felt like she was being drawn in, as though she was going to fall and drift down herself. The cloud of mud when the engine landed ever so quietly.

And that was how it felt. She had been walking along holding the plastic bags after doing her weekly shop when her engine had thudded to the bottom. Nine months after retirement she found herself thinking: I've had enough.

The relief was enormous. She decided to go on living until the end of winter. Then stop before the season changed into the one known as "the sigh", when the snow lay in a thick blanket that would neither take your weight nor give way completely but fall apart every now and then with a muffled sigh.

She went skiing in the woods in March and April. Every day, in sunshine or a blizzard, it made no difference. She would light a fire on the sunny days and sit on the mat made of the skin from a reindeer's skull and have coffee and a sandwich. She didn't read books anymore. She looked inwards and marvelled at the stillness. At the strange power to almost completely dispel the muddy turbulence inside her that had come with her decision.

At the end of April she began death cleaning. But not too thoroughly. The cleaning was not supposed to make it clear she'd committed suicide. The very thought of people cocking their heads and saying, "She must have been so lonely."

No, it needed to look like an accident. There would be fresh produce in the fridge. She took her winter jacket to be cleaned. Would anyone planning on killing herself take clothes to the dry cleaner's? She left the pink ticket in plain sight on the counter beside the kettle.

Outside, water was dripping off the icicles hanging from the gutters, a monotonous plinking sound that sped up as spring drew closer. Snow was slipping off the roofs in a rush and melting off the asphalt streets. The day was fast approaching. The night crust was still skiable and that was a crucial requirement.

During the cleaning she gave a lot of thought to the photos of her daughter. They couldn't remain in their usual places, inserted in Ragnhild's favourite novels on the bookshelves. There was a risk the books would end up at the charity shop for next to nothing. In that event the pictures of Paula couldn't be allowed to fall out. The talk that would give rise to. "Why did she keep pictures of her daughter in her books? What a strange person . . ." They would pity her. And that was not going to happen, under any circumstances.

So what to do? Should she frame them and set the photos out? Burn them? She held them for a while. Here was Paula at the age of two, beaming hugely with ice cream all over her face and a tiara on her head. At five on her first mountain walk to Trollsjön, a warm day, the fell was covered in flowers and all she had on was pants and a cloth hat. She rolled around in the patches of snow. Ragnhild had carried her on her shoulders when she got tired.

I was as tough as a mountain birch tree, she was thinking. Backpack and a kid going up the mountain. That was really something.

She picked up a summer photo from the seaside at Piteå that showed Paula hugging her grandmother, and then there were the usual school snaps with that dull blue background and a smile that wasn't a smile, just the distended mouth of a child, and something akin to fear in her eyes.

Ragnhild looked warily through the pictures, taking short shallow breaths and sitting very still. There was a beast still living inside her that could stir. She had to be on the lookout. She was afraid of the mother beast. It could come crawling up from its lair, rolling its eyes and bristling all over. Angry, hurt, and completely indiscriminate. Filled with a desire to explain, to put right, to seek forgiveness, to point the finger at any accomplices. Make phone calls.

In the end she put the photos of Paula in a drawer in her desk.

The windows needed cleaning; but this wasn't that kind of clean. Only things that were private needed to be got rid of. Besides, a home that was too clean could also make her seem like some poor soul without a life. No, someone else would have to deal with the windows.

When the last day arrived she went ahead exactly as planned. In the evening she packed her rucksack with the kind of heavy objects that would seem natural for her to have brought along: a Trangia stove, an old winter tent, a bottle of wine, her winter sleeping bag, a reindeer pelt, a down jacket.

She gave the plants an extra watering. They hadn't done anyone any harm, after all.

She pulled the Bible off the bookshelf.

"In case you've got something to tell me," she said to God.

She let it fall open at random. And found herself reading a chapter in the Book of Judges where Jael kills the military commander Sisera. While he is sleeping she takes a tent peg and creeps up on him with a mallet and drives the peg through his temple hard enough to pin his head to the ground.

"You're a real laugh, you are," Ragnhild said gruffly to Our Lord. "Like some grumpy old sod in the attic who has an opinion about everything but does nothing."

She shut the Bible on those meaningless verses.

When the nightly detonation in the mine occurred at one o'clock, a faint tremor ran through the building. She lay down on her bed at that point and dozed for a bit.

At 2.30 a.m. she closed the door to her flat for the last time. She didn't feel anything in particular. In her mind she went through her usual refrain, "nothing running, nothing burning", and turned the key in the lock.

She stowed her skis and rucksack in the car. The true midnight sun would not arrive for another three weeks, but even now there was a feeble brightness to the nights. Kiruna was silent apart from the noises from the mine that could be heard even more distinctly at this time of night when there was no traffic to drown them out. There was the screech as the ore trains braked, the thud when the brakes were released and the laden trains rolled away. The sonic overlay of the fans at the shaft.

Though the sounds were still surprisingly subdued now that the mine was devouring this bloody town from below.

She didn't see another human being as she drove out of Kiruna. It felt like it had been abandoned, depopulated. Like it had already been evacuated.

Before long she was on the E10. She thought for a bit about how long it would be before they had to call in a locksmith to break into her flat. She no longer had any colleagues to ask after her, but she had her weekly hobbies, yoga, exercise class and the tail end of her weaving course. It shouldn't be more than two weeks before someone noticed she was missing.

She turned east towards Vittangi. The road followed her home river, the Torne. She was thinking about the thaw, the trees coming into leaf, the chatter of birds, the midnight sun. She cast around inside but was unable to detect any desire to be part of that; there was nothing she wanted to experience yet again.

She did not turn on the car radio; the only other vehicles she encountered were a few ore trucks. The asphalt was dry and full of potholes from frost damage over the winter.

She parked in a spot the ploughs had cleared. She carried her skis and walked along the main road, looking for a place where the bank of cleared snow was a little lower so she could wriggle over its frosty uneven ridge. All she bloody needed was to break her arms and legs and be left lying there.

The moment she had crossed the ridge she was in the woods. She looked behind her, but the car and the road were hidden by the embankment of snow, they were gone.

The bramblings were already at it. Lots of them this year. The sound made you feel like you had stepped into a tropical rainforest. It made the feeling she always got on entering the woods, that she was leaving one world behind and entering another, more intense. And as always she felt the forest was like a mother. A female divinity, the Sami goddess Máttáráhkka maybe, who was bidding her welcome. Like running home from the roughhouse of the school yard to a mother who quietly closed the door of a refuge where no-one could get to you.

Just her and the forest now. The copper sheen on the pines. Tall old fir trees and their grey underskirts. With the low morning sun pale in the south east and the white full moon in the north west, the sky ranged from pink to light blue. They were shining at each other, entwining their lights like the wire the Sami made from pewter.

She fastened her cross-country skis and with a light shove of her poles slid away across the crust the night had frozen. It was hard and shiny. Staying upright when your skis kept slipping to the side required a good deal of skill. Below the trees where melting snow had dripped the crust was extra hard, like thick granular glass. If the sun got too hot this morning, breaks in the surface would form, and she would be forced to ski over the patches that were still frozen.

The crust could still take her weight though, and it was wonderfully easy to ski on. The steel edges of her skis left barely a trace. She could hear a few ravens. At a distance you could easily confuse the sound with the barking of a dog. Just a little while later and they came flying into view above her, scouting the ground and cawing to each other.

She lost any sense of the passage of time and was surprised when she heard the sound of rushing water. Was she there already? She looked at her watch. Half past five. She skied the last bit through pussy willows and osiers, their woolly catkins already out.

She followed the *jokk* downstream until she reached the snow bridge. It was still there. Like a handsome span of snow and ice thrown across the torrent.

She was going to have her coffee first though. There was a little

hillock just twenty metres from the bridge. At its top was a lovely mountain pine, a gnarled dwarf variety. Enough bare soil had emerged from
the melted snow around the trunk for her to sit there and make her fire.

She gathered deadwood and some bits for kindling: grey pine twigs,
birch bark, beard lichen and juniper branches. She made a hole in the
frozen crust and filled the coffee pot and the pan with water. She didn't
dare make her way over to the *jokk* to get water; the banks were too icy.
She had no intention of falling in. The flaw in the logic of her caution
made her smile and shake her head. But she was going to do this her way.

She got the fire going by striking her flint. She was proud of that, of
her ability to light a fire anywhere and in any weather, without having
to get a matchbox out. She had had the same box of matches for over
five years now. How ridiculous, though: bragging to yourself about
something like that.

Her phone rang just as the coffee started to boil. She could have keeled
over in surprise. She lifted the coffee pot off the stove and extricated
her phone from her inner pocket. It was three minutes past six. The
number was a landline. Who rang from a landline these days? And it
was an 0981 number, the area code of the village she grew up in.

She stared suspiciously at the phone. It was several years since she
had spoken with anyone from there. But it kept ringing. And finally
she answered.

A man was on the other end. From his voice he sounded young.

"You Ragnhild Pekkari?" he asked. "*No sitten* . . . Well then," he said
in Torne Valley Finnish, her own mother tongue. "I've got what I think
might be some bad news."

The man at the other end told her his name and explained that he owned the village shop in Junosuando.

"I'm ringing about your brother," he said, "Henry Pekkari. He hasn't been to the shop for the last three weeks."

Ragnhild realised she ought to say something. But that notion went weak at the knees, it had to try and fumble its way to the front of her brain like a patient on Valium. Not a word passed her lips. The shop owner continued:

"It could be nothing though. Only, Henry usually comes in every Thursday when we get the weekend deliveries from the alcohol monopoly. Hello, *oletko sielä*?"

"Yes, I'm here," Ragnhild managed to say.

"Oh right, I thought we'd been disconnected. Anyway, there have been times he hasn't turned up of course. Like now when the ice is getting a bit iffy. He might be stuck on the island. And that could last for weeks. It's just in that event he'd call as a rule. He's out there in that house all on his own, isn't he, so when he can't make the trip, he phones to let us know. The people here in the shop are the only ones he gets to meet and talk to after all. I've been trying to get through to him, yesterday and this morning. But he isn't answering."

"Is that right?" Ragnhild said in a tone of voice she knew made others feel as though they were a Jehovah's Witness on the porch, holding out a colour pamphlet announcing the imminent advent of the kingdom of God.

A tone she had occasionally used on relatives who were being difficult, on the head of the clinic and his team rather frequently.

She looked at the pot. The coffee was already cold. She could re-boil it but it would taste like cat's piss.

Serves me right, she thought. My last cup will be one of those iced coffees.

"In any case," the shop owner said, "I thought you might have heard from him."

"I haven't had any contact with Henry for thirty-one years," Ragnhild Pekkari said. "You must know that. Like everyone else in Junis."

"You're brother and sister all the same, so I thought I should ring you anyway," the shopkeeper said defensively.

She noticed that he said "I thought" in every other sentence. Even though he couldn't really think past the end of his nose.

"Well, sorry for disturbing you," the shopkeeper said in conclusion. "I actually rang the police in Kiruna first. But they said there was no way they could land a helicopter on the island when the snow's like mashed potato."

He was about to hang up. She could imagine him saying to the people who worked with him: "That Ragnhild Pekkari's not bloody right in the head, it was like she couldn't care less."

Then she heard herself asking:

"There's just one thing . . . when Henry came over to do the shopping, did he usually buy dog food?"

"Not a clue," the shopkeeper said. "I hardly ever work the till. Hang on and I'll ask the wife. Don't go away."

To judge by his voice he seemed happier for not having been completely dismissed. Ragnhild regretted her question. She considered hanging up, turning the phone off and pretending the call had been disconnected. But then the shopkeeper was back on the line.

"Yes, he did," he could tell her now. "Henry used to buy dog food."

And Ragnhild turned her face to the pale-blue sky. She tried to ward off the memory of Villa, the bitch whose name meant wool in the language Ragnhild spoke as a child.

Villa who had small kindly eyes and a white star on her breast. Villa who could flush birds, track elk, who herded the cows and spent the summer nights hunting field mice. Villa who slept at the foot of her bed in the winter.

Villa who had stayed on the island with Henry. That would have been, Good Lord she had to work it out, fifty-four years ago. When Henry was eighteen and was left in charge of her island home. When she was twelve and had to move to the town with her mother and father and her foster sister Virpi. Ragnhild had wept and begged for Villa to come with them but what she wanted counted for nothing. "Villa cannot live in a flat in town," her father had said. He had not realised that applied to all of them. None of them were made for flats or the town. As it would turn out.

Ragnhild failed to keep the memory at bay. A wodge of tears was swelling in her throat. Over Villa, who had been dead for so long.

The shopkeeper was speaking at the other end. Ragnhild hawked up some kind of thank you. A phrase that sounded odd in her mouth. Then she ended the call.

She poured coffee over the hissing flames. The grounds looked like an anthill on top. She tore up some moss from a patch of bare soil under the pine tree and cleaned the coffee pot. Then she packed her things into the backpack and put her skis back on.

The snow bridge would still be here. You could still ski over the crust for another week. She would be coming back. Only now there was that dog on the island. She couldn't abandon it to its fate.

Henry, you drunken bastard, what did you need with a dog?

As she was skiing back she came across a hen capercaillie. It was in season and completely unafraid of people, the way they are at that time. It ran across her skis, followed her tracks, and kept rising into the air with a flap of those heavy wings so as not to be left behind. Maybe it was Ragnhild's ski poles that stirred the mating drive in the poor bird. Anything that moved and flapped would seem like a cock playing the same game. It wasn't unusual for game birds to end up in the school yard during mating season. They were drawn to all those lively kids at play. Ragnhild's mother used to say the birds were drawn to children as though they possessed maternal instincts that applied to human kids as well. Ragnhild had dismissed any such notion as completely idiotic. The capercaillie accompanied her for almost two kilometres, a helpless prey to its feelings.

"Just stop," Ragnhild said aloud. "It's not worth it."

Ragnhild skied on. Death behind her for the moment, she thought. But death is always waiting ahead of us. It was so very close now.

Ragnhild Pekkari arrived in the village of Kurkkio just after nine in the morning. She parked outside Fredriksson's old shop, took her skis and poles under her arm and made her way down to the river. The snow had been cleared all the way to the sauna on the shore. She peered across at the island. It was a lot warmer now, several degrees above zero. The ice was treacherous, that she knew; it might be metres thick but it was soft. If you broke through, you'd sink into a quagmire of snow and slush.

There were old snowmobile tracks running here and there across the river to the island though. In the sun they shone like streets of glass. They might be able to take her weight. Otherwise she would have to wait until the next morning and ski over the frozen crust formed in the night. But she didn't want to wait, she couldn't. She was thinking about the dog. About Henry too, of course, but he was dead. She was certain of that. It was about bloody time.

Over there, just two hundred metres away, was her childhood home. Although it looked much the same from a distance, she could see, even from this far away, that half the barn roof had fallen in.

The rucksack had to be left in the car; she wanted to be as light as possible for this. She didn't dare click her shoes into the fastenings. She did not want to be trapped by her skis if she broke through. After an experimental shove with her poles she was off, sliding along a snow-mobile track that led to the island.

The ice in the track was wet and slippery; the skis kept wanting to veer away and her feet kept trying to slip out of them. This was a really bad idea, but once you've let the devil into your boat you have to row him to shore. She used her poles to move forward, keeping one of the skis in front of the other to distribute her weight as much as possible.

She peered at the holiday cottages along the shore. If there was anyone inside they would be watching her through binoculars and wondering who that lunatic was.

She was sweating profusely beneath her cap; so much salt was running off her forehead and into her eyes that they stung. But she didn't dare stop to take it off; that would mean standing still and putting all her weight on a single spot. You had to keep moving.

Now, halfway between the island and the mainland, the crust of ice on the track was getting thinner. The shadow off the edge of the wood and from the banked shore failed to reach this far and it had had sunlight shining on it day after day. She could hear the ice cracking under her skis, the thin sharp sounds of it splitting hammering wedges of terror into her resolve. The main current ran here somewhere as well, which made the ice under the tracks even thinner.

Only it was too late to turn back now, she'd have to get out of her skis for that and would be bound to fall through. She forced down images of cold black water and snowy slush closing over her head. Just keep going.

Forty metres from the island one of her skis went through the crust. There was a plopping sound and her leg disappeared beneath her as she tumbled to one side. An involuntary scream came from her throat, piercing and lonely. She crawled like an insect, pulling her leg out of the melting snow, feeling as if she was going to sink helplessly beneath it at any moment. The fear of death felt like a hare trying to escape from her chest.

She got onto all fours, not daring to stand up, and crept forward instead, one knee on the remaining ski, leaving the poles behind.

She swore her way forward.

"Bloody hell, bloody hell, bloody hell."

When she reached the shore she was hit by a wave of fatigue so powerful she could have fallen asleep sitting there in the snow. It was the second time that morning the fear of dying had caught her by surprise.

After all that was what she had been planning. Cold black water. But when it came down to it, she had fought her way to shore like a beetle whose legs have been chopped off.

So you may be a tablet-and-alcohol type after all, she thought, playing the contemptuous devil's advocate. The coward's way.

No, she defended herself against that accusing voice. Just not here. Not now. Not on my way to Henry.

Ragnhild trudged up towards the house. The sun was burning like a welding torch, a thousand reflections sparkling off the chalk-white snow. The moisture in the snow was forcing its way into her outer clothing and there was slush in her shoes.

She look around with a heavy heart. Thirty-one years since she was last here. She had been to see her brother then to tell him about their mother's death. She had tried ringing, but he had failed to answer. In the end she had driven here. A neighbour had taken her across in his boat.

The human misery that Henry wallowed in had left her cold. She told him he was welcome to attend the funeral but only on condition he was sober, no ifs or buts. He had snivelled something or other with the self-pity typical of an alcoholic and promised. A promise he had of course failed to keep. Someone from the village had dumped him outside the church in Junosuando. He looked like a rubbish heap in a suit that had seen better days. And there had been no shirt beneath his tie. They had persuaded the priest to delay the ceremony while someone went home to fetch one that might fit. The coffin went into the ground, and there and then beside her mother's grave Ragnhild broke off all contact, with phrases such as "never again" and "you aren't my brother anymore".

She hadn't managed to get rid of him though; she had thought of him with rage at some point every day. He kept a spacious two-bedroom apartment in her mind.

Virpi had not attended the funeral. Olle came, neatly pressed and polished to a shine with his stick-thin wife, the chief secretary of the local council. He had not been as unwilling to forgive Henry. Then again, it wasn't Olle who had spent his youth coming out here with *Äiti* to clean the house and wash Henry's filthy clothes every other weekend. In the end – she was over twenty by then – Ragnhild had refused to go with her. But *Äiti* kept at it. Until illness stopped her.

My bitter heart, Ragnhild thought. What am I supposed to do with you now *Äiti* and *Isä* are dead? Virpi too. Olle, God damn him, is in the best of health. So I'm not going to call him to let him know that Henry is dead.

Though maybe Henry wasn't dead. She might find him inside, drunk and incontinent.

She had reached the house now. It was still painted Falun red though there wasn't much paint left on the sunny side. *Äiti* had paid for it to be repainted in the last year of her life. The roof on the northern side buckled inwards like a hammock. A row of sticks as long as your arm stuck out of the gutter, and it took Ragnhild a while to realise they were birch saplings that had taken root and grown out of the muck because it never got cleaned.

The hay sheds were still there in the fields but the doors had fallen off and the snow had collected inside. They looked like dark, rickety creatures; the black holes where the doors had been like mouths open

23

in a soundless scream. Once, in another life, they had been well maintained and stood in the fields packed with dry fragrant hay. She and Virpi used to play inside them. They made cribs for themselves in the hay and read books for girls in the faint light that filtered through the cracks between the timbers. They used to jump around inside too, even though they weren't supposed to.

The whole farm was hunched over now. Aged prematurely. Tumbledown and ugly.

Please let Henry be dead, Ragnhild was thinking. Otherwise I'll end up killing him.

The snow had just about been cleared from the front yard. There were yellow patches of piss here and there.

The dog? she thought. Or Henry?

On the porch she stamped the snow off her shoes. The door was unlocked. The stench when she opened it struck her like a fist in the face. Piss. Booze. Filth.

All those years as a nurse came into their own. She turned off her nose, breathed through her mouth and went inside.

"Henry," she called.

No answer. The tiny hall led to the kitchen. The floor was covered with muck, you couldn't make out what colour it was anymore. Dirt had knocked the starch out of the limp curtains. The sills were covered with dead flies, the windows spotted with their excrement. The counter was cluttered with the packaging from ready meals along with rotting bits of food. Empty glasses and beer cans everywhere.

Under the workbench, in the vacant space where there had once been a plan to install a dishwasher, was a dead rat. Half its body had been eaten. By its relatives? Or by the dog maybe? There were two empty bowls on the floor.

Koirariepu, Ragnhild thought. Poor dog. To have to live like this.

It must be used to going for long periods without food and will have learned to survive on one thing or another.

She whistled up the stairs but no dog made its presence known.

Then she went into the living room. She found Henry there.

He was lying on his back on the sofa. Immobile. His face was turned towards the back of the sofa. Such a small body, like the remnants of the keel and ribs from a worn-out punt you find in a coppice by the river. She moved closer. She could see no evidence of respiration, the moment she saw his face there could be no doubt he was dead. She barely recognised him, matted hair, hollow cheeks. His skin was the colour of death. She touched him and he was cold.

She felt cold as well, like she wasn't really alive. The wet clothes were sucking all the warmth out of her. She sat on the coffee table beside him.

Her hand went into her pocket for her phone. She had to ring for an ambulance. No, straight to the undertakers: it'd just be wasting the time of the emergency services since he was dead. And she had to ring Olle. There were only the two of them left now, siblings in the same town who never spoke. That old rage made its presence felt inside her. Like waves in the darkness of night. Henry and Olle. They grabbed the inheritance when *Isä* died and left it to her to take care of *Äiti* and arrange the funeral.

I will ring, she thought. But not just yet. I've got to be alone with all of this for a bit. The farm, the memories of my parents, Henry, Virpi and Olle. The life I used to have here and that I lost. No-one knows I came out here. What difference would it make if I ring in an hour? And then there's the dog, I've got to find it.

She got to her feet. All of a sudden it felt essential to find the poor dog. If it was still alive.

She wondered about the kitchen for a bit. The idea of strangers coming in here to remove the body. And seeing her parents' home in such a state of decay.

25

But it's Henry's decay, she said to herself. Not mine. It's not my shame. I refuse to accept it.

All the same she opened the windows to air the place. Then she looked all over the house for the dog.

She even opened the wardrobes. The rooms at the top were empty; there were three mattresses on the floor, which struck her as odd. Was that for his drinking buddies who spent the night here? No sign of a dog anywhere.

She fled into the fresh air. Stood on the porch and took deep breaths.

She was going to try and find a spade for the rat corpse. Getting rid of it, that she could do. But cleaning the place . . . not on your life.

Ragnhild yelled and whistled. She saw little dents in the snow that might be dog tracks. Or a fox, perhaps? The shape of the tracks altered in warm weather like this and were more difficult to read.

She trudged over to the long barn, opened the old privy, the woodshed, the storerooms and the outhouses.

She could see for herself that there was nothing of value left on the farm, just junk. With or without permission, Henry's so-called friends had long ago taken anything that could be useful. There was a snowmobile outside the house. Henry had also kept the four-wheel drive and the boat, because he wouldn't have been able to get booze without them. But the tractor, motor saws, the combine harvester, anything like that was long gone. Drunk up.

Beside the privy an obsolete television set emerged from the snow under the run-off from the roof.

Her dismay at the decay, at all the rubbish, the sharp-edged sunshine that made it almost impossible to keep your eyes open . . . she felt so inexplicably tired.

I've got to lie down for a bit, she thought.

Only where could you lie down here? She thought of the mattresses upstairs, but she would never ever lie where his filthy friends had lain. She'd rather stretch out in the old drainage ditch inside the barn.

The barn, of course: there must be a spade in there, she thought. I will make all those calls, but that rat is getting thrown out first.

The door to the barn refused to open. There was too much snow in front of it. It had slid off the roof and turned hard as concrete. She braced herself against the wall and tried to kick it away. Mid-motion she stopped. A sound could be heard from inside. Something moving, a rustling.

She kicked the ice heap until her toes hurt. Then she used the other foot.

It was the eldest brother Olle who had persuaded *Isä* and *Äiti* that Henry should take over the little farm on the island.

Henry had fallen in with the wrong people. He went binging in Tärendö, Pajala and Kiruna. He came home when he needed money but refused to help with work on the farm. "They treat you like a labourer here," he complained when he had to lift a finger. He showed no respect, not for school, the church and the priest, other people's property, work, family.

"If Henry gets to take over here, he'll feel more responsible," Olle told their parents.

Äiti and *Isä* were already riven with guilt when it came to Henry. As a child he had suffered from an ear infection. This was in the middle of the hay harvest and they got him to the local doctor much too late. His hearing was damaged as a result and he often complained of a persistent whistling in his head. The schoolteacher was an impatient fellow and would often slap him for not listening.

Things worked out better for Olle. Although he was only twenty, he already had a job as a supervisor at the mine in Kiruna. He promised to get work for *Isä*.

"They need blokes like you who are good with their hands in the repair shop."

And *Isä* said yes. He'd reached the end of the road with Henry. Arguments and threats were no help. And they couldn't kick him out, because there was nowhere for him to go. Job openings and opportunities had been found and then wasted. And *Isä*'s hip was already beginning to bother him. So the decision was made.

They believed things would get better, Ragnhild thought. Wages, holidays and a flat.

Virpi had been seven and kept babbling on about the playground behind the apartment building; she had never seen it, but she talked about it like a wonderland. Ragnhild was the only one who cried and wouldn't leave. *Äiti*'s patience finally ran out.

"*Heitä nyt,* stop now. You've got to think about someone other than yourself. Dad's not getting any younger. He can't manage the work on the farm anymore. Life will be better for all of us in town."

They were supposed to take the boat across that day. The ice had just thawed. The leaves were like tiny mouse ears on the trees. The cows had been let out onto the summer pasture. The flat in Kiruna was furnished and ready to move into. Waiting for them. Ragnhild ran off into the trees with Villa the dog. The woods on the island weren't that big. She could hear Virpi crying beside the boat and shouting for her to come back. But she didn't care and hid beneath a fir tree. After a while *Isä* came marching along with determined, impatient strides. The moment he called, Villa barked with joy and revealed their hiding place.

Isä grabbed Ragnhild by the arm and pulled her along even though she was crying and refusing to walk. Villa followed them to the shore. But she wasn't allowed to jump into the boat. She stood on the jetty watching them leave. Then she lay down. Beginning her wait for them to return.

Ragnhild came back to herself to discover she had kicked away all the ice from in front of the barn door. It lay around her feet like glass that had been smashed. She turned the heavy key and opened the door.

"Villa," she said quietly as she stepped inside.

What did it matter what she called this dog. She had no idea what its name was after all.

It took a while for her eyes to adjust. Nothing had changed inside. In the semi-darkness she could make out the horse stall and the five small pens for the cows.

She sniffed. How could it still smell of the animals after all these years? She drew in the aroma, and the cows and their hornless heads, their curly tails and clever brown eyes came back to her: Majros, Punakorva, Mansikka, Virrankukka and Sköna. The last horse, Liinikkö, had gone to the eternal pastures when Ragnhild was nine. But the cows had still been here when they left. And now they were almost here again. The sounds they made as they chewed the cud, the stream of milk from their teats as it hit the side of the milk pail, the sensation of their warm breath on your skin, the dinging from the separator in the dairy.

Something was moving over there in the old calf pen. It was the dog. Glossy black eyes. It looked like Villa. How could that be? A village dog crossed with a fair bit of the Swedish and the Norwegian Elkhounds. Pointed ears with black edging and a white bib that ended in a little star at the very bottom. Exactly like Villa.

Ragnhild called to the dog just as they had called to the dogs in her childhood, with a quick "tjo". It refused to come. She took a few steps forward.

As she approached the opening to the calf pen it growled a warning and backed into one corner. Its tail was pressed against its belly, its ears were pinned back and its lips drawn up in a menacing snarl.

Ragnhild stopped. It's been beaten, she thought. It's been taught you can't trust human beings.

She looked around, trying to work out how the dog had got in seeing as the door had been shut. That was when she noticed the old manure hatch. It was open but completely clogged with snow and ice. She could see claw marks in the snow. The dog had evidently got in that way, but then a sheet of ice had plunged down and blocked it off. It might be used to coming in here when Henry drank too much. Living on snow and field mice when he forgot to provide food and water.

"Listen," she said in a gentle voice. "I'm kind. To animals at least."

She took off a mitten, crouched down and extended her hand for it to nuzzle.

"Villa," she said again.

The next moment the dog lunged at her, bit her on the hand. Then it ran off through the barn door.

Ragnhild was swearing as she got to her feet. But she wasn't bleeding. Her hand didn't even hurt. It was mostly from embarrassment. She'd hemmed it in, how stupid could you be?

I understand you though, she thought. I actually feel the same way myself.

She was going to have to lure it out with food, she realised. Create trust. She went out to the courtyard. The bright sunlight and sparkling snow made her squint. The dog had vanished without trace.

She would have to provide something other than the usual dry biscuits. Something it wouldn't be able to resist. She remembered there were three freezer chests in the living room. Typical Henry. The freezers would be filled with game birds and elk. His share from the village shoot because he let them hunt on his land. While he had lived on ready-made meals for lack of a woman's touch.

She went back inside the house, and in the living room was startled to see Henry on the sofa. Christ Almighty, she had completely forgotten about him. And the fact he was lying there dead.

I'm losing it, she thought. I'm definitely not in my right mind.

She really did have to ring the undertakers. Though how were they going to collect him when the ice was giving way? And Olle, she had to ring him. Only it was the dog that was her priority. It might try and run across the river, sink into the deep snow and end up trapped. Starve to death or be killed by ravens or other crows as it lay there helpless. She was going to have to try and capture it.

Purely on instinct she went over to the freezer that must be the oldest. She was practised at making dog food from meat with freezer-burn.

She opened it. It really was old, a miracle that it was still working and humming away.

It was so full of frost you could barely make out the contents. Ice bulged in from the sides. She shoved in her arm and rooted around. To her surprise she came up with empty packs, ancient packaging that had held fried fish, hamburgers, meat balls and blueberry pies. She chucked the packs on the floor. She stopped when she pulled out an empty ketchup bottle.

"What the hell, Henry!" she said incredulously and turned towards him as if he might answer.

Was he using it as a rubbish bin, she thought, leaning over the edge of the chest. So why was it on in that case?

Crossly she brushed the frost away and then caught sight of some check material.

Has he been putting clothes in the freezer? Was he demented at the end? Woozy? Delirium tremens?

Her hand ached from the cold. She shoved it into her armpit to warm it. Then she stuck her fingers in her mouth, Christ they'd got so bloody cold, she ought to put a glove on.

She leaned slightly to one side so that light from the ceiling lamp could reach into the freezer.

With growing horror she realised there was no point in brushing any more ice away. Because in the sleeve was an arm and at one end a shrunken hand.

She didn't scream. She didn't back violently away. She took her fingers out of her mouth and waited for a wave of nausea that never came. Had she been poking at it before she put her fingers in her mouth? She spat on the floor, and kept spitting.

Then she rang 112. Explained the situation. That she was on an island in the Torne river with two dead people in the same room. Yes, that was right. She had to repeat herself. One on the sofa and one in the freezer.

She was worried she sounded too calm. That it all sounded crazy and they wouldn't believe her. In an attempt to increase her credibility she blurted:

"If you're going to talk to the police in Kiruna, you might as well let the district prosecutor know, Rebecka Martinsson? Because Henry Pekkari, the man on the sofa, is her uncle. And I'm her aunt."

She regretted it almost immediately.

The emergency operator said:

"Sorry, I didn't get that last bit, who was it you wanted me to let know?"

"No-one," Ragnhild said. "Forget it."

Virpi's daughter would be told anyway. And Ragnhild really didn't want to have anything to do with Rebecka Martinsson.

District Prosecutor Rebecka Martinsson was standing at her height-adjustable desk when Sergeant Tommy Rantakyrö stuck his head in the door.

"What deep sighs those were," he said.

Rebecka grinned. She hadn't been aware she'd been sighing.

"Sign of age," she said. "I've turned into my grandmother. She was always sighing. And they were very definitely those 'if only the good Lord would put me out of my misery' kind of sighs."

Tommy Rantakyrö laughed and put a paper bag on her desk.

"Afternoon snack," he announced. "Raw food balls, one liquorice and one ginger and cinnamon. They're a cure for sighing."

"Too right! And now the good Lord won't have to deliver me from evil quite yet."

"Not for an hour anyway."

She stuck her nose into the bag to please him. Tommy was kind. She did her best to be kind back. His girlfriend had moved out two months ago and he was devoting himself to being the best and most considerate of colleagues. He was still the puppy of the squad. There was something a bit sad about the way he wouldn't grow up, not properly. Ever since his girlfriend broke it off and Sven-Erik retired, he would often come into the prosecutor's office to chat and then stay a bit too long; she was always obliged to get him to leave with a "Sorry, I've really got to . . ."

"How's it going, reviewing the case backlog?" he asked with a nod at the piles of paper on her desk.

Rebecka gave another of her grandmother's sighs and raised her hands in supplication. Tommy sighed even louder. They both laughed at the little joke they had come up with and now shared.

Rebecka's boss Alf Björnfot had taken all his accrued holidays, added a two-month leave of absence and gone off to Alaska. The trip he'd been dreaming of with his grown-up daughter. Seeing bears and fishing for salmon.

Rebecka's colleague Carl von Post had been appointed acting chief prosecutor. On the last day of work before his holiday, Björnfot had come into Rebecka's office and put a yellow Post-it on her notice board. "TRY NOT TO BE A PAIN". Written only half in jest.

"Try to get along with Calle," Björnfot had said. "I know he's not your favourite person but he's been here longest, so I've got to make him acting chief. But I don't want anyone ringing me on the warpath and spoiling my trip."

"It would never occur to me to ring you on the warpath," Rebecka had said. "And you should be putting that note up in von *Pest*'s room."

"I know," Björnfot said. "But he's the way he is. Bits of paper aren't going to help. He's bound to irritate you, but you'll just have to put up with it. Because if you give Calle any grief he'll find out where I am even if I've managed to hide at the arse end of the wilderness. So please don't."

He had put his palms together and extended them towards her. Then he left the building. Before the door had even closed behind Björnfot, von Post, as acting chief prosecutor and her superior, had assigned her new duties. He put the entire backlog of minor crimes the police had already investigated on her desk for review. Just over one hundred and fifty cases, most involving petty larceny, phone scams and driving over the limit. It would be her task, as the reviewing lawyer, to decide which should be prosecuted and then proceed with them in court. A deathly boring and lonely job.

"So how's it going?" Tommy Rantakyrö asked.

Rebecka gritted her teeth. She had been chained to her desk for three weeks and had been unprepared for the isolation that wore away at her. Von Post had not only dumped the review on her, he had also taken over her current cases. So she could "focus on the backlog". She had not protested. Björnfot's Post-it glowered over her existence like a divine commandment.

Because she no longer had cases of her own, none of the detectives would pop in to her office to discuss what steps were being taken in the ongoing investigations. She had no good reason either to get updates from them or to give them new directives. Her phone was silent as the grave.

I ought to be more grateful for Tommy, she thought. He cares. Why do we never appreciate the ones who do?

"I'm preparing for my days at the Courts of Tedium," she said. "Starting this Monday. Maybe I can get the minor criminals convicted."

"That'll look good in the statistics," Tommy Rantakyrö said.

In von Post's statistics, Rebecka thought.

And just as she had that thought von Post's footsteps could be heard in the corridor. A few seconds later and he appeared in the doorway. Boyishly ruffled hair, neatly pressed shirt and not even a hint of a beer belly.

"Hi there, Tommy," he said in comradely greeting and patted him a bit too hard on the back. "How's it going, Martinsson?"

Rebecka froze. There was a difference between her and von Post, or perhaps between her and the upper class. He was as pleasant as a television presenter to everyone he met, both enemies and allies. She, on the other hand, found it hard to disguise her true feelings and became curt and uptight, her neck stiff and her lips pressed tightly together. She found it difficult to look people she didn't like in the eye. She despised herself for not being able to play the game. Condemned to being the psychological underdog.

Carl von Post gave her a knowing smile. She could loathe him for all he cared. It seemed to please him that she failed to respond when addressed.

"How's it going with the frozen goods?" von Post asked, turning to Tommy.

"The corpse in the freezer? In the end we commissioned a helicopter that finally managed to land. And picked up both the freezer and the old guy who was dead in the house."

"What?" von Post exclaimed. "There were two dead people? Murders?"

"We don't know yet. They're both at the medical examiner's now, so Pohjanen will be ringing when he's got something to tell us."

"Good, good. Anything new on that front take it up with me. Martinsson's got her plate full with—"

"Yea, I know," Tommy cut him off. "I brought her some goodies to cheer her up. That's a hell of a pile she's got to work through."

Von Post's smile got even wider.

"It's really incredibly good for her, you know, to work through the backlog. She didn't get her position as prosecutor the normal way, did she. I was a trainee prosecutor for nine months and then an assistant prosecutor for two years. So there are certain basics she lacks."

Rebecka gritted her teeth and stared at von Post. It was outrageous that he should be talking over her head while making it sound as though she were less qualified than him. In truth she was overqualified, and he knew it. She imagined he lay awake at night tortured by the realisation that she had given up what would be his dream job, a lawyer at Meijer & Ditzinger, for her current position in the Prosecution Service.

And he's bound to think they would welcome me back with open arms if I wanted, she was thinking. Though I'm not sure that's true.

"Anyway, I really should let you get on," von Post said to Rebecka, and gave Tommy an encouraging look.

But Tommy made no move to leave. Rebecka leaned back in her chair and fished a raw food ball from the paper bag.

"Feel like sharing?" she asked Tommy.

Von Post vanished down the corridor.

"That guy," Tommy said.

Rebecka gritted her teeth.

Do not complain, she admonished herself.

At the beginning, when Björnfot went off on his long vacation, she had not been able to stop talking about von Post and how awful he was. She constantly referred to him as von Pest and all her police colleagues had dropped by to see the Post-it note that soon became notorious: She had coined the term "the Pestilence" for the period they were having to endure.

Eventually she began to sense they were getting bored with her harping on. And she had found it difficult to stop. She had made up her mind to say "Good" when people asked how she was, and to talk about something pleasant instead, but after only a few sentences she would hear herself going on about the rat that was von Pest. It just wasn't meant to be.

She was feeling bitter and depressed. Police officers passed her room on their way to see von Post about various matters. She suspected they were telling each other that she wasn't that easy to deal with either. Think about the way she treated their colleague Krister Eriksson.

She and Krister had had eighteen months of what you'd have to call a relationship.

Throughout that time, though, she had said, "We're not a couple." He had replied, "No, no" and smiled. Then he had kissed her hair and dragged her into the woods, or out fishing, or into bed. He wanted more. She wanted less. Then she ruined it all. She was the villain. Everyone knew.

Once Krister had slammed that door shut, she had gone back to Måns Wallgren. He wanted less as well. They were so-called "friends with benefits". He had stopped nagging her to move back to Stockholm. But he thought she was out of her mind to work in the prosecutor's office in Kiruna. "When are you going to resign from that place?" he would ask. "When that idiot von Post tells you cleaning the toilets is part of your job too?"

She came back to the present and tried to smile.

"Screw von Post," she said as cheerfully as she could. "These balls are so delicious, shall we share another one? What was that about a corpse in a freezer?"

"Don't know yet, it looks like it had been there for a long time."

"Butchered?"

"No, apparently not. Shame you're not going to be the lead on this one, von Post is all psyched about it."

"So you're going to have fun together on a freezer murder," Rebecka said. "Don't think about me sending shoplifters and taggers and speeders to prison."

"You're a terror, you are," Tommy said with admiration. "You know we all think that."

"All but one," Rebecka said, before adding, quick as a flash, "not that I'm bothered though."

She rooted around the paper bag with exaggerated interest.

"She'll get over it," Tommy said. "You know what Mella's like."

Rebecka immediately lost interest in the bag and the raw food balls.

"Mella?" she asked.

"Oh hell, you meant von Post . . ."

Tommy swallowed the rest of the sentence; his eyes turned towards the Post-it note on Rebecka's wall.

"Mella!" Rebecka exclaimed. "Is Anna-Maria pissed off with me? Why?"

"Forget it," Tommy pleaded. "I thought she'd been in here to complain. Please forget I said anything."

"Just what have I done to her?" Rebecka said, upset. "I mean, we haven't even seen one another for . . ."

She dropped the bag on the desk and walked towards the door.

"There's no need to say anything. It really won't be that hard to find out."

She strode noisily along the corridor

Tommy debated whether to rush after her but decided not to.

"No, I'm off home," he said aloud. "This is about to blow."

Police Inspector Anna-Maria Mella turned on the coffee machine in the lunchroom; it started up like a wood chipper. When her cup was ready, the word "Enjoy" flashed onto the display. She stared at those red letters.

"Does that drive you mad as well?" Anna-Maria asked her colleagues. "It's not supposed to tell me to bloody enjoy it. I'll enjoy if I want to."

Sergeant Fred Olsson and two new uniforms who were already seated snorted in approval.

"It's like this guy I went with once," Anna-Maria continued, encouraged by their laughter. "When we were, how should I put it . . . being intimate, he kept on like that the whole time: 'Enjoy. Enjoooy!' All I could think was: I might enjoy it if you were doing a better job, OK?"

She scored another laugh but felt a bit of a phoney. Though the story was true, it made it sound like she'd had several men and he'd been one of many, and as though she'd been older when it happened. In truth that was the only time she'd slept with anyone other than Robert. She'd been seventeen and she and Robert had broken it off. She was unhappy and drunk, Jalle mostly just drunk. He was doing the vehicle maintenance programme at school and living in a bedsit in Kiruna with its own front door. A week later she and Robert were back together, a hiccup is all it was. It had always been just the two of them. Why the hell did she have to go and bring up Jalle? What was his surname? Thank God she'd forgotten.

"What's going on with all the machines?" said one of the new uniforms, Karzan Tigris.

He'd started as a junior police officer six weeks ago and had a popular Instagram account where he wrote about the job he loved, posting photos of himself drinking "today's cop coffee" or doing a handstand in full armed-response gear. Anna-Maria thought he looked like he was still at school. Though that was happening more and more these days. Doctors, teachers, priests, it was hard to take them seriously. Many of them didn't look as though they'd even got their moped license. It was so weird.

Karzan continued in the same vein:

"They all beep or make noises. Washing machines, for instance, keep beeping once they've finished. And it never stops. You can't put a wash on before you go to bed."

"There'll be some boffin goes round adding all those features just because they can," Magda Vidarsdotter, the other uniform, said.

Born in Flen, she had no children but a horse she kept stabled in Jukkasjärvi. A junior officer too, but not a complete rookie. She had worked in Eskilstuna and then looked for a job in Kiruna because of the natural environment up here. She could talk horses and dogs with Rebecka until you wondered if you were actually working on a farm. Anna-Maria was desperately hoping Vidarsdotter and Tigris would stay on in Kiruna.

"What do you think it's going to be like in the future, when all that AI technology gets cheaper?" Magda said. "Then it'll be like: Hello Anna-Maria. Your cortisol level is higher than normal. Take three deep breaths and ask yourself if you really need to drink that coffee?"

She said the last bit in a pretend digitised voice. Words without intonation, with slightly odd pauses and a bright and self-affirming voice.

Anna-Maria laughed that bit harder because Magda was normally not one to say much. She was starting to thaw. They were forming a pack, like dogs barking happily. Anna-Maria was good at being the alpha bitch. They had the makings of a great team. Though there was nothing to be done about the emptiness left behind by Sven-Erik Stålnacke; it was still there.

And it felt strange to be the veteran of the team. She had felt like she was twenty right up until Sven-Erik's retirement.

"If your kids aren't going to teach you how to behave, there's always your household appliances," Anna-Maria said with mock resignation. "All you can hope is that . . ."

But her colleagues never found out what she was hoping because Rebecka Martinsson appeared in the doorway that very moment. The lack of expression on her face signalled danger was imminent.

Anna-Maria noticed immediately that her cortisol levels had shot up. She didn't need a coffee machine to tell her that.

"Hi there, Martinsson," Fred Olsson said cheerfully, completely insensitive to the change in atmosphere.

Rebecka nodded curtly and got straight to the point.

"Something the matter?" she asked Anna-Maria. "Tommy said."

Anna-Maria flushed. Bloody Tommy, what did he have to go and blab to Rebecka for? She could feel the officers' eyes on her back.

"Shall we deal with it in my office?" she said.

"Let's deal with it here and now. Since it seems you've been talking about it to everyone except me."

"No, I haven't. I was a bit upset yesterday, which is when I said to Tommy that . . ."

She fell silent and then began again.

"It's about Eivor Simma."

Rebecka raised her eyebrows.

"Aggravated theft!" Anna-Maria said. "The old girl is eighty-one. She was mugged inside the Co-op on Trädgårdsgatan. While some guy asked her if this was the right kind of rice to make rice pudding with, his accomplice nicked the wallet out of her bag. Eivor called yesterday to tell me she'd got a letter signed by you saying there would be no prosecution."

"And?"

"That seemed a bit strange. The shop's CCTV showed Humpty and Dumpty—"

"Wróblewski and Harjula," Rebecka said drily. "I remember the case perfectly well."

"—the camera showed them leaving the shop together while Eivor Simma was inside," Mella went on. "She picked out Harjula from a photo array."

"Right, it was that photo array, you see," Rebecka said. "Ten faces. Eivor Simma identified Harjula, whose photo was the only blurry one into the bargain. I would have pointed to that photo too. Anyone would have. The evidence just wouldn't have stood up, Mella."

"Well, to me it seemed only right it should have gone to court."

"You know the photo of the accused isn't supposed to stick out in any way," Rebecka said in a tone that made Anna-Maria feel she was back at her school desk. "The defence would have picked up on it, and there is no chance in hell they would have been found guilty."

Mella gnashed her teeth. She had taken the photo of Harjula on her mobile. And OK, maybe she had rushed it. It came out blurry and she hadn't taken a new one. But what the hell, the case was cut and dried. And now she was having to put up with being lectured in front of her new colleagues.

"It felt really shitty," she said to Rebecka, her voice tight. "When Eivor Simma rings you at home and you have to explain that we're not even considering prosecuting those bastards. Even though we know they're one hundred per cent guilty. Now she's too afraid to go shopping. That really sucks for us as police officers. And it's the sort of story that spreads like wildfire. You do know it was a thread on 'We live in Kiruna and we're not afraid to let you know what we think', don't you? And we're the ones who have to face the backlash out there. No wonder people spit on the street in front of us and scratch our cars. What's the point of our investigations when all you do is shut them down?"

"So it's us and you now, is it?" Rebecka said. "And all we do is shut cases down? Do you realise this is the only case of 152 I'm not taking to court? I've no intention of wasting tax-payers' money by initiating proceedings that are doomed to fail just to make you feel better."

"That's not what I meant," said Anna-Maria, thinking she was making a really good job of keeping her voice calm. "It's not about my feeling better. It's about our all being on the same team. And a bit of communication from you wouldn't hurt."

Rebecka was looking at Anna-Maria as if she were reading aloud from some cheap self-help book.

"Right then," she said. "I'll take a course in communication and you can learn how to use your camera."

Then she turned on her heel and marched back along the corridor.

Fred Olsson and the new uniforms leaped to their feet and set off for their good deed of the day, busting a few road hogs. In an instant they were gone.

Anna-Maria was left alone in the lunchroom. The coffee machine turned itself off with a sad gurgle. The display showed "Have a nice day".

Rebecka shut the door to her office.

"Fuck . . . the whole lot of them!" she said to the empty air.

She had begun to think she and Anna-Maria were getting to be good friends. And not just at work. But during her time serving in the courts they had barely seen one another. Anna-Maria had her plate full with the newly appointed officers and her family. She got that. But why hadn't Anna-Maria taken up the case with her directly? She'd been talking about Rebecka with her workmates instead. That was so disloyal. Turning her into the enemy of the police.

She wanted to kick something, or go home and binge-watch some series, but she had to finish the job she was doing. Even though she felt she couldn't put up with her lonely office a moment longer.

She took out her phone and rang Maria Taube. The moment her friend answered she regretted it. She was always calling and going on about how frustrated she was.

"Martinsson," Maria exclaimed. "I thought you'd forgotten me. We never talk anymore."

Rebecka had to laugh. "We talked yesterday," she said. "And the day before. And I'm always the one disturbing you while you're doing important stuff."

"I'd completely forgotten," Maria lamented. "How are things?"

Rebecka resisted complaining about the current set-up. She knew

Maria would say anything she wanted to hear. That Anna-Maria had been wrong. That von Post was a nobody, just like all his family. Maria Taube knew all there was to know about them as it happened. She would insist that Rebecka was ludicrously overqualified for the prosecutor's office up there and it was incomprehensible that she wasn't prosecuting tax cases at the regional level.

At the same time Rebecka would be able to hear from her voice that Maria's eyes had not left her screen, that she was still working while talking to her. Mid-sentence Maria would announce she would have to call back later because she had to go into a meeting, or there were a hundred red-flagged e-mails she had to deal with.

And then Rebecka would sit in her office and feel excluded, deeply embarrassed at being such a demanding, boring, needy person. To cap it all she would remember that Maria used to say Rebecka ought to come back to the firm, move back to Stockholm. She'd stopped doing that; Rebecka realised why. There was no place for her now at Meijer & Ditzinger. That train had left the station.

Pull yourself together, she told herself and made an effort to be amusing.

"Things are really happening up here," Rebecka said. "The Kurravaara village association has procured a defibrillator. So we've got to have another meeting to decide where to put it. And they're building the new town hall."

"It's completely crazy, moving the whole town," Maria said. "We really should talk about that at some point. Seriously."

"No way, how utterly depressing."

It was depressing. New Kiruna was going to be built on some old marshland. Ten degrees colder in the winter than in Haukivaara, where the town was currently located.

"Listen, I was actually meaning to ring you," Maria said. "The second weekend in May some girls and I are going to the resort at Riksgränsen. They've still got loads of snow up there. And I was thinking if we left on Thursday we could stay the first night in Kiruna and crash at your place. Wouldn't that be a blast? You wouldn't have to arrange anything. We'd bring food and booze with us. Just turn on the sauna, that's all."

Rebecka felt trapped. She liked Maria Taube, but what about her posh friends from Djursholm?

"So what are they like, these friends?" she said with laughter in her voice. "They can't be the sort that do a detox."

"No, no, none of them are like that," Maria assured her. "They're incredibly nice, you'll love them."

"'Incredibly nice' are they?" Rebecka said. "'Nice' does sound awful. Do they post stuff like 'Friends don't let friends skip yoga' on their Insta accounts?"

"No, they don't," Maria said. "I promise we're all slightly overweight overworked lawyers and economists. None of us work out. No-one's got time for yoga."

"Do all of them eat red meat?" Rebecka asked. "Do they eat carbs? Do they believe that giving children white sugar is the same as injecting them with heroin?"

"Yes and no! We eat anything. Roadkill and refined sugar."

"Oh well then," Rebecka said. "Come and have a sauna; it'll be great. I'll provide beer and a bit of roadkill. Anyone who wants bean sprouts will have to bring their own." And she quickly added, "I've got to go, speak soon."

"Toodlepip," Maria chirped. She wasn't the kind of person to feel left out just because she hadn't been the one to end the call.

At least I didn't complain, Rebecka said to herself. And I was the one to say goodbye. But how the hell did I manage to invite a gang of upper-class twits to a party in Kurravaara?

Barking could be heard from the car park. Rebecka looked out of the window. She had the Brat in a cage in the boot of her car. The boot was open. The weather was perfect, not too cold and not too hot. And the officers would stop and talk to him, stroke him through the grille. Much more fun than life under her desk. The Brat was on his feet, yapping eagerly at a car that was pulling in. Krister Eriksson's jeep.

It wasn't often you got to see him at the station these days. His work as a dog handler took him all over the province and he was mostly away on a job.

The Brat was whirling round inside his cage. Krister Eriksson used to take him along for training sessions in tracking when Rebecka and he were together. The Brat loved him with a completely submissive devotion.

Rebecka watched as Krister got out of his car and said hello to the Brat through the grille. Then he looked up at Rebecka's office. She gave a little wave. He nodded almost imperceptibly. Then he looked down. Just as his girlfriend got out of the car.

Rebecka forced herself to remain at the window. Marit Törmä was sportily dressed in the best way, a faded red anorak from the seventies. Gloves of hand-tanned reindeer skin. Her hair gathered in a blond ponytail. She was a cheerful sort. Pretty too. The local police force had flipped its collective lid when Krister and Marit started dating. Rebecka may have been a catch, but this girl! Marit Törmä had won gold in the biathlon as a junior. In other words, a true mountain lemming. Whenever she and Krister had time off they headed for the hills.

It's the right thing, Rebecka thought. They'll be getting married soon. He deserves someone like her.

Marit looked up at her all of a sudden and gave a huge and enthusiastic wave.

"Hi there!" she called.

Rebecka was smiling so hard her face hurt and waved back. She watched them walking together towards the entrance.

Stop it, she said to herself. Stop making a fool of yourself.

Her phone rang. It was Lars Pohjanen, the medical examiner.

"Hello Martinsson," he croaked. "I've heard your life's been miserable lately."

Rebecka backed away from the window and sat in a visitor's chair that was covered in papers.

"Where did you hear that?"

Pohjanen drew a few wheezing breaths before replying.

"The rumour mill. Von Post has got you reviewing police cases. I thought I might show you a corpse, if you're interested."

"Is it frozen? Rantakyrö came by and told me about it. That's just the kind of thing to cheer a girl up."

He laughed. An appalling sound.

"So get over here then."

"I don't mean to be . . ." Rebecka said hesitantly, "but isn't von Post the one who . . ."

"That idiot," Pohjanen said irritably. "He can read the report when I've finished. Get over here now Martinsson, before I change my mind."

She packed away her laptop, deciding that was enough for today. On the way to Pohjanen's she thought about Krister. He'd looked up at her window, hadn't he? What could that mean?

She kept lurching between Nothing and Something.

Marit Törmä was saying hi to Krister's colleagues. Krister was just handing in a report and then they were heading off into the forest. She was discussing exercise routines with Karzan and asking Magdalena how her horse was doing.

Fred Olsson was a bigger challenge. She knew he had filled his garage with servers and was mining Bitcoin. And while you could always ask, understanding any part of his reply was impossible. And Rebecka Martinsson kept niggling away at her like a lash in your eye. Krister could hardly bring himself to say hi to his former girlfriend. The expression on his face when the Brat licked his hand through the cage. It was gentle and sad. And when he turned back to Marit his face had been wiped clean and was as empty as a flat for sale.

They bumped into Anna-Maria upstairs in the lunchroom. Marit asked how her kids were doing and Anna-Maria told them which ones she had listed under "for collection free of charge". Why couldn't Krister just forget Rebecka? He clearly had good reason to be pissed off at her. But it had been two years since they broke it off and he had Marit now, didn't he?

And I am a catch, she thought.

She could have had her pick. She'd never had any reason to be jealous. So the feeling that she wanted to yank him away from that dog cage was a new and difficult one.

Rebecka was walking along the empty corridors of Kiruna hospital. The county council had closed the maternity ward and emergency surgery. But they hadn't managed to dislodge Pohjanen, the medical examiner. "Go on, shut my department down, transfer it, why don't you, and then I can finally stop working." Which meant that would never happen while he was alive. He continued to be the lord of his subterranean realm.

When Rebecka rang the bell at the pathology department it was Anna Granlund, Pohjanen's technician, who opened the door.

She smiled at Rebecka the way you smile at a relative you're about to share a loss with. Pohjanen was living on borrowed time. He was working only because he wanted to. Granlund made that possible. She undressed his corpses, opened them up, making the incisions as neatly and cleanly as he could ever want. She weighed the organs, sectioned and arranged livers, hearts, kidneys and lungs in neat rows on the steel counter. She split open stomachs, cut out intestines and examined their contents, sawed skulls open, removed brains, changed the batteries in Pohjanen's Dictaphone, got him to sip apple juice and when he had finished she wrote up his notes and sewed the dead up in preparation for their final journey.

"Hello," Anna Granlund said in a hushed voice. "He's asleep, but he wanted me to wake him when you got here."

Pohjanen was sleeping on his scruffy sofa in the break room; his rapid breaths were irregular and shallow. He woke up before Anna Granlund could nudge his arm. His face took on a gentler expression at the sight of Rebecka.

"Martinsson," he said, pleased, getting up on frail legs only to exclaim: "What has happened to you? You look like you've been released from a penal colony."

Rebecka exchanged a look with Anna Granlund. He could insult them as much as he liked, just as long as he didn't go and die.

He worked on the principle that attack is the best form of defence. He was the one who looked like famine personified. His skin was as yellow as cheap paper, he had dark rings under his eyes, his cheeks were caved in and there was a stick leant against the sofa. Pohjanen glared at the stick with disdain and made his way laboriously without it to the autopsy room.

"I don't have to appear in court until next week," Rebecka said. "I'll have a shower before and wear a skirt and jacket. Maybe brush my teeth."

The dead man lay on a steel bench in the autopsy room.

Like something an archaeologist has discovered in a peat bog, Rebecka thought.

There was a pile of clothes she assumed belonged to the dead man on a bench beside the wall.

Pohjanen dropped onto his stainless-steel stool which moved on little wheels and snapped on latex gloves. Rebecka shoved her hands deep into her pockets. One lesson she had learned from working with Pohjanen right from the start. "Put your hands in your pockets, clench your fists and keep them that way."

"This is no fresh corpse, as you can see," Pohjanen said. "It's obvious he was in the freezer for a long time. He ended up being freeze-dried, to put it simply."

"Shot," Rebecka said, looking at the hole in the dead man's chest.

There was a tattoo of a stripper, with boxing gloves hanging on a cord around her neck. The shot had gone through her throat.

"We'll get to the cause of death. *Älä hättaäile*, don't rush me. I thought I could make out tattoos, so I scraped away the outer layer of skin to see what the images were. The tattoos are actually in the dermis so they could be seen quite clearly after a bit. The sixty-four-thousand dollar question: What do they make you think of?"

"Nothing."

"Nothing? That stripper? The sailor's tattoos on his arms. The polar bear baring its fangs? The one with the three dots? Eh, you're too young. This fellow's got the same tattoos as Börje Ström!"

"The boxer?"

"Yup. Odd, isn't it? Ström is still very much alive, after all. So I rang him. We're actually related. His mother and my father were cousins. So that—"

"You rang him . . . you don't think the police should be—"

"His old man, Raimo Koskela, disappeared in 1962 when Ström was eleven. He confirmed that his father had the same tattoos he does. Not something he has ever revealed in an interview as far as I know.

No-one in the family has mentioned it either, not that we talked that much about him, I'll have to admit."

Pohjanen cracked his neck as if he were pulling his skull up out of a bucket of icy water. Rebecka wondered what kind of thoughts and memories had been calling to him – the same ones he was now forced to distance himself from.

"I checked the freezer he was in when he arrived," Pohjanen continued as he pulled off his gloves, throwing them into the waste bin with remarkable accuracy. "It ought to be on one of those antiques programmes on the telly. I took a picture and sent it to a forensic specialist. She said it is perfectly plausible that it was manufactured at the end of the fifties, beginning of the sixties. Which is where we get to my . . . erhh . . . predicament erhh . . ."

Rebecka waited patiently as Pohjanen struggled to clear his throat and catch his breath. Over at the counter Anna raised her head like a reindeer scenting danger.

"Jesus fucking Christ," Pohjanen blasphemed, coughing wetly into a handkerchief he quickly crumpled and tucked into his pocket.

"Your predicament," Rebecka said in a neutral and supportive tone, as if she were in court helping a witness with their testimony.

"Right," Pohjanen said and wiped his forehead with the back of his hand. "As you so percipiently observed he was shot through the chest. The problem is that the crime is barred by the statute of limitations."

"Bad luck for von Post," Rebecka said. "He'd have loved a freezer murder. A real spectacle."

"And a bit of luck for you," Pohjanen countered. "Because I was thinking you could take a little look at the murder. Just for fun."

"What?" Rebecka said. "Why would I want to investigate a time-barred case, a murder that happened more than fifty years ago, 'just for fun'? I'm not an amateur sleuth."

"For Ström's sake then," Pohjanen said through his teeth. "His dad had been gone for all his life. And now he turns up in a freezer. How do you think that feels?"

"That must be really awful," said Rebecka, switching to her gentlest professional voice, the one that signalled there wasn't a snowball's chance in hell of the other person getting what they wanted. "But I'm not going to go snooping around in private so he can have peace of mind. I'm sure you get that?"

A millimetre-wide smile, crossed arms, her head tilted slightly to one side. Her gentle-on-the-outside-rock-hard-on-the-inside pose. Pohjanen took that in and it made him angry. He didn't like being handled.

"No, I don't get it," he snapped. "All I'm asking is for you to take a little look into it in your free time."

"My free time!" Rebecka exclaimed with a chilly laugh. "What free time?"

"How would I know!" Pohjanen barked. "The time you're not fetching your kids from pre-school or cooking for your family."

Rebecka's eyes darkened like marsh lakes in late autumn. Her lips parted slightly as she gasped for air.

Pohjanen immediately regretted his unthinking comment, but saying sorry had never been his strong point. He went on talking instead, but in a softer voice.

"You could have a talk with the sister of the man who owned the freezer, couldn't you? We've got the owner here. So it's too late to have a chat with him."

He chuckled and nodded at the cold store. And then went on as if more words might help to distance him from the insensitive comments he'd just made.

"He died two weeks ago, apparently of what would be natural causes

53

for an elderly alcoholic. Arrhythmias and ultimately cardiac arrest. The heart weighed half a kilo, the fact that he reached the age of seventy-two is something of a minor miracle. His sister skied across that morning to check on things and the brother was lying there dead, and Ström's dad was in the freezer. She rang the police and they winched the freezer by helicopter over to the mainland and drove it here. The sister's called Ragnhild Pekkari. She was going to head back to the island soon, she said. There was some dog or other she had to find. If I give you her phone number—"

He broke off because Rebecka was staring at him as if she had seen a ghost.

"Ragnhild Pekkari?" Rebecka said slowly. "What did you say the name of the island was?"

"I don't remember off the top of my head—"

"Palosaari?" Rebecka prompted. "In Kurkkio? And the owner of the freezer, the dead alkie, is his name Henry Pekkari?"

"It is," Pohjanen said. "Do you know him somehow? We've got him in here."

He pointed over his shoulder to the cold store.

"Do you want to take a look?"

Rebecka flushed.

"No. Though Henry Pekkari is my maternal uncle. Ragnhild is my aunt. Well, my mother was a foster child in their family."

"You're not serious?" Pohjanen exclaimed, incredulous. "Well, then there's even more reason for you to—"

"Not a chance," Rebecka cut him off. "As far as I'm concerned the Pekkari family can rot in hell."

Pohjanen sank into the bobbles on his scruffy sofa. Rebecka had said a hasty goodbye and left. He had tried to ask about her aunt, tried to get her to stay but that turned out to be like stopping an ore train.

It really was a remarkable coincidence. What he knew about Rebecka's kin on her mother's side amounted to less than nothing, he realised. Her mother had died in what appeared to have been an accident, or maybe suicide, when Rebecka was twelve. She had stepped out in front of a lorry. So there was an aunt on the mother's side. Only Rebecka's mother had been a foster child, so what would you call the relationship in that case? Foster-aunt? That just sounded silly. And a dead foster-uncle. Along with a corpse in her uncle's freezer.

"I never cease being surprised," he croaked to Anna Granlund, who was unloading the dishwasher. "They can put that on my gravestone."

Anna appeared in the doorway.

"What were you saying about a gravestone?" she asked anxiously.

But Pohjanen had fallen asleep again. His chin was nodding against his collarbone. Anna crept over and coaxed a cushion in between his shoulder and his ear.

When he next woke it was thanks to a rather cautious nudge. It was not Granlund standing beside him but a nurse he did not know. His mood worsened right away. He didn't like strangers watching him sleep.

And she shouldn't be bloody touching him either. She was wearing a pink top and nurse's uniform trousers in the same colour.

When did they start looking like chewing gum, he wondered. What's going on?

He looked at his watch. A quarter past seven. His wife would be expecting him for dinner.

"There's someone here to see you," the chewing gum said. "I told him you weren't seeing visitors, only . . . it's Börje Ström. He turned up at A & E and asked for you. He drove all the way from Älvsbyn."

There was a man behind her; his shoulders were as wide as a barn door and he had long arms that ended in fists like gnarled birch. His hair was blond and wavy; his eyes were as blue as spring ice though their outer corners drooped a bit which made him seem sad. His nose was broken, of course, the boxer's badge of honour.

Pohjanen got to his feet. He ran one hand over his hair and across the corners of his mouth in case he had been drooling; he adjusted his green coat, gave it a quick glance to make sure it didn't have any stains on it and that he'd done the buttons up right.

"Börje Ström," he said out of breath. "This is . . ."

He put out his hand. The chewing gum took the opportunity to disappear out the door.

Börje Ström gave the medical examiner's hand a gentle squeeze as if he were afraid of crushing it.

They were contemporaries. Ström had turned sixty-five. Pohjanen was only two years older. Twenty would have been most people's guess.

All of a sudden it seemed to occur to Pohjanen that he ought to close his mouth. Only he opened it again to say that they were related, weren't they? Second cousins.

"Though I already told you that on the phone," he continued

apologetically. "And I suppose everyone says they're related to you some way or other."

"That does happen," Börje Ström admitted. "It just struck me . . . after you rang . . . I should drive over and take a look at him."

"I understand," Pohjanen said. "Of course. It won't be pretty though."

"Right, I get that," Börje Ström said.

"He's not his old self, as they say," Pohjanen said.

And immediately wished he'd bitten off his tongue instead of rabbiting on.

16 JUNE 1962

The day Börje's father disappears begins like any other day. He will remember the details of this day, even the most banal of them, for the rest of his life. The vanishing of a flare that shed its light on everything around.

Börje wakes early, just after seven even though it's a Sunday. He creeps into the kitchen and makes two sandwiches. His mother is still asleep. The bread slices crumble because the butter from the fridge is too hard.

Dad is coming to pick him up today, and they're going to be together for a whole week.

He stays in all day, watching the clock, the hands barely move. His mates ring the doorbell and ask if he wants to come out for a bike ride, but he doesn't.

Mum is sitting at the kitchen table, doing crosswords. She has just washed her hair and put it in large rollers. She's smoking and doesn't look up as she asks:

"Why don't you go out and play? He won't be here before evening."

Then she adds almost under her breath:

"If he comes at all, that is. He owes me money."

But all Börje wants is to wait for his dad. Waiting is the only thing he can do. He sits on his bed with a pile of comics. Donald Duck, the Phantom and Illustrated Classics. He can't focus on what he is reading. He is thinking about Dad and the week to come while trying to remember to turn the page because Mum can see him from the kitchen table.

Normally he would have shut the door behind him. And he'd have told his mother he doesn't actually 'go out and play' anymore. He's about to turn twelve. Mum thinks he's still five years old. The important thing now, though, is not to irritate her. So: no closed doors and no backchat.

"Are you going to have fun, then?" Mum asks while they're eating lunch, it's the leftovers from Saturday's deluxe dinner: pork chops and pineapple.

Börje can hear she is making an effort to sound light-hearted. As though she wasn't bothered. But Börje gets the picture. Mum never usually washes her hair on a Sunday. She's taken the rollers out now and put on her best day dress.

"Are you?" she asks, trying to catch his eye. His gaze is locked on a single panel in his Donald Duck comic. "You're bound to have some fun, aren't you?"

Börje shoves the food quickly into his mouth so he can't answer. He shrugs. As though he wasn't bothered either.

They pretend as hard as they can, Mum and him. That Dad doesn't matter. The important thing for Börje is not to let on. Not to seem too happy. Not to seem too keen. Because then Mum might suddenly stub out her cigarette, put her hand on his forehead and decide he's got a temperature. So she can stand in the doorway when Dad turns up and cancel the whole thing.

*

Mum seems to be buying his offhand shrug. She's almost cheerful as she turns on Radio Nord and gets on with the dishes, singing along to the songs.

Then Mum goes round to the lady next door. While she's away Börje looks out of the kitchen window and down at the courtyard hundreds of times. The day goes by. Mum comes back and starts cleaning the blinds without changing into a less fancy dress. Börje gets compote made with mixed dried fruit and a sandwich for dinner. At twelve minutes to seven the doorbell finally rings.

And there Dad is in the doorway.

Börje can hardly bring himself to look at him. It's all he can manage just remembering to breathe. Dad is so big. Tall and broad-shouldered. His waist is narrow and the muscles on his arms make his shirt look a bit tight. It almost feels like he won't fit in the space between the mirror and the coat rack. He stays on the doormat in the hall. Mum, who has taken off her apron, gives him a little toss of her head and Dad takes a half-step inside now he's got permission. He is tanned even though it is only the beginning of summer. His hair is so blond it is almost white and cut very short. Even white teeth and blue eyes. His nose is crooked because Dad knows how to box as well. One of his ears may stick out a bit but that does nothing to mar the overall impression.

"Typical Finn," Mum usually tells her girlfriends when Dad comes up in conversation, "God knows what I was thinking. And then I got knocked up before I even had time to blink."

Only now in the hall Mum's cheeks are flushed. She holds out Börje's backpack, dangling it from two fingers. Dad takes it from her.

"Do you need all that as well?" Dad asks, looking at the paper Co-op bags Börje is holding. "I came on the bike, didn't I," Dad says and strokes his chin thoughtfully.

Mum rolls her eyes so much her entire head rotates in a semi-circle towards the ceiling. Her curls fail to move even a millimetre. Her hair is a sprayed-on helmet.

"I'll repack it," she says and grabs both the bags and the backpack. "Were you planning on him wearing the same clothes the entire week?"

"It'll be OK, Mum," Börje says. "I won't need that much; it's summer."

Mum disappears into the kitchen. They can hear her yanking open the drawstring of the backpack and angrily rustling the plastic bags.

"You owe me money as well," she calls to Dad from the kitchen. "When were you planning on paying?"

Börje is getting worried. She's angry now but Dad is smiling and winking, so Börje smiles back.

He smiles so hugely his face gets tight and his hands feel sticky all over with happiness, like they were covered in fizzy drink.

When Börje and Dad go into the courtyard, the lads are already gathered around his Dad's motorbike. They send envious glances Börje's way when he pulls on the leather jacket and crash helmet Dad brought for him. Dad jokes and chats with them and shows them around his black BSA Gold Flash 650, the 1956 model. Börje lives alone with his mother. So he's usually the one standing there looking on enviously as his mates' fathers pack their cars so the family can drive to their home villages in the Torne valley, or when those dads clear the snow outside the front doors and wax their boys' skis. But this time there isn't a single boy in the courtyard who wouldn't trade places with Börje. With a Dad like that!

"Show us your tattoos," one of the smaller boys says.

Dad laughs and asks which one they want to see. The bigger lads grin in embarrassment but one of the younger ones says:

"The bird, of course."

Dad opens his shirt and shows them the naked girl sitting in the middle of a boxing ring with large boxing gloves hanging round her neck on a cord, hiding the most secret parts of her breasts.

The boys have got loads of questions. Did it hurt? How old was he when he got his first tattoo? How can he have so many? Has he got a tattoo on his cock as well? The bravest of them presses his finger against Dad's chest, as if to check it really wouldn't rub off.

"It does hurt," Dad warns. "Don't get tattoos, lads. Only sailors, ex-cons and drifters get tattooed. If you want a job in the mine, you need to keep your skin clear of rubbish like this."

They are all thinking they'll be damned if they end up working in the mine like their dads. They want to get tattoos. They want to box and ride motorbikes.

Börje and Dad are breezing along the highway in the early summer evening. Börje has his backpack on and his arms are wrapped around Dad's waist. Dad has his backpack around his belly. They pass farms, forests, fields with silvery-grey barns. Dad stops for cows returning from the woods. They fill the entire road so you can't drive past. Börje will always remember the flat-sounding bells around the necks of the lead cows, the way they keep mooing out of longing for the evening milking, their heavy udders like bags under their bellies. He will remember the swallows hunting food for their chicks and the telephone lines glowing in the evening sunlight. The river he will remember for ever. The river that is always there, running beside the road.

In Junusuando they drive over the bridge and head for Kurkkio. Dust whirls up behind the bike.

The last stretch is along a forest road. The exposed sandy soil makes it feel like driving on sawdust. And then they are there.

The cottage is brown with a corrugated roof. The key is hidden in an empty jam jar behind the privy.

"I can borrow it for a week in exchange for building a new set of stairs to the door and painting the woodshed," Dad explains. "We'll get that done in a flash, you and me. We're good at working together."

Börje nods.

"Are you hungry?"

Börje shakes his head. He doesn't dare even open his mouth to speak. That feels so strange, like he might start to cry if he did. Not from sadness. But from this enormous feeling he can't explain. He has a wary look around. At the sun dissolving into the still river. A punt is lying upside down a little way in towards the woods; the jetty is still pulled up, a sign summer has barely begun.

"So let's get fishing. Can you see the rings forming in the water?" Dad says, pointing.

Börje tracks his finger. Rings are expanding across the surface of the river.

The boat takes in some water but it isn't that big a problem, and Börje isn't the least bit scared. They fish in silence. The only sounds are timid ones. The line hissing out, the lure plopping on the water, the clicking of the spool when they wind the lines in. A splash some way off. An animal diving in, a field mouse maybe. A screech in the distance.

"Buzzard," Dad says.

They catch two perch and a trout. Dad has brought salt along and a carton of soured milk. He makes a fire on the bank and they grill the fish and eat it with their bare hands. They drink the milk out of plastic cups. Dad lights the fire in the sauna.

They doze off beside the open fire while waiting for the sauna to heat up.

Then they go inside. Börje sits on the lowest bench, Dad on the highest.

They swim in the river to cool down. Börje dives and swims for long stretches under the surface.

"*Ninku saukko,*" Dad says. Like an otter.

Later they practise boxing for a while by the riverbank. It is way past bedtime but that doesn't matter. The night is light and Dad says that this week they can go to sleep when they feel tired. Dad is good at boxing but a blow to one eye spelled the end of his career.

"You've got to be able to see the right hook coming," he explains to Börje. "Otherwise you haven't got a chance."

He holds up the palms of his big hands and has Börje hit them.

"The jab to the head," Dad says, cheering him on, "means your opponent raises his guard and you can land a blow on his body right away. The second punch is the most dangerous, the first is the one the opponent sees coming. Breathe. If you don't breathe you won't get any oxygen and you'll get tired. Keep your guard up. Wow, that's some clout you've got. A jab and a punch to the bottom rib. Bang. Boom. Nicely done."

"No, more!" Börje says when Dad asks if he's getting tired and wants to go to bed.

So then they practise dodging and ducking, quickly moving your head to the left, to the right, to avoid a blow.

"Duck! Don't drop your guard!"

Suddenly Dad grabs Börje's arm. Not hard but enough to make Börje stop moving.

"Do you hear that?" he says, pricking his ears towards the woods.

Börje can make out the sound of an engine. It is approaching rapidly. He looks at Dad's face. There is a new expression on it. Börje feels a wave of anxiety run through him.

Dad turns the boat over.

"In here!" he says. "Crawl under. And stay inside, don't move a muscle and not a peep out of you. Do you hear me? You're not to move until I say the all clear. Not a moment before. Nod so I know you've understood me."

Börje nods and does as he is told. Dad takes off, moving quickly.

Börje keeps listening. He can hear the car pull up and stop at the cottage. The engine keeps running. Börje can hear voices but can't make out what they are saying.

He can hear footsteps now. Someone is taking a walk around the cottage, they go inside and come out again after a while. They come down to the riverbank. Stop by the boat Börje is lying beneath, tense as a leveret. Börje can see the shoes. They aren't Dad's. The stranger's feet are so close Börje could reach out a hand and touch them.

Without making a sound, Börje manages to squeeze his feet under the sitting board beside the oars and put his hands on the inside of the boat. Then he raises his body. Bracing with his hands, he lifts his backside so his back forms a bow. The effort makes him tremble.

The person outside puts his hands on the ground and looks under the boat. Börje breathes in tiny silent gasps. Then the person gets back on their feet. The steps disappear towards the cottage. Börje drops back with a thud to the ground, but the surface is so soft he makes hardly any noise. His heart is threatening to explode in his chest from the strain on his body.

The car drives off. Börje wants to crawl out immediately because all the mosquitoes in the area seem to have discovered his hiding place. They are biting him in the exact spots he knows will itch the worst. Around his ankles and on the soles of his feet, on his instep and the back of his hands.

Only he wasn't supposed to move from the spot until Dad gave the all-clear.

Börje waits. Dad will be back soon. And before they fall asleep he'll be lying on Dad's arm. They'll make a fire in the hearth and Börje will ask Dad to tell him about the World Championship bout between Ingo and Floyd. Dad knows it by heart, like a newspaper report he's memorised.

But the wait gets longer and longer. Maybe Dad went inside to put the coffee on. Could he have forgotten he told Börje not to move until he got back and gave him the all-clear?

In the end he wriggles out from under the boat. He listens hard. The silence is total. Just the mosquitoes and the river lapping at the bank.

There's no sign of Dad anywhere. Not in the cottage. Not in the sauna. Not in the privy.

Börje starts running back and forth around the area in front of the cottage. In the end he feels brave enough to yell:

"Dad! *Isä!*"

No answer comes in the bright summer night. Just the sound of wings lifting off the water.

Many years later Börje will think that in a sense his life stopped at that point. And he is still there by the riverbank calling for his dad.

Pohjanen went ahead of Börje Ström into the autopsy suite and dropped onto his wheeled metal stool. Börje found himself standing beside the steel counter on which the remains of his father were lying. He inspected the tattoos in detail. He had to take a step back after that and breathe into his sleeve.

"Christ," he gulped. "Though I suppose you're used to a lot worse?"

Pohjanen cleared his throat.

"Yeah, I've seen and smelled almost everything by now."

"Shot through the chest," Ström said softly. "Jesus. What was he mixed up in? What do the police say?"

"The police?" Pohjanen said. "They're not saying anything. The murder is barred by the statute of limitations, meaning the period in which a prosecution would be possible has expired."

Börje Ström scratched his head like a bear.

"Expired? I'm a bit punchy, you know. After all the blows to the head. But I didn't think the statute of limitations applied to murder."

Pohjanen screwed up his face, which made him look like a lemming.

"Quite right. Not anymore. But the change only applies to murders committed after 1985. The new law was passed in 2010, to ensure that the Olaf Palme murder didn't end up being barred by statute."

"I see," Ström said with a lopsided smile. "So I suppose I should have had a dad who was prime minister."

Pohjanen rolled over to the counter on which the dead man's clothes had been piled. He picked up the shirt.

"Do you recognise this?" he asked.

Spellbound, Börje Ström stared at the blue-and-white checked shirt for several seconds.

"That's Dad's," he said in a voice that refused to carry.

Then something twisted in his face.

Pohjanen was afflicted with a feeling of paralysis. Was Börje Ström going to cry? Pohjanen wasn't much of a crier himself. Except when he was watching programmes about past sporting achievements, or about Americans coming to Sweden to look for their roots. He reached out a hand but it only got halfway before turning and stealing into Pohjanen's pocket. Put your hands in your pockets, clench them. Keep them like that.

Pohjanen could see Börje Ström fighting back. Like a boxer on the ropes. Ström's fists lifted upward slightly. True to the habit engrained in them of protecting the head and the body, the heart as well for that matter. But what good is your guard against pain like that. Grief will come at you like a punch from within.

"Take as much time as you need," Pohjanen said and made an attempt to get up from his stool. "I'll wait . . ."

He finished his sentence with a nod at the break room.

Only then Ström pulled back his shoulders and shook his head.

"I'm OK," he said. "Just got to get used to the idea, I suppose. That no-one's going to do anything. That we will never know."

Pohjanen opened his mouth but closed it again – his profession had taught him not to make promises he couldn't keep.

"Are you going to drive back to Älvsbyn now?" he finally asked.

"I'll stay on for a few days," Ström said. "I'm assuming I'll need to arrange the funeral."

He thanked Pohjanen for his time. Then he left.

Pohjanen remained sitting beside the dead man.

He wasn't the sentimental sort, Pohjanen. You have to feel sorry for people but man is wolf to man. All the things he had seen pass beneath his hands. Women and children beaten to death, young people committing suicide, tragic accidents, murder and disease, all of that had led to sorrow bottoming out inside him, a form of resignation his wife called cynicism. It had served as the foundation upon which his professional identity was based.

"And how could I have survived otherwise?" he said to the dead man on the steel counter.

"You've got to stay detached if you're going to do a good job."

Though he realised all the same that the dead had taken part of him with them to the grave. That he would have been a better father and husband had he chosen a different career.

"Hand surgery perhaps," he said with a cough. "Though what do I know, an ENT physician doing one cochlear implant after another, maybe?"

He didn't usually talk to the dead. But this was a special case.

There was a feeling inside him. Rage. At how Sweden had treated Börje Ström after the match in the Catskills. And shame. At how his own family had treated him before his boxing career, when Ström was just a boy.

"My own father included," Pohjanen said to the dead man. "And me too for that matter. Couldn't I just not give a shit for once about staying detached, so I can do something? To help? Because I can. Because I haven't got that much time left."

Rebecka Martinsson stopped the car in her yard. Turned off the engine and stayed in her seat as though she was incapable of getting out.

How can I be this tired? she thought. I'll have to go and have a health check. Thank God winter's over so I won't have to clear snow for a while.

The Brat got to his feet in the cage, wanting to get out and do his rounds of sniffing at the soil.

Rebecka gave her house a listless look. It stared listlessly back. It occurred to her she ought to ring someone about the roof, but not today.

So, Mum's foster sister Ragnhild. And Ragnhild's brother Henry who died out there on the island. And the corpse of Börje Ström's father in Henry's freezer.

There was another brother, Rebecka knew that. Olle Pekkari. He was still actively involved in the family company he continued to run with his son long after he'd retired.

Her mother had been fostered by the family from the age of three. Rebecka knew nothing about her maternal grandmother; on one occasion Mum had said: "I don't know anything either. She was just a girl when she had me so she handed me over to the Pekkaris and moved over the border to Finland." Though the Pekkaris were her mother's only family, they had never had any contact with them. Rebecka's mother had left her and her father when Rebecka was seven. Dad died when Rebecka was eight. Rebecka had stayed on with her father's mother, and Mum had been run over by a lorry and died when Rebecka was twelve. On a straight bit of road.

There was just her grandmother left after that. And Sivving. They were her family.

Every so often the Pekkari name had come up. She had vague memories of Sivving saying to her grandmother that they ought to help out with Rebecka. So she could go on a skiing trip, get a new bike.

"Not on your life," her grandmother had said. "I would never ask them for anything. They chucked Virpi out when she was fourteen."

Her grandmother almost never talked about Mum otherwise. A lesson Rebecka had learned early on. Questions about her parents made her feel sad and her face would be closed off. Did Mum like potato dumplings? I've no idea. What kind of flowers did she like? The questions you ask. How did they meet? It would have been at some dance, I don't really remember.

It was when Rebecka began her legal studies and had to move south that one of the old ladies in the village said it was obvious now she was Virpi's daughter. She said nothing further by way of explanation but Rebecka had understood what she meant. Virpi had been an odd person and Rebecka was the same. That was hard for some of the villagers to accept, of course: Mikko's daughter becoming a lawyer. Their status in the village had been so low. Mikko and that company of his that barely got by. When Rebecka was little and got bullied by the other kids, he couldn't speak out. She understood that better later on. The same kids' parents had bullied Mikko when they were little. Everything got repeated. Like a merry-go-round that couldn't be turned off.

Several years went by, and then she came home on a visit in her boots and long coat. They could stare as much as they liked, she thought. She was upsetting the entire balance of the universe in that coat she had bought at Tiger.

Life in Stockholm became a kind of prison as time passed. She worked and worked and kept on working. And lost herself. She would come home only for the odd week or two in the summer. And for a few days at Christmas. Now the coats were from Prada.

And in the end for her grandmother's funeral.

She could have been there still. Walking across the Persian rugs in the office wearing increasingly expensive shoes. Passing out in front of some brain-dead television series in an ever more expensive flat.

When she left Stockholm and moved into her grandmother's house with its grey Eternit cladding of fibre-cement, it had felt like a kind of liberation. The jaws of the steel trap, a legal career of long workdays, billable hours and rich clients without morals, had snapped shut. She had managed to escape though. Wounded but still alive. She had found her way back to her lair on a south-facing slope, surrounded by all the worn objects that reminded her of her life here, the homespun curtains, beer-glazed furniture, the traditional kinds of flower her neighbours had brought over while telling her they'd got a cutting of it once from Rebecka's grandmother.

Only now it felt like she was back in the trap. Her workload was insane. Who was she doing it for? And for a fraction of her old salary.

And how the hell had she ended up under the heel of von Post?

"I don't give a shit about her," Rebecka said aloud in her car without really understanding who she was talking about.

There was a knock on the side window.

"You dreaming in there?" Sivving asked as he opened the car door.

The sun was low in the sky. The birds were chirring. And the roof was dripping.

"Just spring tiredness," she said.

"That'll be it," Sivving said. "You get this sleepy feeling as winter starts receding, with the sun shining on the snow and spring on its way."

She let the Brat out of the car and he immediately invited Sivving's bitch Bella to play. He kept jumping from side to side, dipping his chest and forelegs and waving his tail so intently that Sivving had to laugh and say it was going to come off if he kept going.

"Oh come on," he seemed to be saying.

But Bella refused even to look at him. She had a Lovikka mitten in her mouth.

"She drives me crazy," Sivving said, giving Bella a loving look completely at odds with his choice of words. "First there was the phantom pregnancy and now she's adopted that mitten. She's been whining and making a den and raising hell. I've barely slept all week. I was actually going to ask if you could think about taking her for a bit. Do you want some veal stew in dill sauce?"

He held out a plastic container, waving it at her invitingly.

"All you need to do is boil the potatoes. Listen, did you take the car in for its MOT?"

"I will," Rebecka assured him and felt such a powerful desire to lie down on the sofa and fall asleep it was making her almost nauseous.

"How are you doing?" Sivving asked.

"I just had a really weird day at work," she said.

"Did you see Krister?"

"What? No, I . . . Krister's got nothing to do with anything."

Except that what flashed through her mind was the way Krister had looked up at her window.

"Well, then," Sivving said. "You can tell me about it over dinner. Have you got any potatoes? Or should I go and get them?"

They heated the veal stew and cooked the potatoes, which led to Rebecka's windows steaming up again. They had dinner while Rebecka told Sivving about Henry Pekkari who had died out on Palosaari and

Börje Ström's father whose dead body had been found in Henry's freezer.

The dogs were stretched out contentedly on the floor. They'd been given a bit of the veal on top of their biscuits.

Bella stuffed the Lovvika mitten under her belly and growled at the Brat if he came too close.

"Ever since 1962," Sivving repeated while probing between his teeth with a fingernail. "Did you speak to Ragnhild Pekkari? Olle?"

"No, the murder is beyond the statute of limitations. And they're not my real aunt and uncle. You know perfectly well we've never . . ."

Rebecka let a shrug conclude her sentence.

Suddenly the dogs leaped up and started barking.

The sound of a car could be heard approaching.

"Who is it?" Sivving asked as Rebecka got up to look out of the window.

In the yard below Pohjanen was extricating himself from a taxi.

"Pohjanen," Rebecka groaned. "He's come to try and persuade me."

Pohjanen said yes to dinner. Then he moved the meat and potatoes around his plate as though he could somehow trick them into thinking he had eaten.

"I've never asked you for anything, Martinsson," he said, contently parking his feet on the Brat who had lain down exactly beneath him. "You ought to do me this favour. Haven't you got anything to drink at this establishment?"

Rebecka got up and went to the corner cupboard. She took out three shot glasses and a plastic bottle. They had two shots each with their food. Then Rebecka said:

"I've got to get up early. We've a lot on with Björnfot away."

She glared at her watch, but none of those present came out with anything like "Goodnight" or "Tomorrow's another day". They were perfectly content in her kitchen and in no hurry. They filled each other's glass. When the bottle was empty, Sivving went and got another without asking permission.

Sivving leaned back far enough to make his wooden chair creak slightly.

"Börje Ström," he said. "His gold at the national championships in '68 was historic. A greater achievement than his gold at the Olympics, if you ask me."

"I agree," Pohjanen said. "Still a junior and his opponents went down like pick-up sticks."

"And after the match in the Catskills . . ."

Sivving shook his head, Pohjanen joined in the headshaking.

Rebecka refrained from asking what happened after the Catskills and what kind of match that was. All she wanted was to go to bed.

"Börje Ström deserved better then and he deserves better now," Sivving said. "We can at least try to find out what happened to his father."

We, Rebecka thought, who's we?

"Rebecka," Sivving went on, a note of appeal in his voice. "Won't you help out with this?"

"I thought you wanted me to look after Bella," Rebecka said curtly. "I can't do both—"

"Is that all?" Sivving cut her off, making a generous sweeping gesture with one hand while pouring more into Pohjanen's and his own glass. "I'll take the dogs. And you can take the corpse in the freezer."

"There must be someone else you can ask," Rebecka said to Pohjanen. "I'm not actually the police, you know."

Pohjanen uttered a contemptuous laugh. It sounded like shaking a bag of empty tins.

74

"Just who am I supposed to ask?"

"Right, right," Rebecka said and began to clear the table.

She knew what was what after all. The police in the county respected Lars Pohjanen but he was not particularly popular.

He got irritated by the way police officers behaved at crime sites. In the courtroom he referred to them as my thank-God-they've-been-fingerprinted friends in the force. Because they had such a remarkable propensity for contaminating both crime sites and victims, it was a good thing the fingerprints of police officers were registered and kept in their records along with their DNA. The officers got their own back by sneering and mocking him behind his back. They joked it was difficult to tell the difference between Pohjanen and the corpses in his cold store. One fine day Anna Granlund was bound to saw open his skull by mistake. They called him Gollum.

"According to Gollum, death occurred immediately," they might say.

"And just how do you think that would look like: a prosecutor taking on work as a private detective in her free time?"

"I don't give a damn how it looks," Pohjanen said.

His voice began to give way.

"I'm begging you, Martinsson. I don't have the strength to do this. You've got to help me. Grant the wish of a dying man."

He rapped his index finger on the tabletop as though his wish was right there in front of her. His words were completely devoid of their usual grumpiness.

The Brat got to his feet and put his head in Pohjanen's lap.

"Seriously," Rebecka said. "Why is this so important to you?"

Pohjanen was getting ready to launch; it clearly went very deep.

"The sins of the fathers," he said. "You may have read about that in the Bible? I owe a debt. And if I could help him . . . it wouldn't free me of the sin . . ."

He coughed.

". . . but it would lighten the load. You could lighten my load, Martinsson. Before I go on my final journey."

"You're shifting the debt onto me," Rebecka said with something close to a smile.

"Uh-huh," Pohjanen said. "Am I succeeding?"

Then he seemed in a hurry to disappear halfway under the table and devote himself to scratching the Brat behind his ears until the dog started thumping the floor with one of his back paws in a futile attempt to assist with that lovely scratching.

Sivving gave Rebecka a look across the table. Stop tormenting him, it said.

"Time to go," Pohjanen said and got to his feet unsteadily. "Will you ring for a taxi?"

"Okey-dokey," Rebecka said. "And tomorrow I'll ring Sven-Erik Stålnacke. In case he's feeling a bit bored and wants to help."

"So you *are* going to do this for me," Pohjanen said, without interrupting the rather laborious procedure of putting his coat on; his arms had to go inside the sleeves and his scarf had to be wound around his neck. "In that case let me thank you. You should be prepared for Stålnacke to need some persuading. I've heard he's been refusing to come into town since his retirement. He can't bear the idea of them moving the place."

"Well, they are digging up half the town, aren't they," Sivving said. "It looks like the councillors buried a treasure and then forgot where they put it. Rebecka, take Börje Ström with you when you drive out to Sven-Erik. Who could say no to the mighty river himself?"

When Rebecka was finally alone in the kitchen, those thoughts about Krister came back. All the times they had eaten dinner with Sivving. She poured vodka into her glass, started on the dishes and while she was doing them, drank what was left in the bottle.

She was thinking about Anna-Maria as well. And about their being friends. Only she really should have been able to accept it was her terrible photo that meant the case couldn't go to court.

Instead she's badmouthing me to the people we work with, she thought. And she's always got her plate full with work and her family.

And it was while she was thinking about Anna-Maria's large family and her messy kitchen that her mind drifted to Marcus, the boy Krister was fostering.

She had to stop doing the washing-up at that point and head for her bedroom. The Brat was lying across the bed in a majestic cross shape. In his dreams he was chasing away anyone who didn't belong there. He grunted in his sleep as Rebecka pulled him towards her.

Ragnhild Pekkari unlocked the door to her flat and stepped into the hall. She had locked the door for the last time that morning but now she was back. Everything was familiar but felt strange. How many thousands of times had she stepped inside exactly this same way, seen exactly this view towards the living room, the back of the sofa, the flowers on the windowsill, the door to the balcony? How many times had she kicked off her shoes at this very spot on the mat while leaning against the doorframe? Nothing inside the flat felt like it was hers anymore though.

Theirs was a relationship that had ended. The threads that had linked the apartment and her, that had made it her home, had been cut. They were strangers to one another. It felt dead. In the same way homes did when they had been empty for a long time.

She looked at herself in the hall mirror. What a strange day it had been, and one that had ended in a long conversation with a policeman called Fred Olsson.

Having to go over what had happened once she had discovered her brother and then the corpse in the freezer had been excruciating.

"So you didn't ring the police or the ambulance or the undertakers at that point?" Sergeant Olsson had asked. "Instead you went looking for the dog? And it was when you were looking for food for the dog that you found the body?"

He had asked if she needed to talk to a psychologist. She had declined.

They obviously think I'm crazy, she thought while taking off her shoes and hanging up her coat. Might be true. Mad people don't know they are mad.

She was in the bathroom brushing her teeth like an intruder with someone else's toothbrush. Which was blue.

She stood in the doorway to the bedroom and stared at the bed and it didn't feel right for her to sleep there. In the end she lay on top and covered herself with a blanket and stared at the ceiling.

Her thoughts drifted to the island and the farm. To the dog she had called Villa, who bit her and vanished. She just didn't have the strength to resist, her thoughts could go where they pleased, what did it matter?

Then she was thinking about the real Villa, the Villa of her childhood. And about when she was small and used to lie down in the sleigh that was full of soft hay *Isä* had brought home from the sheds for the cows. A pack of raisins if she was lucky and one of the books from home that had been read to bits.

She was lying there listening to the sounds from the farm, the chains on the cows that rattled when they moved. And Villa, who would appear from nowhere to lie at her side. She remembered how they used to doze off there in the sun.

And without being aware of it, Ragnhild drifted off to sleep.

WEDNESDAY 27TH APRIL

Rebecka spent Wednesday reviewing twenty-three of the cases and preparing them for the hearing. In the afternoon she drove to Hotell Ferrum to pick up Börje Ström.

They didn't say much. Shook hands. It wasn't awkward the way it can sometimes be with older people from the region. He was used to shaking hands, she supposed, after a long boxing career. And after all those years at the legal firm she had got used to it as well. Cheek-kissing on the other hand, that always went wrong. You went off in the wrong direction, collided and never knew whether it was supposed to be one, two or three times.

You didn't shake people's hands when Rebecka was growing up. You greeted each other with a nod, possibly a curt *terve*, hello. Or if you were of the Laestadian persuasion: *jumalan terve*, the peace of God.

Rebecka had tried to explain it to Måns: "Only Swedes shook hands," she said. "We had to fit in."

"You poor things," Måns replied ironically.

She fell silent then. He sensed she was feeling awkward and immediately started talking about his childhood. He'd had to learn to bow and politely shake hands even as a little lad, hadn't he just. His father's beady eyes watching across the family silver and the linen napkins. If you failed to bow to guests you got a slap to the back of the head. If you put your elbows on the table, Father crept up on you from behind, raised his arm and smashed your elbow onto the table. And that was that. Mind you, a few rules about social conduct never did any harm; it was the putty that held people together.

"I'm sorry," Måns said, "but not being brought up properly and cultural differences are not one and the same thing."

"So you think we weren't brought up properly, do you?" Rebecka said and then they had a row. Rebecka had proceeded to make it very clear to him there actually had been rules for how you were supposed to behave in her grandmother's home in Kurravaara.

I should end things with Måns, she thought.

Not that it was really necessary. They were rarely in touch. And almost never saw one another anymore. Presumably he had a load of other women.

Beside her Börje Ström grunted in appreciation, which yanked her out of her depressing thoughts. They had driven onto Nikkaluoktavägen and the sparkling white peaks of Kebnekaise were spread out in front of them under a cloudless sky. She slowed the car, not for the view but because of some stray reindeer. They were in no hurry to get off the road.

"Nothing we can do about it," Börje Ström said and got out his phone and photographed the reindeer as they slowly trotted past. "We come from the loveliest place in the world."

That's true, Rebecka thought and felt a longing for the mountains stir inside her. She hadn't been on a hike across the peaks for . . . well, that was with Krister. They had camped in winter tents along with the dogs.

She glanced out of the corner of her eye at Ström's hand, the one holding the phone. At the tattoo with three blue-green dots. He was immediately aware of her glance. Obviously used to tracking them. A glancing look could precede a punch.

"The dots were my first tattoo," he said. "A mate did them with a darning needle and the ink from a snapped-off biro. My mum went bonkers."

JULY 1962

It has been two weeks since Dad disappeared. Börje has been out on his bike. When he gets home a policeman is in the kitchen talking to Mum.

"So there you are," she says.

Her voice sounds put on, Börje thinks. It's not for him even though he's the one she's talking to. She doesn't sound like that when it's just the two of them.

The officer asks Börje questions about his father, even though he's looking at Mum the whole time. Börje has to answer. There isn't that much to tell. Dad told him to hide. A car arrived. Someone came over to the upside-down boat where he was hiding. Then that someone vanished. The car drove off. When Börje crawled out Dad was gone. He kept looking. Then he walked to the nearest house and knocked on the door. They rang Mum.

"Did you hear voices?"

"No, I mean yes, but not that well."

"So you couldn't hear any words? Or how many there were?"

Börje shakes his head.

"Can I go now?"

He can.

He bows and shakes hands because he knows Mum likes him to do that. Especially when she uses that voice. Then he sits on the bed in his room with a Donald Duck in his lap. Funny, because the officer said his surname was Fjäder, feather. Just like Donald Duck. Through the door he can hear Mum asking Sergeant Feather if he'd like coffee. Although he says he doesn't really have time, he ends up saying yes please.

Then Mum lowers her voice and Börje gets silently off his bed and presses his ear to the door.

"He's protecting his dad," Mum says. "That's what the man's like . . . and then some. A Finn, you know. So there was drinking to be done. It must have been his friends came to pick him up. And then he fell in the lake. Or went back home to Finland. Just you wait, he'll come crawling back towards autumn. I should never have let him take the boy with him. But what was I supposed to do? A boy needs his father. A role model and that. Only what kind of role model. Tattoos all over his body. No proper job."

When the policeman has left, Börje puts on his shoes. Mum comes out into the hall straight away.

"Where are you off to?" she asks.

"Out."

"I can see that."

She's using her normal voice.

"Where to?"

"Dad didn't go off with his mates," Börje says.

"How do you know?"

"Why did he ask me to hide if they were his mates? He wouldn't have left me there on my own."

"Stop defending him," Mum says, hard as nails. "You don't know him. How could you? I've had to look after you on my own."

"You lied to the police. Said he ran off with his mates. But you weren't even there. How could you—"

Börje doesn't get any further before he gets slapped in the face.

"That's enough of that. Do you hear me?"

He touches his cheek. Then he opens the door and rushes down the stairs. She calls after him but he doesn't care.

He doesn't slow down until he reaches the playground. Matti, one of his mates, is by the swings, pushing his little sister up in the air. She is yelling and screaming inside the tyre swing. The whole world smells of the dust of summer. Everyone who can afford to has gone on holiday. Home to their villages in the Torne valley, home to Finland. One of the kids in his class has gone to Stockholm.

Börje strolls over to Matti.

"Are you going to play with girls all day, or do you wanna tag along?"

"Where to?" Matti says, pretending not to be interested, though he immediately lets go of the tyre and pretends not to hear when his little sister starts yelling: "Higher! Higher!"

"When I get a tattoo," Börje says.

"What? Who's going to tattoo you?" Matti asks.

"You are. If you've got enough *sisu*."

Börje comes home several hours later. His right hand is on fire. He looks aghast at his face in the hall mirror. Even his lips are white. But he did it. He tattooed the three dots. Exactly like Dad's. He looks at his grim face. That's a man with a pale mouth. He's not a boy anymore. Matti and the darning needle have whittled away the boyish flesh from his cheekbones.

"Where have you been?" Mum asks from the kitchen. "Your food's cold."

He tries to conceal his hand from her as he walks past, saying he's not hungry. But she's not slow about things like that, his mother. She latches on to his right hand like a snake. And forces it open, thinking he's got something inside, cigarettes maybe. But when she sees, when she realises, she starts yelling. She screams like she's on fire, yanking at his hair so it comes away in clumps. She shoves him into the kitchen wall first and then the table. "Have you gone mad?" she howls. "Gone completely crazy?"

She lifts him by the hair with her right hand while her left fumbles across the kitchen counter for a suitable implement.

This turns out to be the rolling pin. She takes off his shirt, changes hands, so her left is holding his hair and presses his head down onto the kitchen table while her right hand swings the rolling pin as best she can. As hard as she can, on his back, his bum, his head and neck.

In the end he starts screaming.

"Dad," he yells. "*Isä!*"

She tosses him into his room at that point and locks the door.

He falls across his bed, wailing into the pillow, and while he is sobbing and gasping for breath he can hear his mother bawling her eyes out in the kitchen.

He thinks she's crazy. How can she be feeling sorry for herself? Wasn't he the one who just got beaten?

Fucking crazy old cow, he thinks and is surprised.

He's never felt that way about Mum before. But this is a new Börje doing the thinking. The one the darning needle carved out.

In the middle of the night Börje wakes up. His hand is hot and twice its normal size. It is light outside and silent in the flat. His tongue sticks to the roof of his mouth. He's got to have something to drink. When he tries to get up there's a sudden flash of pain in his head and his body feels like it's broken all over. He falls back on his pillow and deeper into the dark.

The next time he wakes up his mother is standing beside his bed. She is talking but he can't hear anything. It feels like he's got cotton wool in his ears. The flowers on the curtains in his room keep getting bigger and then smaller, and then bigger again. He turns his face away from the light coming in at the window. He notices that the pillow is damp with sweat. Then he drifts off into a merciful sleep.

Mum wakes him. The blinds have been lowered and it is dark in the room. He's got pyjamas on but has no memory of changing into them. He feels so cold his teeth are chattering. Mum wipes his face and forehead with a cool cotton cloth; she helps him put on a jacket over his pyjamas and slips on his socks and shoes.

"The taxi's on its way. We've got to go to the hospital."

Later on. Has a whole day gone by? More than one? A doctor is sitting by his bedside. Börje's tattooed hand is in bandages.

"What a rascal," the doctor says in a kind voice and pats him on the head. "Now maybe you'll realise how dangerous that sort of thing is. It's pure luck you didn't get septicaemia. You'll have to take penicillin for a week."

Börje says nothing. He glances at his bandaged hand.

"You'll have to learn to live with the dots, I'm afraid," the doctor says.

Börje releases the breath he had been holding. When he saw the bandage, he thought they had removed the tattoo. A nurse steps out from behind the doctor's back. She looks very strict: the corners of her mouth are turned down and her nose is sharp but her touch is practised and kind as she undoes Börje's hospital shirt and lays bare his back. The doctor adjusts his spectacles and inspects the red streaks running across it. The nurse says nothing; she moves Börje's hair apart. His scalp is tender. There are hairless patches, clotted blood.

The doctor turns towards Mum without saying a word. The question fills the entire room nonetheless. The law permits the punishment of children but not their abuse.

"He was with his father," his mother says quietly. "We've been divorced for many years. He wanted to have him for a week over the summer."

Then she puts her hand in front of her mouth and lets the tears drip from her eyes.

Börje says nothing. It has been several weeks since he was with his dad, after all. When he disappeared. Not that the doctor knows that.

When they leave the hospital, Mum buys ice cream. Börje eats it even though he doesn't want it. His heart leaps every time he hears the sound of a motorbike. But when he looks round it isn't Dad. It is never going to be Dad.

Rebecka Martinsson knocked on the door to Sven-Erik Stålnacke's detached house with Börje Ström beside her. He really was very tall.

"Just come right in," she could hear Sven-Erik say inside. "Don't stand there knocking like you're the bailiffs."

He hadn't changed, Rebecka thought as she and Börje stepped into the hall. Sven-Erik was sitting at the kitchen table waving them in. His moustache looked like a scrubbing brush. A checked flannel shirt, braces and logger's trousers, his cap beside the crossword, just like a caricature of an old villager from the Far North.

Melancholy invaded Rebecka like a gust of wind. She had missed Sven-Erik at work. Anna-Maria did too, she had no doubt. They'd been wing mates for what seemed like for ever.

They sat in the kitchen. Sven-Erik took two cats off the table; they leaped back onto it straight away.

"If someone didn't keep feeding them the cheese from his sandwiches," Airi, Sven-Erik's partner, said.

Airi put on the coffee and microwaved some buns, apologising that they were from the freezer and not hot out of the oven.

"I was watching when you won gold at the national championships in 1968. Good Lord, you weren't even seventeen," Sven-Erik said to Börje. "You just picked off all his punches. He kept trying to hit you until he was tired and off balance. Your counters: biff-bam-wallop."

"Sounds about right," Börje agreed. "I'd got used to boxing with Finns when we drove over the border on the odd weekend. Their national pride was at stake and they weren't that picky about the stuffing in their gloves either. But when I went south and into the ring to fight against Swedes, I kept thinking: When are they going to start?"

One of the cats marched diagonally across the table and jumped down into Börje's lap before Sven-Erik could stop her. She was streaked with grey and had a black ring around one eye. After pawing around for a bit, she settled and started purring.

"Like an outboard, isn't it?" Sven-Erik said merrily. "She's actually called Boxer. On account of her eye. It's thanks to her Airi and me are a couple. She never seems to age a damned bit. She's looked exactly the same since she was a kitten. Just like you, sweetheart."

He said the last bit to Airi and made sure to pat her on the behind when she got up to get the percolator, which had stopped gurgling.

"Sven-Erik, please," Rebecka said. "It's the third millennium. You don't pat women on their behinds."

"What?" Sven-Erik said. "Not even your wife? In your own home?"

"I'm not your wife," Airi said. "We're not married."

She turned towards Rebecka.

"It's fine. Sven-Erik is allowed to pat my behind. And the boss. And one of our clients, he's important to the firm, so . . ."

She looked dead serious for two seconds and then burst out laughing.

"I'm joking."

Börje Ström raised his hands in a gesture that said best not touch anything at all. Not even the cat.

"Better sit on my hands," he said. "So I don't get sued."

"Except when you're drinking coffee," Airi said. "Get dunking."

They all dunked their buns in the coffee. Airi had put out some cheese as well. Börje explained what brought them here. Sven-Erik listened and scratched his moustache.

Rebecka took a look around. It was cosy, comfortable like Grandma's kitchen. Old cake tins made of copper as decoration on the walls. A row of trays. A neatly pressed decorative tea towel in front of the ones that were actually in use, embroidered with neat twinflowers in cross stitch. Decorations everywhere. Dala horses, bentwood boxes, the Swedish flag on a flagpole made of wood, painted tins from the forties and fifties on top of the kitchen cupboards, candlesticks, crocheted cloths, wooden casks, birch-bark knapsacks and Sami handicraft. There were egg boxes on the window sills containing halved shells filled with soil that had green shoots sticking out of them. Labels made of toothpicks and Post-its announcing they were marigolds, sweet peas, tagetes, poppy and baby-blue-eyes as well as useful plants like tomatoes, squash, lettuce, carrots and mangel-wurzels.

"I'll pay you, of course," Börje Ström said in conclusion.

"I would never accept payment," Sven-Erik said, stroking his moustache as though it were a small animal that needed calming. "It's a murder though, and one that's over fifty years old. They've got private detectives in Stockholm who take on jobs like that."

"I'm not that bright," Börje said and rapped his temple. "All those blows to the head, you know. Makes you a bit punchy. Only the way I see it, if some Stockholmer were to come along and try and talk to the people round here about a murder that happened more than fifty years ago . . . I might just as well pour my money down the drain."

"That's true," Rebecka agreed. "And besides, you know everyone, Sven-Erik."

"Oh, don't talk rubbish," Sven-Erik said, clearly pleased at being praised in front of Börje Ström.

Sven-Erik was looking at Rebecka. Saying no to the legend that was

Ström wouldn't be easy but it would be even harder to say no to her. Once, long ago, when Lars-Gunnar Vinsa shot his lad and then himself, Sven-Erik had held on to Rebecka. Held her as tight as he could so she wouldn't go and drown herself in the river. And now she was living alongside that river. Skiing across it in the winter. Fishing in it in the summer.

"You know," Rebecka said to Börje, "when you're with Sven-Erik in Kiruna it takes half an hour just to go ten metres. Everyone knows him and wants to stop and talk. And then you're related to half of them as well."

That last bit was said to Sven-Erik who waved off her comments.

"Regretfully," Sven-Erik said, "I've got to say no all the same. I've stopped working. And if the police failed to clear this up then the chances of finding out anything more are non-existent."

He fished out the coffee-cheese from his cup. The cats flocked around him. He shared the cheese out fairly between them.

Airi was stirring her coffee in silence, which Rebecka noticed.

Airi was usually more talkative. Though she might be feeling a bit shy with a celebrity in the kitchen.

"The thing is, Sven-Erik," Börje said, "the police never tried to find out the truth about Dad's disappearance. No-one cared. And in the end he was just declared dead. The same year I won the Olympic gold. I got some kind of letter to the effect that there was no 'estate'."

"In any case . . ." Sven-Erik cut in.

There was silence for a second or two.

"In any case Airi needs me here at home!"

Airi opened her mouth. About to say something. Then closed it again.

Börje reached his hand across the table. He had trained himself throughout his career to thank his opponent whether he won or lost.

"I'd like to thank you anyway, Sven-Erik," he said good-naturedly. "For taking the time to listen. And you, Airi, for the best cinnamon buns I've eaten for years and years. I bake myself now and then, but I've never got them to taste like that. You're a lucky man, Sven-Erik."

"Lucky as a leprechaun," Sven-Erik agreed.

"Real butter," Airi said. "And a lot more than the recipe calls for."

From the kitchen window Sven-Erik watched Rebecka's car pull out of the courtyard. He gave directions from the kitchen table but she reversed out through the gateposts without looking at him and without any mishaps.

"Börje Ström should have got the award for the most significant Swedish sports achievement of the year in '68," he said. "Or in '72, when he won at the Olympics. What happened after the Catskills was a scandal. That's an awful business about his father, isn't it? And to think it was a relative of Rebecka's who discovered him. In a freezer."

Behind him Airi was sighing so heavily that he turned round.

She'd taken off her apron and sat down. Her hands rested idly on the kitchen table. It looked like she'd asked him to attend a job interview.

He pushed away his coffee cup. What was all this about?

"My love," she began. "It's not in my nature to tell you how to live your life, how to behave at the dinner table, or how to dress. I don't tell you to change your socks or to get some exercise. You're a grown man and that's the way I like it. You're not some project with room for improvement as far as I'm concerned."

"Do you think I should change my socks more often?" he tried to joke.

"No, though you're welcome to join me at the water aerobics class sometime. No? OK then, you do what you like. We should live together as free companions. But now, just this once, I'm going to ask you: Help Börje Ström to find out what happened to his dad."

"They can manage that all by themselves," Sven-Erik said. "Rebecka Martinsson is an experienced—"

"Not for his sake. For mine."

Sven-Erik looked at her in astonishment.

"What do you mean?"

"That is what I mean," Airi said and pointed at the lamp above the kitchen table. "You've written the date you changed the bulb on every lamp in this house."

"To check if they last as long as it says on the box. It's outrageous what light bulbs cost these days. Sometimes their life expectancy is—"

"I don't care how long they last! And then there's the business with solar time—"

"Why should we bother with Swedish time now I'm finally retired and can live according to the daily circuit of the sun?"

"You tell me," Airi exclaimed. "When you can spend an hour a day working out the true solar time?"

"I hardly spend a whole hour—"

"The thing is, it really drives me crazy when we've decided you should pick me up at two o'clock, and then not knowing if you're going to turn up when my and everyone else's perfectly normal watches say it's two."

She stopped and took a breath. She didn't want to have a row. She could see he was about to seize and splutter like an old engine.

"You spy on the neighbour when he takes the rubbish out. You comment on the way they clear their yard. You get worked up about people who don't keep to the speed limit when they drive through the village. And you've only been retired a year."

"What are you trying to say?" Sven-Erik asked, unable to hide how hurt he felt. "You can't stand living with me? Don't you want me here?

I could move back into town if that's how you feel. The cottage is fully winterproofed, so you don't need me for that now."

"Don't play the victim," Airi said sternly. "You've never been a menial. Not in my house."

Airi put her hands on top of Sven-Erik's to stop him getting to his feet in fury.

"I want you here," she said. "I love you and I want you here. But not all the time. I like the cats around my feet when I'm cooking and washing up and dusting. But I don't want to trip over you. Don't get angry, my darling. It's just when I get home from work, I don't want you to have been waiting all day for me to come back."

His jaw was clenched. Her words had hit him hard.

Airi grabbed his fingers. She could see there was fear there too. Fear of becoming an old man no-one needed and who didn't know anything. She knew he was tormented by the prospect of having to go into Kiruna. The town Sven-Erik knew like the back of his hand that was sliding into the mineshaft bit by bit. And with no place for him in the new one that would replace it. "You won't know where you are soon," he had said the few times he had been there.

"Try it for a few days," she appealed to him. "For my sake. I used to find it so fascinating when you got home and told me about your day. You were the one Börje Ström asked, no-one else. Because you're the best man for the job. If you find it dull, I won't make you go on with it."

Sven-Erik was struggling. Part of him wanted to hurl himself into a ditch of wounded self-pity. Pack some clothes and get in his car. Tell her he could stay in his daughter Lena's guest room for the time being.

But he resisted. He bit back a defensive response. Anna-Maria Mella had been his boss for all those years. And she was far from tactful all the time. He'd had to learn to accept being told what to do by women. There wasn't any room for wounded pride.

"Alright," he said to Airi. "I suppose I could have a look at the case. If I knew you were OK with it."

"I'm OK with it," she said, thanking God for the corpse in the freezer out on that island in the Torne.

THURSDAY 28TH APRIL

At half past four in the morning Börje Ström and Sven-Erik Stålnacke picked Rebecka up from the police station. They had a rubber dinghy on the roof of the car.

"Ragnhild Pekkari said the ice isn't going to break but I'd prefer to be on the safe side," Sven-Erik explained to Rebecka. "So we'll do what they used to do in the old days. Take the boat with us. If the ice starts to break we can just jump into it."

"Jesus," Rebecka said. "Should I have drawn up my will?"

Even before they had driven out of town, Börje had fallen asleep in the back seat.

Sven-Erik looked at Rebecka out of the corner of his eye.

"This is a rum business isn't it?" he said. "Your aunt finding Börje's father. In your uncle's freezer."

"Like I said, she's not my real aunt," Rebecka said. "And Henry Pekkari wasn't my uncle. My mother was fostered in their family. I think she was six, maybe seven, when they moved off the island. She grew up in Kiruna. They lived in a small flat on Träarbetaregatan. Henry took over the little farm and timber yard. We didn't have any contact with the Pekkaris when I was a kid though. They kicked her out when she was fourteen."

Only what do I really know about all that, Rebecka was thinking. She got by abandoning people. And I got by without her. And I've got by without the Pekkari family.

"I don't know them," she said finally. "I've never even met them."

"Isn't there another brother in the family?" Sven-Erik asked.

"Olle Pekkari, he's the oldest child. Though made of sterner stuff. He runs a company that insulates roofs in mining areas. Though now it would be his son who's taken over most of the running I suppose."

"We'll have to have a talk with Olle Pekkari," Sven-Erik said. "Do you know if Henry and he were close?"

"How the hell should I know that?" Rebecka asked. "Were you or were you not in this car a moment ago when I told you the Pekkaris are not my relatives and I don't know them."

"We'll have to ask Ragnhild," Sven-Erik said, unfazed by her grumpiness. "She may have some idea about who her brother hung around with in 1962, even if she was a whole lot younger."

"Is she . . . is she going to be there?"

"Of course. Didn't I tell you? It doesn't matter, does it? There's no grudge between you, is there?"

"No, there isn't."

Just as long as she doesn't want to talk about Mum, Rebecka was thinking.

Just as long as Rebecka Martinsson doesn't want to talk about her mother, Ragnhild Pekkari was thinking.

She'd got up at half past three that morning and driven to Kurkkio, a journey of just over two hours. Then she had sat in the car beside the river, drinking coffee from a Thermos and waiting for Börje Ström, Rebecka Martinsson and that retired police officer whose name she'd forgotten.

The late winter sun was still hanging heavy over the horizon and the sky was the colour of unripe cloudberries. It was just before 7 a.m.

Lars Pohjanen had rung her himself. She'd never met him during all the years she was a nurse in A & E even if she'd seen him in the distance now and then in the car park. She knew who he was, of course.

Rumour had it he was a grumpy old sod, but he had sounded friendly on the phone. A little sad. He was asking for permission to cross to the island while it was still possible. He explained that this was not a police investigation in the usual sense. The man in the freezer was the father of the boxer Börje Ström, and the murder was beyond the time limit for prosecution. Only now a retired police officer, what was his name, the fact she'd forgotten was going to drive her crazy – she'd been the one who never forgot a patient's name – it was some kind of double name, had agreed to take a little look into the case. Would it be alright if he came to have a look at the house? No, they weren't really hoping to find that much in the way of answers after all these years, but all the same. And a prosecutor would also be with him, Rebecka Martinsson. Pohjanen had been told they were related.

"Not really," Ragnhild had replied.

When she said that, she could feel that heaviness inside her once again. It wasn't grief, it was just a weight; it was that worn-out outboard motor sinking, sinking to the bottom. Virpi's daughter was coming to the island.

Hard to find the right word for that feeling. She wasn't scared. Or angry. Maybe she'd death-cleaned her feelings as well. She had chosen not to ski out onto the snow bridge and to turn round and drive to the island. And now everything would turn out the way it was supposed to. It is what it is. Ragnhild hoped all the same that Rebecka wouldn't ask her about Virpi.

Because I don't have any answers, she thought, not a single one. And I'm not under any obligation to tell her anything. What would be the point?

A car was coming over the brow of the hill. There were three people inside and a rubber dinghy had been strapped to the roof. This must be them.

Börje Ström was surprised when Ragnhild Pekkari got out of the car. He hadn't been prepared for the way she looked. She was tall, six foot at least. Big but not square. He had admired other boxers all his life and when he looked at Ragnhild's arms he thought she must have a wonderful reach. He had to force his gaze away from her muscular backside.

He was watching her as she opened the roof box and got down her ski-sled, the ease of her movements. There was something bear-like about her. He had come across a bear once while running in the woods. It had been lying down, sleeping on a little hillock in a bog beside a forest road along the Rautas river. It had stood up just as Börje was passing. Just fifty metres away. With that very same lightness despite the fact that it was so big. Like water flowing upwards. This woman wasn't someone who'd need help getting things down from the top shelf.

When he took a step towards her to say hello, he felt something shift and sway inside him. He was used to looking down on women. But this one was at the same level as him. Which meant her eyes felt very close. They were as grey as a rainy day. He'd always liked rain. Going out for a training run on a rainy Swedish summer morning was the best thing ever. Particularly after the years in the US when he'd had to run in shimmering heat on dusty asphalt and this black stuff came out when you blew your nose afterwards.

Ragnhild Pekkari's eyebrows were wide and blond from the sun. Her braid was sticking out from beneath her woollen cap. She had the typical suntan of a winter skier. The skin around her eyes had been left pale by her sunglasses; the rest of her face was brown and weathered.

She put out her hand. It was dry and had calluses. As rough as bark. Börje Ström was reminded of something he'd been told as a child. There are calluses on the hand of the hard worker, blisters on the hand of the lazy.

She said something. But his mind was still stuck on that rough hand. It was a hand that did things. He wondered what. Chopped wood? Cleaned fish? Renovated houses? Drove a team of dogs?

He gasped as though he were short of breath. Her anorak smelled of an open fire. And then there was another scent, a familiar one, but he couldn't latch on to it. Freshly whipped cream? Sandpapered wood?

He felt an intense desire to put his nose against her skin and take her in.

It felt like he'd been blindsided. Like a punch you don't see coming. He let go of her hand. She said hello to the others, Rebecka and Sven-Erik.

He realised she had introduced herself and that he had failed to say his name. And it was a bit late for that now.

Ragnhild shook them by the hand. Börje Ström's hand was rough like hers. He let go of her hand quickly as though he'd been burned. She could feel herself blushing and getting angry.

What was he thinking? she wondered at first. That it was members of my family killed his father and put him in the freezer?

Then she reached inside for the feeling of contempt.

One of those, she decided. One of those men who've had women at their beck and call all his life. Handsome in a wrinkled way. Like Clint Eastwood. Thinks all he has to do is look at you and you'll just fall at his feet. A celebrity who can't even be bothered to tell you his name.

But she wasn't the fall-at-your-feet kind of woman, as he was going to find out.

"It would have been better if you'd brought your skis," she said brusquely, looking at the rubber dinghy. "The crust isn't going to break. And the ice in the old snowmobile tracks won't either. Not this early in the morning in any case, before the temperature gets above zero."

"I've still got a lot to live for," Sven-Erik said good-naturedly. "But you ski right ahead."

Rebecka Martinsson shook hands as though Ragnhild was nobody special. She busied herself helping to lift down the boat.

She had been afraid Rebecka Martinsson would say something along the lines of "You grew up with my mother, didn't you?" Only she said nothing of the sort. She was calm and pleasant. Seemed relaxed. Obviously, what with her job being a prosecutor you'd have to be practised at not letting your feelings run away with you. Or maybe Rebecka felt nothing for Virpi. It was hard to know.

Ragnhild got the Thermos out of the car. Pushed away her own feelings with arms that had been drained of energy.

Ragnhild had seen Rebecka once at the supermarket; she'd looked like a ghost. That was just after that policeman shot himself and his mentally handicapped son. Rebecka hadn't recognised her of course. Ragnhild had felt conflicted on that occasion. Ought she to go up to her? Tell her who she was? Ask how Rebecka was feeling? Ask her if there was anything she could do to help. But she'd done nothing. They'd never had anything to do with one another after all.

Ragnhild remembered when she visited Virpi during labour. She'd been at work that day so she could go over in her nurse's uniform without turning it into a formal visit. Virpi had let her hold the baby. They talked about the newborn so there'd been no need to tackle anything else. "You could say hello to Isak and Helmi for me, I suppose," Virpi had said in a flat voice. She called *Isä* and *Äiti* by their Christian names.

It was an odd notion that the child she had held in her arms then was the woman in front of her now.

Life passes quickly, indifferently, Ragnhild thought. It doesn't give a damn whether we get time to sort out our relationships or not.

She offered them coffee from the Thermos and told them about the dog still out there on the island.

"I boiled some meat and put it out on the porch before the helicopter arrived. I hope the magpies and the crows didn't get it all."

Rebecka raised her face towards the pale white sun that had risen to just above the treetops, it seemed like she was searching for the scent, like an animal.

"Shall we make our way over then?" she said. "So we can get back before it thaws."

And in that moment she looked just like Virpi. Squinting the way

Virpi did when assessing if you climb to the very top tree and conquer it, the narrowing of her eyes before she fought the boys at school in Kiruna.

Tuiskusapara, wind tail, is what *Isä* called Virpi. *Tuiskusapara*. One of those people whose mood changes like the wind. That was when they were living on the island. When Virpi moved out, he started calling her other things. On the rare occasion she was referred to by name.

Ragnhild hadn't thought of that word for more than fifty years.

You're not as calm as you appear, Ragnhild was thinking of Rebecka.

Then she attached the ropes from her sled to the belt around her waist and skied away. She forced herself not to think about Rebecka and that boxer and tried to think about the dog. She was wondering if it was still on the island. If Henry had given it a name.

The others could follow as they pleased and haul their bloody boat across the ice. She didn't care. She poled her way forward. The sled made the going heavy but she was glad of the physical tiredness, the sense of fatigue in her chest muscles, stomach and back. She wondered if Börje Ström was watching her. She thought she could sense that on the nape of her neck and all across her back. She didn't dare glance back to see if she was right or just imagining things. It was a good thing the distance she'd put between them meant her panting couldn't be heard.

The island was getting nearer. The derelict sheds were staring at her. You again. The black flower of grief began to bloom in her heart once more.

"I'll stay here," Rebecka Martinsson said, tracking Ragnhild's journey to the island with her eyes. "Someone's got to ring the emergency services when you go through the ice." She said the last bit with half a smile to Sven-Erik.

"Uhmm," Sven-Erik said but his mind appeared to be elsewhere.

*

Why would you chuck a body in the freezer? Sven-Erik was thinking as he and Börje Ström started making their way along the snowmobile track towards the island.

He'd intended asking the question aloud. The way he was used to talking things over with Anna-Maria Mella. Only it was the other man's father who had been in that freezer and it didn't seem right to talk about it as if it was just a professional matter.

It was going to be a lovely day. The sun's disc was rising, the sky turning blue. Börje was walking ahead along the snowmobile track hauling the boat. Sven-Erik was pushing from behind.

Sven-Erik soon started sweating beneath his cap even though the work involved wasn't that hard. Ström was taking almost the entire weight. Obviously. He was the kind of man who still ran ten kilometres in the woods dragging tractor tyres behind him.

When they got halfway Börje Ström came to a stop and took a look along the riverbank.

"The cottage Dad and I borrowed is only a little way upstream. But I can't see it from here."

They continued on and Sven-Erik returned to his musings.

So why would anyone chuck a body in a freezer? Ström's father had disappeared at the height of summer in 1962. So it would have been light all day and all night. The perpetrator, because it was by no means obvious that it was Henry Pekkari, wouldn't have wanted to dump the body in the river in case they were spotted. So why hadn't the killer just buried him. Because he, or she, Sven-Erik corrected himself mentally, couldn't be bothered perhaps? Digging requires a lot of effort. You need a big hole for a body. So no, you chuck the body in the freezer thinking that come autumn, when it's dark outside, you'll wrap it up, weight it down and sink it in the river. And then that just doesn't happen. In all likelihood the victim was shot at the farm. Presumably inside the house.

But no matter how hard he tried to free his mind of the idea, he kept coming back to the fact that Henry Pekkari had kept the body in his freezer all these years. Why would he have done that, if he hadn't been the one to shoot Börje Ström's father? And if that was the case, how did he know Raimo Koskela? And why did he murder him?

Ragnhild Pekkari was sitting on the steps to the porch when the two men came trudging up to the farm.

Rebecka must have stayed on the mainland, she thought. Just as well.

Sven-Erik wrestled himself out of his jacket and cap and chucked them onto the steps. His face was red as a tomato from the exertion.

"We're not eighteen anymore," he said with a smile while gasping for breath. "Any sign of the dog?"

Ragnhild nodded towards the empty dog bowls on the steps.

"Could be the crows. Or the fox. I can't see any tracks in the snow, so it's hard to know."

Börje was looking at the house. The drooping corners of his mouth made him look grim.

He must think I'm heartless talking about the dog when his dad was kept in a freezer here for all those years.

Sven-Erik asked if it was OK if he went inside.

"Feel free," Ragnhild said. "I opened all the windows and doors to make it bearable. I didn't dare start cleaning or anything when I was here last. I didn't know the murder was barred, did I? So I thought the police would be coming to look for evidence and I'd best not touch anything."

She fell silent.

Stop babbling, she told herself sternly.

"And that was the right thing to do," Sven-Erik said kindly. "I'd like to ask you some questions about your brother Henry later. If that's OK?"

"Of course. I've been assuming you think Henry killed . . . sorry, what was your father's name?"

"Raimo," said Börje Ström. "Raimo Koskela."

"I just find it so difficult to believe," Ragnhild said. "Henry was a failure and an alcoholic. And nasty with it. But him killing anyone. Though I suppose all relatives say that."

"Do you know if they knew one another?" Sven-Erik asked.

"I don't. But they might have, even though your father was older. Henry still had friends in 1962. People came out to the island and got drunk. He mostly surrounded himself with *ryökälhet*, villains, to use the word my mother would. That was why he was allowed to take over the farm. My mother and father thought he would pull himself together if he was given the responsibility. Only you can see for yourselves how that worked out. After the summer of 1967 my dad had to come out here and put the cows down."

"My father wasn't a villain," Börje said.

How would he know? Ragnhild was thinking. He was only a child, wasn't he, when his father disappeared? People idolise and they demonise. They never manage to create a complex picture of someone.

For half a second of soul-searching she thought about her own mental image of Henry. Of men in general.

"And what about your oldest brother, Olle?" Sven-Erik asked.

"He'd already started working at the mine by then," Ragnhild said. "He was made a foreman even though he was only twenty. Eventually he started his own firm, and he's always done really well for himself. His eldest son is the one running the company now."

Sven-Erik went into the house. Börje and Ragnhild stayed outside on the steps.

*

108

Ragnhild fetched from her sled a roll of black rubbish bags and some tins of dog food. Börje was watching her and thinking he had no idea what to do with himself when he was alone in this woman's presence. He felt his body might suddenly do something without him having a say. It might take a step forward and grab at her. Like a drunkard in a pub when it's time for the last dance.

He'd had a number of very fit women, it wasn't that. There were a great many ladies at home in the gym in Älvsbyn who started boxing because it was good exercise. Particularly if they'd just got divorced. Occasionally they wanted to move in. But that was where he drew the line. It would usually last until some bloke who could actually meet that need for both security and a father figure crossed their path. Or until they got tired of the fact that "the relationship wasn't going anywhere".

But this she-bear. Did she need someone? She'd definitely be satisfied with a solitary life in the woods.

He wondered if she had someone. And just what kind of person would that be?

When she passed him going into the house, he took a large step back so as not to be in her way.

As Ragnhild was passing Börje Ström, he backed away as if she was infectious. That show of his dislike for her hurt in some incomprehensible way.

She had become painfully used to men backing away all the same. Particularly shorter men with a better education. There had been a number of doctors over the years who had found her difficult to bear.

What do I care? she thought the very next second. He can think what he likes about me.

*

Sven-Erik Stålnacke shuddered. Henry Pekkari's house was one of the worst he had seen. And he had seen a good deal. The dirt on the door frames and the banisters was like a colour all its own, and even darker where Henry had put his hand on his way through the house. It required real determination to put your finger on the light switches and touch the door handles. He was grateful Ragnhild had opened the doors and windows and aired out the worst of the smell.

He went into the living room and looked around. Locating where the freezer had stood wasn't a problem at least. The pine floor was a different colour there. A rectangle where the wood hadn't yellowed and wasn't covered in a layer of filth. Thick rolls of dust had collected between the freezer and the wall and when it was hauled out the dust had settled onto the exposed area.

How squalid, Sven-Erik was thinking. Some people just seem to be born with really vigorous genes. It doesn't make any difference how little care they take of themselves. The fact that Henry Pekkari had survived his seventieth birthday must have been a minor miracle.

He could see Ragnhild entering the kitchen out of the corner of his eye. She went on to fill bag after bag with rubbish, old food, empty bottles, packaging. It sounded like she was tearing down all the curtains and wallpaper.

Sven-Erik was concentrating on the living room. The sofa was covered in several layers of blankets. It still looked lumpy even so, sagging and broken. That was where Henry had lain dead.

That would have been where he dropped off in front of the television, Sven-Erik thought.

The picture behind the sofa was a print in a gilded frame. All the colours had been dimmed by age, so that almost all that was left were the bluish-green tones. It showed a shepherd leaning against a stone wall, slicing a piece of meat. There was a dog at his feet begging for a morsel. In the background a landscape from southern Europe with cypresses and rolling hills.

It has been hung very low, though, that picture. It seemed really badly placed: you'd bang your head on it if you leaned back on the sofa.

Sven-Erik leaned closer in. An old hole left by a nail some way above the picture.

It really can't be that simple, can it? he was thinking as he lifted the picture off the wall.

Only exactly that simple it was.

Behind the picture was a bullet hole, clear as day.

Why did I have to come with them, Rebecka was thinking. It was still cold even though the sun had risen above the treetops.

She zipped up her jacket up and tipped her seat back. She was going to try to sleep for a bit.

They would have to hurry, she was thinking as she glanced at her watch. Once it warms up skiing across the river will become impossible. And I really don't think they'll want to spend the night over there.

She tried to fall asleep but failed. If only she could sleep for half an hour, twenty minutes. She would need that if she was going to be working late.

How am I going to be able to prepare all the cases by Monday, she was thinking, and how can I be this tired? I must have something wrong with me. I ought to go to a health food shop. And start making green drinks and going to the gym.

"Hello!"

The sound of a voice made her open her eyes. A very small old lady was coming down the road. She was hunched over and kicking a small sled in front of her. Patches of grit had started appearing through the melting ice here and there and it was hard to get the runners to go across them. She was dressed in an orange anorak that was much too big for her. Two improbably thin legs in heavy boots.

The woman was waving with her whole arm as though she were in a lifeboat on the sea. Rebecka opened the car door and got out. Goodbye forty winks.

"Hello!" the woman called again.

Only then her energy seemed to desert her. She stopped, moved laboriously round the sled and sat on it. She called out again:

"Who are you? Are you someone I know?"

Rebecka laughed.

"Should I come over there so you can see for yourself?" she called back.

"*Tule nyt*, come on then."

Rebecka walked over.

"So whose girl are you?" the old lady asked. "I could see some people going over to the Pekkaris. Who were they then?"

Rebecka explained who they were and what business they had on the island.

"And there's me telling people nothing ever happens in the village anymore. My name is Mervi Johansson. So Ragnhild's over there now?"

"She is, she wanted to have a clear-up and . . . then there was a dog that had disappeared."

"The dog, I see," Mervi Johansson said. "I'll keep my eyes peeled. Henry's dogs usually come to me. Sometimes during one of his spells he forgets to let them in even though it's minus twenty-five outside. He forgets to give them food as well. That's when they learn to find their way to me. Henry and I are the only permanent residents of the village. Then when he's back on his feet he comes to fetch them. I've told him he can't chain them up and he has to let them loose. So it wouldn't surprise me if he'd gone and done that, tied the dog up on the farm, and then forgotten, though I won't have to worry about that anymore, will I? I'm the only one left now."

Rebecka was thinking she ought to take the opportunity to ask if Henry Pekkari had known Börje Ström's father, but Mervi had started listing all the families that were still living in the village when she arrived as a young bride at the beginning of the 1950s, a tale sprinkled with names and fragments of human stories. She seemed to think that Rebecka had some notion of the people she was mentioning. And then she stopped.

"Here I am rabbiting on about the old times. You're bound to have stuff to do?"

"No, not at all," Rebecka assured her. "Do you know if Henry knew Börje Ström's father, Raimo Koskela?"

The old woman peered over at the island.

"You know what. When Ragnhild's mother and father moved from the village to Kiruna, I mourned them for a good few years. Did you say your name was Martinsson? Where do you come from?"

"My father's family are from Kurravaara, but do you know if Henry knew—"

"Are you Viola Martinsson's daughter?"

"No, I'm the daughter of Theresia Martinsson's son. Viola was my dad's aunt."

Mervi Johansson got up from her sled. She grabbed Rebecka's arm as though to reassure herself that she was real.

"Then you must be Virpi's daughter! Virpi lived here with the Pekkaris. You know that, don't you? She and Ragnhild used to come over to my house a lot when they were little. I had bottle-fed lambs one summer they came round to feed. Ragnhild rowed the boat over even though she was just a little girl."

Mervi's bright old eyes lingered on Rebecka.

"And you're so like your mother," she said. "Isn't she just like her mother?"

Rebecka wondered who Mervi was saying that last bit to. She herself often talked to the Brat, which wasn't that far removed from talking to people who weren't there. And how far was it from there to talking to people who weren't there even though other people were, other living people?

You'll be like that too soon enough, she was thinking.

Mervi was silent for several seconds. Slowly she released her grip on Rebecka's arm. Maybe she was remembering how Virpi died.

"No," Mervi Johansson said after a while and for several seconds wrinkled her already wrinkled brow, concentrating hard.

"No," she said again. "I don't know if Henry knew Raimo Koskela. Henry's mates were all good-for-nothings, after all. Forgive me for being so blunt. And fewer and fewer of them visited him as the years passed. In the end he was alone out there on the island. All his old drinking buddies were long since dead. Though come to think of it there was a snowmobile over there, almost three weeks ago, late Friday night. There was still enough snow for the ice to hold. The heat we've been having since then has been almost tropical. It woke me up, joyriding behind my old carriage shed. So there's still someone goes to see him, I thought at the time."

"Who could that have been?" Rebecka asked. "I'd like to talk to Henry's mates. He must have known Raimo somehow. And we'd like to find out what the connection was."

Mervi Johansson shook her head as if there was a puzzle inside and she was trying to shake the pieces into place. A bright pink strand of hair slipped out from her headscarf; Rebecka found herself staring at it. Pink hair? Mervi Johansson noticed her looking and laughed.

"My great-granddaughter came to see me last week. She dyed her hair first and then mine. Lucky I don't go to prayer meetings anymore. What would the Laestadian preachers have said?"

"The Carefree Path," Rebecka said, doomsday in her voice.

Mervi Johansson laughed and squeaked: "Forgive my Great Sins." But then she became serious.

"No, I don't know who was over there on the snowmobile. We had no contact, Henry and I, none at all."

She dropped back onto the sled. Rebecka judged that there would be room for it in the car. She would have to drive her home. Otherwise she might die from the sheer effort of the trip back.

"But I do remember the summer Raimo Koskela disappeared," Mervi Johansson continued. "People were saying he'd left his boy to go off drinking and never came back. The poor lad arrived on foot in the village in the middle of the night. He knocked on the Poromaas' door at the far end, where the forest road begins."

Mervi Johansson pointed over to the road. The village ran in a narrow strip along the edge of the river.

"Did Raimo Koskela have any relatives here?" Rebecka asked.

"No, he borrowed the cottage from Olga Palo. Not that borrowed is all that likely. She was a widow by then. And counted every farthing. It turned into an illness after her August passed away. So I assume she rented it out. She owned some forest land, so it wasn't like she wanted for anything. But she had this terror almost of being poor. You wouldn't believe how angry she got when they extended the main road to the village. That was the summer before. The rest of us were overjoyed. We'd just been joined up with the rest of the world. But Olga had a barrier put up on the forest road and kept it locked. No-one was going to come onto her land to pick berries. She was a real *visukinttu*. Do you speak the language?"

"No," Rebecka said, tapping some notes into her phone. "Though I can understand some of it, although that particular word—"

"It means a skinflint," Mervi Johansson said firmly. "It's such a pity you young people don't speak it. Would you like some blood pancakes? I've made the batter. Or are you one of those vegans?"

"I'll eat anything," Rebecka said with a smile. "Even roadkill. And I'd give my right arm for some blood pancakes."

Börje and Sven-Erik stood in front of the bullet hole in the living room. Ragnhild stayed in the doorway. Sven-Erik drew the knife from his belt.

"Is it OK if I dig around the hole?" he asked Ragnhild. "I'll try not to make it much bigger."

"Dig away," Ragnhild said grimly. "I can get the sledgehammer if you want."

Sven-Erik stuck his knife in the bullet hole.

"So he *was* shot here?" Börje said, clearing his throat several times.

Ragnhild turned towards Börje. She wanted to say sorry. It was the only possible explanation: Henry had shot Börje's father. But her mouth stayed closed.

Börje looked her in the eye and gave a little shake of his head. Ragnhild felt that he understood her torment. That the shake of his head meant she didn't have anything to be sorry for, she wasn't the one did the shooting. The next moment she felt he thought her whole family were scum.

"Thank God my mother and father weren't here to witness this," she said.

In their defence. As though to make clear that *Äiti* and *Isä* were not like Henry.

Sven-Erik fished the bullet out of the wall and put it in a paper envelope he took from his pocket. He turned to Ragnhild.

"We'll have to see if it matches any of the guns Henry owned. Do you think he'd have kept any guns from that time? If he did, we can test-fire it."

"Neither of them, Dad or Henry, used weapon safes," Ragnhild said. "If he's still got any guns they'd be up in the side attic. Take whatever you want."

Sven-Erik and Börje went upstairs. A narrow dark hallway with two closed doors straight ahead and one each to the right and left that led to the box-rooms under the roof.

Sven-Erik opened the door to one of the side attics. A red-checked woollen blanket was lying just inside. The outlines of the shapes beneath left no doubt. He lifted the blanket, a shotgun and a hunting rifle. He broke open the shotgun, no cartridges, checked that the magazine in the rifle was empty and folded the blanket around the weapons.

"This is a bit strange, isn't it?" he heard Börje say behind him.

Börje had opened the door to another of the rooms. It was unfurnished. The paint on the brick stove was flaking off. The wallpaper was peeling away and there were large damp stains on the ceiling. There were three mattresses on the floor, a wide one and two that were narrower. The wide one had two sharp corners and two that were rounded. They looked a bit odd. There were blankets and pillows as well. No bed linen.

His eyes fell on the windowsill. A tube of toothpaste and a hairbrush. He had the feeling they had been left there by accident.

"It makes you wonder who spent the night here," Börje said. "His drinking buddies?"

"With a hairbrush and a tube of toothpaste?" Sven-Erik said sceptically.

He opened the second door which led to a small shower room, pulled back a filthy shower curtain that had flying swans and blue clouds on it. It struck him that the shower had been partially scrubbed clean.

There was a shampoo bottle on the floor. The kind that promised to maintain the lustre and shine of your hair.

Women's shampoo, he thought and went to find a wire hanger in one of the side attics before returning to the shower.

"What are you doing?" Börje said.

"Just checking something," Sven-Erik said.

Using the hanger he fished up the sieve from the drain hole. There were long blond hairs trailing beneath it.

He had a female guest, he was thinking. Only it would have to have been a visit he paid for.

It still didn't quite add up. Three mattresses. Three women? Surely Henry Pekkari was not in that kind of shape?

"Be that as it may," Sven-Erik said and got to his feet. "We're supposed to be finding out what happened to your father in 1962. Not getting involved in Henry Pekkari's leisure activities. Though I'd really like to find out how they knew one another. Are any of your father's old mates still alive?"

"Dad used to box for the North Pole Club," Börje said. "Just like I did. And both the coaches are still alive. Sikke Fredriksson and Jussi Mäntynen, do you know them?"

"Of course," Sven-Erik said. "The club is still on the same premises. I think they're over there from time to time. Have you been back to the place at all? It looks exactly the same."

"No," Börje said. "I haven't been there since the beginning of the seventies. Though it feels like only yesterday I went there for the very first time."

Two months have passed since Raimo Koskela disappeared, and school has just started again when Börje goes to the North Pole Boxing Club. It's his father's club. The idea he might have come back has been fluttering inside him for a while. Maybe Mum has forbidden him from getting in touch with Börje. Maybe he'll be at the club doing some sparring. When Börje steps inside, Dad will break off and smile with every one of those dazzling white teeth of his.

The club is in a basement beneath a bakery next to the water tower. The building is on two storeys with a façade of green-painted corrugated iron and brown trim on the windows. The courtyard is surrounded by barbed wire and is mostly covered in asphalt. Cars and motorcycles are parked on it under tarpaulins. There are yellow leaves lying on top of the tarpaulins. In the light from the street lamps it looks as though someone had been chucking fistfuls of gold coins into the air.

He hesitates, but then summons his courage and heads for the entrance.

This is a brown-painted basement door, a few steps down from ground level. An illuminated sign above it announces BK NORDPOLEN. There's a polar bear on the sign, fangs bared and wearing red boxing gloves.

The door to the club is slightly ajar. The patter of skipping ropes can be heard from inside along with rhythmic thuds and blows as well as snorting sounds. Börje goes warily down the steps and peers inside.

This is a world of men. A boiling cauldron of male scents. Acrid sweat, damp clothes, liniment. Two older men are sparring in the ring in the middle of the floor. Beyond them a huge man is working at a punchbag. Men in shorts with bare chests are pounding away at punchballs or skipping rope. A lot of them are tattooed as well. Börje glances down at his three dots; they won't count for much inside this place.

Despite the pounding of his heart and the fact that his legs seem determined to run away, Börje pushes at the door. He steps inside and stops just inside, prepared to be sent packing like a stray dog.

The walls are decorated with posters from boxing competitions and signed photographs of boxers in fighting poses. Immediately beside the door a sign proclaims: "Anyone spitting on the floor will get punched."

There's a coach with close-cropped blond hair beside the ring. He's wearing long trousers and a white shirt and holds a stopwatch. He keeps calling to the men who are sparring:

"Keep your guard up, Lassi. Don't crouch over with your gloves against your head like an old woman. Move your feet! Are you standing in quicksand or what? Twenty seconds left. Give it all you've got now, lads. Stop!"

At that moment, the men stop fighting immediately. Everyone else stops their exercises as well. Some chat to each other, others lean forward and try to catch their breath from all the exertion.

The coach with close-cropped hair catches sight of him. Börje is determined to keep hold of the door handle because his legs have turned to jelly.

"Are you lost, lad? You looking for someone?"

The coach is giving Börje a searching look. His nose is broad and flat; it looks just like Dad's. His neck is as thick as a tree trunk. His skin is hard and leathery, and looks as if it had been stretched across the bones in his face. Skin that has been broken, healed together and broken again. The voice is of a piece with the skin, hard but melodious. He has a definite Finnish accent, also just like his father. His eyes have something quick and inquisitive about them. Focused intently on Börje, they also keep a check on what is going on at the edge of his vision.

"My dad usually boxes here," Börje manages to say.

"You don't say. So what's your dad's name then?"

"Raimo."

The chat immediately stops. Everyone is looking at Börje.

Börje feels so scared. He tries to lean against the door but since it isn't closed he almost loses his balance when it simply vanishes behind him.

"What did you say?" the crew-cut man says. "Raimo? Raimo Koskela?"

He takes a couple of steps towards Börje. Börje nods. What if he gets a hiding now? Maybe this old guy and his dad were enemies.

Another man comes up to Börje. He appears to be a coach as well, dressed in long trousers and a shirt and holding a stopwatch. He's taller than the other man. And his hair is dark and curly. No boxer's nose either. His eyes look kind. They linger on Börje's face. Börje feels a bit more relaxed.

"Raimo's lad," the guy with the nice nose says and looks both happy and sad at the same time. "Hi there. My name is Sigvard. You can call me Sikke."

"His name's Sisu-Sikke," someone in the gym calls. "Do you know what *sisu* is?"

Börje does know what it is. *Sisu* is the Finnish word for energy combined with drive. Only he can't come up with a reply. The crew-cut guy is examining Börje now from top to toe and his face creases in a warm smile.

"And I'm Nurkin-Jussi," he says. "Well I never, Raimo's lad. So do you know how to box?"

Rebecka entered her office at 11.45 a.m. She had eaten blood pancakes for breakfast at Mervi Johansson's. At half past nine the others had made their way back over the river. No-one had fallen through and drowned, and that was to be considered a success.

Now, though, the neglected piles of paper were waiting on her desk. "What time do you call this?" they were saying.

One case at a time, Rebecka said to herself as a mantra while she chucked her coat on the visitor's chair.

At least she didn't have to take the Brat out today, Sivving was looking after him.

Eva Bergmark, von Post's departmental secretary, appeared in the doorway. Her smile was a bit too broad. Her step just a bit too quick. Bad signs.

"Hi Rebecka," she said. "Calle has gone to Gällivare. For a meeting with the head of Serious Crime. But he had a county court case today he wanted you to take. Nothing you'd have to prepare for, he said. Just turn up, more or less."

"Are you having me on?" Rebecka said. "He's dumped the case backlog onto me for review and now I'm supposed to deal with his court appearances?"

But Eva Bergmark wasn't joking. She tilted her head and smiled in appeal.

"And I still haven't had your on-call timesheets. And your employee survey. And you are the only person not to have let me know when you want to take your summer holiday."

Then she clattered away along the corridor.

Rebecka speed-read the plaint and the evidence report. There was half an hour left before the hearing, and she flipped through the relevant parts of the preliminary investigation while pulling on the suit she always kept on a hanger in her office and stepping into a pair of heels. Although there was a run in the stockings she had folded and stuffed into the jacket pocket, there was nothing to be done about it now. She buttoned up the jacket and hoped it would shut in the smell of sweat from this morning's adventure. She gathered her hair in a ponytail.

Pohjanen rang on her way out the door.

"Report," he said urgently.

"It's been a bit hectic at work today, and I've got to be in court in twenty minutes. Can you ring Sven-Erik and get him to—"

"I've been trying that," Pohjanen said. "But his phone's turned off. Twenty minutes is plenty of time. Just tell me."

She could hear from his voice that he had been waiting for her to ring. He was getting het up. He wasn't used to being overlooked or ignored.

Rebecka told him about the events of the morning while getting into her car and driving to the county court. Pohjanen grunted in satisfaction at the news of the bullet Sven-Erik had found in the wall.

"So we can assume Henry Pekkari shot him, or was at least involved in some way," he wheezed. "How did they know one another?"

"You tell me. Mervi Johansson said she didn't know, but Sven-Erik is going to talk with Börje's old coaches, because his dad trained at the same club."

"Good, very good," Pohjanen said. "We'll have to see what information that bullet can provide as well."

"There was just one thing . . ." Rebecka said.

She parked the car and looked at the clock on the dashboard. Seven minutes until the start of the hearing. She really shouldn't get into this now.

"Shoot," Pohjanen said cheerfully.

"So this is a bit rushed," she said, "but I'm going to have to hurry. Mervi Johansson did say there was some snowmobile traffic across the river almost three weeks ago. And I can't stop thinking about those mattresses on the upper floor and the long hairs in the drain in the shower room."

"What are you trying to say, Martinsson?" Pohjanen asked.

There was nothing cheerful about his voice now.

"You've got to admit it's an odd coincidence that—" Rebecka began.

"Don't even think that thought!" Pohjanen cut her off. "I carried out the autopsy on Henry Pekkari. The only odd thing about his death was that it didn't occur twenty years ago."

"I wasn't going to ask you to do the autopsy again," Rebecka said. "Just—"

"Good," Pohjanen wheezed. "Because I've absolutely no intention of redoing it."

He then had a coughing fit which Rebecka waited out while looking at the clock. Three minutes left to her hearing. Through the glass doors she could see everyone entering the courtroom. The doors were closing.

"You're questioning whether I can do my job, that's perfectly clear," Pohjanen said when he'd finished.

"No, I just want you to take another look at the autopsy report," Rebecka said. "I've got this really bad feeling."

"So we're back to that, are we? You and your feelings. You keep your emotional whims to yourself, do you hear?"

124

"I've got to finish this call, you know, now," Rebecka said. "My hearing . . ."

There wasn't time to say anything more because Pohjanen had hung up.

She got out of the car and hurried towards the entrance.

You're welcome, she thought angrily. Welcome that I got up in the middle of the night and spent almost an entire working day on your private investigation. And then spent the rest of it doing von Post's job.

She found her way into the courtroom and went laboriously through the case. The impression she made was of someone ill-prepared and uncertain. Which left her hating herself.

Once she had gathered her things and pulled on her coat, the defence lawyer found time to come over and say hello. He had tried to ask her out on several occasions. She didn't have the energy to wriggle out of it with more excuses.

He told her it was nice to see her.

"I thought this was von Post's case," he said.

"He had to meet the head of Serious Crime," she said. "So I had very little time to prepare."

She closed her mouth. She felt angry at herself. What in God's name was she doing apologising for herself to this . . . small-town lawyer. The bottom of the legal barrel.

"Uh no, I don't think that can be right," the lawyer said. "The Head of Serious Crime is on leave both today and tomorrow. Her husband's celebrating a big birthday."

"Oh really?" Rebecka said. "I must have misunderstood. There was something Calle had to do in any case."

She smiled at the lawyer as if she had suddenly realised how handsome he was, a diversionary tactic, and managed to utter a hasty goodbye before it could occur to the lawyer to try his luck again with a dinner date.

Rage was seething away inside her like a witch's cauldron as she chucked her bag onto the back seat. That bloody fucking arsehole von Post. He had handed the case over to her just to be a pain. And because he could. Because Alf Björnfot had given him the power to give her grief. She wondered what von Post had been doing today. Driven up to Riksgränsen and gone skiing perhaps. While she was working like a dog.

She drove home to Kurravaara, forgot to go shopping on the way, decided to eat just anything at all for dinner instead of turning back towards town. Popcorn with melted butter.

In her anger she kept the accelerator depressed the whole way home. She was angry at von Post. Angry at Pohjanen. Angry at Björnfot. Angry at everyone who took her for granted.

"Fuck the lot of you," she said aloud in the car.

Sven-Erik Stålnacke arrived home to a house redolent of fish stew and freshly baked bread. Airi met him in the hallway.

"Well," she said. "How did it go?"

But she could see from his face how it had gone. Very well indeed. He had life in his eyes and a lot to tell her. She had been able to make that out through the kitchen window. From the way he was walking.

"Typical of you," he said with feigned indignation. "You always have to be right."

"I know," she said and smiled so much her face hurt. "It's a dreadful quality."

"Back so soon?" Sivving said to Rebecka. "It's not even six yet. I thought you'd be taking the opportunity to work late now you're dog-free."

He was standing at the stove in the downstairs boiler room of his house, reheating ready-made soup. He had his bed there and a little dining table. He rarely used the upstairs anymore.

"Haven't got the energy," Rebecka said. "Is there enough for me?"

"Of course there is," Sivving said. "I bought a new kind of crispbread. With those . . ."

He reached for the packet and read aloud:

". . . chia seeds and sea salt. And you've got to tell me all about today. Did you get the car MOT'd? You'll lose your licence if you're not careful."

Rebecka looked under the table. Bella was lying beneath it with her woollen mitten.

"Where's the Brat?" she asked.

"At Krister's. Didn't you get my message?"

"What? No!"

"What do you mean, no? Did you even look at your phone?"

"All the time. I check my phone constantly. Can I see this message?"

"No, my battery's dead. But I sent it by twelve. I couldn't have the Brat here any longer. The growling started immediately now Bella's the way she is with that mitten. And the Brat wanted to grab it and play with it. So I asked Krister to come and get him. I said you'd pick him up."

"From Krister's?" Rebecka asked, and suddenly she felt so utterly exhausted it was a miracle she didn't keel over.

"Call him," Sivving suggested. "And he'll bring the dog here. Tell him there's soup for him too."

"That's a no," Rebecka said. "You do know he's got a new girlfriend? You can't just call up and ask him to look after dogs and fix stuff anymore."

"Are you going to start in on me again, about clearing the snow away that time? You were in Stockholm and if he hadn't come over and dealt with the yard you wouldn't have been able to drive into it. It was snowing, thawing and freezing. Look at Anna-Lisa Aidanpää. She didn't clear the snow and then she had to park on the street. You could barely get past. A traffic hazard."

"You said you were going to look after the Brat. If that's not working out, you need to call me first. So I can sort things out, OK?"

"Should I call Krister and ask him to bring the dog here? I can say there isn't enough soup for him."

"Oh, for God's sake, no. I'll drive over there. Wasn't your phone dead?"

Rebecka Martinsson pulled up outside Krister Eriksson's house. Just a single car in the yard. And it wasn't Krister's. So Märit Törmä drove a Toyota Corolla. Rebecka tried to come up with what that said about Marit, preferably something negative, but couldn't work it out.

Did she really have to get out of the car, walk up to the house, ring the doorbell, chat with Marit and ask for her dog? Yes, she did. Fuck Sivving.

She opened the glovebox and got out her cigarettes. She smoked in the car without opening the windows.

It occurred to her that Marit would notice that she stank not only of old sweat but ashtray as well. She wound down the window and chucked out the butt. Then she rooted around both the glovebox and her bag for chewing gum. She finally found three loose bits at the bottom of her cup-holder, stuffed them in her mouth and chewed away like a wood-chipper before thinking "just do it" and getting out of the car.

Krister's car came round the corner just then and pulled up behind hers. All she could think about was her dirty hair. Why hadn't she had a shower that morning? Because she got up at 4 a.m. All the same. She swallowed the chewing gum.

The next second she forgot all about her hair as three boisterous dogs came leaping out of the car. They greeted her with all the canine joy their bodies were capable of displaying. Their tails swung and their tongues flapped like flags on parade. They kept barking and trying to get so close to her she almost fell over. The Brat found a stick he ran at her with in the hope it would make him popular. Roy, the old guy, growled at the younger dog and pressed his backside against Rebecka's leg to make her scratch his croup. Which she did. Tintin sang a song of devotion. Rebecka did her best to have hands enough for all of them. She crouched down and let them lick her face. They had just enough time to cover her in slobber before they abandoned her as if they'd been given a signal. Which was when Krister appeared and they all capered around him, telling him with their barking that they had a guest, could he see? Hey you, the best guest ever! And then they went back to Rebecka.

You couldn't help laughing and Krister and Rebecka were laughing together. The dogs had just whisked away everything that still grated, everything old and unresolved between them. Then Rebecka got to her feet. The dogs tore away across the yard, sniffing around to check on whatever might have happened while they were away.

He was so attractive. She had never thought his badly burned face was ugly. And his body. Strong, genuinely powerful. Not the way you get from pressing weights at the gym. He said a brief hello. When she heard his voice, something tottered upright inside her to test the air. Like a little animal that has got lost in the forest and hears its owner calling. A voice from home. She gulped. Said hello back. Asked him how he was. He said everything was fine, just fine. She was thinking about her awful hair again.

Marcus came running over from the house in his socks.

"Rebecka," he yelled.

He threw his arms around her and buried his face in her chest while he was talking.

Rebecka put both hands on the back of his head. His hair was still baby-soft. Eleven years old. How was that possible?

"I can't hear what you're saying when you're talking onto my clothes," she said with a laugh. "Though I'm sure it's really interesting."

"I'll have to text it to you later," he mumbled. "Because right now I've got to hug you for a really long time."

"You've got no shoes on," Krister said. "Run back inside. Is the food ready?"

Marcus turned his face up to Rebecka.

"Marit has made Indian lentil stew. Do you want to eat with us?"

"I can't because then Sivving would be sad, I promised to eat with him."

"We can go and pick him up. And the Brat wants to stay here and play with Tintin and Roy. Don't you?"

He let go of Rebecka and started running around with the dogs.

"Go indoors," Krister said. "Or else I'll put those wet socks of yours on your evening sandwich."

"OK, OK, slave driver!"

And he ran inside.

Krister took the opportunity to look at Rebecka while she was watching Marcus run with arms and legs flapping just before he went indoors.

She looked skinny. There were dark circles under her eyes. Not that it mattered. She was like Biran, his favourite mountain, a solitary peak between Kårsavagge and Kärkevagge. He had seen that mountain in all weathers. Fog. Snowstorm. When the flowers and the sun were out in June. In late winter covered in fresh snow like some kind of meringue. When the hail was the size of ping pong balls. He never got tired of

Biran. It was his mountain for all seasons. That went for Rebecka too. In all her various guises. He was filled with such a powerful desire to throw his arms around her, he had to stuff his hands in his pockets straight away. He could see Marit at the kitchen window out of the corner of his eye.

It's Marit and me now, he was thinking. We've got a good life.

A feeling of rage at Rebecka took him by surprise. An impulse to punch her.

"Is Marcus doing OK?" she asked. "With his friends at school and so on?"

He said "just fine" again, like when she asked how he was doing. He felt sheepish. An idiot who could only say "just fine" over and over again. What do you think about the climate crisis? Just fine.

"Thank you," she said. "And sorry. I never meant for you to have to look after the Brat. It was Sivving who . . ."

She finished the sentence with a sigh and a resigned gesture.

"Uhm, that's OK," he said. "I have to go in now."

She tried to smile. With rather limited success. Her mouth twitched involuntarily. It made him strangely pleased she couldn't fake it. She opened the boot and the cage, and called for the Brat who came wagging his tail.

"Hop in," she said.

He ought to go in to Marit. Instead he took a step towards the Brat and scratched him behind the ears.

"He's got a good nose," he said. "I set out a lure for him to trace. He could have been a good tracker."

If you hadn't . . . he was thinking and felt the ridges of his teeth clash together inside his mouth.

Tintin tried to jump into Rebecka's car as well. Rebecka had to push her away and shut the Brat inside. Tintin licked Rebecka's hands. She jumped up and put her front paws on the boot. Roy knew better. He stayed close to his master.

"Come here," Krister said to Tintin, but she wasn't listening.

He had to drag her by the collar towards the house.

Rebecka drove away. She felt heavy, she must weigh several tons. And it was far too light outside even though it was already evening. She wanted it to be dark. She wanted the darkness to wrap itself around her. It felt as if the motorists she encountered on the road were examining her. She felt forced to grit her teeth.

Krister touched the door handle; he was trying to fend off the flutter of a maternal longing to take Rebecka with him into the woods. Watch her stare into the fire or fall asleep on a reindeer skin while he was making the food. The dogs spilled around her. She had looked so tired and worn. That was von Post, of course. He was making sure to muck her about while Björnfot was on his long vacation.

Marit loved going out on their trips as well. But, and he was ashamed of the thought, Marit was a celebrity. She had won a gold medal in the biathlon as a junior and was also part of a mountain rescue team, just like him. She had more than thirty thousand followers on Instagram. The last time they were out on a trip she had asked him to take a photo of her as she was fetching water from a cold spring. He had taken the phone and she had pulled off her top and carried the buckets just wearing her undershirt. Her thin muscular arms with the mountains in the background. She got so many likes for that. He was proud of her. Happy for her sake. But it felt like they weren't alone on the mountain. It was her, him and thirty thousand followers.

Rebecka wasn't any better, he corrected himself. She was always thinking about work or lost in her own thoughts.

When he and Marit became a couple and she posted about it on her Instagram account, the reaction had been a powerful one. Some people were revolted by the sight of his mottled pink and burned face, the lack of a nose. The comments were brutal and suddenly there were trolls on her threads who wrote: "Fuck an alien, why don't you", while others were quick to tap Unfollow.

And he'd been irritated that Marit felt she had to console him. "Don't let it bother you," she said. Though in fact he wasn't bothered. "All the people who matter love you," she assured him. He didn't know those people. He couldn't care less whether they hated or loved him. "Most people think you're wonderful," she went on. Great, there were a lot of people who thought he was wonderful. That was almost even worse. Those "beauty is on the inside and you are perfect" comments.

Marit had posted just a bit too much about that. And the fact that he was in a mountain rescue team as well. A dog trainer. A man who had taken in a traumatised boy. As though she had to try and sell him to them.

He opened the door to his house. Marit met him in the hall and threw her arms around him. He wrapped his around her and thought how incredibly lucky he was. She really was perfect.

He was regretting having agreed to look after the Brat. Only it was Sivving he had done a good turn. Not Rebecka, as it turned out.

The dogs strolled in and said a quick and nonchalant hello to Marit; they had a sniff around and then went into the kitchen to check their bowls. They didn't even give her time to pat them.

How many times had Marit told him how tiresome it was that he had so many one-man dogs.

He kissed Marit, compensating for the dogs. He said something appreciative about the aroma of her Indian cooking.

"Darling, before you take off your shoes," she said, "could you please go out there and pick up Rebecka's cigarette butt. I saw her chuck it on the ground. A cigarette butt can kill all the microbes in seven litres of groundwater."

He found the butt and chucked it in the rubbish bin. He was thinking about the fact that Rebecka had smelled of mint chewing gum. Strongly of mint chewing gum. What was all that about? What had she been imagining? That they were going to kiss?

It's that time of the night they call the hour of the wolf. The thin membrane between night and dawn when most people die, most children are born, when sleep is at its deepest and nightmares most real. The Germans call it the *Hundewache*, the dog star Sirius is shining brightly. The same hour that is called the cock crow in the Bible, when Peter realises he has betrayed his master three times.

In his hotel room Börje Ström is woken by the subterranean rumbling of the nightly detonations. He lies there unable to sleep until half past three in the morning. Then he goes out for a run in the bright night. The sun is rising and his shadow is a daddy longlegs. The roads are free of snow but still covered in the winter grit which twists and turns under his feet so even running on asphalt feels laborious. The first few kilometres are really hard work and sometimes quite painful. It takes longer to get going as you age.

He leaves the city behind him and runs up towards Luossavaara – the mountain where they used to mine iron ore. They are going to be moving some of the city's buildings here to save them from subsidence. The mine is devouring the city he grew up in. It keeps sliding down an ever larger hole. The ore has to be mined. The young have to have jobs. He understands that.

The path gets steeper. While he runs he is thinking about his father lying in that freezer on the island all these years. He has to know what happened. If that is even possible. But maybe everyone who could tell him is dead. Truth decays, just like this city, and turns to dust.

All he can do is go on running. One step at a time now his legs have turned to spaghetti. He is remembering how Nyrkin-Jussi used to preach that as gospel. You had to run. Preferably in bogs and wet snow.

AUGUST 1962

"Raimo's lad, well I never," the coach with dark curly hair says. "So can you box?"

"A bit."

Börje hardly dares look up at the men around him.

"Alright then lad," one of the men in the ring calls. "Come up and show us what you can do."

Widespread laughter.

"Back to work," the curly-haired man yells. "The holiday's over!"

He and the other coach look Börje over for a moment, while the others all go back to what they were doing: the skipping ropes swish, the bags get punched. Börje holds his breath. He has a strange feeling that his fate is being decided here. He is scared they'll just shrug and say: "Right then lad, it might be best if you went home." He is more afraid of that than dying.

The short coach with the close-cropped hair clears his throat. His name is Nyrkin-Jussi.

"So your dad hasn't turned up yet?" he says.

Börje shakes his head.

"He was teaching me how to punch the bag," he says quietly.

"Do you want to have a go, then?" Sisu-Sikke asks. "You can borrow your dad's gloves. If I wrap your hands they'll fit OK."

And that is what happens. Börje has a go at one of the bags. Punching it as hard as he can to start with in case they're watching. But then the bag swings back and almost knocks him off his feet. His arms are trembling from exertion but no-one seems to care, so after his introductory struggle with the bag he starts hitting it more lightly. The bag is a training partner rather than an enemy. His body remembers what his father used to teach him and he runs through his series of punches: jab-hook-low uppercut, jab-jab-right cross.

No-one says anything to him the whole evening. No-one else at the club is as young as he is. The other guys in training are maybe fifteen or older, a lot of them are as old as his dad. Their bodies are drenched in sweat like they've been standing naked in the rain. The coaches devote their time to the other boxers. At one point he gets the feeling someone is watching him but when he turns both Sisu-Sikke and Nyrkin-Jussi seem immersed in the stopwatches they are holding.

Sisu-Sikke pops up behind him later and puts a hand on his shoulder. "That's enough for today," he says.

He helps Börje take off the gloves and carefully unwraps his hands. The tiredness in his body and the sense of calm feel nice. So does being looked after and not just because he's a child.

Then Sisu-Sikke asks him: "Do you want to come back?"

Börje nods.

"So bring your training clothes next time. You can keep them in your dad's locker. We're here in the afternoons and evenings. Your mother will be keeping dinner for you now, won't she?"

Then Börje is on his way home. He is feeling something akin to astonishment. At the fact that the world outside is still there: for more than an hour he forgot that this other world existed. The one in which he has a home and a mum and school. The smell of the boxing club stays with him; he can still hear the noises.

And they said he could come back.

The adult Börje Ström is standing at the top of Luossavaara, panting. He jogs slowly on the spot to get rid of the lactic acid. He looks at his watch. Four thirty. The city is spread out below. It looks lovely, actually, saddling the low Haukivaara mountain between the two ore mines of Luossavaara and Kirunavaara.

He blows snot out of his nostrils and gets out his phone. He has a woman in Älvsbyn called Lottie. She sent him a text last night. She's really lovely. Well preserved. And she can cook too. He sends her some hearts and a winking smiley.

Then he jogs down the hill. He is thinking about Ragnhild Pekkari. About the rough skin on her hands and that anorak of hers that smells of a wood fire. He is thinking he has to come up with a way to see her again.

In the hour of the wolf Ragnhild Pekkari is dreaming of Börje Ström. They are naked. Sweaty. Slippery. Embracing as if they wanted to hug each other to death, melt into one another. She straddles him.

Her orgasm wakes her; she can't tell if she cried out. Loud enough for the neighbours to hear?

You just have to hope God doesn't exist, she thinks, she doesn't want anyone witnessing what just happened.

Sweaty and hot from the dream and from embarrassment she lies there looking around in the dark. The brightness of the night outside is pushing in through the gap between the roller blind and the wall. The outlines of the furniture slowly emerge. That sense from childhood that they are coming alive in the dark. The desk and the chair, the clothes valet and the laundry basket: silent black animals standing still, watching her. Wondering what she is.

Rebecka falls asleep on her kitchen sofa and wakes at 3 a.m. Her mouth tastes of nappy and her clothes are stuck to her body. She puts the wine glass and the empty bottle in the sink and closes the laptop. Has a pee, splashes water on her face but doesn't have the energy to get out the make-up remover and cotton pads, so when she looks in the mirror a panda stares back at her. She tries to rub off the make-up with a towel, with only limited success. She brushes her teeth and tells herself she has to start sleeping properly, go to bed early, not watch box sets. Leave her phone outside the bedroom, the things they always tell you.

She is afraid of depression. It skulks around her house like a shadow: a giant, slow and remorseless. It will be like leaving the door wide-open if she keeps on like this, messing up her routines. So all the giant has to do is crouch down, step inside and get her.

The Brat is sleeping on his bed in her room. He doesn't even lift his head when she comes in.

It hurts a bit that he has chosen to sleep on his own in here and not pressed up against her on the sofa. He always used to sleep at her feet before.

It's because everything I've been feeling is so dark, she thinks, and can't help the beginnings of a grin when she sees him lying there. So lovely, rolled up like a little fox in his bed, nose to tail.

He's avoiding me, she thinks. I'm not good for him. Just my being here must be so hard on him, my darkness is infectious.

She immediately feels desperately sorry for the Brat having to live with someone as awful as her. She feels sorry for herself as well for being that awful person who can never be someone else.

She wants to cry. The corners of her mouth turn down, but the tears refuse to come and ease the pressure. She can't even cry.

Cold, she thinks about herself. Emotionally inhibited. Disturbed. Mentally ill. Bad for everyone.

It strikes her that she will have to give the Brat to someone else. He has to be free of her. Sivving wouldn't take him. Maybe Krister.

She thinks about Krister. And then immediately about his new girlfriend. Sod Marit Törmä. One of those perfect mountain girls. Rebecka hates her so much. What can they possibly have to talk about, her and Krister?

The dark voice inside her says Marit is definitely not the sort of girl who suddenly starts crying when they are having sex. Or feels overwhelmed by her own darkness and has to be on her own for a whole week.

He did the right thing getting together with her, Rebecka thinks, and she's filled with self-hatred the way an old well fills up in the rain. I've got nothing left, and it's all my fault.

Then she falls asleep.

Pohjanen is smoking on his sofa in the subterranean part of the hospital. He has his work computer open on his lap showing the autopsy report on Henry Pekkari. His wife has sent him five furious texts but he has not replied. She knows perfectly well where he is. And she should bloody well stop writing "Let me know you are alive at least."

He didn't go home this evening but stayed at work. He's still an adult man, isn't he, or do you suddenly stop being one when you're dying? And she is still his wife, isn't she, so when did she become his kindergarten teacher? Or his carer? If he does die here, some chewing-gum-pink person will inform her.

The fit of rage he suffered at Rebecka Martinsson faded a long while ago.

Martinsson. And those bloody feelings of hers.

The moment he hung up he looked in fury at the autopsy record again. And she was right. Henry Pekkari had not died of what would be entirely natural causes for an ageing alcoholic. He had been killed.

Although anyone could have missed it, he thinks and lifts his glasses up his forehead; they fall off the back of his head and he can hear them land on the floor behind the sofa.

He feels absolutely no inclination to retrieve them. He rubs the bridge of his nose.

I have lost it, he thinks.

How many old men had he autopsied because they hadn't had the sense to realise the time had come to stop driving? And how many of their victims?

Time to stop then. Drive home to the wife. Lie down on the expensive sofa, start munching the valiums and listen to music for the rest of his life. John Coltrane's *Giant Steps*, Kanye West's *The College Dropout*, Björk's *Vespertine*, AC/DC's *Highway to Hell*, Madonna's *Confessions on a Dance Floor*, Beethoven, Symphonies 5 and 7 played by the Vienna Philharmonic under Carlos Kleiber, the aggressive forward march of the 5th, the allegro in the 7th. Kiri te Kanawa, when she's literally turning anything to gold, the Flower Duet, for example. There are worse ways to go.

He's going to close his eyes for a moment. In an hour or two it will be morning. He will ring Martinsson then.

Martinsson and those bloody feelings of hers.

FRIDAY 29TH APRIL

Pohjanen rang Rebecka early the next morning. She got up with the phone clamped between shoulder and ear, the blanket round her shoulders. While he kept having to clear his throat, she went down the stairs and let the Brat out for a pee. Out in the yard she crouched down herself; there was no-one to see, after all. She shook off the drops and pulled up her pants.

"I took another look at Henry Pekkari's autopsy notes," Pohjanen said. "Everything would indicate that he was affected by arrhythmia and died of a heart attack as a result of long-term alcohol abuse."

"Right," Rebecka said. "Sorry I—"

"I haven't finished, Martinsson," he said cutting her off. "What has, however, since become clear is that Henry Pekkari was the victim of a Burke and Hare-style killing."

"What is a—?"

"Anyone could have missed it!" Pohjanen exclaimed and she could hear he was looking for a quarrel. "It was the discoloration, post-mortem lividity."

"I don't understand," Rebecka said, calling the Brat to come inside. She fed the dog while Pohjanen explained.

"Tiny vascular ruptures. Do you know what spider veins are, Martinsson?"

"I do but I—"

"Be quiet while I'm trying to explain. Otherwise I'll ring your boss, your temporary boss. And talk to him instead. I noticed the patches, of course. But the haemorrhages were only on the upper part of the front of the body."

He had to catch his breath. Long, tortuous inhalations, as if through a straw.

"What kind of qualifications did the drivers of the transport team have?" he went on after a moment. "Winning a pancake-eating competition in Överkalix? They didn't think it important to inform me that they had turned him over. So I based my assumptions on their having found him lying on his stomach. I assumed that the burst capillaries, those patches, were post-mortem."

Rebecka had begun to measure coffee into the pot, but lost track.

A murder, she thought excitedly. Or not?

"He also had haemorrhaging in the muscles at the temple. That would have occurred while he was still alive."

"Intravitally," Rebecka said like an eager schoolgirl.

Pohjanen barked out a cough and quickly became serious.

"The forensic team will have to examine him," he said.

"What is a Burke and Hare killing?" Rebecka asked, setting the pot on the stove.

"They were murderers who sought out society's rejects at the beginning of the nineteenth century, so they could sell the bodies to physicians carrying out anatomical studies."

"You're joking . . ." Rebecka said both to Pohjanen and to the Brat, who had lain down on his back on her bed, his head on her pillow. He obviously thought this was entirely appropriate for the King of Kurravaara.

"Let me assure you I am in no mood for joking," Pohjanen said. "The victim was subjected to thoracic compression as would be caused

144

by the offender sitting on his chest. Owing to the chest's natural flexibility it becomes increasingly compressed each time the victim exhales without being able to re-inflate. No external signs of damage occur but the pressure inside the chest cavity is ultimately so high that the blood cannot return to the heart. Instead it is squeezed into the veins in the upper part of the thorax and throat. Simultaneously you suffocate the victim by holding the nose and mouth closed or pressing a pillow over the face. This results in petechial haemorrhages on the face, throat and around the shoulder joint. Make sure the forensics team look for fibres on his face. From the pillow."

"Mhmm," Rebecka said. "Can you wait until after five today to report this officially?"

"Of course, this would never have become a murder inquiry if you hadn't . . ."

He stopped. There was silence at the other end.

"I missed it," Pohjanen said finally. "I thought it was just post-mortem lividity."

"You said anyone could have missed it," Rebecka said.

"I'm not anyone though," Pohjanen said and hung up.

Mervi Johannson was woken by the sun shining into her bedroom. Heavens above, what could the time be? Past seven! When was the last time she slept that long?

She got out of bed and looked at herself in the mirror. Thin pink strands of hair stuck out in all directions. She had to laugh at herself. She'd never been a beauty, now though! She took a selfie and sent it to her great-granddaughter.

In her youth she used to dream of being able to sleep late in the mornings. But her mother had told her to get out of bed. And then she had had to work and before you knew it there were the children and after that any hope of getting more sleep was gone. When they were still small and on the breast or round her feet. That whole time she had longed to be able to sleep. To sleep until late in the morning. To sleep until she wasn't exhausted, until she was actually rested. She had longed for that for many years. Then the children fled the nest but the sleepiness of her childhood never came back to her. She woke up early and never lay in and dozed.

She dunked rusks in her morning coffee and thought about the previous day. About Rebecka Martinsson, Virpi's daughter, and about Ragnhild. Ragnhild really could have come round to say hello. Though maybe she had a lot to deal with now her brother had died. A funeral would be fun in any case. Although funerals had been at their most entertaining when she was between seventy and eighty. That was when

crap on her to deal with. And then he'd played truant at his own court hearing the other day; he had lied about having a meeting with the Head of Serious Crime. Made her rush over to the hearing and stammer like a terrified legal trainee.

And she knew he was saying things behind her back. It wasn't hard to guess what. He would be telling people he was concerned, insist that Björnfot was worried and that Björnfot regretted having recruited her. He would insinuate that she drank too much, suggest that she had a habit of missing work-related matters, and maintain – correctly – that she had refused to have therapy after the suicide of Maja Larsson, adding that she was moody and found it difficult working in a team, that she ruined all her relationships, Krister being the most recent example.

Her thoughts decided to settle in the same place they had settled so many times before. How she could have been made a partner at Meijer & Ditzinger and earned five times as much as von Post. How in hell had she ended up here in the district prosecutor's office, being humiliated by him? The cockless worm. Why the bloody hell did Björnfot keep letting this happen? How in God's name did she manage to make the same bed for herself time and time again? Just how the fucking hell?

There is something seriously wrong with me, Rebecka thought. Von Post is completely right about that.

She was going to take over this murder all the same. Because leading investigations, working with the police, closing the noose, getting the guilty properly punished, was what was fun about the job.

Besides, there was something about this murder, she was thinking. It could have been your usual dreary drunken killing if it weren't for those mattresses in the attic. And the long blond hairs in the drain.

Rebecka spent Friday evening on the murder of Henry Pekkari. She drew up a memorandum on the visit to the island and the reasons for the trip, namely the discovery of the body of Raimo Koskela in a freezer in the living room.

She took the official decisions required for cordoning off the site and the issuing of a search warrant.

She e-mailed the forensics team in Luleå and issued instructions for the examination of Henry Pekkari's residence and of his corpse.

She registered a pro-tem decision about telephone surveillance, to find out which calls had been made to and from Henry Pekkari's phone. She would be requiring cell-tower dumps as well, to find out which phones had been in the vicinity at the time of the murder. And when was that? Pohjanen couldn't give an exact time of death.

Though come to think of it, Mervi Johansson had mentioned snow-mobile traffic out on the island almost three weeks ago. Late one Friday night, she had said. That would have been the night of April 8th.

Rebecka tried calling Mervi Johansson to ask her to confirm the date, but she wasn't answering. Maybe she'd already gone to bed. Rebecka looked at her watch.

It was 8 p.m. on a Friday night. She was the only person left at police headquarters. She rang Sivving. When he picked up he sounded so happy. He said there was enough food for her too. Hurry on back.

And he didn't nag her about the MOT or the roof either.

SATURDAY 30TH APRIL

"I really don't care," Anna-Maria Mella said. "It still feels really shitty though."

The family were sitting at the breakfast table. Her teenage son Petter was shovelling down muesli and soured milk as if he was going for the world record. Jenny was standing by the mixer turning cabbage and chia seeds and spirulina and bananas into a brownish goo while snapchatting with her friends.

"Mhm," Robert said, absorbed in his phone. "Remember to wash that up when you've finished," he said to Jenny.

"Why didn't Pohjanen ask me to help with the freezer murder?" Anna-Maria said. "It feels really weird for Rebecka and Sven-Erik to be working together. And Sven-Erik didn't even pop in to say hello when he was in town. Besides . . ."

She bit into her sandwich as if it had upset her and went on with her mouth full.

". . . besides I can't stop thinking that she didn't take my case to court. You build up a reputation as a police officer in the same town over twenty years, and it only takes her three minutes to ruin it. That thread on Facebook. Everyone knows it's me even if they don't say so. The whole town will be talking about the fact I can't even take a photo or present the supporting evidence properly, which is why all the villains round here are still free."

"Now you're exaggerating just a tiny bit," Robert said, without looking up from his phone.

"And why didn't she talk to me about it face to face."

"Ask her. You're mates, aren't you?"

"That's what I thought."

Anna-Maria turned to her youngest son, Gustaf, who was staring listlessly at his sandwich and his glass of juice.

"Eat, you've got a match today, haven't you?"

"I can't," he said. "I'm depressed."

Anna-Maria put down her coffee mug.

"That's a big word, darling," she said. "Has something happened?"

She could feel her stomach contracting with fear as she took in his woebegone expression. Relationships between kids at school were so tough nowadays. And Gustaf was a gentle boy. Was he being bullied? How long had he been bullied for? Why hadn't she noticed anything? Because she'd been working too hard. Or maybe he was unhappily in love with a girl? Anna-Maria wanted to strangle the little heartbreaker, whoever she was.

"You know last week when I was so happy because I got invited to a Minecraft server?" Gustaf said.

"Yes," Anna-Maria lied.

"I was on the server yesterday evening, I was supposed to be building my house. I didn't have time to cut down all the trees so I scorched them. And started a forest fire."

His voice was threatening to break as he went on:

"The fire burned much hotter than I expected and my neighbour's house was almost completely burned up, it was made of wool and wood and two blocks were scorched and he was the one who built the forest and now it's been burned down. I tried to put it out. I'm going to be banned from the server. And if you hadn't forced me to turn off the computer and go to bed I could have rebuilt the forest."

"Oh darling," Anna-Maria said.

She was so relieved she had to bite her lip not to laugh.

"The word is 'torch' not 'scorch'," Petter said.

Anna-Maria gave Petter a look.

"What?" Petter exclaimed. "Like you don't correct me when I get words wrong."

"Thanks, sweetheart," Anna-Maria said to Jenny who was placing glasses filled with the dung-like smoothie in front of the members of her family.

"Make sure you wash that up," Robert said to Jenny who was putting the liquidiser beaker into the sink.

"I will," Jenny said. "Breathe!"

"I'm not having your diarrhoea for breakfast," Petter said.

"Stop it!" Anna-Maria said to Petter. "Don't use that word about food."

"You eat meat, don't you?" Jenny said to Petter. "You won't drink a smoothie cos it's got the wrong colour but you eat the grey parts of corpses. *And* you've taken my charger."

"I am breathing," Robert said to Jenny. "But I swear if that mixer isn't washed up by the time we get home from the match I'm going to put it in your bed."

"You do that," Jenny said to Robert. "And I will put every bit of washing-up you don't do in your bed for the rest of eternity."

Anna-Maria's phone rang.

"That's work," she said. "I have to take it."

She rushed out to the hall. In the kitchen a row broke out between the cast members of the soap know as "Saturday Morning with the Nuclear Family". She could hear Gustaf start to cry.

It was Police Constable Magda Vidarsdotter.

"Sorry," Anna-Maria said and put her hand over one ear. "Could you repeat that? I couldn't hear over the harmony of my family life."

"Everybody's been called in," Vidarsdotter said. "You know that dead guy in the freezer in Kurkkio?"

"Yeah?"

"The old guy who owned the freezer, he didn't die of natural causes – he was murdered, according to the report Pohjanen sent in."

"You're kidding," Anna-Maria exclaimed. "Who's leading the investigation?"

"Martinsson. And we've got another two dead bodies in Kurkkio. Two women have been found less than a kilometre from the house."

"Seriously? Murder too, or what?"

"There's a case review here in fifteen minutes, so—"

"On my way," Anna-Maria said and hung up.

When she came into the kitchen there was a pause in the family harmony.

"What's happened?" Petter asked.

"Looks like three murders," Anna-Maria said and she could feel herself flush. "Four, if you count the guy in the freezer. That'll set the cat among the pigeons."

She put on her jacket and shoes.

And just like that her family were patching things up.

"Has your server got a mob farm? If so, you should have endless amounts of bonemeal," Petter said to Gustaf. "And in that case you can get the trees to grow incredibly quickly. I can help you rebuild the forest if you want."

"Delicious!" Robert said as he downed the mud smoothie in two swigs.

"Thanks," Jenny said.

She threw her arms around her father.

"Pretty please could you wash the mixer up? I've got to study today."

Robert muttered yes.

Anna-Maria looked at her family. How come the rows had stopped as soon as she was removed from the equation? Why couldn't they feel responsible for one another like this all the time?

It's enough to drive you mad, she thought. You love them, but they drive you crazy.

She said goodbye on her way out, but barely anyone replied.

As Anna-Maria Mella was getting into her car before skidding off to the police building in Kiruna, Carl von Post's wife was eating breakfast with her husband in the dining room of Niehkus Hotel in the ski resort of Riksgränsen. The boys were still asleep. They were sharing a room and ate breakfast as soon as they got up and lunch when they were hungry. They had to have dinners together as a family, that was her only rule. They did so dutifully, shovelling down their food and not taking part in the conversation but fiddling with their phones under the table. Calle didn't tell them off. She did it every other time. After ten minutes they would have finished eating and ask if it was OK to leave. Family time, a word beginning with f just like fucking.

And speaking of fucking.

Calle had stayed in the bar after she had gone to bed at eleven. She felt she was being boring, but she was exhausted. She had worked like a slave all week, and then there was the packing and having to interrogate the boys to make sure they had brought everything they needed. Sun, masses of fresh air and skiing. When Calle decided to sit at the bar and have a night cap, she felt so tired she could cry.

So he had stayed there on his own. And the night cap really had sent him to bed. With someone else.

He had come up at half past three. He hadn't even bothered to sneak in. The bar closed at two, that she knew.

He had flopped into bed reeking of alcohol, sweat, sex, some other woman's perfume.

And now he was fiddling with his phone. Checking the comments and likes for his latest post from the slopes. "Genuine snow." Today they were supposed to take a five-peak lift. So he had something impressive to post on Instagram.

His phone buzzed and for a moment she thought it was his companion from last night.

"Rebecka Martinsson," he said, his eyes on the display. "That pisshead on the island where they found Raimo Koskela, he was murdered apparently."

"Are you driving back to Kiruna?"

"No, I'm not. Who the fuck cares? Some stupid row between two drinking buddies and then one kills the other by mistake. Be my guest, Martinsson. She's welcome to take the case. Along with the backlog of petty crimes."

She noticed that he put the phone in his pocket when he stood up to go and get more coffee. Just how long had he been making sure to keep it out of her sight?

"Do you want some more?" he asked with a glance at her cup.

She shook her head.

She could hear him talking to someone over by the juice bar.

"I really hate Kiruna, you know. Especially now the whole town is tipping into its own arsehole. But March, April and May up here in the mountains. You can't beat it."

He hates Kiruna, she thought. He hates Rebecka Martinsson. Why's that?

Then she surprised herself by thinking *Why does he hate me?*

That was so aggressive on his part. Not even sneaking around, not even showering before crashing into bed beside her. She had simply turned her back. She hadn't had a row or questioned him. She knew how rows like that began and what they were like in the middle and how they ended. They ended with him saying she worked too hard, which was a form of unfaithfulness according to him, that her boss was always more important, that she was boring, showed too little interest in sex, and the latest: she was pathologically jealous and paranoid.

She looked down at her hands. They were no longer the hands of a young person. The skin around her wedding ring had shrivelled.

He hates Martinsson and me for the same reason, she thought. Because he's a mediocrity. And I am so tired of pretending that he isn't, to the boys and to our friends.

She hadn't even told him about her recent pay rise. It wasn't the sort of thing he would be happy about.

The small queue that had formed at the steaming waffle iron was making her strangely depressed. Everything felt so hollow.

"I want a divorce," she said.

Not loud enough for anyone to hear. Calle was still chatting and laughing over by the juice bar. But *she* heard. She was listening to her own voice. To how it sounded. Very calm. Sad.

Everyone had gathered at the police headquarters by a quarter past eleven. The coffee machine was humming and beaming ENJOY in blazing red letters at passers-by.

Anna-Maria said hello to her squad and then Rebecka took over.

She began by telling them that Henry Pekkari had been subjected to a Burke and Hare-style killing.

"And," she went on, "when Sven-Erik and I were over there, I met Henry Pekkari's neighbour Mervi Johansson. This morning Mervi's daughter found her in the snow. She was unconscious and hypothermic, but still alive. Unlike the other two women behind the barn."

She clicked forward through a series of images on the screen on which two dead women could be seen lying in the snow. Both had blond hair with dark roots. One of their faces looked like it had been subject to serious abuse. An arm at an impossible angle. A ripped quilted jacket. The other one had barely any face left and was clad in no more than a leopard-print blouse. Both were wearing jeans and trainers.

"They weren't outside pursuing leisure activities, as you can see," Rebecka said. "The ambulance staff took the pictures. The closest police officer in Eastern Norrbotten was in Karungi, so it would have been another hour before he got there."

"What happened to them?" Anna-Maria Mella said.

"Was it birds pecked out their eyes?" Karzan Tigris said.

"Probably, though we'll have to wait for the autopsy," Rebecka Martinsson replied, "but we're obviously working on the assumption they were murdered."

She ran through the measures she had taken. Anna-Maria was impressed by how good Rebecka was. Quick and systematic. She had to stop herself nodding, as colleagues around her were doing. It felt as though Martinsson was preaching the gospel to her born-again flock.

"Only, have we got any reason to believe there's a link to the murder of Henry Pekkari?" Tommy Rantakyrö asked.

"Definitely," Rebecka Martinsson said. "When we went over to Henry Pekkari's because of the freezer murder, Sven-Erik Stålnacke discovered long blond hairs in the shower drain hole. We will be checking to see if there's a match, but it seems likely that the hairs are from one of these two women."

The mention of Sven-Erik sent a gentle ripple of happiness through the group of officers. Of course Svempa had been the one to discover the hairs.

"And," Rebecka continued, "there were mattresses in a room on the

161

upstairs floor. Sven-Erik, Börje Ström and Ragnhild Pekkari will have contaminated that murder site, but as far as anyone knew at the time, Henry had died of natural causes and the murder of Raimo Koskela was barred by the statute of limitations and so . . ."

She sighed and puffed out her cheeks.

"The forensics team are not going to be best pleased with us though," she said. "And I'm the one to blame. I was the one who sent them in."

She paused and Anna-Maria was wondering if Rebecka was expecting her to make a snarky comment. She had no objections though. How the hell could they have known they were trampling all over the site of a recent murder?

"As soon as we get the results from the cell-tower dump and Pekkari's phone, perhaps one of you could—"

"I'll do it," said Fred Olsson, putting his hand up like a schoolboy at the front of the class.

"And maybe someone could check with the National Operations Department in case there are any women listed as missing?"

Another hand went up.

Rebecka went through the list of steps to be taken at the start of the preliminary investigation, writing them up on the whiteboard and adding the initials of whoever was going to deal with them.

"Anna-Maria," she said by way of conclusion, "I've commissioned a helicopter. Getting to the island over the ice would be extremely dangerous at this point. And I was wondering if you would be willing to take someone with you to have a look around the scene of the murder."

That was the most important job of all. And the most fun. Checking out the scene of the murder. Talking to the forensics team. Anna-Maria appreciated the olive branch.

They smiled briefly at one another, reading relief in the other's eyes.

Just a hiccup, let's forget it. She knew that Rebecka had been working herself into the ground with the case backlog. And Anna-Maria's plate was full dealing with new arrivals on the squad. She would ask Rebecka to lunch with them when the opportunity arose.

"Yup," she replied. "Tommy?"

"Oh yes," he said and stood up. "I've just got to get some chewing tobacco. Going without baccy in the forests of the Torne valley calls to mind that old saying: 'No fucking way!'"

The others burst out laughing.

From the puppy of the squad to the right-paw of the alpha bitch, Rebecka was thinking.

"So how is the old lady, Mervi . . .?" Karzan Tigris asked.

"Mervi Johansson," Rebecka said. "She's got pneumonia and she's in a pretty bad way. We're hoping she'll pull through. The moment she can talk we'll want to question her of course. I'm going to inform Henry Pekkari's relatives as well."

Ragnhild Pekkari ate breakfast as slowly as she could. She read the newspaper from cover to cover. Did the little washing-up there was. Dried and put away the plates and cutlery and then there was absolutely nothing left to do. The flat was horribly clean.

She rang Olle.

"We should talk about the funeral," she said after a few introductory phrases.

"Do what you think is best," he said. "It'll be fine."

What do other people do, Ragnhild was thinking. They talk about their memories of course.

"The lad can arrange the inventory for probate," Olle continued. "Not that it'll amount to much. The place is a ruin, isn't it?"

"It is," she said and thought: *So that's the way of it. They'll want*

163

to buy me out for nothing. So let them. She was thinking about the snow bridge.

The lad was his eldest son Anders. The sort of man who changed his car every year and took his family on expensive foreign vacations but couldn't help stealing those little packs of salt and sugar from restaurants.

"If there's nothing else?" he asked.

"No," she said.

And then that conversation was out of the way.

She barely had time to put the phone down before it rang again. A number she didn't recognise. But she recognised the voice immediately: Börje Ström.

"So . . . uh . . . hi," he began hesitantly.

She wasn't going to give him any help. It would be interesting to hear how he managed on the phone. When he has only his voice and words to use. When he couldn't just stand there being so bloody handsome.

"I thought I'd go and check out a coffin for Dad," he went on. "And since you're likely to need one for your brother, maybe . . ."

"Maybe?" she said, even though she understood perfectly well.

"Maybe we could go together," he managed.

She was appalled to discover how happy that made her.

She said yes. The suspicion that he simply needed to have a woman with him started clawing away at her immediately. Just like Olle, he'd be used to having women take care of the practical matters. The fact that he'd asked her had nothing to do with it of course.

But she couldn't afford to be all that picky. It would be a relief to have company. And to be completely honest, he was the only person she wanted as company.

Madness, she said to the old man upstairs in the attic, to God.

She was like an animal taking its first tentative steps out of a cage.

Everything outside was life-threatening. But the only thing it wanted was to run on the legs it had never had a chance to use.

She had said yes! Börje looked at his phone in astonishment. He hadn't believed she would, though he must have had some hope or he wouldn't have called her. He thought again about those rough hands of her. And that anorak that smelled of wood smoke.

And then he was thinking about the funeral. About the first funeral he had ever attended. Dad hadn't ever had one. He had just up and vanished, after all.

OCTOBER 1962

Börje's grandmother is dead. She died of stomach cancer. On the morning of the funeral Börje and his mother take the bus to Övertorneå. The first snow has not yet fallen and autumn seems unwilling to let go even though the crops in the fields have been harvested and the potatoes dug up.

The seats smell dusty. A cold drizzle is tapping against the windows like a thousand needle pricks. They pass all the familiar places: the ruins of the old iron mill in Kengis, the small country shops and the ESSO petrol station. The road follows the river. The water level is low, any moment there will be a cold snap and ice will form. The river runs from poor to rich. To the north there are steep sandy banks, with small strips of arable land, the farms are smaller, the sheds and barns as well. As they travel southwards the banks get flatter, the fields broader and the farms are not only bigger but have decorative woodwork and elaborate porches.

Mum has three older brothers. They belong, like his maternal grandparents, to the West Laestadian faith. There are West Laestadians and East Laestadians.

The West are the worst people say, in order to distinguish the different doctrines. The West Laestadians are the most strict. They're not supposed to be frivolous so they have no curtains or flowers in their windows. They don't have television or radio. The women wear simple long skirts in dark colours. They hide their hair under headscarves that are knotted under the chin at weekends. The men do not wear ties. Ties are carefree and vain. They sing psalms in shrill voices and with excruciating slowness at their assemblies, always lagging a bit behind the organist. The sermons are very dour and go on for ever.

Mum is the only member of the family who does not belong to the true faith. She does not attend their services. Mum wears trousers and does not cover her hair. She even has short hair – a sin – and cuts other women's hair for a living – that's a sin twice over.

When Börje was younger his uncles' wives would take him to the services sometimes. He hated it. Mum calls her brothers "the men without ties". It suddenly occurs to Börje that he has never heard her talk about her life when she was a kid.

Börje has no desire to see his uncles. Erkki, his mother's eldest brother, took over the forestry business and the farm when her father died five years ago. He never says very much but everyone knows he is the top dog now Börje's grandfather is dead. Every member of the family, including Mum, takes time off and returns home to the farm to help out with the harvest. But Börje has never heard Erkki say a word of thanks. Instead he appears to think that the others are living off him while they are there. He walks into the kitchen wearing muddy boots and one of the women is always quick to wash the floor after he has left. He eats in silence and the others shovel their food down quickly because once Erkki is finished he expects everyone else to be ready to go back to work.

The middle brother Daniel is a woodwork teacher; he can build punts and make absolutely anything out of wood. He's always got some project on the go. His boys are allowed to help – Daniel teaches by demonstration – but Börje is never given anything to do and has to look on like a girl, or he might just be allowed to do the most basic tasks like pulling nails out of old planks and straightening them with a hammer.

Mum's youngest brother, Hilding, is the one Börje likes least. He lives in Kiruna and is a raise drill operator in the mine. Hilding is also a preacher in the West Laestadian community. All the preachers are laymen; they are expected to make their own living and not to be a burden on the community the way Swedish priests are.

When Grandma was alive, even she was afraid of Hilding. Before he came to visit she would hide anything that could be considered frivolous.

The embroidered and fringed tablecloth was swapped for a simple one, all the decorative objects and the pelargoniums in the windows were hidden away. She took down the paintings, only the photographs of her wedding were allowed to remain.

Buying things is a sin so rag rugs will do, bought carpets are completely unacceptable. The non-essentials of the Swedes are a sin as well. You can have a short curtain at the very bottom of the window to stop people looking in, but long ones are both unnecessary and sinful.

Börje has a lot of cousins. Contraception is a sin. Erkki has got seven children, Daniel eight and Hilding five with another on the way. The children use the formal pronoun "Ni" to their parents. Börje uses the informal "du" to his mother.

Börje is remembering one time when Mum had bought him a hula hoop. He took it with them on the bus. He and his cousins took turns spinning it around their waists out in the yard. Hilding burst out of the house all of a sudden. Just a few quick steps and he had reached them. He grabbed the hula hoop with such force that one of the little girls fell over.

"What are you doing, showing off like whores?" he roared.

His own children began crying straight away and yelling "*anteksi, Isä, anteksi*": sorry, Father, sorry. The others stood there afraid to move. Hilding disappeared into the woodshed and hacked the hoop into bits with the axe. And that was the end of that.

And now Börje Ström and his mother are on their way to the funeral, which means they will have to see the whole family. A lump has formed in Börje's belly. Mum is feeling it too, that's obvious. She stood in front of the mirror all morning changing her clothes and putting her hair in rollers and they almost missed the bus because at the last minute she decided to wash the lipstick off her mouth.

Börje wants to tell her how nice she looks but that won't help.

During the bus journey she talks aloud to herself so much he gets embarrassed. The other passengers must be thinking she is crazy.

"I don't give a shit," she suddenly yelps very loudly.

The interment goes on for ever. It was drizzling in Kiruna. It is colder here. The air shimmers with ice crystals and Börje's feet are so cold his toes hurt, his best shoes are much too thin. He has to remind himself that it is Grandma who is down there in the hole. He keeps thinking about his dad. It has been almost four months since he disappeared. The smell of wet woollen clothes in the church later is enough to make him feel sick.

There is coffee in the parish hall afterwards. It is crammed with people. Now they can talk at last. The buzz gets louder, people are eating sandwiches and cakes or chewing baccy.

Uncle Hilding is likely thinking this is getting far too frivolous. He looks very strict eating his sandwich. There's a furrow between his eyebrows like a dent left by an axe. All of a sudden he gets to his feet and takes a look around. The talk stops immediately. The women gather the little ones together and shush them.

Hilding thanks everyone for coming today to accompany their mother to her last rest. His voice is tight with suppressed tears as he talks about their mother. A hard-working person. A good wife, mother and neighbour. Her deep faith. A faith she wished to share with all her children.

Mum turns pale in her seat. Her eyes are wide with fear. She knows where this is headed. There is a tradition among the Laestadians of pointing out individual members of the congregation during the sermon and accusing them of sinful living and a lack of the proper reverence for God, while encouraging them to seek atonement and to better themselves. And she is the biggest sinner in the congregation.

The faithful sigh, utter small cries. There will be tears and handkerchiefs.

"Our poor mother," Hilding says, his voice trembling. "She wanted all of them to share in the truth. And it was her greatest grief that her only daughter, her youngest child, who should have been their heavenly joy, failed to join the other members of the family on the narrow road that leads to eternal life."

Although no-one is looking directly at Mum, everyone's attention is focused on her. Her shoulders sag and her chin drops towards her chest. She is crouching with her back against the ropes, waiting for the rain of blows to stop. Hilding talks about the broad road, the carefree road that leads to the sinkhole in the mire.

Börje is wondering if he has ever seen a road across a bog.

No-one says anything afterwards about Mum being put through the wringer. Instead, people seem almost friendly. And smile kindly at her. It feels like they have got something off their chests. Dumped it on that woman with a child born out of wedlock, with short hair and wearing a dress and make-up who works at a salon. And now that they have unburdened themselves, they can afford to appear kind. The hum of conversation gets louder once again. More coffee is served, the first cup had time to go cold.

When Börje reaches for a bun, he feels an iron hand clench round his upper arm. Uncle Hilding has appeared behind them. His eyes are as pale blue as spring ice. His lips are narrow. He says that Börje is frail. Built like a girl.

"He's doing training in gymnastics," Mum informs him.

That's what Börje told her. That he is training to be a gymnast. He's in no doubt at all she would never allow him to visit the boxing club.

Uncle Hilding's narrow mouth gets even narrower. An anaemic pencil line across his face. Gymnastics is worldly.

"So that's what they're getting up to nowadays? What's wrong with a bit of honest manual labour? My Antti is only six but he is helping Erkki raise the new barn."

Though Mum has the sense at this point to say nothing, Börje can feel his heart clench at the thought of being lent out to the relatives as a handyman. His uncle's children are identical copies of their parents. Dour eyes and pencil mouths. Börje has watched the way Hilding's children keep manoeuvring out of the way of their father. They shy away like dust bunnies. Hilding has to command their attendance if he wants something.

Then someone else starts talking to Hilding and he goes off.

"Let's go, now," Mum says to Börje and looks at her watch.

It is three hours before the evening bus leaves. Mum wants to be sure of having enough time to take a look at the cottage.

When the inheritance left by Börje's grandfather was settled, the brothers shared the forest. Erkki got the farm. As for Mum, she got a little cottage.

Mum and Börje get changed into jeans, anoraks and rubber boots. It's a half-hour walk through the woods.

The cottage isn't much to look at. It isn't insulated and there's no double glazing. But the location is lovely, on a south-west facing slope that leads down to a stream from a cold spring. The water is clean and fresh, and you can swim in it in the summer. They get the evening sun on their little set of steps. And almost no mosquitoes in the summer because there is sandy soil beneath the old spruces, the lovely broad-leaved trees and the tall pines that turn copper and gold in the evening sun. Mum loves those tall pines.

"These woods, you know," she will sometimes say.

Mum makes coffee on the wood-fired stove even though they've drunk several cups already.

Mum's shoulders relax. Her face softens. Börje knows she thinks this is the loveliest spot on earth. And he agrees with her.

Börje has time to take a dip in the stream. A thin crust of ice has formed along the edges but he breaks it up with his feet and Mum is laughing as she holds the towel up for him when he surfaces with a snort. And then it is time to go back.

Uncle Hilding drives them to the bus stop. When he says goodbye those heavy hands of his are at it again. This time he grasps Börje by the scruff of his neck and yanks him back and forth by it. It feels like Hilding wants to shake Börje. Give him a proper seeing to. Educate him.

Mum will be giving Hilding the chance to do just that. But none of them have a clue about that at this point. Mum least of all.

Anna-Maria Mella and Tommy Rantakyrö got to Kurkkio just after lunchtime on Saturday. The forensics team were already there. Their cars were parked in Mervi Johansson's yard. One of the team came over to give them a quick run-through of their findings.

"Behind the cart shed over there," she said, pointing. "Extremely difficult site to work. We couldn't get to it without destroying any traces because the snow is over a metre thick and soft as mush. We flew drones over it and filmed the site, and then all we could do was trudge through the snow carrying stretchers to salvage the bodies: they're in the van. Do you want to look at them right away?"

They moved over to the van.

"We're supposed to be here to collect trace evidence," the forensic technician told them. "The idea is we clear the snow away centimetre by centimetre. Martinsson commandeered a copter so we can get over to the island as well, but the pilot says he may not be able to land on that much slush. He's afraid the helicopter might tip over. They managed to salvage the corpses of Börje Ström's father and Henry Pekkari the other day, though that turned out to be far from easy. Is it true Stålnacke got out there on foot with just a rubber dinghy for a lifeboat?"

"You know Sven-Erik," Anna-Maria said with a wry smile.

The technician opened the back doors of the van and they stepped inside. They squeezed together between the bodies.

"Pohjanen will have to give his verdict," the forensics woman said. "But the bodies are of two women, twenty-five to thirty years of age. They were run over by a snowmobile, several times; there is visual evidence to support that in the snowmobile tracks we filmed with the drone. When we lifted them you could sense their pelvises were no longer stable, so definitely pelvic fractures on both of them: that alone would lead to massive and fatal blood loss."

She was pointing from one to the other while speaking. Anna-Maria was recording on her iPhone.

"The thigh bone is quite obviously out of alignment here and you

172

can see for yourself how swollen it is: they both suffered haemorrhaging in various parts of their bodies. Notice the asymmetry of the thorax, it's been crushed on one side and I would guess she didn't die immediately, because air has leaked into the fatty tissue under the epidermis, you can hear the crackling sound if you press the skin."

She pressed her rubber-gloved finger against the dead woman's skin. Anna-Maria and Tommy listened to the sound.

"Crush injuries on the ridge of the nose, one ear torn off along with defensive injuries. The skin has been completely scraped off, especially on the face of one, as you can see. The reconstruction's going to be tricky."

"We've got to identify them," Anna-Maria said. "I'm going to need dental records and DNA as soon as possible. And any other identifying characteristics."

"I checked into that," the technician replied. "No jewellery. But one of the women has a tattoo of a red umbrella on one ankle. Here. The photo I took is pretty good; I'll send it to you."

Tommy had had enough. He turned on his heel and vanished through the doors. Anna-Maria followed him. She was watching his back. Best to let him recover for a moment. Some deaths were worse than others. Her stomach wasn't that easily turned, it never had been.

She peered across the river at the island.

There were three mattresses on the upper floor of Henry Pekkari's house, she was thinking.

Wearing trainers and only one of them had a jacket on. Where do you go when you're trying to escape? To another house, of course. In the hope there'll be someone to save you.

Two people on the run, another driving the snowmobile. Though maybe not. Three people on the run and one got away? Could it have been some kind of weird accident? People did manage to run themselves over with their own cars. Maybe the snowmobile had got stuck and two of them got off? No, they had been run over several times. Back and forth. Murder, most definitely murder.

Though murder was awful, she actually found investigating murder cases fun. Not that you could ever really admit that to anyone. And only as long as it wasn't children or women who had been killed in the home, because then it was just awful and not fun at all.

She was thinking about the girls in the snow. Then she found herself thinking about her own daughter. Who made mud smoothies in the kitchen.

Anna-Maria has been doing this job for so many years. You had to remind yourself that these dead women were someone's daughters as well; you always had to find the resources within you to think of the victims with sympathy, and not lose all hope in humanity.

What a strange job I've got, she thought, one that's hard for other people to understand.

Tommy was standing beside her all of a sudden, and being unusually silent. He seemed depressed. He looked pale. Dark skin around the eyes. She knew things had been difficult since his partner had moved out; she had met someone else: a heating engineer from Altajärvi. That was the reason she had asked him along, thinking it might liven him up a bit. Only maybe it had had the opposite effect.

"Anna-Maria," Tommy suddenly said.

As if he had something to tell her, something that was weighing on him.

But when she asked: "What?"

He said: "Oh, nothing really."

And then the technician came over to tell them the helicopter was on its way.

MONDAY 2ND MAY

Carl von Post went back to work at 9 a.m. on Monday morning and was informed by his secretary Eva Bergmark that Rebecka Martinsson's investigation had expanded over the weekend. Three murder victims, two unidentified women and the alcoholic Henry Pekkari. Four, even, if you counted the statute-barred murder of Raimo Koskela.

Eva Bergmark was also able to report that the press had started calling. It was the freezer murder that had attracted their interest. "Murdered and Put in the Freezer. World-Famous Boxer's Father Found After 54 Years." The headline generated so many hits that the television news as well as the newspapers had been calling to find out more. Interest in the dead women was just part of the package.

"And it didn't occur to anyone to inform me?" Carl von Post said with evident displeasure.

"I really thought Martinsson had done that," Eva Bergmark said defensively. "I asked her, in fact . . ."

But by the time she had got the words out von Post was already on his way to Rebecka Martinsson's office.

The Brat greeted von Post with a vast, submissive joy. He waggled around, chucking his damp cloth rabbit into the air in the hope that a jealous von Post would actually feel tempted to grab Ninen and they could have a tug of war over it. And then be really great mates.

Von Post tried to push the dog out of the way with his foot. The smell of the sopping rabbit made him feel slightly nauseous. He promised himself that the most important factor in any forthcoming recruitment of office staff would be that the successful candidate was allergic to animals with fur. So they could put a non-negotiable rule in place against dogs in the office.

"So things have been happening, I hear," he said to Rebecka.

"Uhm," she answered, without taking her eyes off the screen.

Her hair had been freshly washed and gathered in a loose knot. Her blouse was ironed and she was wearing dark-blue suit trousers and high heels.

Dressed to meet the media, he thought in annoyance.

"You can do a quick overview of the investigations up to this point, and then we'll assign them to my division."

Rebecka looked up.

"Why would we assign them to your division?"

"Because, in my view, you haven't got time to lead the preliminary investigations of three murders while simultaneously dealing with the petty crimes backlog. And I don't take the murders of women lightly. This has to be dealt with by a strong hand."

"I've already put in three working days on this," Rebecka said calmly. "I've been to the sites. I have set out the parameters for the preliminary investigation. It would be a waste of resources to assign it to you. I couldn't agree to that."

"You can keep Henry Pekkari so—"

"Henry Pekkari. The women in the snow. I'm keeping them all. They are all linked in some way. It's ninety per cent certain that we've found hairs belonging to the dead women in Henry Pekkari's house. It looks like they spent the night there."

Carl von Post could sense straight away that something huge was in the process of getting away from him.

"Since I am the head—"

"Acting head, you mean," Rebecka cut him off. "I spoke to Björnfot over the weekend. He promised that if you decided to take over the investigation he would return to work and clear up the mess."

Carl von Post felt forced to take a deep breath.

At the beginning of the twentieth century scientists came up here to measure the skulls of Martinsson's relatives, he was thinking. In their view, miscegenation in the region was the greatest threat to the purity of the Nordic race. Quite appalling, of course. They hadn't been completely on the wrong track though.

"You contacted Björnfot," he said. "You're so bloody pathetic, Martinsson."

He turned on his heel and left the room.

A degenerate, he was thinking. Depressed. Unstable. And she was contaminating the entire workplace.

The notion that he would have to follow the entire case from the sidelines was making him ball his fists.

But there are more ways than one to skin a cat, he thought. Just make one mistake, Martinsson, and it'll be into the ring for round two.

Fred Olsson stuck his head into Rebecka's office.

"I've got the location data from the cell-tower dump and the list of people who rang or were rung from Henry Pekkari's phone. I thought it was going to be a bit difficult at first because we can't be certain when the murder took place. One call a week was his average. To the shop in Junosuando."

"The weekly alcohol shop," Rebecka said.

"That's right. But! He made a call at 23:13 on Friday April 8th that was *not* to the shop."

"Who to, then?"

"His brother, Olle Pekkari."

"Well done," Rebecka said encouragingly. "It would be great if someone could find out what that call was about."

"And another thing," Fred Olsson said. "I googled the image of that tattoo one of the women had . . ."

He cut himself off and looked down the corridor where happy voices could be heard. Then his face lit up.

"So good to see you," he exclaimed. "I was beginning to think you were dead."

Rebecka could hear Sven-Erik Stålnacke replying: "Can't keep a good man down, you know."

The next moment Sven-Erik appeared in the doorway.

"Am I disturbing you?" he said. "I was going to ask if you wanted to tag along and talk to Börje Ström's former coaches."

"You're not," Fred Olsson assured him. "You two keep talking. I've finished."

"Hang on, Fredde," Rebecka said. "You googled the image of the tattoo. The red umbrella?"

"Oh right, yes, I did: it's a symbol used by activists campaigning for the rights of sex workers. The campaign's called Red Umbrella."

"The rights of sex workers?" Rebecka repeated.

"So their interests are taken into account when laws are passed, that kind of thing. I don't know any more than that. It's all new to me actually. You can google it yourself."

"So they were prostitutes," Rebecka said. "Oh hell."

She pressed the tips of her fingers against her eyelids and sighed.

"That could really make the identification a whole lot harder," she said.

They all knew that sex workers habitually moved around. They would often lie to their families about where they were and how they were making a living. Sometimes they had no contact with their relatives at all and no-one would be looking for them if they disappeared.

Then Rebecka took her hands away from her eyes and stared at Sven-Erik as if he were manna from heaven.

"Only, if the girls were working in Kiruna and the area around it, some of their clients might know who they are," she said loudly. "The johns tell their whores everything, that's what you usually say isn't it, Sven-Erik. And you—"

"I know where you're going with this, but the answer is no!" Sven-Erik said, a note of warning in his voice.

"—and you've got a CI who's a prostitute," Rebecka said. "Or you used to when you were still working. She might have some customers who don't just visit her. And in that case we might be able to find the identity of the dead women. Their first names and nationalities at least."

"Like I said, no," Sven-Erik insisted.

"Take a look at this," Rebecka said and reached for the photo of the dead women in the snow before handing it to Sven-Erik.

"Some madman ran them over with a snowmobile," she said. "Back and forth."

Sven-Erik took a quick look at the photos, sighing at the sheer awfulness of the real world and handed them back.

"Alright then," he said reluctantly.

Although this is what he really likes, Rebecka was thinking. Being a part of things as they're happening. Putting all that experience and all those contacts of his to use.

He got out his phone and sent a text. It pinged at him a short while later. He grunted with satisfaction when he read the reply before shoving the phone back in his pocket.

"Let's go then," he said curtly.

"What?" Rebecka said. "Where to? To see her? Can't we just do the questions over the phone? I've got court this afternoon."

"She'd just say no," Sven-Erik said. "We're asking her to put us in touch with her clients. Buying sex is a criminal offence. So a bit of persuasion is going to be necessary. She has agreed to meet us and listen to what we have to say. I wasn't taking that for granted. You'll be back in time for your court thing."

"Persuasion is your Olympic speciality though," Rebecka said and put her coat on. "What do you want me along for?"

"Don't make yourself out to be any more stupid than you really are," Sven-Erik said in a kindly tone. "Any information you obtain in this way cannot form part of the preliminary investigation as I hope you realise. And a CI has to get something in exchange, money or something else. That's the way it works. She doesn't need money. She needs a police contact now I've retired."

They drove out of town, passing huge machines being driven by young people, dumpers, bulldozers, diggers, plate compacters, cranes. Over wet drifts of snow mixed with mud.

Sven-Erik was driving, swearing when he went the wrong way. New roundabouts. Roads closed off.

"I never know which way nowadays."

He hissed when Rebecka tried to help him so she let him drive around until he knew where he was going.

"Makes you wonder how long Kiruna's going to be a construction site," Rebecka said.

"For ever," Sven-Erik said. "I'm so tired of all this nonsense about moving a town. All over the world the media keep referring to Kiruna as the town that has to be moved because the mine is expanding. But the truth is that they're going to tear it down. Tear it down and build

180

a new one. Only a few buildings are actually going to be lifted and transported to new sites."

"Right," Rebecka said. "Only without the mine—"

"—we wouldn't exist," Sven-Erik filled in. "I know that. I know."

They fell silent. They drove past the building site of the new town hall.

Sven-Erik was thinking that come what may the local politicians would be getting a palace of their own, a lavish creation costing several hundred million. But he wasn't going to say anything out loud. He had no desire to sound like a grumpy old man.

The moment you had a dissenting opinion nowadays you got branded. A white, middle-aged guy who has no idea how privileged he is. If he got a krona for every time his thirteen-year-old granddaughter came out with the word 'mansplaining' he'd be . . . he'd be able to afford a slap-up meal with all the trimmings, at the very least.

Sven-Erik's former CI was called Anna Josefsson. She lived twenty kilometres outside of Vittangi. Sven-Erik steered cautiously into the yard so as not to tear up the water-logged soil. A barn, a stable and in between an old timber house with an attractive porch.

"Lovely," Rebecka commented. "And a view over the river!"

"That's right," Sven-Erik said. "The Vittangi farmers were rich and powerful in the old days. Anna's father helped her renovate the house. Though he often used to say to me it would have been better to level it to the ground and put up a prefab."

"Ahem," Rebecka said, wondering just how well Sven-Erik knew Anna Josefsson. She was rather hoping he hadn't been her client when his wife Hjördis left him. Was that fifteen years ago?

We know so little about people, she thought. You know one side of them and think that's all there is.

It wasn't the kind of thing you could ask about though.

Hands in your pockets, she thought. And keep those fingers clenched.

There were some horses in a fenced paddock. As Rebecka and Sven-Erik were getting out of the car, one of them came cantering up to say hello, extending its neck over the electric fence. It was black with a long mane and snorted affectionately at Sven-Erik while sniffing for sweets in his pockets.

"So who's a lovely gee-gee then," Sven-Erik said and patted the horse on its throat, which led to its winter coat coming off in huge clouds of hair. The horse snuggled up to him, closing its eyes.

Anna Josefsson came out onto the porch, pretty and fit in jeans, an Icelandic sweater and high-topped rubber boots. A remarkably long brown plait was uncoiling from beneath her knitted cap.

"Rebecka Martinsson," she called out. "So you brought Rebecka Martinsson with you, did you Svempa? I thought you were bringing a fellow officer."

She moved briskly forward to meet them. Smiling with her entire face.

"Do you recognise me?" she asked. "I got my nose fixed; you need to imagine it a bit bigger."

Rebecka ransacked her memory but the corridors were empty.

"I went by Isa when I was in school so I didn't have to put up with all the Anna jokes.

"Isa who was in my class in primary school?" Rebecka said.

She must have looked suspicious. Isa had been a quiet, fairly plain girl.

"So you're classmates?" Sven-Erik said with a laugh. "Rebecka's always saying I went to school with everyone, or I'm related to them."

"We were good friends," Rebecka said. "You and me and—"

"—Maret-Anna and Lena," Anna Josefsson said. "Do you remember when you taught us the times tables while we were skipping?"

"I did not . . ."

"The goal was to keep skipping all the way through the times tables until you got to nine. I still sometimes catch myself bending my knees a bit when I'm counting. And you used to write stories. And plays that we acted. Do you remember?"

"No, I don't. God, that's embarrassing."

"I've got one of them," Anna Josefsson said, pecking at the air with one finger. "I've got a story you wrote. About Paiju the Elk."

"Paiju the Elk," Rebecka said. "And I wrote about her?"

"So, Svempa, seems like you've got a new best friend?" Anna Josefsson said.

She was referring to the horse which was brushing its muzzle across his broad moustache.

"He's a real teddy bear," Anna went on. "But when he arrived three years ago he was thin as a rake. He bit me on the back as soon as he got the chance. Terrified of the curry-comb, he grabbed my arm and dragged me towards the partition once when I tried to curry him."

"Who was so horrible to you?" Sven-Erik asked the horse, stroking it along the top of its head . "Have you still got Svante?" He looked over at the other horses in the paddock.

Anna burst out laughing.

"Good Lord. I took Svante in fifteen years ago; he was twenty-two then. He left for Shangri-La ages ago now. Rebecka, you really should have that elk-storybook. I think I know where it is."

She disappeared into the house.

While Sven-Erik patted his new best friend, Rebecka thought about her elk. She had forgotten her entirely. One autumn her father had shot an elk-cow. The very next moment a calf had stepped out from the edge of the woods. Rebecka had not been there but she had heard him telling her grandmother about it and had gone into the kitchen. "Hasn't it got a mummy anymore?" Rebecka had wept. And then she had persuaded her father to promise they would save the calf. He agreed they would feed the calf over the winter. They had called it Paiju, willow.

Anna came out of the house holding an exercise book. She handed it to Rebecka. On the front cover was an elk head with horse's eyes and the name Paiju in large letters filled in with red crayon.

"Here, you can have it," Anna said.

"So how did you get to know each another?" Rebecka asked, coaxing the exercise book into her bag.

Sven-Erik had stopped petting the horse and it buffeted him to remind him of its existence.

"Me and Svempa got to know each other back in the day because I had a client who got really difficult," Anna said. "He fell in love with me – the client I mean, not Svempa. Or at least that was what he said. He started buying me clothes. He used to ring and check if I was wearing them and got upset if I wasn't. Upset if I put them on and someone else saw me in them. He started stalking me, he'd turn up here and note down the registration plates of my other clients and threaten them. He wanted me to go on holiday with him. When I tried to put a stop to it, he began threatening me as well. He used to ring and say these horrible things. And he was going to inform on me to the tax authorities and get me assessed unless I was 'nice'. If he'd done that I'd have lost the house, my home, everything. But one of my cousins knew Svempa, and you were able to talk some sense into him."

"Total nutcase," Sven-Erik said and shook his head at the memory.

"Forgive me if I'm being naïve," Rebecka said. "But the law would be on your side, wouldn't it? I mean, it isn't illegal to sell sex. It is only

184

illegal to *buy* sex. So why didn't you tell the police? He would have gone down for assault and for buying sexual services."

"That's a misconception," Anna said calmly. "The law against buying sex does not protect me; it protects 'public order'. It exists to protect you from living in a society where men purchase sex. If I went to the police, they'd confiscate my phone on the spot so they could go through my texts in order to find johns they can imprison. They'd also want me to appear in court to testify against my clients. Then they would maintain surveillance on my home. If I were renting somewhere they would prosecute my landlord for sexual procurement. Or they'd come bursting in here and drag my clients off to be arrested. You know, if I take a taxi and the taxi driver knows I'm on my way to a client, he is making himself complicit in the crime of procurement, because he's making money off my selling of sex. So we sex workers will go to any length not to turn to the police for help."

Though it must have made her feel safer knowing Sven-Erik, a police officer she could trust, Rebecka thought. And now she wants to add me to her list.

And it turned out they'd been school chums long ago. She didn't like owing people favours. But sufficient unto the day.

Rebecka told Anna Josefsson about the dead women in the snow. Sven-Erik stood there in silence, stroking the horse which looked as though it had fallen asleep with its head on Sven-Erik's shoulder.

"So there could have been three of them? But two are dead?" Anna said.

"Murdered," Rebecka said.

The law against buying sex puts a curb on demand at any rate, she was thinking. And until now there have been no murders of prostitutes in Sweden, not since it came into force. Not reported cases at least.

Anna Josefsson groaned.

"No-one wants to know," she said and her gestures got larger; her fingers were crooked as though she was holding something huge. "Just to be a bit Red Umbrella myself, this is exactly what I'm talking about. People who sell sex often work abroad; they prefer not to sell sex in their home countries and the market insists on variety. Clients in Kiruna want pretty Russian women one month and something different the next. So sex sellers move around. But a sex worker who wants to set up in business can't simply advertise for premises or employ a bodyguard, a cleaner, a driver, because they could all be prosecuted for procuring. So the sex worker has to buy those kinds of services from criminal elements. Which immediately makes the job a lot more dangerous. You become dependent on guys who sell drugs and weapons and have a really hateful view of women, and when they cheat the sex worker or try to force them, well then . . ."

"I get it," Rebecka said. "So what are we supposed to do?"

Anna looked at the ground.

"Do you know how many crimes of violence against us actually lead to arrests and guilty verdicts?" she said quietly.

Then she looked up with a warm smile.

Her work face, Rebecka was thinking.

"I'll check with my blokes," Anna said. "Some of them don't just come to me. They may know the two blondes who were working in this area recently. The umbrella tattoo might be something they noticed."

Anna turned to Sven-Erik.

"So what's it like being a pensioner then?" she asked. "Is it bingo and genealogy all the way?"

"Not really, it's . . ." Sven-Erik cleared his throat.

But he didn't get any further. With no warning at all, he started crying soundlessly. The muscles round his mouth twitched, his moustache seemed to jump up and down. The tears kept flowing.

Aghast, Anna and Rebecka glanced at one another. The hands of both women landed on Sven-Erik's arms.

"Sorry," he managed to say. "I was just thinking about my mother. Those last years. She couldn't remember who I was. Her memory just kept wandering around in the woods without a compass. My brother never came north from Karlstadt to see her. 'She doesn't know who we are, does she?' he said. So I was the one who sat with her."

A sex worker, a horse and a broken prosecutor were standing around him in silent sympathy.

He pulled himself together and managed a little smile. Anna gave a little smile too and made a sound, a soft humming. Rebecka got the feeling she was used to men crying.

"No idea why I suddenly got so soppy," Sven-Erik said. "Maybe it's the horses. They had horses when she was a kid. Her dad was a haulier."

Sven-Erik was thinking about those sudden tears of his as Rebecka and he were driving back to town. Odd how a feeling could suddenly flare up like that, and then vanish entirely. He kept thinking about his mother. On her deathbed he found things out she had never told him.

She had talked about her childhood. The dire circumstances. People today had no idea of the hardships they endured. About how she worked as a cleaner for rich men's wives and begged for cast-off clothes for her children. One of the wives had taken back a box of discarded clothes, saying, "It can't be a good idea to give poor children such nice clothes. It might make them uppity." When she told him that they had both started crying.

Rebecka asked him to look for her sunglasses in the glove compartment, which meant he had to stop reminiscing.

"I must have left them in the office," she said. "The sun's so bright it's making my head hurt. Can you do me a favour?"

"You can always ask, and maybe your prayers will be answered," Sven-Erik said.

"Henry Pekkari rang his older brother Olle the evening he was murdered. I'd like to ask Olle what that conversation was about. But I don't want to step on anyone's toes, the police I mean, butting in and doing their job can be a touchy business. Only, if you were there as well, no-one would mind. Everyone ends up happy."

"Why not ask Anna-Maria or Fredde or Tommy in that case?"

"They've all got so much on at the moment," Rebecka said casually.

Sven-Erik stroked his moustache thoughtfully, then came out with a short, joyless laugh.

"You haven't told them," he said. "You haven't told them that your mother was fostered by the Pekkari family. And you're scared it's going to come out. Fuck, Rebecka, that's really not clever."

"It isn't a secret," Rebecka replied. "But Mum moved out when she was fourteen. I've never had anything to do with that family. I don't know them. I don't care about them."

"You're investigating the murder of a family member! That's a conflict of interest."

"It's not a conflict of interest. I'm not related to the Pekkaris. I don't even know them. And it's not like Olle is a murder suspect. Or Ragnhild. Anyway, you're related to half the city and you went to school with the other half. If you weren't able to investigate cases where you knew those involved or were related to them—"

"The difference is I'd have been open about who I knew and who I was related to. And now and then I did have to step aside. Full disclosure, Rebecka. Ring a bell?"

"I'm going to be transparent," Rebecka said to appease him. "Just not right now."

188

"Yeah, right, you want to solve the case first. Scared the Pest will steal it for himself."

"If I were to give von Post any cause to try and take these murders over, he'd grab them faster than you can say 'media-whore'," Rebecka said glumly. "So? You coming with me to have a little chat with Olle Pekkari or not? And we can be sure to ask him how Henry Pekkari knew Börje Ström's father."

"Yeah, yeah, I'll go with you," Sven-Erik said. "But I'm worried you're only going to make things more difficult for yourself." Rebecka's phone chirped. It was a text from Maria Taube.

Can't wait, can't wait, can't wait was the message, along with hearts and dancing women.

Rebecka groaned and texted a row of happy face emojis back.

"Bad news?" Sven-Erik said.

"No," Rebecka replied. "I'm having a girls' night in on Thursday. A former colleague from Stockholm and her mates are coming north to go skiing, so they're taking the opportunity to visit. I've have absolutely no idea how I'm going to find time to arrange anything. And I ought to clean the house."

"Ah, offer them *surströmming*. A dish for any occasion."

He searched out a YouTube video on his phone in which a group of Americans were obliged to eat the rotten herrings. Rebecka watched while trying to keep her eyes on the road. They ended up laughing and the car did veer a bit. Absolutely no regard for the law.

Olle Pekkari lived in a detached timber-clad house on Föraregatan. His wife opened the door. Astrid Pekkari was born in 1942, the same year as Olle, Rebecka had looked it up. She had looked up their taxable income as well along with the balance sheet of the company. She knew the average age and average income of their neighbours. She found out from the civil registry that Astrid had two siblings, and on Facebook she had seen pictures of the grandchildren, knitted sweaters, and of Astrid and Olle hiking on Tenerife last year.

Astrid's hair was styled in an attractive light-grey pageboy cut, with a slanting fringe; she was wearing a neatly ironed blouse, a pearl necklace and a skirt that looked a little loose. Rebecka thought it would have been a classic look twenty or so years ago; a simple jumper that looked expensive. Was she expecting visitors? Or were there really people who dressed like that when they were at home? That prompted Rebecka into thinking about how she mooched around at home in sweatpants, her unwashed hair in a topknot.

"Come in," Astrid Pekkari said amiably after they had introduced themselves and asked to see her husband. "Have a seat in the living room."

There was an open birch-bark knapsack in the hall containing blue plastic slip-on shoe covers.

"Would you like us to . . ." Sven-Erik said, glancing at the knapsack.

Astrid gestured dismissively.

"Not at all. Olle's the one who fusses. What I usually say is if I'm the one doing the cleaning, then it's my rules apply. You don't need to take off your shoes."

She gave Rebecka an extra long look.

"I can't get over how like Virpi you are," she said.

When Rebecka failed to respond, she turned towards the staircase and shouted:

"Olle!"

Rebecka had no idea how to deal with being told she resembled Virpi. She felt no obvious emotional response. Grandma and Sivving had always said she was like Dad.

There was no reply from upstairs.

"He's got his headphones on," Astrid said. "Just have a seat in there and I'll go and get him."

She vanished up the stairs.

"It's probably best to . . ." Sven-Erik said softly while slipping on the shoe covers. "If it's that important to Olle."

Rebecka followed his lead and they moved squeakily into the living room. They heard a knock at a door upstairs and an indistinct murmur.

The living room matched Astrid Pekkari. Furniture in the Gustavian style, polished to a shine. Glass display cases and a chandelier. Oil paintings. You got the feeling nothing had been changed for at least thirty years. Spotlessly clean and free of dust. There was nothing to indicate the room was ever used. Not even a newspaper or a book. No knitting. No crossword.

Rebecka's thoughts turned to her grandmother. When she was little and living with her, they slept in the kitchen, Grandma on the pull-out bench and Rebecka on a mattress on the floor. What was now Rebecka's bedroom had been the parlour, and it was kept spotless and untouched. It contained the only upholstered piece of furniture in the house: the best armchair. Tablecloths with lace embroidery covered the folding table. The parlour was used only on special occasions. When the priest came to visit. When Rebecka finished grammar school. For festivals.

That had been the set-up in many a home in the Torne valley. Possessing a room that did not get used may have been an important means of distinguishing yourself from the common folk, from manual labourers: You might have been poor, but at least you weren't living under a pine tree along with your goat.

Her eyes scanned the rows of books. Were there any photo albums here with pictures of her mother?

They perched on the edge of the sofa without leaning back against the plumped cushions.

What did Olle and Astrid say about Mum? Rebecka wondered. If they talked about her at all. Maybe they were one of those couples who never said anything to each other anymore. Him up there on the upper floor and her outside pole-walking with her friends.

Not everyone needs to talk, she thought. About what had shaped you. About what made you head for the hills, find yourself a hidey-hole and raise the drawbridge. What did Marit say to Krister? What did they talk about? It was bound to be about much nicer things.

Olle came into the room. He was tall, just like Ragnhild. Fit for someone who would soon be seventy-five. He moved smoothly without any obvious hitch. He sat on the sofa without having to steady himself on the armrest. He resembled Ragnhild in the face as well: something about the eyes and the cupid bow of the lips. Smartly dressed, just like his wife, neatly pressed and with a white shirt.

Rebecka and Sven-Erik introduced themselves.

"Obviously I know who you are," he said with a dismissive gesture.

He barely looked at Rebecka. Only there was that glint of recognition in his eyes. Virpi again.

He turned so he was facing Sven-Erik. Rebecka was glad Sven-Erik had accompanied her. Sven-Erik and Olle danced around for a bit about the latter's granddaughter who played hockey in the women's junior league. Their team would be in the second division soon, or so they both thought.

"We wanted to ask you one or two questions," Sven-Erik said once the hockey had been dealt with. "About Raimo Koskela who was found in your brother Henry Pekkari's freezer."

"Right, good Lord," Olle Pekkari said, running a hand across his face. "I hope you realise that I didn't have the slightest idea—"

"Any prosecution for the murder of Raimo Koskela would be barred by statute," Sven-Erik said, "but we'd like to find out what we can. I'm retired now, but I promised Börje Ström I'd do a bit of asking around. So he can have some closure, you understand."

"I see," Olle Pekkari said. "Just ask away. Only my family and I have no wish to be involved in this business. The papers have got hold of it, you know."

"Do you know if Henry knew Raimo Koskela? If there was some link between them?"

Olle Pekkari shook his head.

"Henry was, I'm not sure how to put it, weak. I sometimes think I took far too much of the responsibility when we were young. We spoiled him, and he never developed any backbone. He kept on drinking and could never hold down a job. And he ran around with a lot of the riff-raff from Kiruna and the surrounding villages. Raimo Koskela would have to have been ten years older though. I never heard Henry mention him."

"If anything occurs to you, please let us know," Sven-Erik said. "And there was one other thing."

He looked at Rebecka to give her the floor.

"Your brother Henry was murdered," she said.

Straight to the point. Sven-Erik almost leaped out of his seat beside her.

"What?" Olle Pekkari exclaimed. "That can't be right; he died of a heart attack. Or a stroke."

"That was what the autopsy initially indicated," Rebecka said. "But when the findings were reviewed it became very clear that he had been killed. A thoracic compression."

Rebecka briefly explained what the autopsy had revealed. She told him about the women in the snow. Olle listened with his lips clamped shut.

"We read about the women," he said.

Astrid Pekkari appeared in the doorway.

"Would anyone like coffee?" she asked.

Olle Pekkari shooed her away as if she were a bug.

"That has to be a mistake," he said. "Murdered?"

"When did you last talk to your brother?" Rebecka asked him.

"Ages ago," Olle Pekkari said. "It's no secret that Henry was severely alcoholic. We had almost no contact."

"Speaking of which," Rebecka said. "A call list has shown us that Henry rang here, to your landline, the evening we think is the evening of the murder: Friday April 8th. Could someone else have answered? Your wife, perhaps?"

"Henry would ring occasionally when he got drunk," Olle said and tried to catch his breath. "It was almost impossible to work out what he was saying, you know, it was that muddled and usually slurred. The kind of conversation you want to finish as quickly as possible. And I never made an effort to remember them."

"I understand," Rebecka said. "Could your wife just confirm that she wasn't the one who—"

"Of course. Astrid!"

Astrid Pekkari reappeared in the doorway.

"Would you like some coffee?" she asked again.

"Did Henry ring?" Olle Pekkari asked. "And talk to you. Before he . . . I mean?"

"No."

"Well, if that was everything?" Olle Pekkari said, getting to his feet to make it clear the conversation was over.

He was white in the face. He attempted a smile but failed. As though he had suddenly realised it wasn't appropriate. His mouth was only slightly open. Rebecka noticed that his chest was heaving beneath his shirt.

He accompanied them into the hall where the shoe covers were taken off and consigned to the bark knapsack. Astrid was standing in the doorway to the kitchen.

"Just to be clear. My family had nothing to do with Henry. We do not want to be involved in this investigation."

Sven-Erik smoothed his moustache with two fingers.

"Is there any reason you might be involved?" Rebecka asked.

"Not apart from any resentment you feel towards us Pekkaris," Olle Pekkari said.

"Olle," Astrid said with a note of caution in her voice.

"Your mother," Olle Pekkari said, now sounding agitated. "She should have been grateful that we looked after her. Instead she did her best to muck things up for both my mother and father. *Kansainvälinen*. She shortened their lives, I'm certain of that."

"It's odd you should say that," Rebecka said. "Anyone else would realise it was her life that got shortened."

A warm hand was placed on her back. It belonged to Sven-Erik. He led her out of the house.

*

When they were sitting in the car once again, Rebecka said.

"What does that mean? *Kansainvälinen?*"

"Anyone's," Sven-Erik said. "You really should tell them you are related . . . OK, OK . . . that there's a family connection with the Pekkaris."

"He's lying."

Rebecka slammed her hand against the wheel.

"About the phone calls, I mean. He was lying when he said that Henry Pekkari hadn't called him," she continued. "And when he was confronted with the truth in black and white, he changed his mind and said Henry used to ring every now and then when he was drunk. Only the list from Henry's phone didn't show any other calls to Olle Pekkari for two months."

"You're right, there's something there," Sven-Erik said.

"I want Olle Pekkari's call history," Rebecka said and tapped out a text to Fred Olsson. I want to know if Olle Pekkari rang anyone immediately after he spoke with Henry. And . . .

She snapped a screen dump of the clock on her phone.

. . . I want to know if he's calling anyone right now

"Mmm," Sven Erik said. "At least we didn't have to wear hairnets in there. Although Astrid, the wife, seemed OK, didn't she?"

Rebecka laughed out loud.

"I just fell so completely bloody in love with my messy home all over again," she said.

"Too right," Sven Erik said. "Makes you want to go back to cat litter scattered all over the bathroom floor."

"Dog hairs and the dribble their willies leave on sofa cushions."

"You just can't beat it," Sven-Erik said warmly. "Willy dribble. It's severely underappreciated as a contribution to a cosy domestic environment."

*

Krister Eriksson was in his sister Linda's kitchen, drinking a cup of rooibos tea.

He and Marit were supposed to be flying to Stockholm to spend the night at a Japanese spa. They had been given a special discount in exchange for Marit posting five pictures of their stay. Linda was going to be looking after the dogs.

Roy was staring fixedly at the broom cupboard. Linda laughed.

"He knows the toys and chews are in there. Don't you, old boy? You know perfectly well I usually get something new for you, something fun."

She got up and opened the cupboard and held out a rubber duck that squeaked, which Roy flung himself at.

Tintin couldn't care less about ducks. She had parked herself in the hall and lay sighing by the door, giving Krister long and accusing looks.

"How can she possibly know you're planning on leaving her here?" Linda asked.

"She knows everything."

"Tintin," Linda said in appeal. "You're going to have a lovely time with me, you know that don't you? Your master needs to have some dog-free time just for a bit."

He must have made a face, because she immediately asked:

"Won't it be nice to get away?"

"Sure, it'll be fine."

Before she could say more he asked her how she was getting on at work. And she told him about the building of the new school, and the architect who thought having windows between the classrooms and the corridor was a good idea.

"As if my kids didn't have a hard enough time concentrating," she said.

Then she told him how crazy it was that they had ordered chairs with wheels, because it would be impossible to get the kids to sit still on them. And that you had to be a qualified engineer to put the new tables together. And what was the point of all those meetings with the architect since no-one listened to what the teachers wanted the classrooms to be like.

As she finished, she realised her brother didn't seem to be listening either.

"Hello," she said gently, putting a hand on top of his. "Anything the matter?"

"It's fine," he said.

Only a bit later he said:

"What do you really think of Marit?"

She withdrew her hand.

"The important thing has to be what *you* think," she replied, trying to avoid the question.

He stayed silent for so long she felt forced to say something.

"I think that Marit is a . . . good person," she said. "Everything in order and she's nice to people. Extravert . . ."

She tried to catch his eye, but his unblinking gaze had drilled its way into the tabletop.

". . . happy," she added.

"You're not answering the question, though, are you," he said with an edge of anger to his voice. "What do *you* think of her?"

She got her box of chewing tobacco out of her pocket and inserted a wad under her lip. She offered him some, but he shook his head. He had stopped for Rebecka's sake. One good thing the relationship had done for him at least.

"Does it matter?" she asked. "I mean, you're the one who has to live with her."

He stiffened and closed up. He shoved away Roy, who was trying to put the chewed and saliva-coated rubber duck in his lap.

"OK," she said. "I don't dislike Marit, definitely not. But I suppose I think she's a bit shallow. And I always get kind of nervous when you both come round because all of a sudden I'll see my kitchen on her Instagram account. I always feel I've got to clean the place up and dress nicely. There's something else about the Instagram business as well; it feels like everything has to be about 'likes'. Sometimes you wonder if anything you do has any value of its own. Like when I did a birthday dinner for her here; it was incredibly sweet of her to post pictures and write 'my darling sister-in-law'. But I think I would have preferred it to remain a private moment between you and me and her. It feels like she's converting what is genuine into some kind of celebrity currency."

She stopped.

"Now I'm being unfair," she said. "Can I take it all back?"

She made a sound like she was reversing a tape at maximum speed.

Not even a hint of a smile from him. Instead he said:

"So what did you think about Rebecka then?"

"You know I like Rebecka. But she's more of a roller-coaster person. I mean, I could see that she was hurting you. And no-one gets to hurt my big brother. When you were together I used to sometimes wish you would meet someone like Marit instead."

"You know," he said, and it came out more forcefully than he intended. "When Rebecka and I were together she never even left her toothbrush at my place. She brought her overnight bag and she'd take it away with her every time. It felt like she was ready to walk away at a moment's notice. If it was going to end, she wouldn't even have to come over to pick up a sweater. Or her fucking toothbrush."

"I get it."

"Then she flew down to Stockholm to fuck Måns."

Tintin sat up in the hall.

"Lie down!" Krister said.

He was remembering Rebecka that time. She'd come straight from the airport and just stepped right inside his house. She didn't have her overnight bag with her. It was still in the car. He understood immediately. She stayed in the hall. She didn't take her shoes off. The dogs surrounded her, crazy with joy at being reunited. She was completely rigid. What he was feeling was close to fear.

"I had to tell you," she said. "I slept with Måns. We're not a couple; I haven't gone back to him."

"What about us?" he had asked.

But she didn't seem able to answer that question.

He had moved to the front door and opened it without a word. Stepped to one side and stuck his hand out in a gesture that she should leave.

She had taken the Brat with her and left. Just got into her car and drove away.

And that was that. They hadn't even had a row.

He had taken the dogs with him into the mountains. They were away for five days and nights.

They slept in the winter tent on reindeer skin. He climbed a new peak every day to get reception on his phone but there was never a missed call from her or a message.

He looked at his sister.

"Marit is the best thing that has happened to me," he said.

"Yes," she said, and you could see from her face she wished she could take back every word she'd said.

But she couldn't, could she. The words had been said and they were still dangling in the air, reverberating, like the peal of church bells.

He said no to lunch. He gathered his things and fled the scene.

Anna-Maria Mella could hear Sven-Erik's voice as she went into the lunchroom.

The air was heavy with the smell of ready meals that have been microwaved. And there was Rebecka sitting with Sven-Erik eating Thai take-out. Karzan Tigris and Magda Vidarsdotter were tucking into their plastic boxes. Fred Olsson had dished a vegetarian curry onto a plate, a piece of kitchen paper folded neatly beside it, folded neatly like a serviette.

They were all laughing at something Sven-Erik had just said; in Magda's case so hard that some food had dribbled out of her mouth.

Hurt feelings sliced through Anna-Maria as if she was made of butter.

Sven-Erik Stålnacke. She missed him so terribly. Even though she'd been his boss, somehow he had been the one to make her feel safe. Never mind they'd always been partnered on the job, he was the person she could talk to about problems, problems she had with her bosses and their colleagues and, yeah, problems at home.

But apparently the sense of loss wasn't mutual. He was sitting there laughing with the others and telling one of his anecdotes. He hadn't even come by her office to say hello. Of course Rebecka was the one who mattered now.

And no-one had texted her to say it was time for lunch. Only the other day she had decided to take Rebecka to lunch with the new employees. But that goodwill only worked in one direction apparently. She could feel her resentment taking hold once again. Like flypaper in her hair.

"Hi there," Sven-Erik called to her. "Come and have a seat."

"I don't want to disturb you."

"Meh. Don't talk nonsense. You wouldn't be disturbing us. Come and sit here." His voice was full of laughter and he pulled out the chair next to him.

Anna-Maria made her way over to the table. She was smiling and trying to think of something to say.

Karzan repeated what Sven-Erik had just said. The conversation got going again and she no longer had all eyes on her. The morning papers were on the table. The headlines were all about the body in the freezer and the women in the snow. Soon they'd be writing about Henry Pekkari's murder as well.

"Are you going to tell them we found blood and cloth fibres under Pekkari's snowmobile?" Anna-Maria asked.

"Not yet," Rebecka said. "Press conference at 5 p.m. I'd really like you to sit in on that."

"I knew I should have had a shower this morning," Anna-Maria said, raking in a laugh or two herself.

"Where's Tommy?" she said, looking round.

"He went home," Magda replied. "He was feeling lousy."

Anna-Maria made a mental note to check on Tommy Rantakyrö's days off sick. She needed to have a chat with him.

"Are you wondering what to wear to Rebecka's party?" Sven-Erik asked.

"What? Uh . . . no, I'm not . . ." Anna-Maria replied before losing her thread.

"It's not really a party as such, just one of my former colleagues and her mates," Rebecka began, and then said: "You should come. They're really nice."

"Mmm, thanks," Anna-Maria said.

Caught in a cleft stick. She realised Rebecka had felt obliged to invite her. Bloody Sven-Erik. What was she supposed to say in front of all the others? "No, I don't want to go to a party with your mates from Stockholm."

Sven-Erik's phone rang. He got up and nodded pointedly at Rebecka before vanishing into the corridor.

He came back a moment later.

"Yup, she had a client who thought he knew who those dead girls were."

"Who?" Anna-Maria asked, but got no answer.

"Do you want someone with you?" Rebecka said. "Maybe Karzan could . . ." Sven-Erik waved away the suggestion.

"He's refusing to talk to the police, but a retired officer is fine. And I had to promise to keep his name out of it. He doesn't want to end up part of an investigation or as a witness. So I'm going to go straight there."

"It would be so helpful to get them identified," Rebecka said. "Oh my God!"

She looked at her watch.

"I've got to be in court in quarter of an hour. To get the bad guys convicted."

"Not all the bad guys," Anna-Maria said just loudly enough as Rebecka left the lunchroom.

Börje Ström took the stairs down to the dining room of the Hotell Ferrum and chose cod with egg sauce for lunch. He was joined by the hotel caretaker, a friendly chap. Pleasant company. The caretaker was born in Merasjärvi, and they spent a while working out any family connections. They found a blood tie from the middle of the nineteenth century. Then they got on to boxing, of course. Followed by a few words about Börje's dead father.

"What a terrible story," the caretaker said sympathetically.

Börje told him he was going to the undertakers and then on to the church. Preparations for the burial. He was on the point of saying something about Ragnhild but didn't.

"Still, it will be good in a way to get your father properly buried," the caretaker said.

"Yeah, it will," Börje said. "I just wish I'd brought a shirt along."

He pulled at his washed-out sweater, thinking of Ragnhild Pekkari and what she would think of it.

"I didn't get changed when I drove from Älvsbyn. I just jumped in the car and took off. I don't even think I locked the front door. I'll have to go and buy something."

"Come with me to the storeroom," the caretaker said, keen to help. "You know, people leave clothes in the rooms and never ask to get them back."

"Are you going to have anything in my size, though?" Börje Ström said with a smile.

He was a head taller than the caretaker, who wasn't exactly small either.

There was a shirt. It was purple and made of cheap cotton.

"Just help yourself," the caretaker said generously. "It's been hanging here for ages. It'd get chucked soon in any case."

Börje Ström did up the cuffs: he had to be helped with the one on the right. He stood there like a child and offered his arm. He was thinking about the other people who had helped him during the Kiruna years: Sisu-Sikke and Nyrkin-Jussi. All the times they had taped up his hands and helped him on with his gloves.

1962–1966

"A boxer who can't last all the rounds might just as well give up," Nyrkin-Jussi yells as they keep skipping as part of their training routine. "You're going to skip and you're going to run. Run," he thunders like a Laestadian preacher. "Run every day."

Then he quotes from Paul.

"'Do you not know that all the runners in a stadium compete'," he bellows. "'But only one receives the prize? So run to win. Each compet-itor must exercise self-control in everything. So I do not run uncertainly or box like one who hits only air. Instead I subdue my body and make it my slave.' That's in the Bible, lads. Keep at it!"

And Börje runs. Eleven years old and he runs every day, all the time. To and from school. (That's running for free, lad, Nyrkin-Jussi says. You just let the others laugh, the grins will be wiped off their faces soon enough.)

By the time he is twelve he is running in the forest around Luossavaara, the old mine. (Every now and then feel free to imagine that the äpärä are thrusting their spindly childish arms up from the underworld to pull you down, that'll help you speed up, ha ha.)

He punches the bag at the gym. (Don't give it your all, concentrate on being fast instead, your punch should be relaxed until it makes contact, that's when you clench your fist, think of it like capturing a fly in flight.)

He turns thirteen and starts upper secondary school. Now he is running the whole way up Luossavaara. (Right then lad, you'll have to run the last uphill bit yourself. Looking at you go makes me feel like someone's great-granddad. "Strength is the pride of the young, white hair the honour of the old." I'm just going to catch my breath now for a bit.)

Going on for fourteen he gets his growth spurt, and all of a sudden he is big and tall. Sisu-Sikke gives him a mouth guard. It tastes of inner tube. One of the older lads usually drops a bit of mouthwash into his mouth-guard box, but the others think that's being sissy, so Börje does what the other lads do and gets used to the taste. In the end he will start to like the taste of inner tube, strange how things can turn out.

He gets a head guard as well, but no-one uses head guards, they feel loose when you get hot and slide down over your eyes. He's sparring now, with the seniors as well.

Nyrkin-Jussi and Sisu-Sikke are postmen and help him get part-time work. They give him the worst districts, the ones with hills and lots of stairs. He runs as he delivers the post and flyers after school. He hauls his bike, weighed down with postbags, through the snow in winter before rushing up the stairs in the high-rises with the postbag over his shoulder and then down again in record time, feinting lightning-fast to left and right on every floor to get the envelopes into the letterboxes.

He goes to train at the boxing club every day. He punches the bag, does abdominal exercises with the medicine ball and keeps skipping.

He has to hold the pads for the older boys. One of them says he smells of cat piss. What's he supposed to do about that? He's only got one lot of training gear. Mum does the washing in the communal laundry every other week.

But the day after that comment was made, his only top and pair of shorts are hanging freshly laundered in his locker. And it stays that way. Every week his training clothes smell freshly washed. He realises it must be Sisu-Sikke, but neither of them ever mention it.

He holds the pads and learns to read the way the older boys punch. He can see how the muscles move beneath their skin, signalling a hook is coming; he becomes strong enough to stand firm and keep his guard up.

He turns fifteen in the spring of 1966 and starts taking part in club matches. It turns out he is useless at them. When it comes to it, he cannot punch.

"You're too defensive," Nyrkin-Jussi yells. "You know you can do it. Just attack. Being nice is for your mum."

There is a difference between sparring and holding the pads on the one hand and boxing on the other. He's never been able to fight. And at school he's the same person he's always been. You have to keep out of the way of the tough guys as best you can. He sometimes turns up for training with a bust lip and a black eye.

"What's this?" Nyrkin-Jussi says as he examines him. "It's one thing for you to leave this place looking like that now and then, but you shouldn't be turning up like that. You've got to give as good as you get."

It's not that easy. The fear is like a worm in his spine. And there are a lot of them. One time one of the worst bullies forces him to kneel on all fours and eat a pinch of baccy that's just been spat out. He's got no choice. All he can do is obey. In front of everyone in the middle of the break hall. And they keep yelling how fucking disgusting he is. And laughing. Afterwards he spews like a cat outside the woodwork room.

But all that vanishes the moment he gets to the club. He becomes calm. The smell of sweaty gloves and liniment. All the rhythmic noises made by punches and skipping ropes. Nyrkin-Jussi's rough voice, sometimes he shouts like a preacher, sometimes like a booze smuggler: "Everything you do has got to be done hard. Hard, boys. *Helvetin saatana piru* – hard! *Päälle vain!*" he yells in Finnish.

Steering clear of women feels great as well. At home there's Mum. At school the girls of his age have started wearing make-up and smoking. They're completely impervious. If you happen to look their way they start hissing: "What you looking at, you spotty Finnish git."

Mum's pleased about his part-time post job and isn't bothered that he sometimes gets back after nine at night. He's dropped the lie about gymnastics. She's just pleased when he gives her half his wages. She needs it because he eats like a horse and she doesn't earn that much at the hair salon.

But he knows it's only a question of time before she finds out about the boxing.

"You're not getting up to no good, I hope," Mum says, looking at the cuts on his eyebrows.

It's just a matter of time.

Not that it matters, Börje Ström thinks. She can beat me to death. I won't stop boxing.

At exactly two o'clock on Monday afternoon Börje Ström rang the doorbell. By then Ragnhild had changed her clothes several times. She was about to change again, but too late now.

She was wearing a skirt. Wearing a skirt was what she actually hated most because then she had to wear stockings. And stockings were hell for tall women. She usually brought two identical pairs in the largest size and cut off one of the legs, then she'd use both pairs one on top of the other. That stopped the crotch slipping down as much. She was a trouser person. So why was she putting herself through this skirt misery? And that was him ringing the bell. Nothing to be done about it now.

She glanced at the mirror before opening the door. True, there were 66-year-old women who looked worse. The Icelandic sweater with a simple black skirt. Her hair tied back in apparently careless fashion. You couldn't see all the effort she had made. She shut the door to her room and that tell-tale pile of clothes on the bed.

They walked to the undertakers. They didn't say much. They did comment on the fact that May was the ugliest time of year in Kiruna. Grit on the pavements and the roads. A black layer of dirt on the snow drifts that had almost entirely melted. No greenery. In southern Sweden people were posting pictures of cherry blossom and lilacs in flower, crocuses and daffodils.

Ragnhild was thinking that she knew nothing about either boxing or sport in general and she had nothing in common with this man. And where in the world had he got that hideous purple shirt?

Börje Ström was dwelling on the large shelf full of books he had seen in Ragnhild Pekkari's home as he stood there in the hall while she put her coat on. He had read a book once at school but couldn't even remember what it was called. Marvin Hagler said in an interview: "If they cut my bald head open, they will find one big boxing glove. That's all I am. I live it."

They may have found the silence between them oppressive to begin with, but after a while they got used to it. They fell into each other's rhythm, taking long powerful strides. Like two majestic stags they trotted along the street drawing looks from everyone they passed.

Just you go on looking, Ragnhild thought.

She was keeping pace with this large man as they surged ahead, and feeling just as much at home as she had only ever felt in the woods.

And then all of a sudden they arrived at the undertakers. She could have kept walking for days.

The funeral director remembered Ragnhild from A & E. He'd had appendicitis. There had been an acute surgical unit in the town then.

"Luckily for me," he said. "God knows if I'd have made it all the way to Gällivare."

She looked around. IKEA curtains, IKEA furniture, IKEA posters in cheap frames on the walls. It made her feel depressed. Not so much because it was ugly, but because it was all the same, everywhere the same. And that went for people with money as well: William Morris wallpaper and Svenskt Tenn.

She thought about her childhood home on the island. About the furniture that *Isä* made. The curtains *Äiti* wove. Olle and his wife wouldn't want to keep them. They just didn't get it.

Not that I'm going to be responsible for the furniture or the fabrics, she thought then. I'm just going to get Henry buried.

Börje Ström was chatting happily with the funeral director, without any apparent effort.

"You'd have to be good with people to run a place like this," he said.

"You do," the funeral director agreed. "When I was in school, I could never understand how Mum could keep doing it. I hated helping out at weekends. But now I get it. It really does give you an opportunity to interact with your fellow man in a rewarding way. From time to time you have to be a bit of a psychotherapist as well."

They picked out the urns and talked about the practical details. She looked at Börje. He was the spring sun that thawed everyone out. They melted like snowmen until their carrot noses fell to the ground. She couldn't decide if that made her furious or not.

She found herself thinking about the funeral director's mother. She had dealt with the funerals of *Isä* and *Äiti*. A good person.

"No flowers," she said. "There'll be hardly anyone there anyway. Just me and our older brother and his wife."

"But you'll be there," Börje objected. "Of course you should have a few flowers."

So she chose the second cheapest wreath. Börje chose the same one for his father.

Once she'd done it, it felt right though.

It's what *Äiti* would have wanted, she thought. I'm doing this for her. Not for Olle. Not for me. And definitely not for Henry.

If Henry had been the only one involved, she'd have collected the ashes in a shoebox and just driven to the dump. Along with all the glass, the paper and the stuff that could be incinerated.

211

The funeral director made notes about coffee and sandwiches.

"No other relatives will be attending?" he asked. "Your daughter, will she be coming?"

The last was directed at Ragnhild.

"No," she said, her voice completely steady. "She didn't know Henry."

"She doesn't live in Kiruna anymore, does she?" he asked.

Not everyone knows, Ragnhild thought. You think everyone does, but people are mostly preoccupied with their own lives.

She shook her head and before he could go any further down that road, she said:

"So, are we done?"

Sven-Erik felt his mood sour as he turned into the car park where he was supposed to meet the client Anna Josefsson had put him in touch with. Thirty or so pale-grey units of barracks housing piled on top of one another. When did they put those up? It had been ages since he'd been into the town's industrial zone, so he had no idea. He felt a pressure on his chest. Were people really meant to live that way?

The client was a young man, not yet thirty. He was wearing a knitted cap and an expensive down jacket. He rapped on the windscreen.

"Would you be Sven-Erik?"

He got into the passenger seat, took off his cap and said his name was Simon.

His skin was very pale. This was not a bloke who spent any time in the forest as winter gave way to spring, Sven-Erik was thinking.

"You live here, do you?" Sven-Erik asked with a nod at the barracks.

"I do. Cosy, isn't it?" Simon said with obvious irony.

"Not really, it doesn't look that nice at all."

"You should see what it's like inside," Simon said. "You share a room with another guy, work twelve-hour days seven days at a time, then you're off for seven days. That's when people go home to their families. And two other guys will be living in your room. There are twelve of us sharing a kitchen. We're supposed to do the cleaning and keep it tidy, but it's like a fucking monkey house."

"I see, and where's home?"

"Tollarp. Only I don't do that anymore."

"Really? Do you want a Yoggi Yala?"

Sven-Erik reached across Simon to open the glove compartment. I'm back to my bad old eating habits, he was thinking. Gulping something down on the run.

"It's like a jungle picking out a flavour these days," Sven-Erik said. "You can have a . . . what the hell does it say? . . . cactus-lime one. Or do you want strawberry-lemongrass?"

"I'm good thanks," Simon said with a faint smile. "I'd rather have some baccy." Simon got out his tin and put a portion in his mouth.

"Good choice," Sven-Erik said. "I gave up twenty-eight years ago."

"Christ," Simon said. "I wasn't even born then."

"So why aren't you going home anymore? If you don't mind my asking."

"Just, you know . . ." Simon said, running a hand over his face. "While I was working up here, my partner took the liberty of seeing one of my mates. And they were more than mates if you get my drift. And all of a sudden there's no home for me to go back to. So I live here full-time now. Do three shifts instead."

"Can't you move?" Sven-Erik asked. "To somewhere of your own?"

"There are no flats to be had in Kiruna. Though I've heard it's supposed to be really nice in the town."

"What? You've never been into the centre? To Kiruna itself?"

"Never worked out, has it. The mine bus fetches us when we start and drives us back here when the shift is over. And it costs money to have a flat of your own besides. I've got to pay maintenance for our two kids, and then I've also got to be able to afford the trip to Tollarp every other weekend to see them. And live in a hotel when I'm there. That's how it is."

"What do you do in the mine?"

"Transport the waste rock."

Sven-Erik felt he had to get to the point. Simon would be in tears soon and then the conversation might go completely off the rails. He'd often had to deal with men in tears, which either led to them telling him everything or closing up for good because they had revealed a weakness they could not stand in themselves.

He had the photo of the dead women in his inner pocket, but decided to wait a bit before getting it out.

"You'll have seen on the news that we found the bodies of two sex workers," Sven-Erik said. "Anna Josefsson said you knew who they were."

"She promised I wouldn't get mixed up in anything if I spoke to you."

"I'm not a police officer anymore," Sven-Erik said, "I'm just interested in finding out who they were and who . . ."

He allowed a little shake of his head to finish his sentence.

"So I've been with Anna a few times," Simon said. "She's the one I get on best with but I have to hire a car to drive there. That makes it expensive. Some of the guys here club together to have these women come over. They turn up in a camper van they drive into the car park."

"How does that work? In purely practical terms I mean?"

"They've got two beds in the van. So there are two of them inside with a client each. And another in the driver's seat. For anyone who only wants a wank or a blowjob."

"So who's driving the van?"

"Some Russians I think. They talk payment and stuff in English. Two guys do the driving and deal with the money, preferably dollars or Euros. Cash is king."

"And the girls?"

"The last few months they've been three girls from Eastern Europe. Could be Russians as well, I don't know."

Three, Sven-Erik was thinking. But only two of them dead. Where did the third one go?

"Can you describe them?"

"Two blondes, they had silicon boobs. I prefer natural ones. I never had the third one so . . ."

"Do you know what any of them were called?"

"Yeah, well, Mary was the name of the one I had last. 'Virgin Mary, you know. Easy to remember.' Seriously though, they never tell us their real names. And you shouldn't believe anything they tell you about themselves. They'll spin these tales about how they're studying or that they've got kids at home they need to feed. But that's just to make the clients feel they're sort of helping them somehow. You'd rather think your money was going to families in need than being spent on drugs and shit, wouldn't you? Some of the guys here can be easily duped, let me tell you, only if you ask me they start lying the moment they open their mouths. The girls know I don't swallow any of their bullshit so they respect me. And then I'm a bit of a favourite customer I suppose, being young and not like . . . one of those old gits."

In his mind Sven-Erik kept shifting between sympathy and contempt. Aloud he said: "When were they here last?"

"A month ago maybe. They were supposed to turn up the first Thursday in April, only they never showed."

Sven-Erik checked the calendar on his phone. The first Thursday in April, that was the 7th.

"You said you call them to come over. Have you got the phone number?"

"Negative. It's more like all of a sudden the news does the rounds that they're coming and then you have to say if you want anything. Sex or drugs. The guys who drive the van sell a bit of that as well."

"Who tells you when they're going to come?"

"I'm not saying. That could land me in deep shit, you must get that."

"I do," Sven-Erik said and fished out the photo of the dead women from his pocket.

Simon glanced at it but immediately looked away.

"Fucking hell," he mumbled.

"Is that them?" Sven-Erik asked.

"Yeah. Maybe, I mean you can't look . . . the faces . . . put it away."

"I don't suppose any of you who bought their services wished them any harm," Sven-Erik said, putting the photo back in his pocket. "So if you can think of anything that could help the police find out who they were or where they came from. Or how to get hold of those Russians."

He held out a handwritten note with his name and phone number.

"And listen. Give me a ring sometime and I'll show you Kiruna. You should definitely see the town. Before it falls down the mineshaft."

The priest had cropped hair and tattoos on her forearms. And a ring through one eyebrow. It took quite a while for Ragnhild and Börje to realise she really was the priest and not someone going to confirmation class.

The priest laughed at that.

"I'm used to it," she said. "I look like I'm twelve and on the run from justice. Genes. My mother still looks like a twenty-year-old."

She asked them to follow her to the corner of the church where Sunday school was usually held. A little group of chairs in a ring. There was a children's Bible and a candle on the table. The priest lit the candle and invited them to sit down.

"It's cosier here," she said. "Why don't you start by telling me about your relatives, the ones we're going to bury."

Börje told his story. About his father who vanished when he was twelve and had now turned up in a freezer. The priest had seen it on the news of course.

"Were you close to him?" she asked.

"Depends what you mean," Börje said. "I didn't get to see him that often. I grew up with my mother. But he was the one who started teaching me how to box. And after he went missing I kept at it. I've had all my tattoos done the same way I remember his." He rolled up his sleeves to show her. An anchor on one arm and a compass rose on the other.

"It sounds like he was a big influence on you," the priest said, rolling up her own sleeves so her tattoos could be clearly seen. A cross on one arm and a Bible verse on the other.

"So not that dissimilar after all," she said with a smile. "The anchor is a symbol that derives from Christianity. The crossbar makes it a kind of camouflaged cross."

"And the compass rose was so you could find your way home," Börje said.

He smiled at Ragnhild to draw her inside the circle, the talk-to-the-priest circle.

"It's crazy when you think a priest can have tattoos nowadays. In Dad's day it was only criminals, prostitutes and sailors that went under the needle."

Ragnhild was feeling conflicted as she listened to Börje talking about his upbringing.

So easy, she was thinking. So bloody easy for men to turn up as the guest star. When it was obviously his mother who actually brought him up. Made sure there was food on the table and a roof over their heads.

She would lay odds that the priest was a feminist. So where was all that critical thinking then? She just sat there, smiling and comparing tattoos. Being seduced. By the stories men tell about men.

Then all of a sudden it was her turn.

"Could you tell me a bit about your brother?" the priest said.

But Ragnhild couldn't come up with a single word. There was a ton of rubble in the way.

Her eyes were caught by a felt board with some cardboard figures on it. A boat and a whale.

"Is that Jonah in the belly of the whale?" she asked. "Don't children think that's a silly story?"

She folded her hands and squeezed them together to stop them shaking. The rubble was filling her up, all the way to the crown of her head.

"That's right, it is Jonah," the priest said. "We follow the church year with the children as well. And it's the tall tales in my view that are the truest stories."

"I can't remember," Börje said. "How did he end up in the belly of the whale?"

"Jonah was a prophet," the priest said. "And just like all the prophets in the Bible he was unhappy and discontented and depressed. I've always thought that's so wonderful. The fact that all the prophets are not happy-clappy-people. Anyway, God told Jonah to travel to Nineveh and preach to the people there about the need to atone and mend their ways because God was going to destroy them."

"Time to face the music," Börje said good-naturedly.

"But instead of going to Nineveh Jonah jumped onto a boat to Tarshish. Then a storm blew up and everyone thought they were going to sink. Jonah told the crew to throw him overboard because it was his fault. So they did. The sea grew calm, and Jonah ended up inside the whale. When God rescued him, he went to Nineveh and preached. And the people of Nineveh mended their ways so God decided not to smite them. That made Jonah absolutely furious. He thought God was undermining his reputation as a prophet; after all he'd told them that they were going to perish. The whole story ends with Jonah sulking and God trying to explain things to him and staying with him even though he's being so bloody-minded."

The priest laughed.

"Sorry, that turned into a sermon all its own. But the story feels so true to me because I'm often running away from my own Nineveh, doing something else instead and sometimes I prefer death – spiritual death – to doing what I should be doing."

"Like what?" Börje asked curiously.

The priest shrugged.

"Asking someone to forgive me. Feeling what I am really feeling. Getting sober was like that for me. I took the boat to Tarshish hundreds of times."

"Shouldn't we be selecting the hymns?" Ragnhild said.

They choose which hymns they would have. They sang two of them. In the middle of the singing, Börje's phone buzzed and Ragnhild noticed out of the corner of her eye that he was holding it away from her as he read the text and tapped in a short reply.

Of course, she thought. A woman.

And Börje's phone rang as Ragnhild and he were outside the church saying goodbye to the priest. He apologised, said he just had to answer. He went round the corner of the building. She could hear the murmur of a conversation.

She looked at her own phone. A former colleague had texted her to offer condolences. She texted back to thank them for their concern. She kept it brief. It meant nothing. Almost nothing. People were just being polite.

She and Börje had decided to have dinner together. But she couldn't bear the thought. It had become perfectly obvious she was just a convenience for him, just as she was for Olle. She was the one who had called to set up the appointments with both the undertaker and the priest.

A social worker, she thought. That's what I am. Börje's usual social worker is ringing him now, to find out when he's coming home to Älvsbyn.

She started walking. As fast as she could without running.

It was as she was trotting along Lappgatan that the Kiruna police rang her. An officer called Anna-Maria Mella told her that Henry had been murdered. The funeral would have to be put off for the time being, she said, the forensic technicians would need to examine the body. And the police wanted to talk to Ragnhild again. So, if Ragnhild could drop by . . .

Börje Ström finished his call with Lottie in Älvsbyn. When he went back to find Ragnhild, she had gone. It felt like going down in a knockout when you still had all your energy left. The punch you hadn't seen coming. A blow to the nerve along the jawbone that makes the bone give way.

At the police station Ragnhild had to tell them all over again how she had skied across to Palosaari and found her dead brother and then Raimo Koskela in the freezer.

She told them all of it, the phone call from the shop owner, the dog that got her to make the crossing. And still hadn't turned up. Maybe it was dead. Eaten by carrion crows and foxes.

It was only as she was sitting there trying to remember the details of her movements on the island that she realised how much she had already begun to invest her hopes in Börje Ström. She had been dreaming of him, even while wide awake.

What were you expecting? she asked herself.

What was it Moa Martinsson wrote: "Trust a man and you deserve a hiding."

Inspector Anna-Maria Mella kept up the questions. Part of Ragnhild kept answering. The other part of her wanted to scream with embarrassment because she had actually been thinking about whether she should start a relationship with him. She had thought he was the kind of man who went round seducing women. But he wasn't even a seducer, really; he didn't need to bother seducing them. All he had to do was exist and hordes of women came tapping along in high heels bearing casseroles and leaving the top buttons of their blouses undone.

And she was one of them. She'd turned into one of them just like that. Changed her clothes hundreds of times to look nice. In her mind she'd already been lying against his shoulder; she had leaned into his arms and let them surround her. She had been thinking "yes". As though she had a choice.

She had no great opinion of men in general. She never *had* had. When she was a young child you had to watch out. Boys came looking for fights. And if you got a hiding at school, the adults just shrugged and said, "Boys will be boys." Later they would get what they wanted by other means. The men, that is. The boys. They had gone by many names in their time. They included layabouts, good-for-nothings and slackers. Gigolos and Don Juans. There was wickedness in some of them, an evil streak like the recurring stripe in a rag rug. Or they were nice. Most of the women in her family appeared to agree that if you found a nice one who didn't drink too much or use his fists, that was good enough; even better if he was hard-working and good with his hands. You fed a man like that and cleaned after him and slept with him every now and then. You even had feelings for him, a bit like you would for a plough horse or a faithful dog.

I should have found a faithful dog, she thought. Then, when I was young. As a father for Paula. Everything would have turned out differently. But I was a bloody idiot.

Inspector Mella asked her about the people Henry usually consorted with. No-one, as far as she knew. Did he have a grudge against anyone? Everyone, she supposed. But that was all so long ago now. Who would have the energy to care about someone like Henry? Killing him was so . . . over the top.

She had been thinking about men. Even Henry had been one of the masters.

"God preserve us from passion," she'd heard female relatives say. Physical desire always led to misery.

And just look what happened the moment the body started whining, wanting. Börje Ström, he was the kind of man who ripped you apart from the inside. Hadn't she had enough of all that? She'd gone and stepped straight into the jaws of the trap all the same. She was absolutely certain she'd done the right thing to leave him there at the church.

When the interview was over, she said:

"Have you told our brother, Olle? Does he know Henry was murdered?"

"Yes, he knows," Anna-Maria Mella said.

As she was walking home from the police station she was struck by the thought that Olle hadn't even got in touch with her about it.

Just a social worker, she said to herself once again.

"So there were three of them," Rebecka Martinsson said, downing a swig of yoghurt. "What's this one supposed to be . . . cactus-lime!"

"What will they think of next?" Sven-Erik Stålnacke said, and looked fondly at his own apple-vanilla. "Cheers to a demon prosecutor!"

He gulped down his drinking yoghurt and leaned back, getting comfortable in her guest chair. He had treated them to the yoghurt when Rebecka got back from her hearings. She was on a high. The court had ruled for her in every case. Tick-tick-tick!

"Two of them were run over and killed, you heard they found trace evidence on the underside of Henry's snowmobile, didn't you? If I can get some overtime arranged, would you consider coming onboard and working the case?"

Sven-Erik waved one hand dismissively.

"Someone's got to look into what happened to Börje Ström's father.

Seeing as you're hardly going to have time for Raimo Koskela as well now, are you?"

"Where are we at with that?" Rebecka said.

"Not sure, I was going to ask Pohjanen if he'd heard back about the bullet. And then I'm going to talk to Börje Ström's former coaches. They knew Raimo after all."

A rap on the door and Fred Olsson stuck his head inside.

"Hey there, Svempa," he exclaimed.

Then he waved some call lists at Rebecka as if they were winning lottery tickets.

"Your turn," he said.

"Is it Christmas Eve?" she replied in jest. "Is it my birthday?"

It was wonderful, Rebecka was feeling. Wonderful to be part of a team again. To have officers coming in and out of her office, handing over reports and asking for decisions. And then there were all those court cases she'd cleared today. The whole building now knew what an operator she was. The press conference had gone like a charm, too. And von Post had been sulking in his office the whole time with the door closed.

"There you are," Olsson said, pointing to the rows he had high-lighted in the call lists. "Friday April 8th Henry Pekkari rings his brother Olle. And as soon as they've hung up, not even a minute passes before Olle rings Frans Mäki."

"You've got to be kidding!" Sven-Erik exclaimed. "Is he still alive?"

"Who?" Rebecka asked.

"Oh, come on," Sven Erik said. "You must have heard of him. How old would he be now? A hundred?"

"Eighty-eight," Olsson replied. "Lives over towards Esrange. Married for the fifth time from what I've heard. To some Russian mail-order bride."

"Mail-order bride?" Rebecka said. "Do they still call them that?"

"He's always been a bit of a criminal by profession," Sven-Erik said. "He used to own a load of restaurants and clubs up and down the country. Properties too. He organised burglaries and ran drugs in the sixties and seventies. Only then other people took over the narcotics trade."

He kept twisting the lid to his yoghurt on and off. Rebecka realised that Sven-Erik was the kind of man who did his best thinking when his hands were busy with something else. Her own thoughts switched abruptly at that point to Krister, whose hands were endlessly busy. She had to run to catch up with those thoughts and rein them in.

"He was as crooked as any man with an eye on the main chance," Sven-Erik went on. "He was always coming up with new ideas for doing business. To give you just one example, he owned a garage at the beginning of the eighties and bought luxury cars that had been written off in accidents. Cars that had been totalled. He unscrewed the number plates and dumped the cars in water-filled mine holes around the province. Then his guys would steal identical luxury cars. They screwed on the old plates and then made out they were geniuses at repairing wrecks. It wasn't that long ago that the new owner was extending the garage. When they were digging the foundations they found over thirty number plates buried in the flowerbeds. By then the crimes were way past the statute of limitations."

"He was still active at the beginning of this century," Fred Olsson added. "He was involved in smuggling diesel from Finland at the time. And that was big business because people used it to heat their homes with. This was before the Hells Angels entered the picture and took over the whole operation."

"Just imagine if your average Swede could grasp that simple equation," Sven-Erik erupted. "If you buy smuggled cigarettes, or alcohol or diesel, or a bit of amphetamine on the cheap for your Saturday night out, you're paving the way for criminal elements to take over what is a lucrative trade. Criminal elements who will go on to shoot people in the street and sell drugs in school playgrounds. By then of course you can bet the same idiots will be calling on the police to act."

"Why did Olle Pekkari ring him?" Rebecka wondered aloud.

"For several years afterwards he was involved in that berry-picking business," Sven-Erik continued because he had started down memory lane. "He brought people over from Thailand and Bulgaria. Promised them you could make money hand over fist by picking berries. And then they were just left here. They didn't have a krona between them when the snows came. They still owed him money for the plane ticket and board and lodging. Even though they had worked all summer. In the end the local authority had to intervene and pay their return fares."

"Was he the one the papers called the Lingonberry King," Rebecka asked.

"I told you you'd heard of him," Sven-Erik said. "He'd been known as 'the King' for a very long time, but after that business the label 'Lingonberry King' stuck. He was already headed downhill. He had been for ages. So that didn't exactly make him happy. He wrote to the paper and threatened to sue the reporter who coined the nickname. Only they published his letter."

Sven-Erik looked up at the ceiling as he searched through his memory.

"A libellous name that is associated with the time of the month . . . It was something like that. Owing to the colour, obviously."

"How ghastly," Rebecka said with mock gravity. "To be associated with something so utterly shameful."

"You also wanted to know if Olle Pekkari called anyone after the two of you paid him a visit," Fred Olsson said to Rebecka. "And he did."

He leafed through the call lists and pointed to a yellow highlight.

"This one," he said. "He rang his son straight after you left. They spoke for seven minutes and thirty-two seconds."

"That doesn't necessarily mean anything," Sven-Erik said. "He'd just been told his brother had been murdered. He may have needed to talk about it."

"But it could mean something," Rebecka said. "Olle lied to us, don't forget. He said he hadn't spoken to Henry either and then the story changed when we told him we knew Henry had rung him that night. I want to have a talk with the Lingonberry King. You want to come along, Fredde?"

"I've got an appointment with the chiropractor. Shouldn't you take Mella? She's in charge of the investigation, after all."

Börje Ström went back to the hotel. It had just gone five. He rang Ragnhild Pekkari again, but she didn't answer.

He sat in one of the chairs in the lobby and read the local paper from cover to cover. Then he went into town and bought some shirts, underpants and socks.

It was close to six when his phone rang. It was Sven-Erik Stålnacke.

"So what do you say?" Sven-Erik said. "Fancy going to see your old coaches? To find out if your dad knew Henry Pekkari?"

Börje jogged back to the hotel, took the stairs up to his room and ripped the price tag off one of the shirts. When he got back down to the lobby Sven-Erik was waiting, talking on the phone.

Pohjanen, Sven-Erik mouthed, and they moved towards the swing doors of the hotel and out into the car park.

"Börje just arrived," Sven-Erik said on the phone. "I'll put you on speaker."

Börje and Pohjanen said hello to each other.

"So how's it going?" Pohjanen croaked, demanding to be informed.

"I'm going with Börje to talk to his old coaches," Sven-Erik said. "All good."

"Fine. Now listen," Pohjanen said. "I just heard back about the bullet you found in the wall. Fired from a nine-millimetre calibre handgun."

"Well, I'll be damned," Sven-Erik said.

"You said it. It's going to help limit our search, though . . ."

A wet coughing fit followed. Sven-Erik and Börje looked at one another and shook their heads. That really didn't sound good.

"Who had access to handguns in the sixties?" Pohjanen said once the coughing had stopped. "The officers of the Lapland Rangers and the Home Guard. I presume there would have been a local shooting club."

"Might be good to get the public to help a bit," Sven-Erik said.

"Exactly what I was thinking," Pohjanen managed to say as he tried to suppress another coughing fit. "I rang the *Norrländska Socialdemokraten* and the *Courier*; people are talking about it on social media as well, so let's hope it gets spread about."

They brought the call to an end.

"Did you hear that?" Sven-Erik said to Börje. "The bullet was from a handgun. The same ammunition the military use."

Börje was thinking about this as they got into the car and Sven-Erik steered out of the car park.

"What was my dad involved in?" he finally asked.

"You tell me," Sven-Erik said. "Speaking of which. The Lingonberry King, you must have known him? Or known of him?"

"I did, though in my day he was just called the King. He owned the premises of the boxing club. He used to hang around quite a bit. His son was only a year or two older than me."

JANUARY 1966

A furious blizzard is whining and howling outside. Nothing is moving. Drifting snow has been piling up on the roads, making them impassable. Only a handful of people have made their way to the boxing club. Inside, the atmosphere is almost sleepy. A car heater is humming away rather loudly, but they're all in long sleeves anyway. Someone is shadow-boxing in front of the mirror. Another two are sparring in the ring. The sound of punches landing on bags and balls can be heard. Börje is dancing back and forth as he hits his sandbag.

As the King comes into the boxing club with his son Spike, so much snow blows in that the door refuses to close. It fills the entire doorway, melting and then freezing to ice in a few seconds. One of the younger boxers hurries over and scrapes the lintel clean and shuts the door. It is impossible to look out through the basement windows; they are completely obscured by snow. The storm is pummelling the walls of the building.

The King stamps the snow off his shoes; water pools in front of the door, even though towels and cloths have been put down. The look in his eyes as he glances around would silence any form of greeting from the men training here today.

Börje has a quick peek but then goes back to working on the sandbag. He was at the Palladium a while ago. They were showing a nature film from Africa. The way the lions looked into the camera with eyes that seemed to be made of glass was completely impenetrable. All you knew for sure was that you were meat. That's what it felt like with the King as well. You are just meat to him. And he can move from zero to sixty in less than no time. You know that too.

The King had been a light middleweight in his time. But he stopped.

230

Boxing for points had nothing to offer him as he regularly tells the younger boxers at the club. Too many referees who are idiots. "I'm the sort of boxer who just went for the knockout," he will frequently say. "Like your professional boxers."

You keep your eyes on the floor when he goes on about that because you know he can see through you. He knows you're thinking that going for the knockout has never been forbidden in amateur matches, you're allowed to punch as hard as you like. As hard as you can. But you keep your eyes down. Because you don't want that meat-look on you, the one that knows you don't have enough *sisu* to say what you're thinking out loud. The King is happy for you to think he's a shit just as long as you don't utter a peep. The King owns the club premises. He's fair, the rent he charges is low. Recently one of the King's lorries delivered some new bags to the club. A present. It's useful to the King to have the North Pole Club on site because no-one dares steal the cars that are concealed under the tarpaulins outside. And some of the lads at the club collect debts for the King or go with him to meetings that might prove tricky. Only no-one ever mentions that. Not to Börje in any case. But he has been training at the club for three years now, so there are one or two things he has begun to realise.

In Spike's eyes you are meat too, though his face is usually anything but expressionless. It is narrow and full of contempt for little boys. Spike is three years older than Börje. He always punches too hard when he spars. And you have to be on the lookout for that extra punch when the coach blows the whistle for a break and you lower your guard.

This time, though, there is no look of any kind. Spike appears to be studying the floor and isn't brushing off the snow. It is melting on his clothes. The vertical quiff, the spike of the hardened greaser that gave him his nickname is drooping like autumn grass after rain.

The King moves towards Nyrkin-Jussi. He drags Spike along with him, holding the scruff of his neck in a fatherly grip. He gets straight to the point.

"Jussi, why isn't my lad going to Gamla Karleby at the weekend to compete with the others?"

He speaks loudly. So no-one will ever think he's one of those people who scrapes their feet and apologises for their existence.

Nyrkin-Jussi takes off his pads and asks the boxer he's coaching to do some skipping for a bit. He turns to the King and his son.

"Because only three lads are supposed to be going," he says calmly. "And Spike isn't one of them."

Some of the boxers have stopped training to listen. Börje is attacking his bag and minding his own business. Though eavesdropping is not something people can actually see.

"I know Spike isn't one of them," the King says just as loudly, even though the men are now face to face. "So are you just going to go on telling me what I already know? Are you going to disrespect me when I come here to ask you a question?"

Nyrkin-Jussi's leather face furrows into a contemplative expression.

"The Finns are not going to be easy pickings," he says, and everyone in the club can hear the self-control exerted in his voice, "they're bloody good. I don't think Spike is in the right shape for—"

"But I say he *is* in the right shape," the King cuts him off. "I haven't said anything about this before, I didn't want to cause a fuss, but it was a fucking shame you threw in the towel during his last match. Spike went down on points but he could have won. Isn't that right, Spike?"

"I would have won," Spike says and looks Nyrkin-Jussi straight in the eye. The meat-look is back. Börje is thinking the only thing capable of turning Spike into meat would be his own father.

Nyrkin-Jussi purses his lips and takes an audible breath through that broad, flat, boxer's nose of his and then lets it out.

The King throws his hand out in a gesture that says, "Or do you see things differently?"

"You only got to your feet on seven. And didn't get your guard up until after eight," Nyrkin-Jussi says with restraint. "Much too shaky in my view. My lads can lose, that isn't the problem. But they don't need to get thrashed."

"He's not going to get thrashed," the King says. "And he's not going to lose either."

He raises one finger and is about to poke Nyrkin-Jussi in the chest but something in Nyrkin-Jussi's eyes makes that finger stop. The finger points around the club instead.

"Nice here, isn't it?" the King says. "Brand-new stuff. Lucky I contribute a bit of money, don't you think? A lot of space and a low rent."

"OK," Nyrkin-Jussi says. "He can come along, but at your own risk."

The King suddenly turns all friendly, now he has got his way. He laughs heartily as though the whole thing was just a joke. He pats Nyrkin-Jussi on the shoulder.

He goes round saying hello to the lads. Exchanges a few words. Then he opens the door to the snowstorm and is gone, Spike after him like his tail. Absolute silence reigns when the door closes.

Nyrkin-Jussi's leather face is blank. Those huge fists which lent him his nickname, *nyrkki* means fist in Finnish, are hanging loosely at his sides. But his shoulders are rising and falling in time with his chest which is expanding and contracting, expanding and contracting. Then he turns on his heel and heads for the changing room. Börje has just completed a long sequence of body blows against the boxing bag. The bag is swinging back at him and Börje gets in some solid hooks. As he is passing, Nyrkin-Jussi puts his hand on Börje's shoulder and pulls him back. Börje has to shift his feet. The bag thuds against him.

"Where's your balance," Nyrkin-Jussi hisses. "Never lean back, lad. How many times have I told you that?"

He disappears into the changing room. Ten minutes later he is back, his gloves clenched under his arm, and asks Börje if he wants to give it a go.

Börje nods. If he was a bit pissed off before, it is already forgotten as he puts resin on the soles of his shoes. Nyrkin-Jussi has never sparred with him before.

"You've got a quick left, lad, but where's the right? If you'd followed up with the right you could have hooked me on the head. And then you punch with your left at the liver. Don't be afraid to give it some clout, the other guy can still push back. But if you land that punch, your opponent is not getting up again. The liver's the death blow. Your opponent will have nothing left for the rest of the match."

Börje slams in a punch with his left fist at Nyrkin-Jussi. It's not that hard but faster than Nyrkin-Jussi was expecting. Börje can see the surprise in his eyes.

"Thou shalt break them with a rod of iron," Nyrkin-Jussi intones. "Now back it up with your right. Thou shalt dash them in pieces like a potter's vessel."

Börje shifts his feet, always moving, ducking and weaving when his coach tries a jab. Then he punches as hard as he can when Nyrkin-Jussi forces him back.

"You can't stop," Nyrkin-Jussi yells. "Keep attacking and unsettling your opponent, use that left fist of yours when you're backing off as well. I hate seeing a guy backing towards the ropes, crouching with his arms around his head like a bloody *huivi*."

Sweat pours off Börje like the run-off from spring snow. Nyrkin-Jussi's hoarse voice is the voice of God on Sinai.

"Keep your guard up and your chin down. Relax your shoulders.

Don't hold your breath or your muscles will be starved of oxygen. You can't keep going without oxygen, no-one can. Breathe! Breathe! Don't twist your body so much, you'll lose your balance. Imagine someone has driven an iron spike through your skull and all the way down through your bollocks and into the ground. You've got to rotate around that spike."

When they have finished Börje is shaking like a newborn calf. He spits out the mouth guard, bent forward and panting, and puts his hands on his knees. Nyrkin-Jussi is also red in the face and out of breath.

"You're ready," he says and raps Börje lightly on the back as though he were giving him a stamp of approval. "We've got to take an extra car to Finland at the weekend now. Do you want to come along for a match?"

Börje just stares at him: Is he joking? In Sweden he's not allowed to fight until he's seventeen. He's not even fifteen. He knows the rules are not as strict in Finland. And they're not as fussy about recording all the details when it comes to boxing.

The key thing as far as the Finns are concerned is that their lads get to fight matches without having to spend a fortune travelling south. Still, as far as he knows no-one as young has ever been allowed to compete from the North Pole Club.

What's he going to tell Mum? He'll have to come up with some lie about going to the Torne valley with one of his mates.

He straightens up. His eyes wander to the mirror on the wall. Facing him is a big lad. Not particularly beefy, but tall and broad-shouldered. His fair hair has been neatly cut: his mother is a hairdresser, after all. Shorts and a tee dripping with sweat. Eyes on watch for blows that might come from the right or the left. A boxer. Someone like his dad. All he needs are some more tattoos. He looks at the three dots on his hand.

*

Börje crosses the border and gets his arse kicked. It feels like the Finns are able to punch unbelievably hard compared to the Swedes. Many years later it will be revealed that their Finnish brethren used old gloves and poked the filling round towards the inside. But no-one has a clue about that now. The only thing the Kiruna lads know is that when the Finns land a punch it feels like being hit with iron bars. They've got bruises everywhere.

Börje's problems are not in the gloves the Finns use, though, but in his head.

"You've got to finish him off," Nyrkin-Jussi scolds him after every round. "I know you can do it. You can't wait around for your opponent to recover once you've landed some punches and he's feeling a bit dazed. *Päälle vain.* You're just stepping aside, for Christ's sake, and letting him climb off the ropes. No, you've got to . . . attack him again. When Joshua conquered Jericho, first they wandered around the wall once a day for six days. Then they stepped it up. Seven circuits on the seventh day. What happened after that?"

Börje shrugs. Waiting for the gong.

"Then the walls came tumbling down and the warriors went straight in and sent the whole town to the Lord," Nyrkin-Jussi yells. "They finished them off."

Sisu-Sikke doesn't say much. He looks more concerned than anything else. Börje is thinking he's going to finish him off. That he can do it. He wants to finish him off. Only what goes on in your brain isn't always enough. Your body seems to be thinking something else. He loses on points in Karleby.

As winter turns to spring, he fights matches in Rovaniemi, Kemi, Kajani and Otanmäki. He can't remember the match in Kemi afterwards. He remembers Sisu-Sikke helping him tie his gloves. Then he can remember being outside the sports hall, looking for his skis in the snow. Sisu-Sikke came to bring him inside. The match was already over. "What are you saying, lad? You didn't bring any skis with you." Börje stopped rambling on about the skis and lay on the stretcher outside the showers while the others had a sauna. He heard Nyrkin-Jussi say that, though the lad is technically proficient, he hasn't got punch.

Börje has no punch and what's more he's a bleeder. The moment he gets punched on the eyebrow Börje starts bleeding – so much he can't see.

All those nights on the rear seat of the car. Through the snow and the forests going back across the border to Sweden. Hurting everywhere. But it doesn't matter when your body hurts. In some strange way it feels almost good when you've been beaten black and blue.

It's the pain in his mind that eats away at Börje. When you know you're better than your opponent. And you still don't win. When Nyrkin-Jussi gives up and stops preaching at you.

"When did you last see your old coaches?" Sven-Erik asked as they were approaching Indian Summer Court, the residential centre for elderly people. "Was it a long time ago?"

"I haven't seen them since I won the Olympic gold medal. And after the Catskills I didn't want to come back here, did I? Then I moved to Älvsbyn. Let's see . . ."

He failed to complete his sentence.

Let's just wait and see if they are willing to meet me, Börje Ström was thinking. You're young and dumb to start with. Then the years pass.

But Börje was worrying unnecessarily; it was like Christmas Day at the orphanage when Sven-Erik Stålnacke and Börje Ström made their entrance.

Sisu-Sikke and Nyrkin-Jussi embraced Börje and ruffled his hair.

"You come about our clogged pipes, have you?" Nyrkin-Jussi said.

It was Sisu-Sikke who lived at Indian Summer Court. He was in a wheelchair, one of his arms was slow to respond and that went for his speech too, but his eyes were as clear as a mountain lake.

Nyrkin-Jussi was still straight-backed. Tough as willow wood and those huge fists. He and Börje did some shadow-boxing.

"We've got special guests," the staff exclaimed and made fresh coffee. Then they took an endless round of photos of the residents together with Börje Ström, their right fists clenched and raised. Even the frailest resident, a 97-year-old raisin who had hair like cotton sedge after a rainy autumn day and was dressed in a fluffy red sweater, managed to get her fingers well enough aligned for a boxing pose. She stared resolutely into the phone camera.

Sven-Erik, who had been dreading the odour of disinfectant combined with the smell of decaying bodies, plastic flowers in the windows, and shipwrecked lives crying "Help me, help me" out of the fog they were in, was in a good mood.

When the worst of the commotion had died down, they were quick to wheel Sisu-Sikku into his room to have a conversation in private.

Börje Ström stopped in the doorway. The walls were plastered with his career. The headlines from when he won Olympic gold. The puns on his surname: "The Punches Kept Coming in a Steady Stream". Framed newspaper articles and head shots that had been taken for the fans. He recognised his old gloves hanging on a hook. No headlines about the Catskills. Which took a load off his mind.

He had wondered how they really felt when he decided to turn professional. When he left them behind. And here was the answer. He was still their lad.

"Tear . . . tear . . ." Sisu-sikku said and pointed at Nyrkin-Jussi who was hastily wiping his cheek.

"Eh, stop talking rubbish," Nyrkin-Jussi said. "They're not tears. Got something in my eye, that's all. Have a seat, lads."

Nyrkin-Jussi put another pot of coffee on. Sven-Erik could feel the acid forming in his stomach. It would have to be camomile tea tonight. They talked boxing for a bit and then moved on to more serious matters.

"That's right, your dad did a bit of work for the King," Nyrkin-Jussi said. "But he wasn't involved in anything criminal. He didn't do that kind of thing, I can vouch for that."

"Who knew they were at the cottage in Kurkkio?" Sven-Erik asked.

"We did, of course," Nyrkin-Jussi said. "It was Sikke's aunt's sister-in-law, Olga Palo, who lent it out. But Raimo told everyone near and far. You made him so happy, your dad. He was looking forward to the week you were going to spend together. Your mum wasn't always that keen on the idea of him seeing you."

"No, she wasn't, they separated before I was a year old," Börje said. "And they never even got married. So Mum was kind of a scandal in the family."

"Did he know Henry Pekkari?" Sven-Erik asked.

"Henry used to come in to Kiruna now and then to go drinking," Nyrkin-Jussi said. "He'd hang around the club with some of the lads. Though he didn't box."

"King . . . King . . ." Sisu-Sikke said. "Bas . . . tard."

"Yes, he was," Nyrkin-Jussi said. "The Lingonberry King was a right bastard even then. So there was riff-raff hanging round the club. From time to time they'd arrange matches of their own with lots of drinking and betting on the weekends. But we kept well away from all that. Minded our own. And like I said, your dad. He didn't bloody well hang around with the likes of Henry Pekkari."

He shrugged and shook his head.

"He was shot with a handgun," Sven-Erik said. "Military ammunition. Did you have any soldiers or Home Guard people in your team?"

Nyrkin-Jussi scratched his head.

"A pistol, eh," he said. "Only the officers had those. There weren't any officers prepared to sully their reputations with boxing. People didn't see the sport in the same way then. And the officers in the Home Guard were upper class, business owners and headmasters, that sort. We didn't have people like that coming to the club."

It wasn't just posh people who thought boxing was corrupt though. Börje Ström's thoughts turned to his mother. And her brother.

FEBRUARY 1966

Börje does his best to keep his boxing secret, but Mum finds out in the end. And then all hell breaks loose, and it's worse than he expected.

It was one of her customers at the salon who told her.

"As if that wasn't enough," Mum screamed. "Having to find out from a customer. People will be wondering what sort of mother has no idea what her own son gets up to."

Börje didn't even have time to take off his jacket before Mum was in the hall yelling at him. About him lying. Lying to her face. For several years! She had trusted him. He must really think she's dumb. He and his boxing mates must have been having a good laugh at her expense, at how easily she could be deceived. She's so bloody gullible and so kind.

She pursues him into his room and yells that must have suited him down to the ground. Having a mother who's that naïve. Because eating home-cooked food and sleeping in a bed that's been made for you is ever so convenient.

"Nice hotel this, isn't it?"

He's just like his father. Raimo treated her like a maid, too. And now Börje's doing the same.

When she stops yelling, she starts crying. Is he going to turn out like that? Without a proper job. Running around with that pack of thieves at the club. Getting his nose smashed and his brain as well. Going out drinking and getting tattooed.

Mum is demanding a response.

"So say something then!"

And when Börje remains silent, she says there'll be no more boxing. She's not going to allow it. Not as long as he lives under her roof.

He shakes his head at that point.

"You can't stop me," he says.

At first he thinks she's going to slap him. He'll let it land if she does. He just has to turn his head a bit and take it on the cheekbone rather than his ear. It won't hurt. He'll be fifteen soon and he's a head taller than she is. She's complained about all the new clothes she has to keep buying.

But the slap never comes. Mum leans back against the wall and puts her face in her hands.

"Why?" she sobs. "Raimo never paid a penny. He left us. And you do everything to be like him. You treat me like rubbish."

Börje observes her. Her tears leave him cold. She can cry and scream all she likes. He can't actually believe he's managed to keep his boxing secret this long. He does up the zip on his jacket and puts on his cap. He walks calmly out the front door and takes the stairs in three steps. He jogs over to the club. The snow creaks under his feet and the northern lights ripple majestically across the sky. The crazy old cow, you could hear her all the way out in the courtyard.

When he gets home from training, his school bag and a suitcase are in the hall. Uncle Hilding is in the living room, sitting in the centre of the sofa. Pencil-thin lips, arms crossed. Mum is sitting at one end.

Hilding is doing the talking. He says Börje's mother can't cope. Börje has grown up without a father's firm hand and the time has come for someone to take on that responsibility. So Börje will be coming to live with Uncle Hilding for a while. Until things have been settled. Hilding's voice is gentle and calm. He talks about love. About real love. Real love is tough. Tough just like the hand a child feels as it is pulled from the railway line the moment before being run down by the train.

Mum looks like she is regretting this. But it is too late now. Börje imagines she is expecting him to beg forgiveness for the lies. That he'll beg to be allowed to stay with her. But Börje still feels strangely indifferent to everything that is being said and done. He says almost nothing. He carries his bag down the stairs to Uncle Hilding's car. There are two things he knows. One: nothing is ever going to be settled if he has to stop boxing. Two: He's never going back to live with his mother. Ever.

His uncle lives with his wife and their seven children in a three-room apartment on Tallplan. Börje can hear the sound of children's voices as he and Hilding are coming up the stairs. But the voices fall silent the moment they come in the front door.

There is no radio in his uncle's home. No curtains. No flowers in the windows. Frugal, austere, sober. And very clean. You would never think children lived here. Börje is told to put his bag in the children's room. There are two bunk beds. The bedspreads have been tucked in tightly over the mattresses.

Hilding's wife Maria makes a bed for Börje on the floor. The baby, a girl, sleeps in the same bedroom as Hilding and Maria. The eldest two sleep in the living room.

After that the family have their tea in silence. The children peek at Börje. The baby is the only one to make a sound, babbling incomprehensibly away and showing everyone her sandwich which looks increasingly like soggy paper.

For his part, Börje is stealing glances at Maria. At the skin that is exposed when she reaches for the cheese and the sleeve of her blouse slides up. The bruise around her wrist. At the faint mustard-coloured marks on her throat. At the violet impression left by a pinch on her cheek.

He lies on the mattress that night and cannot sleep. He allows himself to think about Dad. He has been doing that more as he gets older. He has realised that your memories start to blur if you drag them up too often. They take on strange colours they didn't have to begin with and then start to fade away. Just like bruises. But tonight he has his arms around Dad, his cheek against his father's back. They are riding through the Torne valley. Ghostly birch trees, cows crossing the road on the way home to be milked. Evening sun and the wind in his hair. Dad's back. Dad's broad back.

Börje skips training for a week. His uncle has laid down rules. He has to go straight to work at the post office after school and then come straight home. No detours. On Sunday he will go with them to the prayer meeting, or he can stay indoors.

Börje does not want to obey the man, but what choice has he got? He needs to come up with a plan.

At night he dreams he is locked inside a black building with a grunting bear that keeps sniffing out his hiding places in cupboards and under beds. He wakes up. It is unbearably stuffy in the bedroom. The sounds of dreaming from the little boys. The hot, sour smell as they sleep. During the week he wrestled with them on the kitchen floor.

Chased them between the hall and the kitchen and their bedroom. And he heard Maria's laugh.

But a quarter of an hour before Hilding is due home the family straightens out all the rag rugs and rakes the fringes so they lie right. And become so silent and serious that Börje can barely breathe. He is desperate to get away. He just wants to run straight out of this place. Home to . . . not to Mum, home to the club. That's how he feels.

So in the end he makes his way there. After he has delivered the post.

Nyrkin-Jussi and Sisu-Sikke nod at him. Their faces are grave but encouraging. They know how things are.

Börje spars all evening until his body is tired and calm and the lump he had in his belly all week has gone. It is past eight when he chucks his gloves and mouth guard into his locker. Then he walks all the way back to Lombolo. He can feel winter's teeth on his skin.

It is past nine when he gets back to the flat. Uncle Hilding calls to him from the living room. He is standing with his hands behind his back, and he orders Börje to sit on a chair he has placed in the centre of the room. Maria and the children are lined up against the living-room wall, pale and silent. Börje sits down. He gets a sense that this is how the family usually end up. One of them against his uncle in the ring. The others are forced to look on.

Börje is used to his mother's rage. A hot saucepan boiling over and spitting. And then it's over.

His uncle's rage is the exact opposite. It is cold and still. It goes deep like permafrost. It can break stone and will brook no opposition.

And, oh, his voice is so soft. As soft as the down of fresh snow. But there is a thick crust of ice beneath that snow. A crust that starves the reindeer to death. The downy voice asks where he has been. Börje does not answer. Didn't they agree that he would come home immediately after delivering the post? Börje remains silent.

Uncle Hilding is circling around Börje. He says that Börje is corrupt. It is Satan, the Great Destroyer, who has trapped Börje's soul in his claws. Only Satan could make a person want to pound his fellow human beings to pieces? And for what? For a shiny trophy? For earthly glory?

His uncle wants to hear from Börje's own mouth that he will not be going back to the boxing club again. That he will turn a deaf ear when the old snake tempts him to eat of the fruit that will turn to poison in his veins. His uncle is not going to allow Börje to walk the broad path, the golden path, the carefree path that leads to eternal torment, to Hell. His uncle's love is too strong to allow that to happen.

"Say it," Uncle Hilding exhorts him. "Tell me you won't go back there."

Börje looks at Maria and the children. The little girl is sitting on Maria's hip with her thumb in her mouth. The boys are crouching; they have backed up against the wall as far as they can.

It might be Satan who has trapped Börje's soul in his claws. There's someone doing the thinking inside Börje's head in any case. Thinking that his uncle is surrounded by people who sob and crouch. At the prayer meetings. In the family. No-one dares answer back.

At work, though, it occurs to Börje, among the other miners, among the communists and the Finns and ordinary people, it must be very different.

Inside Börje's head the old snake is telling him Hilding's shoulders won't look as broad at work in the mine. And all of a sudden he feels no fear at all. He is imagining a silent Hilding feeling very ill at ease among the coarse-spoken miners who would never put up with any of his stuffy God talk.

"Now then," his uncle orders him again. "Say there'll be no more boxing."

"No," Börje says, and makes to get up because he is not going to stay here any longer. If he hurries there may still be someone at the club. He can sleep on the floor of the changing room.

But his uncle shoves him hard on the chest so he falls back, almost falling off the chair.

"You're not going anywhere until we've finished talking."

"Oh yes, I am," Börje says calmly. "You're not my father."

He gets up again. His uncle moves a hand towards him. He is taller but not that much taller. And this time Börje is prepared. He slips to one side, his uncle misses and loses his balance, so he has to take a step forward and strikes the chair with his leg. A little grunt passes those pencil-thin lips.

Maria lets out a terrified cry. And Börje takes a moment to glance at her and the children. The mustard-coloured marks on her skin. He catches the eye of the eldest boy, Antti.

Börje has occasionally seen boxers trying to catch the referee's eye. When the opponent is in a really bad way, hanging off the ropes, barely knowing where he is, although his legs don't have the sense to give way. The winning boxer will then try and catch the ref's eye to ask him to stop the fight, or do I really have to knock him out?

Börje is trying to find that appeal in Antti's eyes, for him to say: Stop the fight now. But the ten-year-old is not appealing to him; instead those eyes are darting barbs at him, wordlessly conveying: Finish him off!

Finish off the creeping, the crouching, the deferential silence, being on your knees and forced to swallow a wad of baccy that came out of someone else's mouth. Time for this to end. It's over. More than enough.

His uncle grabs at Börje's arm but isn't able to get a grip and catches on his shirt. Börje engages his stomach muscles, drops his chin, there are springs in his knees though his feet are glued to the floor. He refuses to be knocked off balance or shoved back onto that chair.

246

"Sit," his uncle gasps. "Sit down. You devil child. You bastard."

And his uncle's left hand comes flying. Open. Aimed at his cheek. Börje's right hand is free. It blocks the slap and then drops before turning into an uppercut aimed at his uncle's chin. Bang.

Uncle Hilding falls to his knees. Maria puts the little girl down and catches her husband to stop him falling over.

Börje asks the boys to help him gather his things together. That is quickly done. In less than a minute he is out of the door.

The day after Börje knocked down Uncle Hilding he leaves school and starts working full-time at the post office. He moves into a bedsit near the water tower, close to the club.

A week later he goes up against Jari Kuusela, a threshing machine from Kittilä. Kuusela is eighteen. But then the Finns are known for not being particular about the age of their fighters.

In the second round Kuusela rushes at Börje, lashing out in a series of blows to his head. Half the skin on Börje's back has been rubbed raw by the friction against the ropes and his eyebrow is bleeding. He has difficulty seeing. Blood is pouring into his eye.

Sisu-Sikke patches him up between the second and third rounds, ices his eyebrow and applies his home-made salve. The wound refuses to stop bleeding. Bloody fucking eyebrow always getting torn open. If you can't see the punch coming, you're done for.

Sisu-Sikke mumbles something Börje can't quite make out. In some strange way, though, he understands that Sikke is talking to his eyebrow, no, to the blood itself. Börje can sense the eyebrow sort of responding to being addressed. It feels like when the tide is going out. Or someone pauses for breath. And then the bleeding stops. The mouth guard is shoved back in and he is back on his feet.

Kuusela pummels away at Börje, chasing him round the ring and soon he has him on the ropes again. He punches at his head, aiming for the eyebrows.

Börje goes into a crouch. He is beginning to feel groggy from all the blows to his head. Black mist is drifting in from the sides. And then he hears the Finn calling him a devil child and a bastard. It is his uncle's voice, although he doesn't understand that until afterwards. It doesn't seem odd either at the time for Kuusela to be speaking Swedish.

The rest of the match is over quickly and it all happens entirely by reflex. There is a gap in Kuusela's guard. While the Finn is pounding away with left jabs, his right follows along. His jaw is left unprotected.

Börje's counterpunch happens in a flash. His left hook swings up from below. The way a cat strikes with its paw. So fast that afterwards some people will say they never saw it coming.

And then Kuusela is lying on the mat with the ref counting him out. Nyrkin-Jussi grabs Börje's head between his hands and yells:

"That's how it's supposed to work, lad. God's hand. God's mighty hand. You've got punch!"

Sisu-Sikke stays sitting in his corner, pale and smiling. He doesn't seem to have the strength in his legs to get up and hug his young boxer.

Sven-Erik Stålnacke was watching Sisu-Sikke, who was drooping precariously in his wheelchair.

"Time to wrap things up maybe," he said. "Airi will be expecting me for dinner."

"Come back," Nyrkin-Jussi said, "not a lot happens here at the Last Stop Hotel."

"St . . . sto . . ." Sisu-Sikke said.

"Last Stop Hotel," Nyrkin-Jussi clarified, putting a hand on Sisu-Sikke's shoulder.

"You ought to get a boxing club started in the common room," Börje Ström suggested. "Do you ever go to the club?"

"Now and again," Nyrkin-Jussi said. "Though the young folk barely know who we are."

"Sto . . . stop." Sisu-Sikke sounded distressed.

"I think we may have overdone it a bit," Nyrkin-Jussi said, looking at Sisu-Sikke with concern. "Thanks a lot for coming, though."

When Börje Ström and Sven-Erik Stålnacke shut the door behind them, they all but tripped over a small man in a wheelchair. His shirt was haphazardly buttoned up and there was a sizeable stain on its front. He was holding a couple of single dentures in his fist that he quickly inserted the moment he saw them. There was a bit of a clatter when he spoke.

"Hello there," he said. "Would you be Börje Ström?"

Börje admitted that was the case.

"I read about your father in the paper," the clatterer said, wiping brown bits of baccy out of the corners of his mouth with the cuff of one sleeve. Judging by the cuff this was a habit.

"I know why he was bumped off! I can tell you for two grand."

"What utter rubbish," Sven-Erik said. "Anyone who really knew something wouldn't ask for money. Come on, Börje, let's go."

"Thank you anyway," Börje Ström said with a big smile, holding out his hand.

He shook hands with the man in the wheelchair, who then introduced himself.

"Lars Grahn," he said. "Didn't mean any harm. Though it's true I knew your dad. And I know why they bumped him off."

He glared at Sven-Erik.

"I can't pay," Börje said, scratching his head. "I'm a bit punchy by now, you know, after all the hits I've taken. And if I was to pay people for tips about my dad, they'd be inventing one tall tale after another. What Svempa says is right."

"Eh, bugger the money, then," Lars Grahn said. "Come along."

He wheeled in front of them to his room. Börje and Sven-Erik glanced at each other.

"What the hell," Sven-Erik said with a little shrug. "It can't do any harm, I suppose."

The blinds were drawn in the little room and Lars Grahn heaved himself out of his wheelchair to crash into an armchair that was positioned facing a wall-mounted television.

"*Istu*, lads," he said, with a gesture at the unmade bed.

Sven-Erik and Börje sat on the edge.

"We can't stay long," Sven-Erik warned, checking his watch.

Airi would be expecting him for dinner. He suspected Lars Grahn knew nothing about Raimo Koskela. And that the temptation to have a moment alone with the legend that was Börje Ström was the only reason they were sitting here.

"Did you know my father?" Börje asked.

"It wasn't like we were mates, but he drove lorries for the King. We used to hang around the club, both of us. I had a hell of a left hook in those days. Middleweight. Åke Forslind used to drive for the King as well. Have you heard of him?"

Neither Börje nor Sven-Erik knew the name Forslind.

"Forslind, a bloody clown if you ask me, was involved in a fraud case in 1960," Grahn said. "The American government sold printing presses to . . . where the hell was it?"

Grahn fumbled in his pocket for his box of chewing tobacco, opened it and then seemed to realise he had to choose between the dentures and a wad of baccy, so he closed it and came up with the memory.

"Bahrain," he said. "That was it. The Yanks were supposed to be updating their technology for printing bank notes. With new machines. And the old bank of machines was destined for Bahrain. A lot of transport companies were employed for the delivery, including a Swedish company that Forslind drove for. And in the course of the various transports there was some kind of plate that should of course have been destroyed but got left in one of the vehicles. And Forslind thought it might be worth something, so he took it home. In any case he knew some high-up in Stockholm. A lawyer, I think. One of those guys who collects luxury cars and had a small printing shop. Yup."

"So they started printing bank notes?" Börje Ström cut in.

"That's right, the posh guy in Stockholm could produce the back of the note; the plate they had, the genuine one, could only print the front. They printed several hundred kilos of hundred-dollar bills. They sold them to some interested speculators in what was then the Soviet Union. But the idiot lawyer made two mistakes. First, they printed the stuff on bloody awful paper."

Grahn paused and grabbed hold of his front teeth, pressing them back and forth. Presumably his denture was protesting.

"What was the second mistake?" Sven-Erik asked. At least he would have a story to tell Airi this evening.

"Secondly, he sent Forslind over the border carrying two suitcases of fake hundred-dollar bills. Forslind kept drinking on the ferry to Finland, to calm his nerves. So he was sloshed when they reached the border. Finnish customs grabbed him on the spot, but the fact that the bills were printed on such bad paper was a blessing in disguise; it meant it wasn't treated as a serious crime. Forslind was only inside for just over a year. The lawyer would have got some kind of penalty as well, I suppose, I'm not sure about that, but posh gits like that usually end up OK."

"Like I told you, I'm a bit punchy," Börje said. "So what's this got to do with my dad?"

"Your dad was mixed up in it," Grahn said. "He and Forslind got paid for that fake currency and then he didn't pay it back. That would have screwed up the whole deal. The Russians were flaming mad. In the end it was the Soviet mafia came over and knocked him off."

Sven-Erik took a peek at Börje Ström. He looked like he had witnessed a train collision.

"Did you tell the police this?" Sven-Erik asked. "I mean, someone must have asked after him at the club when he vanished."

"Yup," Grahn said. "Police Constable Adrian Fjäder."

Adrian Feather, Sven-Erik was thinking. What sort of a name was that? Something Grahn had seen in a Donald Duck comic?

"Thanks, but we've got to be going," Sven-Erik said, getting to his feet. He dragged Börje out into the corridor with him.

"You'd never have thought that, would you?" Lars Grahn called after them. "You'd never have believed that about your dad?"

"He's talking nonsense," Sven-Erik said once both men were standing out in the street.

"Umm," Börje replied, moving away from the drips coming off the roof. "All I wanted was to be like Dad, you know? I even had myself marked like he was. But the truth is, I never knew him."

"Balls," said Sven-Erik. "Horse bollocks. Elephant testicles."

Börje Ström shook his head. The sense of devastation was overwhelming. A forest that had been felled. Around a pitiful wreck of a cottage that had become worthless.

JUNE 1966

Mum rings Börje. They speak from time to time, which is nice.

"You coming with me to the village?" she asks.

Since he left home he has gone with her to the cottage every now and then. There's always something needs fixing and when they are in the cottage with the old woods around them they get along despite everything that has happened. Like Mum says: "You just can't be miserable, not completely, when the wind is in the tops of those pine trees."

Börje borrows one of the post vans. He hasn't got his licence yet but no-one makes a big deal of it. They don't talk that much during the trip. Börje is going to fight at his first junior national championship once the summer is over. Only Mum doesn't like talking about boxing, does she?

They park the car and then start on the hike towards the cottage. Börje loves this trail. Even when he was little something used to change in Mum and him when they put on those heavy backpacks and started making their way towards the eastern side of the mountain. You forgot what day of the week it was almost immediately. Time took off its weekday suit and any and every day became huge, filled with weather and wind, forest and animal life.

They pass all the resting stones of his childhood: the juice rock, the lizard, the king's throne, the magic rock. Mum was never in a hurry when she came here; she let him take his backpack off and climb up the big stones he'd made his. She used to light a fag and turn her face towards the sun until he had finished visiting his special places and they could go on.

They can hear the sound of the water tumbling down the gully. Mum says something about how good a cup of coffee is going to taste.

But when they get there all they can do is stare in horror.

The entire stand of trees the cottage was nestled in has been chopped down. It looks like a theatre of war. What was virgin forest has become a field of death.

The great willows, covered in the kind of gorgeous lungwort that changes colour and turns a lovely green when it rains, are lying there dead. The aspens, whose leaves used to make a sound that called a rippling stream to mind when the wind rustled them, have been felled. The leaves on the fallen birches are still small like they are in early summer and shiny green. But they will never blaze with the colours of autumn again. The tall firs, the pines that are hundreds of years old with tops like clouds and a home for nesting birds of prey, lie lifeless on the ground. The cottage looks like it has been stripped to the bone.

Börje cannot get a word out. These woods. They were their home. All those times he skied down the mountain slope at high speed and always managed to find a gap between the trees. All the animals. Their blueberry patches. The softness of the moss. It has all been destroyed for ever.

Mum is crying. She gets out a cigarette, shoves it in her mouth but drops the matchbox on the ground.

There is a strong smell of freshly sawn wood. Apart from the smell of the boxing club, the scent of fresh wood is one Börje loves best but now it is stabbing at him like a knife and he has to bend over and vomit onto the path.

This is Uncle Hilding. They both know it without having to exchange a word. This is his revenge for Börje knocking him to the floor. The brothers own the stand of trees. All Mum owns is the cottage. So on paper it is their wood and they can do with it what they want.

I'm going to kill him, Börje is thinking in the van as they drive home. Though he knows he will never do that.

*

Sven-Erik Stålnacke touched Börje Ström on the shoulder to drag him back to the present.

"Listen to me. If it was the Soviet mafia that shot your father, why didn't they do it there and then? At the cottage in Kurkkio?"

"Maybe they . . . wanted to check if he had any money to give them," Börje suggested.

"And so they drove out to Palosaari? Why would they have anything to do with the island? No, this smells fishy to me. Speaking of fish, do you fancy coming back with me to eat? Not that we're going to be eating fish."

"Thanks, my friend. Some other time maybe. Right now I've got to . . ."

Börje paused. He had been about to say he had to be alone, but it wasn't true.

"What do you know about Ragnhild Pekkari?" he asked.

Ah, so that's how it is, Sven-Erik thought and felt almost idiotically pleased.

"Well, you'd have to say she's a real battle-axe. A white-water rafter in the eighties, the only woman to make it down the Kengis rapids. She worked as a nurse in A & E. Unlucky with men, according to what I've heard. The father of her daughter drank too much. Though he got back on the straight and narrow once they went their separate ways."

They said goodbye, and that they'd be in touch soon. Börje Ström stood there a while, listening to the dripping from the eaves.

There was a time when he longed to fight matches again. There was no room in the ring for anything complicated or muddled. It was about life and death. Just his body and that of his opponent, burning with exhaustion. Everything else was blocked out.

And there had been the bottle every now and then. After the Catskills and for a while after he moved to Älvsbyn. But that was long ago.

And of course there had been women. They had strutted around half-naked with signs in the breaks between the rounds. They had sat in the first row, made up to the nines. They had shared his bed. And depending on the state of his finances he had bought them jewellery, dresses, furs.

It was Ragnhild's arms and her rough hands he was longing for now though, the same way he had longed to sit behind Dad on his motorbike.

Even if he couldn't understand it, the longing he felt for her and for her smell of wood smoke, her rain-coloured eyes, was just as intense.

She had left him there at the church.

But it isn't over until the ref has counted to ten, he thought.

He started walking.

Inside Indian Summer Court Sisu-Sikke had broken down in tears. He was weeping, uttering:

"Sto . . . sto . . . stop!"

"What's the matter?" Nyrkin-Jussi said anxiously and tried to hold his hand. "What is it, my love?"

But Sisu-Sikke swiped at him.

The coffee cup smashed on the floor. He refused to let anyone calm him. The staff had no idea what to do. In the end they decided it would be dangerous to leave him in this state and a nurse was called to give him an injection. Nyrkin-Jussi and one of the staff had to hold him down.

"What happened?" Nyrkin-Jussi said afterwards when he lay down beside the sleeping Sisu-Sikke.

Though he didn't know if he meant what had just happened, or what happened then, in 1962, when Börje Ström's father disappeared.

Rebecka had to wait for ten minutes in the car before Anna-Maria Mella came traipsing out of the police building. Her eyes on the ground, like a child who had been forced to go to school. She parked herself in the passenger seat with a curt hello.

"Mind if I drive?" Rebecka asked.

"It's your car," Anna-Maria said with a shrug.

Not a word was exchanged after that. Rebecka spent the trip gnashing her teeth. "Mind if I drive?" What a way to behave, like an underdog. The mood in the car could hardly get any worse.

They drove out towards Esrange. The Lingonberry King's house was a prefabricated eighties model: a one-storey detached house, painted pale blue. It had been merged with two buildings on either side, making the courtyard look like a square-shaped horseshoe. They drove inside and parked.

The "wings" appeared to be for storage. One had a large new garage door at one end and at the end of the other was an empty dog run.

They got out of the car.

All the windows in the storage buildings were covered in sheets of particle board that had been screwed in place. In the forecourt were three unremarkable cars and a four-wheeler with a snowplough mounted on the front. Apart from that the area was full of junk. A rusting car body without wheels, a mountain of rubbish, soggy cardboard boxes, a discarded hoover, plastic bottles and all the other stuff a more orderly person would have driven to the recycling centre. A huge red patch on the snow.

Anna-Maria tapped Rebecka on the arm and nodded upwards. There was a surveillance camera on every corner.

"They're watching us," she said.

Rebecka rang the doorbell. Nothing happened. She rang it again. The only sounds to be heard were a dripping from the eaves and a bird trilling some way off.

"What do you think?" Rebecka said.

Anna-Maria walked over to the red patch in the courtyard. It was covered in coarse animal hair.

"Elk," Anna-Maria said. "Though it bloody well isn't hunting season."

Rebecka moved over to the windows of the main house and tried to peer in through the lowered blinds. She was beginning to feel uneasy. A powerful sense that they were not alone.

She knocked hard on the door.

"This really isn't on," Anna-Maria said. "I'll go round the back and check."

She rounded one corner of the building. Getting all the way round and back to the main house felt like it would be an almost impossible feat.

Her jeans were soaked through and her shoes full of snow. She really wasn't dressed for an adventure like this. And she was going to miss dinner with her family.

I'm going to get stuck and I won't be able to get out, she was thinking.

But she had kept the promise she made the previous New Year and had been training at the police gym three times a week. So she struggled on. Finally she reached a window and looked inside.

She could see straight into a living room. A woman was lying on a brown sofa with a laptop on her belly. Anna-Maria pounded on the window.

"Hello! Open up. This is the police."

The woman raised her eyes. Anna-Maria got out her police badge and pointed through the house to the front door. Once the woman had got to her feet, she started trudging back.

"She's coming," Anna-Maria gasped to Rebecka. "She was lying on the sofa in the living room."

The door opened, and the woman poked her head out.

Rebecka had been expecting someone with dirty hair in a bun and jogging pants. But this one looked like a million tasteless dollars.

She was young and slim with long legs. Black stockings, high heels and a leopard-print silk blouse that was unbuttoned far enough so the black-lace edging of her bra could be seen. Her hair was long and streaked blond and bright red. Huge stiff lips that had been fixed. False eyelashes like greasy fly legs and absurdly long glittery-blue nails like claws.

"Yes?" she asked.

"Police," Anna-Maria said and cleared her throat to crank up her school English. "We want to speak to Frans Mäki. Can we come in?"

The woman drew her hand to her chest in a purely mechanical gesture of deference.

"I can't . . . I don't . . . Wait a minute," she said and shut the door.

After a short while the door was opened again, this time by another woman. She was in her thirties. Her hair was done up in a severe topknot. No make-up, no jewellery. She looked briefly but intently at Anna-Maria and Rebecka. Anna-Maria felt like she was being scanned and evaluated by an android.

"What can I do for you?" she asked in impeccable though accented English.

Anna-Maria repeated that they wanted to speak to Frans Mäki.

"What do you want with him?"

"We'll tell him that ourselves," Anna-Maria said, and tried to look inside. "Is he at home?"

"My husband is ill. He is not receiving visitors. Wait."

She disappeared but was back in a minute, waving a piece of paper. It was in Russian but the heading was in English: Medical Certificate.

"You can speak to me," she said.

Rebecka and Anna-Maria exchanged looks.

"OK," Rebecka said. "On the night of April 8th, Olle Pekkari rang here. We'd like to know what that conversation was about?"

The woman got out a cigarette packet. She shook one out and lit it. She took a drag and shrugged.

Just then Anna-Maria turned round.

Two large men were standing beside Rebecka's car. Two rough-looking men. She read their faces. The kind who had put on real muscle, necks like tractor tyres. They hadn't been working out the last few years though and had put on a good deal of weight. The sheer physical strength was still there all the same; that was obvious. They both had close-cropped hair. The scalp of one of them shone a chapped pink.

Easy to get burned in the early spring sunshine, Anna-Maria was thinking. Even on your scalp.

It was as if they had appeared out of nowhere. One of the tyre-necks had a pitbull-like dog on a leash. There was almost nothing left of its ears, just frayed remnants. It had very visible scars on its body.

The other man had opened Rebecka's car and was getting into the driver's seat.

"You there," Anna-Maria said. "Stop that now. Get out of the car!"

She started to walk towards them, the man got out of the car and took a step towards Anna-Maria. He said something in Russian to the woman. She answered in Russian. Rebecka and Anna-Maria could make out the word "politsiya", police. The dog produced a menacing growl.

"Get that dog away!" Rebecka said.

The dog made a lunge. The man shortened the leash. It clawed at the air, drew its lips back and bared its teeth, barking hoarsely when the chain was taut round its neck.

Anna-Maria felt scared. The dog must weigh at least as much as she did. She backed off a step or two, knocking her leg against the car.

There was something about the way the men were looking first at each other and then at the woman. As if waiting for a signal. They both moved calmly but in less than a second Rebecka had one of them in front of her and the other behind.

Professionals, Anna-Maria thought.

The ice-cold kind that cut off people's fingers with garden shears as a warning. Who pulled bags over people's heads before they shot them, to stop getting the spray on their clothes. Who made sure the victim was standing on cheap carpet that could easily be rolled up.

The one with the dog wore only a shirt. The other was wearing a black down jacket buttoned with one stud in the middle. It had to be at least fifteen degrees in the courtyard. Why would you put on a down jacket before going outside?

To conceal a weapon, Anna-Maria was thinking. But we're the police. She told them that. What are they going to do? They wouldn't dare do anything, would they?

She had her own service weapon on her. But her hands felt frozen and she had pins and needles in the tips of her fingers. She would drop it on the ground.

The woman went inside and shut the door behind her. Rebecka and Anna-Maria were left with the tyre-necks.

The men exchanged some words in Russian. Anna-Maria could feel fear twitch in her stomach.

But then the men backed away a bit. One of them nodded at the car. A sign that meant it was time for Anna-Maria and Rebecka to leave. The dog kept barking incessantly, rearing up on its back legs. It wasn't easy for the man to hold him back, he must weigh a good 120 kilos.

"Let's go," Rebecka said curtly.

They got in the car and Rebecka reversed out of the courtyard. The men stayed where they were, watching them turn and drive away.

"What the fuck was that?" Anna-Maria asked once they had been driving for a bit.

Rebecka shook her head and squeezed the steering wheel so tightly her hands hurt. She noticed she was having difficulty keeping her foot steady on the accelerator. Their speed was erratic.

"I mean it!" Anna-Maria exclaimed. "Who were they? How come the police don't know about them? I've never heard of any Russian mafia gang living round here. Are they up to something in Kiruna?"

"And that poor dog," Rebecka said.

"Are you out of . . ." Anna-Maria began, but then bit off the rest of her sentence.

A dog like that should be shot on the spot, Anna-Maria was thinking. No two ways about it.

They sat in silence for a kilometre or two, both overwhelmed by the sense of having stumbled onto something huge. More or less by mistake. Like turning over the potato patch and suddenly the spade makes a clanging sound. And you wonder what the hell your spade has hit. Who were those people?

"We're definitely on to something, though," Rebecka said. "Henry Pekkari rang his brother on the night of the murder. And Olle Pekkari rang the Lingonberry King a minute later. And those Russians are living in the home of the Lingonberry King. That's no coincidence."

She slowed down for some reindeer moving at a leisurely pace across the road.

"We just drove past a house," she said. "Let's go back. We ought to talk to the neighbours."

"Shouldn't we call for backup?"

"Backup?" Rebecka asked. "To talk to the neighbours?"

Anna-Maria said nothing. She was filled with rage at being made to feel embarrassed.

Bloody Rebecka, she thought as Rebecka turned the car around and drove back. What's going to happen if the tyre-necks see us? Rebecka doesn't have children. It's easy for her to be smug.

The neighbours were in. It was ten to seven in the evening. The man who opened the door had a large white beard and heavy-knit long socks pulled up over his jeans.

Anna-Maria introduced herself and showed him her police badge. The wife, who was sitting on the kitchen sofa with her knitting, called out:

"Who is it?"

"The police," the man replied over his shoulder, inviting Rebecka and Anna-Maria in.

The woman came into the hall with her knitting.

"Oh my God!" she exclaimed, her free hand covering her mouth.

"No, don't worry we're not here to inform you of a death," Anna-Maria said. "Sorry if we alarmed you. We just want to ask you a few questions, if that's OK?"

"What about?"

"About your neighbours," Rebecka Martinsson said.

Right away there was something defensive in the look on their faces.

The woman clamped her lips together while the man stroked his beard and shook his head regretfully.

"We don't know anything about them," he said.

"We don't know anything," she repeated, and her fingers tightened round her knitting.

"You must know something," Rebecka said. "You must know what they're called, at least. There's only you and them on this stretch of road after all."

"We can't help you."

"OK," Anna-Maria said and held out her card. "We're interested in finding out who they are and, well, anything else really. If anything occurs to you, ring me. OK?"

The man accepted her card.

"Chief Inspector Anna-Maria Mella," he read aloud. "Is that you?"

"Yup, though my name was Nygård before I got married."

He laughed out loud.

"Good Lord, I didn't recognise you at first. So you cut off your plait? I don't suppose you remember, but you took care of our son one time when he ran away from home. You won't remember, I'm sure."

"No," Anna-Maria admitted.

"It was more than fifteen years ago," the man said. "God, he kept running away – all the time. Ants in his pants, that was the diagnosis in those days. And one of those times a woman handed him in to you; she didn't think six-year-olds wandering around on their own could be just left to their fate. In all the excitement he'd wet his pants as well."

The man smiled softly, a smile mixed with sadness at the memory.

"When I came rushing in to the police station with my heart in my mouth he was sitting on your lap drinking hot chocolate. He'd been given a key ring with a police motorbike on. And you'd become best friends. You used to say hi to each other in the town centre afterwards."

"Yeaah," Anna-Maria said, ransacking her memory; the truth was she could barely remember when her own kids were small.

"You didn't say a word about his wet bum. Your trousers were soaking. Not a peep out of you. And my little lad was spared any embarrassment."

"He was made to feel really embarrassed about that in any event," the wife said. "He went on wetting himself long after his mates found out."

"Only you pretended nothing was the matter," the man said to Anna-Maria. "I'll never forget your pee-soaked lap. I hope you had a change of clothes."

"I'm sure I did," Anna-Maria said. "What's he doing nowadays, your son?"

"He works with special-needs students at the Rocket School."

There was silence for a bit.

"Do you promise it won't get out if we tell you about the neighbours?"

"I protect my sources," Anna-Maria said.

And we can deal with any discussion of the legal duty to give evidence at a later date, she was thinking.

"Come in and sit down," the wife said. "Don't bother taking off your shoes, the snow on the ground out here is clean."

"Right, the same can't be said for in town," Anna-Maria remarked. "You're a bit more firmly in the grip of winter out here."

Despite the couple's protests they took their shoes off anyway.

"Coffee?" the woman asked. "We were just going to have coffee after dinner, so it's freshly made."

They sat in the kitchen. The woman offered them some little cakes and strong coffee from the percolator.

"Tell them about Bengt," the woman said to her husband.

"Bengt, your son?" Anna-Maria asked.

"Oh no," the man said. "Bengt was our dog."

"A Borzoi," the woman said. "The kindest dog in the world."

"They killed him anyway, didn't they," her husband said.

"Your neighbours?"

"No, their dogs."

The man put his hand in front of his mouth while the woman continued:

"I was about to drive into town. Bengt had jumped into the car boot; I went back into the house because I'd left my reading glasses on the table. I didn't shut the tailgate because he never jumped out of the car without permission. Anyway. They appeared out of nowhere. Two killer dogs. All I heard was this terrible screaming. I looked out of the window and watched those dogs leap up into the trunk and drag Bengt out. I rushed outside, screaming as loud as I could. Then they ran away. And Bengt . . ."

She stirred her coffee to pull herself together before continuing:

"He limped over to me. His belly had been torn open, his guts were hanging out. He lay down at my feet and then he died in my arms. At least it was quick. You came down from upstairs."

"That's right," her husband said. "This is still so . . . My mind went blank and I got my hunting rifle and went over there."

"I tried to stop him," the wife said.

"I wasn't thinking clearly," he said. "I went over there and one of the men who lives there was in the courtyard. He had put the dogs in the run. I had only taken a step into the yard when he took out a gun and pointed it at me. I was holding the rifle but the safety was still on. Then he called towards the house in Russian and a woman came out. She asked me in English what I wanted."

"Christ Almighty," Anna-Maria said with feeling.

"Yeah, you could say that. I started crying, I was bloody terrified as well. I said their dogs had killed ours and I was going to ring the police. She told me to wait and then went inside. She came out with a bundle of banknotes. Thirty thousand. Just like that."

"What did you do?" Anna-Maria said.

"I took the money; I didn't dare do anything else, because the man with the gun was aiming it at me, urging me to take the money. And she kept saying: 'No police. Remember. No police.'"

"When was this?" Anna-Maria asked.

"Six months ago," the woman said. "We've been thinking about selling up and moving, but we can't afford to. The loans on this house are just too high; we had to help our boy for a while when he messed up financially. Before he got himself straight."

She shook her head in resignation.

"They just had the one dog when we were there," Rebecka said.

"One of them must have been killed. They hold dogfights over there every now and then. Betting on them for money."

"How do you know that?" Anna-Maria asked.

The couple exchanged looks and got to their feet in concert.

"Come upstairs," the woman said. "None of what we've told you or are about to show you must ever get out."

The couple went ahead of them up to the bedroom. The bed was neatly made with a crocheted bedspread and decorative cushions. Behind the curtain at the window was a camera with a serious lens on a tripod. You could clearly see the roof of the neighbours' house and the dog run.

"I'm a birdwatcher," the woman said. "That was why we moved here twenty-three years ago. We've had rosy starlings and hawfinches here. Occasionally, though, you find yourself looking at other kinds of things. And taking photos, too."

"I understand," Anna-Maria said, feeling love for Detective General Public swell inside her. That wonderful detective, the best ever.

A quarter of an hour later and Anna-Maria and Rebecka were driving away with a stack of photos that had been printed out. They clearly showed all four people in the house, the two women and the two tyre-necks. One photo showed someone who had to be Frans Mäki, a thin old man in a wheelchair, a cap with a slogan on his head and a blanket across his lap.

"This is really good stuff," Anna-Maria said, looking through them. She was thinking to herself that the decent thing for Rebecka to do would be to acknowledge that they had been given the pictures only because Anna-Maria was such a good police officer when the couple's six-year-old had run away. But it seemed like Rebecka only noticed when you did things wrong. Anna-Maria hardened her heart.

"You really mustn't feel obliged to invite me to your party," she said, desperately wishing she had come up with a good excuse when the whole thing was first mentioned.

"I want you to come," Rebecka said, without a spark of feeling.

After that they said nothing more.

Now there was no way of getting out of it that wouldn't seem glaringly obvious, Anna-Maria thought. She wanted to groan out loud at the thought of an entire evening with Rebecka and her posh lawyer mates. As if that wasn't enough, what was she going to wear? Now she'd have to spend a small fortune on a new dress too.

Rebecka was in a world of her own. Olle Pekkari knew who those Russians were. No doubt about it. He had rung there the same night his brother was murdered. And she was going to keep squeezing him until he told her what that call was about.

*

Krister Eriksson was padding along the corridor of the spa in a hired dressing gown, with a basket under one arm in which you were supposed to keep your phone and other valuables. He had skipped the gong meditation and was looking forward to a snooze alone in their room before dinner.

Sleep let him down like a bad insurance policy, though, and on the spur of the moment he sent a text to Rebecka: It's all go, not a moment to myself. I feel like a complete flake. Only my feet are extremely smooth following my fish pedicure. The fish gnaw away your calluses. Would you really want to eat sushi though in a place like this?

Ragnhild Pekkari was lying on her bed, thinking about men and love.

And just what was love? Fear of loneliness. The body's instinct to reproduce. A repetition of all the shortcomings of childhood: if I couldn't save my brother from disaster, I keep trying to with new men who are like him; if my dad wasn't able to love me, then I find men with cold hearts and try to be good enough.

She had made up her mind long ago to steer clear of the madness people call love.

Over the years she had witnessed her female colleagues serving their husbands, taking responsibility for the children, the cleaning, the home, relationships, parents, the husband's as well. At best those women felt unseen and unloved, at worst they were worn down, bullied, mentally and physically abused. But they kept going. They made sure not to learn how to change fuses or winter tyres so they could continue living in a fantasy that they wouldn't be able to manage on their own.

And then there were all those women who came into A & E, who had fallen down the stairs, slipped in the bathroom, fallen out of bed. The fear in their eyes and lips sealed tight about what had really happened.

It wasn't until long afterwards that she realised she too had been programmed to ruin her own life aided and abetted by a man.

When they moved from the island to Kiruna, *Äiti* had become a different person. At a stroke all her skills had become worthless. On the island she had been a powerful woman who knew how to do everything, how to look after the animals, how to butcher, preserve, bake, churn butter, stack hay, card wool, spin, weave, knit, and how to cure ailments with herbs.

That kind of knowledge had no place in Kiruna. *Isä* was an employee at the LKAB mine and they shopped for food at the Co-op. The doctor treated even minor ailments and their clothes were bought in a shop. *Äiti* became a housewife, did the cleaning and changed the curtains in spring and autumn. She shrank.

Ragnhild is remembering late one evening when she was fourteen. She was in bed listening to *Äiti* and *Isä* in the kitchen. *Äiti* was washing up and *Isä* was talking about the job in the repair shop while turning the pages of the regional newspaper. Ragnhild was going to steal out when they had gone to bed. She had started staying out at night. Running around with boys and drinking. Virpi was deeply asleep in the bed beside her.

She could hear *Isä* talking about how awful it was having the time-and-motion guy there, following the workers around with his papers stuck to a masonite board and a pencil held aloft.

"They time how long it takes to fetch a screwdriver," *Isä* complained. "They count how many steps it takes, make a note if you discussed matters related to work with your mates or if you happened to be talking about fishing. They stand guard outside the bog with their stopwatches and they're there when you sit down for a break and when you go and get spare parts. Then if you take more time than normal, they deduct it from your wages."

Bloody bean-counters and their goddamn UMS-System, *Isä* was complaining. It led to discord among the workers and meant it paid to do a poor job. As long as it was done fast, it was fine. And then there was Henry, who was ruining the farm. Selling off part of the forest to make money.

"I'm not suited to this life," *Isä* said. "It feels like there's no ground under my feet."

And then *Äiti*'s voice could be heard, withdrawn and dismissive: "It's what you wanted."

Though by then Ragnhild had long since stopped begging to be allowed to move back to the island. She wanted to sneak out at night, get off with boys and get drunk. She still went with *Äiti* to the island to do the cleaning for Henry, because she had to. But she was already searching for an unhappiness all of her own.

Ragnhild dragged her thoughts away from her younger days and got up off the bed. She felt weak at the knees and looked at her watch. Already seven. She was supposed to be having dinner with Börje and it was definitely dinner time now.

She got down a Bible from the bookshelf. Looked up the story of Jonah. Jonah who refused to go to Nineveh and took the boat to Tarshish instead.

Ragnhild had to sit on the sofa while she was reading Jonah's prayer: "Water engulfed me up to my neck" and "I went down to the very bottoms of the mountains; the gates of the netherworld barred me in for ever."

There is a Nineveh for every person, Ragnhild thought. You try and escape it. You'd rather ask the crew to chuck you overboard than end up there.

She went down on her knees beside the bed. She gathered her thoughts to pray. She hadn't prayed since she was a child. It felt like calling out in a huge empty warehouse.

She thought about Rebecka Martinsson. And about Virpi. Then her mind was drawn to Paula. They were her Nineveh.

She began to pray, just like the many other people who were unused to prayer before her:

"I don't know if I believe in you. But I've got no idea where to turn."

And then the doorbell rang.

Through the peephole she could see Börje Ström in the stairwell.

I'm not opening the door, she thought.

But her hand did it anyway.

He had a shopping bag with him.

She looked into his eyes. They had lost all their self-possession. Neither of them looked away.

Two lost souls who happen to find one another in the middle of a winter storm, Ragnhild thought.

"Hello, little one," he said. "You left me."

"Yes."

"I've been shopping," he said, and raised the bag a little.

She opened her mouth to say she wasn't hungry. And to tell him to push off. Ask him if his woman knew he was giving her the run around.

Her mouth refused to obey. It choked off the attempts to reject him before widening into a grateful smile. Her legs moved a little to the side so he could come in.

Little. No-one had called her that since she was eleven and had grown taller than all the boys at school. And a life began in which she would be called everything from "Long-legs" and "The Mountain" to "Gorilla".

Little. She is remembering all the men in her youth who came up to her at dances. If she had sat down and they had failed to realise. She could see they were far too short and would politely refuse. That would make them angry. All the drunken phrases that came out of their mouths when she did. "You too posh for me? What the fuck are you doing here if you don't want to dance?" They would keep at it, keep bothering her. Until she gave up and got to her feet. Then they almost shat their pants. Looking up at her on shaky legs. "No fucking way," they would say. "Fucking freak."

And now, little. She wanted to lean into that word.

Börje Ström removed his size sixteen shoes and moved ahead of her into the kitchen. She followed like a stray dog.

"This is a kitchen to fit me," he said, and tapped appreciatively on the counters she had had raised.

"I've done the same in the bathroom," she croaked. "Raised the mirror and the sink. I didn't want to have to bend down in my own home."

He chopped onions and whipped together an omelette. He fried it golden brown and grated a generous amount of Västerbotten cheese on top. He folded it and made a salad as well.

She was battling those dark thoughts of hers. She had shifted from thinking he was just a spoilt man who wouldn't be able to boil an egg to suspecting this was his seduction trick. And that hundreds of women before her had watched him put together an omelette.

The next moment she was thinking that she had been waiting for him all her life. That she had got lost and had turned down the wrong path that just led further and further away from what ought to have been her life. But now she was back on track. With this man who was as tall as her. On the island where her life was still the right life for her. Was this pure chance? Or was it God?

He kept talking about his memories of Kiruna, about some of the people he'd come across in town; they'd said hello as if they'd known each other for ages. And he wasn't wearing that hideous shirt anymore either.

They ate. She drank several glasses of water. Felt her energy returning.

He washed up. She dried. Then he took her hands in his.

She let him. Contact, touching another person. It was so terribly long since she had experienced that. She used to touch her patients. She didn't have that anymore. All winter long she had held books in her hands.

Her skin was filled with hunger. She was totally starved of the human touch. She let the sensation trickle from her hands into her body and down to her loins.

He had someone else. But that would have to wait.

His hand was on her hair. She was so afraid she had to stop herself from pushing him away.

"I don't know if I can deal with this," she said, so as not to be alone with that feeling.

"My dad was a criminal," he said.

That came out of nowhere. She realised it had been lying in wait inside him. He told her about the trip to see his old coaches, the old man and his story about forging banknotes.

"I always thought so highly of him," Börje Ström said. "To me he was . . . And it all turned out to be a lie."

"Welcome to the club," she said with a joyless laugh. "My brother . . . Not that I ever thought highly of him. We're not them, though."

"Almost," Börje said and looked at his tattooed arms.

"Would you like to lie down?" she said. "We don't have to . . ."

He nodded gratefully.

"We can just rest our heads," he said. "We don't have to get undressed."

And they went into the bedroom. All the changes of clothes from the day were lying there like skins that had been sloughed off.

She lay there with her head on his shoulder. He kept his free hand around her ear and the back of her head. The sound she could hear in her head as he slowly moved his hand across her ear was like water, lapping against the shore maybe. Or like the water a child hears when it is in the womb.

"You have to take one day at a time," she said.

"You get one day at a time, you mean," he said.

She wasn't going to argue and fell asleep in the calming murmur of his hand cupping her ear.

TUESDAY 3RD MAY

The Brat woke Rebecka before her alarm went off. She put the coffee on, had a shower and fixed her hair all in the space of ten minutes. She was supposed to be in court today, but she was familiar with the cases so she could allow herself a moment on the porch with her coffee.

This is what life is about as well, she was thinking as she sat on the steps with the mug in her hands. There was no heat from the morning sun as yet. But it was going to be a really warm day. The Brat was racing around the yard with a stick he had found. He tossed it in the air, slipped on patches of ice as he leaped after it, infecting her all the while with his canine joy.

She pushed her phone away to stop her hand calling up Marit Törmä's Instagram page all by itself.

You have to decide what you're going to think about, she told herself, pointing her nose at the morning sun. This is enough for me. Working. Dogs. Sivving. A bit of sun. A cup of coffee.

She dropped off the Brat at Sivving's. He insisted she ate a sandwich before she was allowed to drive away.

An hour later they were holding a case review at police headquarters. Rebecka Martinsson and Anna-Maria Mella gave an account of their visit to the home of Frans Mäki, the Lingonberry King, his Russian wife and the two men with the fighting dog.

"And who's the young woman?" Anna-Maria wondered aloud. "The shared girlfriend of the two men?"

"Weren't there three girls who catered to the punters in that camper van?" Karzan Tigris asked. "Maybe these were the same guys who drove it. Which we'd have to assume is very likely. If two of the women are dead, could she be the third?"

"Shouldn't we bring them in for questioning?" Magdalena Vidarsdotter asked.

"If we haven't got anything conclusive on them, they'll just deny everything," Rebecka said. "All of it. Or just remain silent during the interview. You know the type."

"It's strange that we don't know anything about them at all," Anna-Maria said. "No reports, suspicions, nothing."

"Couldn't they just be a really unpleasant bunch that happened to move here?" Tommy Rantakyrö suggested.

"The phone connection is no accident," Rebecka said. "It can't be. On the night both Henry Pekkari and the two women were murdered, Henry, or someone else, called Olle Pekkari on Henry's phone. Less than a minute after that conversation Olle, or someone else using his phone, calls the Lingonberry King."

"One of them had a gun under his jacket," Anna-Maria said. "And trust me, they were a lot more than an unpleasant bunch. They felt like . . ."

She searched around for the way she had felt and then found it.

". . . professionals," she said finally.

"I suggest we take a break," Rebecka said. "You can all call your informants and people who know people in the right places, if I can put it that way. Someone has to know who they are."

Everyone went off to phone around. Rebecka read the text from Krister again. Would you really want to eat sushi though in a place like this?

She had delayed responding. But enough time had passed.

The Brat says he'd love to eat those fish direct from the foot baths, she texted.

We can still be friends after all, she thought.

After that she kept checking her phone to see if Krister had replied, right up until the team reassembled forty minutes later.

No-one had anything to tell them about the Russians. But Fred Olsson said that one of his informants had seemed scared.

"He knew," Fred said. "That's the feeling I got in any case. But he insisted he didn't. And another thing: Rosa Larsson and Heikki Vinberg have left town."

"Who are they?" Magda Vidarsdotter asked.

"They've been supplying the citizens of Kiruna with a whole range of addictive substances for the last twenty years," Anna-Maria said.

"Apart from four at the beginning of the noughties, when Rosa did a long spell inside," Fred Olsson added.

"So they've moved?" Anna-Maria exclaimed. "When? Where to?"

Fred shrugged.

"Just over six months ago. Outside the country in any case my source said."

"I can hardly believe it," Anna-Maria said. "Heikki Vinberg can't ever have been south of Gällivare. I don't know what you think, but when the little fish hide in the reeds and the medium-sized ones disappear . . ."

". . . it's because there's a big fish swimming in the lake," Fred completed her thought.

"We'll just have to try and scare someone into talking," Anna-Maria said, and thought with a pang of Sven-Erik who had rarely considered scaring people a good method.

"Do we know for certain the dead women were prostitutes?" Tommy asked.

"That tattoo with the red umbrella is pretty difficult to ignore," Rebecka said.

"Can't we bring the Lingonberry King in for questioning?" Magda Vidarsdotter asked. "As a witness in the preliminary investigation?"

"We'd have to run a check on that medical certificate first, the one she waved at us," Rebecka said. "In any case I'm going to start by issuing a search warrant and I'll be sequestering Olle Pekkari's accounts, all his contracts and receipts, everything to do with his business operations. If he's got any kind of fiddle going with the Lingonberry King I'm going to dig it up. That might make him a bit more inclined to talk."

"Have we got anything new on identifying the women?" Anna-Maria asked.

"The dental records have gone to the National Operations Department," Fred Olsson said. "Can I get pictures of those villains by the way? I thought I could run them through a facial-recognition program."

"They're on my desk," Anna-Maria said. "Just dig down a bit and you'll find them."

"Anything new on Henry Pekkari's snowmobile?" Rebecka said.

Anna-Maria shook her head.

"No fingerprints apart from Henry's. But it was definitely what ran over the women in the snow."

If we hadn't discovered that Henry Pekkari was murdered, we would have assumed it was him, Anna-Maria thought. He ran them over and then died. What really went on over there?

"I think we've stumbled onto something major," Rebecka said. "Organised crime. An operation that has managed to keep below the radar for a pretty long time. We need to get a sense of the scale and nature of what they're up to. Is it just drugs and sex? Or is it bigger than that? The longer we can investigate before they feel threatened, the better. They've already had one visit from the police."

Rebecka looked at the clock. Her criminal cases were due in court.

But before that she had to issue a search warrant and drive over to Olle Pekkari's firm. Something would emerge.

She had one missed call from Pohjanen and one from Sivving.

I'll do it, she thought, even though she had no idea what they wanted, I'll do it.

Marit Törmä's eyes darted towards Krister's phone when it lit up on the hotel bed. They had been having a good time on what was a spontaneous mini-vacation. A break from the everyday routine. She had taken her photos for Instagram when he wasn't around. There was always an air of suppressed impatience about him when she posted her stories. And to be perfectly honest she found it annoying. It was her Instagram account that was paying for the lion's share of their trip. Other influencers had husbands who were happy to hold the camera when they were doing yoga or at the gym. She felt she had to do it quickly and be stealthy about it. Like there was something bad about having an account that was such a success.

Krister flushed inside the bathroom.

A text from Rebecka. Marit leaned over his phone and read: The Brat says he'd love to eat those fish direct from the foot baths.

"I'm going to have my massage," she said loudly, and he barely had time to answer before she was out the door.

She wanted to run down the corridor even though there was still half an hour until her appointment. She forced herself to walk. The corridors were incredibly long in this place. The group of women that she and Krister had met as they were coming back from breakfast were now walking towards her. They were a chatty, giggly group, and pretty loud as well. When they had caught sight of Krister and her they had fallen silent. They were chattering away and laughing this time, and one of them said hello.

He was held in high regard in Kiruna. Everyone knew who he was, the mountain rescuer and dog trainer for the police. South of Luleå it was very different. People either stared or made an obvious effort not to stare. Children asked him straight out, to their parents' horror: "Why are you so ugly?" "Why haven't you got any ears?" He was incredibly patient and kind with children. He told them about the fire. She admired him for it. She loved that.

The masseur commented on her strong body and asked about her fitness routines. He talked too much. Marit just wanted to be quiet, but felt she had to be friendly and respond.

So he was texting Rebecka now. She shouldn't feel bothered by that. But he hadn't mentioned it. When his sister or Marcus texted, he told her.

She had been the driving force behind their becoming a couple. It had been over between him and Rebecka for some time. She got in touch with him because she was going to the caves in Björkliden and wanted to know more about the underwater passage. When the thread ended, she was the one who made the final post. She didn't know whether it was her competitive instinct or interest on her part that made her get back in touch with him. She wasn't used to men letting go when she showed an interest. She had sent him a photo of her fully laden backpack. And then written: "Come along if you like."

She had devoted two years of her life to this relationship. She had been patient. He wanted to delay living together for Marcus's sake. To give the boy a sense of stability in his daily life. Only, something had to start happening sooner rather than later. She wanted to have children further down the line. Children of her own.

She didn't like to think it, but Krister should thank his lucky stars for having her. Only he was texting Rebecka. Looking after Rebecka's dog. And Marcus was sharing YouTube clips with Rebecka. Every now and then Marcus would realise he was missing the Brat and Sivving and then he got taken over there.

Is this worth it? she was thinking.

As she was walking back along the corridor, the masseur followed her on Instagram and liked twenty of her photos.

After breakfast Ragnhild Pekkari got in the car and drove to the hospital in Gällivare. It was a hundred and thirty kilometres but if Mervi Johansson wasn't going to make it she wanted to have said goodbye. It kept gnawing away at her that she hadn't taken the time to stop by when she went over to the island, not the first time or the second. Rebecka Martinsson had been there. Mervi must be wondering.

She talked to a nurse on the thoracic ward and was promised she could go in once rounds were over. She passed the time in the cafeteria, sipping her coffee and leafing through an evening paper from the day before. She watched the relatives and the hospital staff. All lost in their own thoughts. About work, or worries about illness. She felt at home. The girl at the cash desk was putting sandwiches on the chilled counter. She had been friendly without making you feel it was put on, and when Ragnhild looked at the clock she was surprised to find that in what seemed like no time at all it was already a quarter past ten.

Mervi's skin was thin and soft as silk. Ragnhild took her hands in her own. She had become so tiny. The hospital nightgown was like a huge sail around her shoulders.

"I'm Ragnhild Pekkari," Ragnhild said. "Do you recognise me? Isak and Helmi's daughter?"

"Ragnhild, oh yes," Mervi Johansson said, sounding distracted. She closed her eyes.

Maybe she doesn't remember me, Ragnhild thought.

"Did you drive all the way from Kiruna?"

"Yes, but it's really not that far. I listened to the radio."

"Let me give you money for the petrol."

"Don't be silly. Did you dye your hair?"

Mervi hauled herself upwards. Ragnhild took her time arranging the pillows.

"Listen," Mervi said, "I can really recommend pink. The attention you get is quite different. One of the nurses here, he's got dreads. And he thought I was lovely. You're never too old."

She winked knowingly.

"Have you got someone new?"

Ragnhild made a dismissive gesture.

"No, God save me."

"You were so unlucky with Tord. *Huja*. You handled it so well all those years."

Ragnhild could feel an ache under her cheekbone and on her forehead. She wanted to shake her head. She hadn't handled it well.

"And how's Paula doing?" Mervi said.

"Fine."

Ragnhild was thinking about Paula. She was doing fine. She could see from Facebook that she was doing fine. But they had no contact. She usually sent presents when the grandchildren had their birthdays. Though sometimes she wondered if they got them. Or if Paula just chucked them away unopened. She never even got a thank you.

"Ragnhild Pekkari!" said a voice behind her. "It's been absolutely ages."

A woman of her own age was standing in the doorway. Light-grey hair and Mervi's eyes.

"Stina, Mervi's daughter. Hi Mum, I've brought some clothes and some other stuff. How are you doing?"

"Just fine," Mervi replied. "Are we going home?"

Stina rolled her eyes at Ragnhild.

"My own children want to move me into an old people's home in Pajala," Mervi said to Ragnhild.

"They've got a place," Stina said. "She can't go on living on her own in the village. We're worried about her."

"Haven't I had to worry about them all my life?" Mervi said to Ragnhild. "I will make the decisions affecting me. Or has someone been appointed my legal guardian?"

Stina sighed in resignation and unpacked the clothes and a wash kit from a paper bag.

Ragnhild squeezed Mervi's hand.

"The police have been here to talk to Mum," Stina said. "It was really awful what happened to your brother, but all Mum knows is that a snowmobile drove past the cart shed."

"When they asked me the same thing for the third time I told them we were done talking," Mervi said.

She was blinking with tiredness like a child. Ragnhild stroked her upper arm the way she used to with Paula to get her to sleep.

"Guess what," Stina said to Ragnhild. "When Leif and I went over to Mum's to fetch her things the dog was there. Henry's dog, Mum," she said more loudly because Mervi had shut her eyes again. "It was on the front steps when Leif and I arrived."

"The dog," Ragnhild said. "Where is it now?"

"We've got it in the back of the car," Stina said. "Leif said he would take his rifle to the woods and put it down. Or it'll starve to death. That would be cruelty to animals. Has she fallen asleep?" Stina began to whisper. "She can't stay on there. She was this close to dying. What if she has a fall? She can't keep the place clean anymore and are we supposed to go over there and do the cleaning? All she needs is to get food poisoning. I've told her straight up that it's selfish to refuse. But you know her. Stubborn as a mule."

Ragnhild nodded. She was thinking about the dog.

Oh God, she thought. Only what can I do about it?

"I understand that Mum wants to live in her own home. She was determined to stay behind in the old world. We moved, didn't we, and got an education. Learned Swedish. It's not that I don't think back to the simple life we had in the village. The cows, the haymaking, the fishing, Dad coming home from the forest, the games with my brothers and sisters. But times change. And you have to adapt when they do. We never really had to suffer any kind of hardship, not really."

"No," Ragnhild said, thinking about the way her *äiti* used to light up and become her old self again when they stopped at Mervi's for some women's talk and a coffee once they'd finished cleaning for Henry.

Then she said:

"The dog. You mustn't shoot it. I'll take her with me."

"*Älä houraa*, what do you want it for? It's completely wild, you know."

Stina's husband Leif was waiting in the hospital car park.

What is it about men? Ragnhild thought. Why didn't he come in with her?

Leif also thought it was crazy to keep the dog.

"It can't live in a flat, can it?"

Only then he added it was a blessing not to have to kill a healthy animal. And Ragnhild could call him if she changed her mind.

The dog was docile but rigid with fear when he lifted it into Ragnhild's car. He handed Ragnhild a bit of rope to use as a leash.

"You can use that; I've put a knot in it so it will shorten if she tries to run away but hang loose otherwise. Like one of those retriever leashes."

"That's right," Stina said to Ragnhild. "You've always been an animal person. Do you remember that calf you and Virpi ran around with one summer? It followed you everywhere apart from in the boat. You built fences and made it jump over them. What was its name?"

"I don't remember," Ragnhild said truthfully.

The dog was lying in the boot like an exhausted prisoner the whole way back to Kiruna. She kept talking to it.

"I don't know if I'm doing you a favour," she said. "Sometimes it's difficult to distinguish love from selfishness."

When they got to Puoltikasvaara she remembered that the calf she and Virpi had played with one summer was called Onnenkukka, Lucky Flower. She remembered how she and Virpi gave it milk to drink from a pail. And when it had finished drinking they stuck their fingers in its mouth and it went on sucking. It had a strong mouth. The sensual feeling as their fingers were squeezed between its gums and that rough tongue.

She wondered whether the dog thought about the island as well. About hunting field mice and roaming wherever it liked.

And Börje Ström hadn't been in touch. Perhaps he'd driven back to Älvsbyn.

On Tuesday morning Sven-Erik Stålnacke drove into town even though he didn't have anything particular to do. For Airi's sake perhaps, so he didn't spend the whole day on the sofa at home.

On the spur of the moment he drove to Luossavaara. They were supposed to be moving some of the town's lovely old wooden houses up here.

He stood on the summit facing the wind and looking out over Kiruna. He could see the building he grew up in with his single mother; the church where Hjördis and he had got married. The residential area where they lived when Lena was at nursery school. He was familiar with every street and almost every building. He knew who owned the properties and who had lived in them. He was remembering the way his life as a policeman had been intertwined with that of the town itself. The streets where they had arrested speeding motorists, the detached houses he had taken runaway dogs back home to, the ones he had turned up at with the news someone was dead, or had to intervene to stop abuse, drunken rages, drugs and burglaries. There were some buildings you couldn't look at, not ever again. Places they had had to rescue children from, or execute deportation orders. It could sound like one bout of misery after another but the fact was he had always had a rather hopeful view of human beings. He had seen a great deal of good over the years as well. The people who stood by their nearest and dearest when things got really bad. Witnesses who had defied their fear of reprisals and done the right thing. People from the school board and the social services who had fought for young people. The Kiruna he knew and was remembering would disappear in a landslide that had been meticulously planned. The very foundation of his memories would be obliterated. New buildings and streets would be constructed that he would never have any relationship with.

All the same it had been the right thing to do: driving up here to take a look at the town. It hadn't felt as awful as he expected.

There's no point trying to run away from what troubles you, he thought. It will keep pursuing you nonetheless. The only way to get through your cares is to accept the pain and work through them; there just isn't any other way.

He grieved for his town for two minutes until the phone in his pocket started ringing. A number he did not recognise.

Someone selling something no doubt. Though they were people too.

It wasn't a salesperson.

"Hi Sven-Erik, this is Simon."

The lad from Tollarp he had talked to in the car park at the barracks.

The one who had told him about the sex workers and the Russians in the camper van.

"So you were asking about the third girl," Simon said. "I found out where she is. She's working at the Mården Hotel in Riksgränsen. Her name's Galina, apparently."

"Thanks Simon," Sven-Erik said. "Has she got a surname as well?"

"No idea."

"Who told you about this?"

"One of the blokes here, I can't say who. But Galina had his number and rang him and said she was in trouble and he helped her get a job. They get completely booked up there during the season."

They ended the call. Sven-Erik was thinking that seeing people in person was always worth it. He tried ringing both Rebecka and Anna-Maria but only got their voicemail. He left a message for Anna-Maria. For one blessed moment he felt like a police officer.

Karzan Tigris and Tommy Rantakyrö went with Rebecka Martinsson to fetch Olle Pekkari's accounts and the rest of the documents relating to the operations of his company. The office was next to a detached house belonging to his son, Anders Pekkari, on Kengisgatan. White brick on the outside and potted plants that were easy to look after on the inside. Blond furniture and no rugs to trip over.

Anders Pekkari was in. Just on his way out to lunch but he took his jacket off again.

He was a fit man in his fifties, as neatly pressed as his father. Tall, just like the rest of the family.

He read the warrant that Rebecka showed him; he appeared to remain calm, though his nostrils flared in mute testimony to the way his breathing had sped up as he got his phone out of his pocket and rang his lawyer. Then he asked his secretary, the only other person in the office, as it happened, to help the police find whatever they were looking for.

Karzan and Tommy took the folders of receipts and end-of-year accounts along with what seemed like everything else bar the kitchen sink out to Rebecka's car. Rebecka remained in the office to ensure that nothing suddenly vanished during the process.

Karzan and Tommy went out the door. Anders Pekkari brought a brief call on his phone to an end and gave Rebecka a look that made her feel like she was in a cage and he was poking her with a stick between the bars.

"Odd to think you and I could have been step-cousins," he said.

Rebecka said nothing.

"But shit always sinks to the bottom, is what they say," he went on. "Granddad and Grandma provided Virpi with a good home. And then she didn't even come to their funeral. Bloody dreadful if you ask me. She jumped from one bloke to the next until she finally found someone simple-minded enough to get her pregnant."

Rebecka was thinking about her father. He might have been a simple man. But he died before she was old enough to know. He only rarely put her to bed, preferring to sit in front of the telly with a beer. Sometimes she managed to nag him to the point where he lay down beside her for a moment. Then she would lay her head on his shoulder and he would tell her about the life of Paiju the elk in the woods: "Paiju the elk thinks it's lovely that summer has come. She has stepped into the lake and is grazing on water lilies on the bottom. It looks like she is diving. She disappears under the surface and then pops up to breathe and chew."

I loved you, she thought. I loved you so much.

"You were a lawyer in Stockholm before, weren't you?" Anders Pekkari went on. "What really happened there? Rumour has it you slept with the boss and eventually you got fired. And now you're getting a kick out of abusing your power at the prosecutor's office. It's obvious you're related, you and Virpi."

Rebecka could see the secretary doing everything she could to pretend she wasn't listening. And the next moment Karzan was back.

"This one too?" he asked, pointing at a cardboard box. "Is that the last one?"

"Just that one left," Rebecka said. "Was there anything else?"

This was said to Anders Pekkari.

"Oh there'll be more," Anders Pekkari said. "I can promise you that."

"Thank God this kind of thing is a complete mystery to me," Karzan said once they were back in the car. "How long does it take to read all of this?"

He peered at the box on the rear seat.

"I don't have to read it all," Rebecka said. "I'm just trying . . ."

She gave a goofy kind of shrug.

. . . to find a needle in a haystack, she was thinking. If there *is* a needle.

There is, she thought a moment later. And I am going to find it. I'm going to stick it straight into that family and their stuck-up notion of themselves.

She peered at Tommy. She was waiting for him to say something encouraging but he remained silent and looked out at the town which seemed to be dissolving in the damp spring.

I'm arguing with ordinary, decent people, she thought. And he doesn't like being part of that.

She had to steel herself against the sense of being alone. By trying to keep the rage inside her going.

*

Anders Pekkari locked the door once the law had left. He told his secretary she could go. He then made three phone calls. The first was to Carl von Post. They were members of the same rotary club after all.

"We're having huge problems with her," von Post said when he stopped speaking.

Then von Post promised he would get a grip on the situation.

Anders Pekkari's second conversation was with a journalist on *Norrländska Socialdemokraten*. The reporter's daughter played on the same hockey team as his own. The Pekkari family company had been supporting the team financially for many years.

The last call was to Maria Mäki, the wife of the Lingonberry King. Because he had to. He told her what had happened and about the steps he had taken. She was curt and her tone harsh.

"They've got nothing," she said. "Stay calm. This is just like turbulence, you know, like when you're in a plane. Though you feel it in the very pit of your stomach, it's really nothing."

He wanted to contradict her, to yell down the phone. "What do you mean, nothing?"

"So tell me," she said. "How's your daughter doing on the hockey team? And your son, he's doing well at school?"

Icy terror squeezed his innards.

"Very well," he croaked and they ended the call.

He sat at the desk in his empty office with the phone in his hand. When he noticed the drips falling onto it, he realised he was weeping. He was crying like a scared little boy.

Rebecka dropped Karzan and Tommy outside the police station. The boxes of folders were on the back seat. She was going to go through them this evening. She might try and find her trainers and go for a run before dinner.

And we're off! she thought, and felt her good mood return.

Then she cured herself of her good mood by going onto Marit Törmä's Instagram account. Marit and Krister were lying in a Japanese bath with the Stockholm archipelago in the background (3572 likes) while being massaged with bamboo sticks (6213 likes).

She peered at her phone. Nothing new from Krister.

She rang Måns on the spur of the moment.

"Martinsson!" he exclaimed heartily. "There's so much happening in Kiruna. Corpses in freezers and whores in the snow."

"This is where it all happens," she said.

"I hear Taube's coming to visit when she goes skiing up north."

"Uhmm," she said.

Maybe he was expecting her to suggest that he join them, it was hard to know with Måns.

"Do you know anyone who works on organised crime?" she said. "Who really knows their way around?"

"Don't you have that kind of expertise in the prosecutor's office?"

"We do."

"Only the best people happen to be somewhere else," Måns said. "Well, you were the one who chose to play in the minor leagues. I can check. What's actually going on up there?"

She really ought to throw him a bone. Every lawyer liked to know more than the media did. They were a gossipy lot. They wanted to know which celebrity had been arrested for drunk driving. They wanted to be in on the truth behind the resignation of the politician who cited "personal reasons".

Only she didn't have a bone.

"I think we've found something," she said.

Then she changed her mind.

"Or rather, I think we may have stumbled onto something."

She told him about her trip to see the Lingonberry King. And those terrifying men and about the dog Bengt.

"You really would have to call that a 'bonus family'," Måns said, sounding excited. "I know someone you could talk to. An expert who used to be at the National Tax Agency. The kind who had to have a secret address because of their job. Then she went over to the private sphere. She's an investigator for an insurance company. I can ask, but don't get your hopes up."

"I never get my hopes up where you're concerned," Rebecka said. "You and the people you know, a lot of show and not much content."

He laughed. "Fuck you, Martinsson."

There were too few people in his life who dared to speak to him without respect. More and more people who were simply afraid of him. It got boring in the end.

"What are you really doing up there?" he said. "I just don't get you."

"I've no idea. Come and kidnap me."

She could see there was coffee in the cup left over from this morning. She took a swig. Cold but not that revolting.

He laughed again but said nothing about coming north. Besides, it wasn't a real invitation. And she had stopped saying she missed him.

I just don't want to be alone, she thought.

He had stopped nagging her to move back to Stockholm.

He liked her. But he liked her when she was like this. Full of energy. On the hunt. Pretty and freshly showered.

But what about the rest of me? she thought. Who's going to love that?

She and Måns were over. Or they would be soon, in any case.

He started talking about a watch he had bought. A Gustaffson & Sjögren, the Skadi model. Only five were made: black Damascus steel, red gold and mother of pearl.

"Forty-two thousand dollars plus tax."

She listened patiently. This was a side of him she could never fathom. The importance objects held for him. Cars, boats, houses on Majorca, watches. Suits made by a tailor in Iran who Måns drank coffee and smoked cigarettes with whenever they met. He often talked about that minor friendship, at dinners and parties. Måns belonged to a family whose members only consorted with one another; they were what counted. But everyone in his group loved to know a few authentic examples of people from real life, the farmer in the country, the baker on Österlen, the tailor from Iran.

"I'm envious of you," she surprised herself by saying.

Måns lost the thread of what he'd been saying about the intricacies of the mechanism.

"What?" he said, with laughter in his voice, prepared to defend himself against any possible seriousness.

"You seem to be content," she said. "Content with your life."

Something is always making my skin crawl, she thought. No kind of life has ever suited me. They all start to itch after a while.

"Good God, Martinsson," he said. "I've never been content, not for a single day in my entire life."

Then he said quick as a flash:

"Got to go now. Lunch appointment."

He rang off before she even had time to say goodbye. He was always doing that.

Carl von Post took a two-hour lunch break and spent ninety minutes of it in the gym. He rowed three kilometres on the rowing machine and then did a whole-body session with his personal trainer. With sweat dripping off him, he got a lot of encouraging whistles and felt incredibly strong.

Afterwards he studied his reflection in the changing-room mirror. A towel around his waist. No love handles on him, no sir.

He was looking good, better and younger than his contemporaries.

He was ready; he was going to take Rebecka Martinsson down.

And he hadn't even had to do anything. At least, not much. She had made her own bed and now she was going to have to lie in it.

You messed it up right from the start. You thought you could give me grief and get away with it. And now the time has come for you to take the consequences.

"Open wide and swallow, Martinsson," he said out loud.

He was alone in the changing room, after all.

Rebecka cleared herself a path through the court proceedings. Operating like a snow blower, she barely had to look at the papers in front of her. Like a machine she rattled off a list of charges, pleas and the penalties she was asking for. The court complied with her recommendations in every instance. The defence lawyers looked tired and geared up to lose even before the verdicts were announced, consoling themselves with the thought of their fee. Half of the accused didn't even bother turning up.

Right at the back of the courtroom sat Stefan Oja, a freelance reporter from the town. He would attend court hearings from time to time. Minor items about less important crimes were a recurrent element in the local press. If there was a comic twist to the story, Stefan could sometimes sell it to one of the evening papers. He made a few notes during the hearings. Somewhere in the middle he got out his phone and appeared to be reading a message. He gave Rebecka a look that was hard to interpret and after that was busy with his phone to the exclusion of all else. Rebecka had thought no more of it but when the last verdict had been announced and everyone was starting to gather their things together, Stefan Oja came up to her.

"Hello Rebecka, good job today," he said. "Listen, one of the national papers has asked me to put something together about you being accused of harassing your relatives."

"Well, I haven't . . . Where did this come from?"

"Have you got any comment?"

"Are you recording this?" Rebecka asked, looking at the phone Stefan Oja was holding.

"I can get fifteen thousand for this crap, Rebecka. You're a bit of a celebrity, you know. Don't take it personally."

"I haven't harassed anyone. The police in Kiruna are investigating a case involving three murders."

Rebecka leaned deliberately over Stefan Oja's phone and spoke into it.

"And I am not related to the Pekkaris."

"So you think only biological children count as family?" Stefan Oja said. "Your mother was Olle Pekkari's foster sister."

"Oh, give it a rest," Rebecka said. "Just stop."

She picked up her belongings, stomped out of the courtroom and drove a bit too fast to police headquarters.

Rebecka chucked her briefcase on the visitor's chair. The door to Carl von Post's office was shut.

He's up to some mischief, she thought.

But there was only a quarter of an hour before they would have the final case review of the day. She exchanged her high heels for trainers and hurried along the corridor towards the police section.

The first person she saw there was Fred Olsson.

"I've got something," he said, waving some sheets of paper. "I think you'll want to see this before we get started."

"Hit me," Rebecka said and followed him to his desk.

She could hear the rest of the team gathering in the conference room. Tommy Rantakyrö and Magda Vidarsdotter said hello on the way to the coffee machine.

"I'll get you a cup, Rebecka," Tommy said.

"First off," Fred said, spreading out his papers. "I think we've got an ID for the woman with the umbrella tattoo. Adriana Mohr from Balvi in Latvia. Her sister reported her missing having heard nothing from her for three weeks. We've requested dental records. The sister has confirmed that Adriana was a sex worker and plied her trade in northern Scandinavia. She was currently drug-free and had been involved for a while in campaigning for sex workers' rights. Ten years ago, when her daughter had just been born, she had a red umbrella tattooed on her right ankle.

"That does sound like her," Rebecka said, dismayed. So she had a daughter.

"It's awful. The sister is a single mother of two. And she takes care of . . ."

He looked down at the papers.

". . . Adriana Mohr's child. It appears that Adriana was the sole financial support for all of them. She used to go home once a month. She should have been back last weekend."

"Good work, Fredde," Rebecka said, thinking that if she had stayed in company law at Meijer & Ditzinger she could have avoided being continually confronted with how fucking awful the world was.

"Listen, though," Fred said, breathing a long sigh while playing the fingers of one hand over his mouth. "This may seem a bit weird but I'm going to run with it anyway. The photos you and Mella got from the neighbours. Of the big guys and the women who live at the Lingonberry King's house. I ran them through a facial-recognition program."

"And?"

"I got a hit off one of them, only this isn't one hundred per cent, you've got to bear that in mind."

He opened his laptop and scrolled through to an image. It was a black and white photograph that looked like a picture from a newspaper. The headline and text were in Russian.

The photo showed a group of people walking down a broad set of steps outside an imposing building with huge leaded windowpanes, columns and archways.

"There," Fred said and pointed at a woman. "There are three images from this event and the program identified her with 72 to 84 per cent certainty."

"That's her," Rebecka said with complete conviction. "It is, isn't it?"

She compared the two pictures.

"Elena Litova, a member of the jury at a trial in Novosibirsk that garnered a lot of attention," Fred said. "I didn't get all the ins and outs, but it was about the hijacking of a major Belgian company in the telecom industry operating over there. The Belgian CEO said in an interview that the hijackers had drained the company of almost two hundred million American dollars."

Tommy Rantakyrö appeared in the doorway.

"Are you coming?" he asked. "Everyone's here."

"What's that on your face?" Fred said to Tommy. "You growing a proper beard?"

"Could you send me a link to that corporate hijacking piece?" Rebecka asked Fred.

Carl von Post came down the corridor at that very moment.

"Are you about to start?" he said. "I've got something to bring up with all of you."

Rebecka followed him into the room. She had a bad feeling about this.

Carl von Post took up position in front of the police squad. Rebecka sat on a chair to one side. She folded her arms, raised her shoulders and crossed one leg over the other. A perfect illustration of "defensive" in the dictionary of body language.

Carl von Post felt relaxed. He had laid his jacket across his desk and pulled on a cashmere sweater before coming here. A leader with a casual look.

"I'll get straight to the point," he said. "Rebecka Martinsson has been taken off this case with immediate effect."

He paused briefly, and into that pause, exactly as he had predicted, Rebecka Martinsson said:

"Come off it. Why?"

"I thought we could discuss that just the two of us," Carl von Post said, giving her a look that was both sympathetic and grave.

Oh, she was so easy, he thought. You've just got to wind up that key on her back and off she marches exactly where you want her to go, straight to the edge of the cliff.

"Let's deal with it here and now," Rebecka said. "It affects us all and everyone is going to know about it."

"You've been reported to the CSIP," von Post said. "The Commission on Security and Integrity Protection. You authorised telephone surveillance without sufficient grounds."

"Says who?"

"Says the complainant, the lawyer for the Pekkari family."

"But the CSIP isn't saying that, are they?" Rebecka said. "Anyone can be reported for anything at all."

"We are taking this –" von Post appeared to be fumbling for the word – "very seriously. The decision to remove you from the case has been taken higher up. You concealed the fact that you are closely related to the Pekkari family. Your mother and Olle Pekkari were siblings."

"They weren't brother and sister . . ."

"She was a foster child in their family, so that makes it a conflict of interest given the degree of relatedness."

"That is assessed on a case-by-case basis," Rebecka said, cutting him off. "It wouldn't automatically count as a close relationship."

"Your mother was in conflict with the family," von Post said.

"Conflict? What conflict was that?"

"And you authorised telephone surveillance of Olle Pekkari without him being accused of any crime. Furthermore, for three days you delayed informing the family that Henry Pekkari had been murdered."

"For technical reasons to do with the investigation," Rebecka said.

"Or because you didn't want people to know you were related to them?" von Post asked softly.

The officers were looking suspiciously at Rebecka.

"What the hell, Rebecka!" Anna-Maria Mella exclaimed.

"The report is baseless," Rebecka said. "I'm going to talk to Björnfot about this."

"You do that," von Post said. "I've just been speaking to him. He wants you to call him."

Rebecka got to her feet.

"I'll do that straight away, then," she said and almost ran for the door.

Gloom spread the moment Rebecka Martinsson had left. Carl von Post had to control his face like a hawk; it was so hard not to smile.

"The investigation will continue as usual," he said, stroking his chin in a gesture meant to signal he was shouldering the burden, taking on a responsibility he would have preferred to avoid. "I will take over as preliminary investigator and the proscribed telephone surveillance will be removed from evidence. I do not hold any of you in this room responsible for these errors. We're going to be doing this differently now though, and we're going to do it right. There'll be a delay of an hour before the case review and Anna-Maria is going to brief me on where we stand."

He looked at his phone.

"So, we'll meet again at . . ."

He was interrupted by Sonja from reception sticking her head around the door.

"Hello everyone," she said. "Sorry for the interruption, but we've had a report of a death up in Riksgränsen. Suicide by the looks of it."

She looked at her notebook.

"It's a woman. The boss at the Mården Hotel couldn't remember her surname, he was pretty upset. But she was called Galina. She'd been working on probation there for three weeks, he said. Wasn't a Swedish citizen. And now . . ."

Anna-Maria got to her feet. Her face was as pale as a winter sky. She got out her phone.

"Galina," she said. "Sven-Erik texted me. One of the three prostitutes who operated out of that camper van was called Galina. She'd found a job in Riksgränsen. He got that from his source."

"When were you planning on telling me this?" Carl von Post said.

"Now! I was going to bring it up during the case review."

What an idiot, von Post was thinking. I am completely surrounded by idiots of every conceivable kind.

Rebecka stormed into her office and slammed the door behind her. She dropped her phone on the floor as she was calling up the number for Alf Björnfot and had to start all over again.

You bastards, she was thinking. You fucking bastards.

Alf Björnfot answered after the first ring. It didn't sound as if he were far away.

"Right then, Rebecka," he said. "So there turned out to be problems after all. You may not be able to see it, but I'm taking you off the case for your sake as well."

"Thank you," Rebecka said. "For your concern."

"There's no need to be sarcastic. Do you really not grasp what you've done? You authorised telephone surveillance of an individual who is not even a suspect. You failed to disclose that you were related to him. The press is already looking into the incident."

"So you're worried about the press."

"No, I'm worried that people inside the legal system believe that the rules don't apply to them."

"So I think the rules don't apply to me?"

"What do *you* think? And I'm concerned that you have been lying to me and manipulating me."

"What?"

"You took this murder case on in a very high-handed manner. You lied to Calle and said that if he tried to take it away from you I'd make sure it was given back to you."

"That was a lie, of course it was," Rebecka said. "Because you'd never take my side against Carl von Post. The men in this place have got each other's backs."

"Stop that right now," Björnfot roared. "And just fucking stop trying to lay this all on me. This isn't the patriarchy. This is you committing an abuse of office. And this is us trying to repair the damage."

"Damage?" Rebecka said. "You want to see the damage? I could text you photos of the two sex workers so you can see what damage looks like. But you seem very sure of where you think the priorities lie."

There was silence at the other end. Seconds passed. When Björnfot's voice could be heard again it was calm, almost lethargic.

"You're saying terrible things about me right now, Rebecka," he said. "And I don't think you can really hear what you're saying. But there's one favour I want to ask you for before we end this call."

"Don't be a pain?"

"Don't quit. Don't go on holiday. Don't take sick leave. You are needed."

"Of course. Someone has to empty the ashtrays and clean the toilets. You do know your boy made me take on the entire backlog of petty crimes the moment you left?"

There was a deep sigh from the other side of the Atlantic. She realised he had not been told about that.

"We'll have to talk more about this later," he said. "Look after yourself."

"Right," Rebecka said and ended the call.

She looked at her phone. It crossed her mind to call Maria Taube.

They can't come now, she was thinking. The party is cancelled.

But she couldn't bring herself to make the call.

Fred Olsson had sent over the link to the corporate hijacking of the Belgian telecoms company, an interview with the CEO. It was a can of worms. Russian mafia, the CEO maintained. No reason to suppose anything else, a whole slew of individuals involved, corrupt police officers, judges, officials at the Russian tax authorities. They had hijacked the company's control document and its electronic seal, signed scam agreements on behalf of the hijacked company that instantly left it with gigantic debts. Then the false creditors had sued the company for the scammed debts. Neither the court nor the jury checked the authenticity of the agreements but ruled in favour of the creditors. And because the telecoms company was operating at a loss they were able to get the Russian tax authorities to pay back an enormous amount of withholding tax as a result, almost two hundred million dollars. The sum was paid into the new accounts of the hijacked company and then channelled to the accounts of the fake creditors.

"Who would ever bloody believe it?" Rebecka said aloud.

Elena Litova was a jury member who had been bribed. And she

might be the same individual who was married to the Lingonberry King. The woman known as Maria Mäki on the census form. Not your everyday mail-order bride by any means.

What is she doing here though, Rebecka wondered.

She could hear Anna-Maria and von Post's voices in the corridor. They went into his office and shut the door.

She found herself sitting on the floor with her back against the visitor's chair. She didn't have the energy to get to her feet.

I'm finished here, she was thinking. They can sort this out. I am never, ever coming back here. She stuck a leg out and kicked over the waste-paper basket.

"This is completely insane. I can't get my head round it."

The manager of the Mården Hotel in Riksgränsen was standing on the paved rear courtyard of the hotel annex. He wiped one hand across a face tanned by the early spring sun and adjusted the bandana that was wrapped tightly round his head. He was wearing a blue apron with leather detailing and smelled faintly of cooking. His moustache was stylishly groomed, with the tips pointing upwards. According to the badge on his apron his name was Mange Eriksson.

They were so cool, all these mountain people in the tourist industry, Anna-Maria Mella was thinking. The last time her feet had been attached to a pair of downhill skis was, well, it was before the kids.

The dead woman was lying on the ground under a blanket. The ambulance staff had been waiting for them. Then they had driven off to get a meal somewhere; the hotel restaurant was too expensive. They would come and get the body when the police were done.

Anna-Maria lifted a corner of the yellow waffle blanket. The woman was short. Slender, like Anna-Maria's daughter Jenny before she got her curves. There was a little pool of blood under her head.

I take it back, Anna-Maria thought. I don't like working on murders. I want to arrest people for traffic offences. More admin please.

"So she was working up there?" she asked, pointing to an open window on the third floor.

"Yeah, she was cleaning."

"But no-one saw anything?"

"No, lunch had been over for quite a while. Basically everyone had gone off to the slopes, the snow's awesome right now, so . . . The restaurant staff were busy clearing things away, tidying up, getting ready for the dinner service."

"Only it was a guest who found her?"

"Yes, someone who'd gone out the back for a smoke. She's gone off dog-sledding but she left her name for you, I've got it written down."

Anna-Maria stifled a dismayed sigh.

"What was her name?"

"The guest?"

"Her too, but I mean Galina? What was her surname?"

"Uh, Galina Ko . . . Ku . . . no, I don't know."

"Maybe you've got it in your employment records?"

The manager was shuffling his feet, shifting his bodyweight from one to the other. The sound of a snowmobile could be heard far off.

"Right, only that's where we've got a bit of a problem, you see. She was on probation, sort of. We were supposed to get the records sorted and so on but there's just been so much to do, what with it being high season."

"I see," Anna-Maria said. "So she was working unregistered."

"God, I hope I'm not going to end up in trouble over this. We were going to get it sorted there was just a . . . delay on the admin side. She didn't come here as the result of an employment interview, if you get my drift. She was in trouble and needed somewhere to sleep and a job straight away."

"What kind of trouble?"

"I don't know."

Anna-Maria let the seconds pass. She wished Tommy was beside her to back her up, but he was a few paces away, looking in a different direction.

"I think she was a prostitute," the manager finally said. "But I don't know any more than that."

"You don't know any more than that? You must have heard on the news that the Kiruna police are investigating the murders of two prostitutes? And it never occurred to you that there might be a connection?"

"Not really."

"I see. So when did she start working here?"

"Less than a month ago."

"Did she come here off her own bat?"

"No, there was this guy who moonlighted here when we were extending the dining room. He got in touch with me about her."

"We're going to need his name and telephone number," Anna-Maria said.

"Really?"

Anna-Maria looked up from her notebook and raised her eyebrows. The manager raised his hands in a gesture of surrender.

"I get it. His name is Kristoffer Westman."

He got out his phone and read off the number.

"What did he say when he contacted you?"

"Not a lot. He knew this girl who needed a job. We always need people at this time of year."

"Was she depressed? Did she talk about taking her own life?"

"She didn't talk much at all. Not with anyone here. She used to Facetime now and then when she was off. Though she was pretty down, I think. I used to see her crying quite a bit. When she was cleaning the rooms and on her own."

"So you think she killed herself?" Tommy Rantakyrö asked.

"Of course I do. You're not thinking she was . . . What?"

"One thing at a time," Anna-Maria said. "Why do you think she was feeling down? Tommy, could you get us a pair of plastic gloves from the car?"

"I don't know. She just said she'd ended up with 'bad men', 'very bad men'. She didn't want to talk about it. You can hazard a guess, though."

Tommy came back with the gloves. Anna-Maria pulled them on and turned part of the blanket over so she could go through the dead woman's pockets.

"No phone," she said, folding back the blanket and taking a look around. "Did she have one?"

"Sure, like I said I saw her Facetiming every now and then. She was using our wifi."

Anna-Maria asked to see the room Galina had stayed in.

It was small. The bed had not been made. Some pants and a T-shirt with the slogan "REAL SNOW REAL HAPPINESS – RIKSGRÄNSEN" had been hung over the radiator to dry.

On the bedside table were some pictures cut out of glossy magazines featuring beautiful homes, lovely gardens, a woman in a long dress reclining on a divan. There was absolutely nothing else in the room apart from some sweet wrappers in the waste-paper basket.

There was a toothbrush and a mini-sized tube of toothpaste in a plastic beaker in the bathroom, probably from one of the hotel's guest kits. A piece of paper was folded over the edge of the mirror, and written on it in pencil: "Smile, Breathe and Go Slowly."

"Where are her things?" Anna-Maria asked, without taking her eyes off the message on the bathroom mirror.

"She didn't have any when she arrived," the manager said. "Not even a handbag."

They raised the thin mattress on the bed; there was a passport underneath.

"Galina Kireevskaya," Anna-Maria read, laboriously working through the Cyrillic. "From Kurchaloi."

"No phone, though," Anna-Maria said again. "Can we have a look at the room she was cleaning?"

The corridor was empty apart from a cleaning cart outside the room. The manager unlocked the door. Sheets were piled on the floor. A cloth just under the open window.

"Have you been in here since she fell?" Anna-Maria asked.

"No, I mean, I watch telly you know," the manager said. "I pulled my sleeve over my hand as well, when I shut the door."

"The door was open when you got here?"

"Yes."

"We'll cordon it off. And get the forensics team in."

"OK, and sorry to ask, but when will that happen? We've got guests arriving tonight. And the hotel is packed to the rafters."

"Hard to say."

"I'll have to sort it," the manager said. "Only, are you thinking something else happened? I mean, she jumped, didn't she?"

Anna-Maria did not reply. She walked over to the window and looked down at the body. A teenage boy and girl were approaching.

"Hey, you," Anna-Maria shouted. "Get away from there."

Tommy leaned out as well. Yelled at them to clear off.

The boy glanced upwards before giving the girl a nudge. A quick and coordinated move saw the girl raise the blanket while the boy took some snaps on his phone.

"What the hell!" Anna-Maria yelled.

She stormed out of the room and down the stairs with Tommy immediately behind her.

I'll strangle them, she was thinking. But when she rounded the corner to the rear of the building the girl and boy had disappeared. Tommy was running round the far corner.

She put her hands on her knees and tried to catch her breath while pulling the blanket back over the body. Then she heard shouts from the other side and ran after Tommy.

She found him and the two teenagers in front of the hotel entrance. Tommy was straddling the boy. He pulled his jacket open and got the phone out of an inner pocket.

"Stop it," the girl screamed. "Are you out of your mind?"

"Are you out of *your* minds?" Tommy yelled back. "Taking pictures of a dead person. A human being. What were you going to do? Post them on Facebook?"

"Tommy," Anna-Maria shouted as she grabbed his arm and pulled him up.

"Who the fuck has Facebook?" the boy said as he got to his feet. "Give me the phone."

Tommy chucked the phone against the stone wall of the building; the sound of hardened glass cracking offering conclusive evidence its life had come to an end. Then he picked it up and hurled it as far away as he could. It ended up in deep snow among some birch trees.

"You can fetch it if you want," he panted.

"I can't believe you did that," the boy shouted. "That was a 6S Plus!"

"Go and sit in the car!" Anna-Maria said to Tommy. "Right now."

She had to tell him several times before he shuffled off.

"I'm going to report you," the boy said. "Don't think I won't."

Tommy Rantakyrö flipped him the bird without turning round.

"Are you intending to report this?" Anna-Maria asked.

"Yes, I am. Are you police? Is he police?"

"That's correct. How old are you?"

"Seventeen."

"In that case we'd best get in touch with your parents. Are they here?"

It was noticeable how the boy and girl quietened down immediately.

"They're on the slopes," the girl said sulkily.

Anna-Maria could see they were siblings. Twins maybe.

"We'll have to tell them what you did."

"It's not illegal, is it?" the girl asked.

"No, not yet," Anna-Maria said. "It's immoral and revolting, and it makes you wonder what kind of people would do something like that. I'll have to ask your parents what they think. But it isn't illegal."

Both teenagers were staring grimly at her. Like Jenny when she didn't get her way. In the end the boy shrugged and turned on his heel. The girl ran after him.

Anna-Maria marched towards the car. She was seething.

They said nothing for the first ten kilometres of the return trip, Tommy in the passenger seat with his collar turned up, his cap a long way down his forehead. As if he were hiding away.

He's always been such a brat, Anna-Maria was thinking.

She had been so pleased when he moved in with Milla, hoping she would provide the stability he needed.

Like one of the "cushion girls" at school, it occurred to her. She'd been one of those herself, seated between rowdy boys to calm them down.

She felt paralysed by her own helplessness. The bits of her brain that were supposed to come up with the right thing to say had obviously left for the day.

There came a point when you had to learn to cope with life, she was thinking. Divorces, illness, death. You can't just lose it when they happen. Start boozing and end up in a ditch you've dug yourself.

She was going to have to talk to him now though. Because it couldn't go on like this.

Only she had to do it gently and be sure to listen. So he didn't become defensive.

She let her eyes wander across the lake, across the Torneträsk. Soft, white mountains, pale-blue shadows, blazing sunshine. It was lovely, really beautiful. Just looking at it ought to make her as calm as one of those people who rub crystals.

While he was perfectly happy to just sit there not saying anything. That was so childish, as well.

You could at least say sorry, she thought. How hard can that be? Then again, that's an adult quality. Being able to understand that everything isn't always someone else's fault.

The last thing she needed right now was an assault claim being filed against one of the members of her squad. She was hoping those rotten kids would keep quiet. Though that was so wrong as well.

She took a breath. Counted to five on the inhale and five on the exhale.

Robert used to joke with her about that. Because they had five children. "Breathe," he would say and then he would count: "One idiot, two idiots, three idiots . . ." All the way up to five.

"What a couple of fuckheads," Tommy suddenly said.

"Those kids?" Anna-Maria said. "The boy was seventeen, Tommy."

And when he failed to reply, instead appearing to sink deeper inside his collar as if determined to disappear, she said:

"What you did was completely unacceptable. You get that, right? I had a talk with them so if you're incredibly bloody lucky, he won't report you. But this can't go on."

She stopped. She was being far too accusatory.

"I'm worried about you," she said. "Very worried."

And then it all came pouring out of her. His taking sick leave so often. And smelling hungover at work. He had to pull his socks up and comb his hair and buck up, and for God's sake go and talk to someone.

"Someone professional, I mean. Because I've no idea what to say. I'm not your mother."

"Well you sound just like her," he said from inside his jacket.

She felt so sad she lost her train of thought entirely. They drove another twenty kilometres before she said:

"I'm driving you home. And you're to stay home for the rest of the week. I'm going to book you some therapy sessions starting next week, and if you cancel any of them I'll get HR involved."

They were silent for the rest of the trip. Anna-Maria switched on the radio. At one point he turned quickly away and wiped a hand over his face.

And when she dropped him outside his block of flats and watched him move slowly inside, shoulders hunched, she thought:

You really handled that brilliantly, Mella. You listened and you were gentle. So he didn't get all defensive.

Then she revved the engine and drove off.

She was thinking about Galina Kireevskaya's thin body lying there under the blanket.

Wouldn't you take off your rubber gloves? she was wondering. Wouldn't you take off those thick rubber gloves if you were going to kill yourself? And where was her phone?

Tommy Rantakyrö went into his flat. Or rather, his and Milla's old flat. Inside there were gaps everywhere left by the things she had taken with her and he had not replaced. There was a screw in the wall in the hall where the mirror used to hang. An inflatable mattress was lying on the floor of the bedroom. He couldn't understand her new bloke; he didn't seem to mind having sex in the same bed she and Tommy . . . he, Tommy, would never have been OK with that. That was what he usually told himself even though he knew in his heart it wasn't true. He'd have agreed to anything. She'd taken the table in the living room and the large rug in there as well. He'd been allowed to keep half the potted plants. They had all died.

He was thinking about Galina Kireevskaya. He was thinking about the teenagers who'd been taking pictures. He'd never been the kind to resort to his fists, not ever.

Anna-Maria thought the problem was him drinking too much; she was angry he had lost his temper with those teenagers. She didn't have a clue. He'd done something much worse. Something really terrible.

The image of the women who'd been found in the deep snow behind Mervi Johansson's shed flared in his brain. His heart kicked in his chest.

He should never have become a policeman. He wasn't suited to it. Only, it was what he'd wanted ever since he was ten. That was when an officer visited their class. Even the tough guys had been impressed and flocked around the man in uniform. Tommy had made up his mind right there and then. One day he would be the man in dark blue everyone looked up to. He had got in on the second attempt.

After training he had applied for a post in Kiruna and got it. Mum had been over the moon. Dad too, even though he wouldn't show it the same way. He always kept in the background, Dad. He had started work on the railways when he was fifteen and done the same job for forty-three years. It might be called the Transport Administration nowadays, but it was still the same job and when Dad retired he'd have been working there for fifty years exactly. Five days off sick his entire working life. He could have got Tommy into the railways. Everything would have been different then.

They hadn't had any more children. Tommy was their only child. Always thrilled when he dropped by. Mum and her endless "Why don't you have a little lie-down", which was an invitation to lie on the kitchen sofa and shut his eyes. And when she woke him by tentatively patting his leg there would always be something to eat on the table, coffee and sandwiches, a pile of pancakes, supper or lunch if it was that time of day.

What would they say if they ever found out?

He had fucked up a pretty good life as a police officer, what with Anna-Maria as his boss and Sven-Erik, everyone's anchor at the station. He knew he'd been the young pup of the squad, but he'd accepted that role and was always teasing Sven-Erik. Cats had been a recurrent theme; he'd say they kept rubbing up against Svempa to scent-mark him, not as a sign of affection.

Milla's words from one of their many rows still haunted him: "It's sweet being boyish when you're twenty-three; it's a turn-off when you're thirty-three."

A few months ago he and Karzan Tigris had been out on traffic patrol and had stopped one of the tough boys from Tommy's time at school. "Just let this one go, Tommy," his old classmate had pleaded. A hint of a command in his voice nevertheless. And Tommy knew in his heart he would have let him go if it had been up to him. But Karzan had laughed and said it wasn't up for negotiation and a fine had been issued. The classmate had mouthed the word "cunt" and Tommy had said nothing, hoping Karzan hadn't seen.

Karzan was younger than him and twice as strong. He had overtaken Tommy more or less immediately. And Tommy no longer felt comfortable in the role of squad brat. Sven-Erik had retired. Milla's voice in his head again: Grow up, for fuck's sake.

The anxiety threatened to overwhelm him. Those women. It wasn't his fault. It was his fault. His upper body rocked to and fro as he breathed in rapid bursts through his nose while dragging his fingertips roughly across his face, from his cheekbone down over his throat until the skin was sore.

He wasn't police material. Never had been. And now he had gone and proved it beyond any doubt. Messed up so badly there was no getting out of it. Just like a thousand times before, he was thinking he had to tell Anna-Maria everything. But then he thought, like he had a thousand times before, that he couldn't. It just wasn't possible.

He wiped his face with the dish cloth; there was no more kitchen paper.

His phone rang. His other phone, the new encrypted one. It was bound to be Yury. He was the one who did the talking. The other one never said a word. Tommy didn't answer. Which meant they would be here soon. You weren't allowed to ignore them.

He had to get out of here. This very moment. He would stop at Systembolaget. He needed something to calm himself down, to stop his thoughts whirling round and round.

"So come on then," Ragnhild Pekkari said softly. "I'm going to stay completely still. See if you dare."

Villa was in the doorway between the hall and the kitchen. Ragnhild was sitting on the floor. She was holding a messy clump of wet food in her outstretched hand. The bitch was sniffing the air, she took a stiff step forwards and then backed off and disappeared down the hall so Ragnhild could no longer see her. Then she appeared in the doorway again. Two steps forward. Hunger was warring with fear.

Her phone rang. Börje Ström. She hadn't entered his name in her contacts but she recognised the number.

Ragnhild answered and put the phone on speaker.

"What are you doing?" he asked.

"Building trust," she said and told him about how she had acquired a dog. "This will take a while," she went on.

Yesterday at this hour she had fallen asleep on his arm. When she woke up he was gone. She had felt very alone. Villa was here now though.

"Are you out for a walk?" she asked.

She could hear it in his breathing.

"I am," he said, and asked if he could drop by. Maybe they could have dinner together. He could go shopping.

"I'm not sure," she said hesitantly.

He hadn't gone home to Älvsbyn. She could feel her face smiling.

"Maybe you're seeing someone?" he asked.

"Hardly," she blurted.

She remembered her last relationship. Fifteen years ago. She had been just over fifty and still attractive. He was a science teacher in Gällivare. They had started getting together every other weekend because he had his teenage daughter living with him one week in two. She didn't want to meet his children. No children, was what she had said. And definitely not daughters, was what she had thought. He drove a hundred and twenty kilometres to see her on Fridays and the same distance back to Gällivare on Sundays.

They always met at her place, never at his. She cleaned the flat, bought flowers for the kitchen table, and shopped for food at the deli. Three months into the relationship and he had suggested she pay half the cost of his petrol. She had refused. And gone on to explain that she had extra costs as well, as a result of their seeing one another. He had backed down but had been unhappy about it, that much was obvious. It lasted for two years. She had thought about that business with the money afterwards. With petrol at roughly ten kronor a litre, every trip he made would definitely have cost less than two hundred kronor as the car he had couldn't possibly consume one litre every ten kilometres. The flowers alone had cost that. But she had never asked him to contribute for the flowers, the food. Loo roll! He took ages to have a shit and used to wipe himself at half-time.

And once he had allowed himself to express that minor discontent, she had never felt she could ask him to stop and get something on the way. She had gritted her teeth on those occasions when he brought a bottle of wine and always, always, told her how much it cost. She had told herself she wasn't going to sink to his level. She had never told anyone else about the relationship. Her embarrassment at not having immediately ended it with a cheapskate like him was too great.

The science teacher had also felt right at home in her tidy flat with its lovely cushions and paintings and books.

She had made up her mind at that point that enough was enough. She couldn't put up with the imbalance. She had neither the energy to fight it nor the strength to bear it. And there was nothing lonelier than feeling lonely in a relationship.

"Where did you just go in your thoughts?" Börje asked.

And just like that she told him about Kenneth, the science teacher. She didn't care that it made her appear weak and afraid of being alone.

Börje Ström was laughing at her story.

"What an idiot," he simply said.

She laughed too. He was the kind of person who dealt with things a lot more casually, and it was infectious.

Carefree, she thought at the same time as a dark voice inside her said: Carefree is no different from being spoiled.

All the same, sitting on the kitchen floor while patiently outwaiting Villa and talking to him on the phone was the nicest thing she had done in ages.

"I want to tell you," he said then. "I had someone. In Älvsbyn. It's not like we were living together though, only . . . I called her in any case. So it's over."

A whole gymnastics squad of joy was leaping up and down inside Ragnhild. She was entirely unprepared. A team of young girls were doing cartwheels and vaults in pink outfits. Though she kept yelling at them to sit down on the benches by the wall bars.

"I've fallen for you," he said.

Contempt for such a simple way of expressing himself hit her like a switch being tripped. The very next moment she realised it was crazy to get hung up on his choice of words.

Silence fell. Villa was in the doorway. Her movements had become less tentative. More curious than scared. Her ears were pointing forwards and she was tilting her head first to one side then the other.

Ragnhild reached for the Bible and her reading glasses on the kitchen table.

"In Genesis there's the story about when Adam and Eve sinned and ate the forbidden fruit in the Garden of Eden," she said. "And then God curses them, he curses the serpent and the man and the woman. To the woman he says . . ."

She put on the glasses and read aloud:

"I will greatly multiply thy sorrow and thy conception; in sorrow thou shalt bring forth children; and thy desire shall be to thy husband, and he shall rule over thee."

"I see," Börje Ström said. "That was one way of responding, I suppose."

Poor bloke, she thought. He doesn't understand anything.

"It's not a commandment, you see," she said. "It's a curse. We desire you. You rule over us. And when it comes to falling in love, or passion, experience tells me it often strikes when we're trying to escape. From depression or grief."

Villa sat down. She was giving her new human an exploratory look.

"So what did God say to the man?" Börje asked.

Ragnhild looked down at the Bible verses.

"In the sweat of thy face shalt thou eat bread, till thou return unto the ground; for out of it wast thou taken: for dust thou art, and unto dust shalt thou return."

She put her glasses on the table.

"We're cursed," she said. "Although we try to live together, we just can't break the curse."

"So you and me," he said. "Are we cursed already?"

Sure enough, Ragnhild was thinking. Maybe even now. The very fact that I'm sitting here trying to explain. Having to keep explaining to someone who doesn't get it.

"I've a small property I rent out in Älvsbyn," Börje said. "So I've had to learn how to tinker with all kinds of things. And the way I see it, as long as things work, you don't have to try and fix them. I don't get my toolbox out until one of the tenants actually tells me the pipes are blocked."

"So tell me, then," Ragnhild said. "Tell me about your relationships with women. Have you ever had to get out your toolbox?"

1970

Her name is Marjut and she comes from Kemi. Börje meets her in the People's Park. She is a real beauty in the old-fashioned sense. Modern girls cut their hair off and tease it. They dress in trouser suits and short skirts with shiny boots. Marjut's hair is like Rita Hayworth's. She makes her own dresses and jackets so they cling to her curves. She has a generous laugh and likes boxing, "though sometimes I have to shut my eyes," and doesn't ramble on about the Vietnam War and Nixon.

This is September 1970. Börje is treated like a hero in Kiruna. He's won the light heavyweight national championships three years in a row. This year he won on a knockout. He never has to pay for his own drinks when he goes out, people jostle for the chance to do that for him. The worst of the bullies from secondary school even popped up one time he was in a pub, with a glass of beer in his hand, though Börje said in front of all the onlookers: "You can fuck off, we're not mates, you and me." Someone took the glass of beer and handed it back to the bully, who skedaddled.

He parties hard, on Wednesdays, Fridays and Saturdays at least. And he is not one to turn down a free drink either. There are lots of women willing to spread their legs. He has already lost count.

He asks Marjut if she would like to go for a walk. But she doesn't want to. And he can't offer her an alcoholic drink.

"I'm here to dance," she says, drinking something fizzy through a straw.

"It's just . . . I can't dance," Börje says, "so I thought we could get some air."

"You'd better learn in that case," Marjut says with a merry twinkle in her eye. She disappears onto the dance floor with a lad from Tuollavaara who might have won an ice-fishing tournament – at the very most.

Börje does not give up. He strolls over to Marjut a bit later on.

"I've thought about it," he said. "I'll learn to dance, if you give me lessons."

They do a passable imitation of a dance. Marjut laughs a lot. They went out on walks for a whole week after that before they ended up in bed. By then Börje had put clean sheets on the bed in his flat. Marjut is only just eighteen and has a room at one of her aunts, so they can't get together there.

"Who's that?" she asks with feigned indignation when she sees the tattooed pin-up on Börje's chest, almost identical to the one his father had.

"That's you, isn't it," Börje Ström says.

So she laughs again and gets down from the wall the gloves he wore during his most recent national championship match, and hangs them around her breasts. She asks about his other tattoos as well; there are quite a few now. He had the polar bear with the bared fangs, the emblem of the club, done when he won the international match in Berlin; the Three Things that Will Ruin a Man – the girl, the playing cards and the bottle of spirits – he had done after winning the last but one national championship. When he wins the Olympic gold he will have a huge ship with a snake twined round it done on his back. She laughs at his cockiness. And at those three damned spots that were his first. The three spots have turned into an amusing anecdote with the passage of time: the way his mate had jabbed him with the darning needle, and how he got beaten and came down with a fever and how, ever since, he had spent the rest of his nineteen years getting jabbed and being beaten.

On Christmas Day Marjut tells him she is pregnant. Börje goes and buys a ring. Nothing else to do. Their little girl is born in July, in the maternity ward at Kiruna hospital. He doesn't have a tattoo done.

"What happened then?" Ragnhild asked once Börje had finished.

She was looking at his number on the screen. Pondering whether to add him to her contacts. Whether to write Börje Ström into her contacts list.

"Well," he said. "I did a lot of drinking. The rest of the time I was training for the Olympics or working. She got fed up in the end and went back to Kemi. Aina had just learned how to walk."

He didn't fill her in on the details. About being so drunk when he got home that Marjut had to help him up the stairs. Though he wasn't so drunk he couldn't insult the neighbours who opened their doors a sliver. About being sick all over the floor. Or the time none of his mates would have him in their cars when he couldn't make it home under his own steam. They found a wheelbarrow at a building site to cart him home in. Tipped him out at his front door. That also turned into a funny story that did the rounds. How they had to take it in turns. And how the wheelbarrow kipped over several times.

"Are you in touch with your daughter?" Ragnhild asked.

"Yeah, we speak on the phone. She comes to visit with her kids from time to time. They're fourteen and twenty. Time marches on."

Villa moved in and felt brave enough to take the food from Ragnhild's hand. She gobbled it down and backed away.

"Good girl," Ragnhild said just as what Börje had told her was making her feel melancholy.

They had it so easy, the men. They could do whatever they liked and still be forgiven. Börje had been drinking. In between, he'd been training and working. Until Marjut couldn't put up with it any longer.

"What about you?" he said. "You've got a daughter too. How did that turn out?"

"You tell me," she said. "How did it?"

She cleared her throat; it felt sore.

"I had just finished training as a nurse when I met Todde. And I was a white-water rafter. He was one too. So . . ."

New to the team, she was thinking. Happy, funny, easy-going. Full of stories and anecdotes. Tall and handsome.

The fact that he loved the bottle was noticeable from the start, though. He always got the most drunk. He could fall asleep anywhere. He used to tumble into the river.

Only I, she was thinking, I had to move in with him, get married to him, have a child with him, start a company with him.

"It didn't last?"

"No," she said curtly.

Although the real answer was that it lasted far too long. He could never keep a job. His bosses were always fools. It was odd how life always had to give him grief. So in the end they started a white-water-rafting company. Ragnhild would look after the administrative side and join them on weekend trips now and then. Todde would manage the practical stuff. That didn't even last two seasons. By then the hotel that sold the trips had grown tired of his incompetence. It wasn't much of a funny story when you'd kept the dinner warm for too long and all the punters on the trip came down with food poisoning and filled their sleeping bags with diarrhoea.

Everyone got tired of him, she thought. Me too. I was so exhausted by all the rows and nothing ever being his fault and the promises to shape up and nothing ever changing. Apart from his drinking, which got worse. I was so tired of myself, of the person I was forced to become, the one who repaired his relationships, the one who was always sullen, the policeman, the fixer, the mother to a grown man.

The company went to pot. The equipment had to be sold for next to nothing because he hadn't looked after it. He left rubber dinghies out in the sun; he'd put a tin of roofing tar in one of them that got overturned. She started doing extra night shifts at the hospital so they could keep afloat. He was off on trips, rafting with her old friends.

I thought he needed that to get back on his feet, Ragnhild thought.

And the similarity with her brother Henry was so obvious she'd laugh if it weren't so bloody tragic.

"Not exactly an ornament, was he," she said.

She was silent after that because she sounded so bitter. What did it say in the Book of Proverbs: "A quarrelsome wife is like the dripping of a leaky roof in a rainstorm." She was thinking about Paula. She couldn't push the thought away. When Paula was six months old. The sound of her first giggle; she could split her sides laughing even though she couldn't walk. She remembered the way Paula's head had smelled; the way her tiny hand had gripped Ragnhild's finger. The sucking sensation at her nipples that travelled all the way to her womb when she was breastfeeding. Why oh why had she not understood then how happy she was with that little person.

I should have left, Ragnhild thought, and it feels as though her eyes are on fire. I should have taken my kid under my arm like Marjut the Strong and moved out. But I held out and kept holding out. Until he left.

Börje Ström made a sympathetic sound that she couldn't bear, didn't deserve. It was like a grunt of consolation. Like a reindeer cow to her calf.

She ought to press the red button on the phone. She had to end this call.

"Little one," Börje mumbled as if she really were a little child.

That was when she burst. Ripped in two like a piece of paper. The tears came with such force it was a struggle to breathe. She had nothing to block them with. She wasn't doing the weeping. She was being wept. Like the ice breaking up. She had broken and it came pouring out of her.

She shoved her back against the radiator. Hard. She forced her nails into the skin along the inside of her forearms.

"Shall I come up and hold you?" Börje asked. "I'm outside the building."

She said yes. The next minute they were standing in the hall. She was crying and he was holding her in his arms. He just rocked her as they stood there without pointless words or questions. She didn't say anything about Paula. She wasn't capable of talking about her.

All the while she was being racked by tears, she kept wavering between the idea that his embrace was salvation, or a trap.

How high a price was a woman prepared to pay to not have to cry on her own, she thought and leaned into his arms.

Anna-Maria Mella was heading for the living-room sofa. She went through the kitchen and its pizza boxes. The family had eaten and there was some left for her. She ignored the washing-up in the sink. Shut her eyes at the scraped-off bits of food filling the sieve in the drain. She couldn't be bothered to empty the dishwasher of its clean load, making up her mind that cold pizza would do just as well as hot, and cut off a few slices. She sank into the cushions and turned on the television.

One last call for work. Then it was thank you and goodnight for today. She called Sven-Erik Stålnacke.

"We're making osso buco for dinner. It's Mella!" he called.

She could hear Airi shouting in the background: "Say hello from me."

"It has to simmer for three hours," Sven-Erik said cheerfully. "The cats are going crazy. They got a little bit when I was cleaning the kitchen."

"What?" Anna-Maria laughed. "Are you letting the wine breathe as well?"

"Actually, we are!"

She told him about Galina Kireevskaya up in Riksgränsen.

"That's just awful," Sven-Erik said. "Poor girl."

"I don't think she jumped," Anna-Maria said. "We ought to bring those Russians in for questioning."

"Of course we should, but on what grounds?"

"Well, it was Russians who drove the camper van, wasn't it?"

"You can't just bring them in because they're Russians."

"They're not just any Russians," Anna-Maria said.

"True. Only, if you've got nothing on them and you bring them in . . . Let's stay calm and wait for Pohjanen's report. The risk is they'd skip town the moment you let them go."

"I know. Listen, your CI, the bloke from down south. Could you show him those photos and ask if he can identify them?"

"Of course," Sven-Erik said. "How's Rebecka doing? I heard the Pest and Björnfot booted her off the investigation."

"She's not the only one who's been working on this," Anna-Maria said and could hear how bitchy that sounded.

"Of course not, and when did I ever say anything to suggest she was?"

"Rebecka isn't a team player," Anna-Maria said. "She just hares off – making decisions and running riot – and the rest of us have to clean up after her as best we can."

"Maybe," Sven-Erik said thoughtfully.

He fell silent. Anna-Maria knew they were thinking the same thing. The time Anna-Maria had acted recklessly, drawing her gun and running straight into the Regla estate belonging to the financier Mauri Kallis. Sven-Erik had been forced to shoot a human being. It had taken him a long time to get over that.

"Rebecka isn't someone who's always thinking about saving her own skin, though," Sven-Erik said. "And when she turns everything over, things tend to get shaken loose for us to work with. You'd have to agree with that, surely?"

Rebecka, always Rebecka, Anna-Maria was thinking gloomily.

"I just get so tired of it," she said. "You and I have worked together for many years. Am I a good police officer?"

"The best," Sven-Erik said with feeling. "A good boss. A good colleague. A good detective."

"Do you miss the job?" she asked, even though she really wanted to ask if he missed her.

"Giving it up was bloody awful," he said. "Just ask Airi what it was like having me at home after I retired."

"OK," she said. "I've got to hang up. We're not having posho bucco at our place tonight. I'm lying on the sofa with cold pizza."

"You'll have time to work the saucepans when you're a pensioner," Sven-Erik assured her. "Chin up, Mella."

They ended the call and Anna-Maria folded a pizza slice dejectedly and shoved it into her mouth. The cheese had congealed, she was feeling useless and what was she watching?

Jenny appeared in the doorway.

"Hi Mum. I didn't hear you come in. How are you?"

She came and sat beside Anna-Maria.

"Alright," Anna-Maria said and tried to put on a credible smile. "Sometimes you just have a bad day at work."

"I was reading about that girl in Riksgränsen on the Internet," Jenny said. "Is that what this is about?"

"That too."

Jenny stroked her hair. Glanced at the television.

"What are you watching?"

"I've got no idea. That woman seems to be a doctor who squeezes gigantic spots on people. Tell me to get off the sofa and do something useful with my life."

"No," Jenny said. "Sometimes you just need to lie back and watch terrible telly. You can't be a capable, hard-working person all the time."

So it's come to this, Anna-Maria thought. When she was little she was always reaching her arms up. Now I'm the one reaching out to her. Longing for these moments. She's thinking about other things, wanting other people.

"Promise me you'll be careful," Anna-Maria said.

"What? About what?"

"All of it. Life. When you're overtaking juggernauts. Men."

Jenny smiled. She was so lovely when she smiled that it hurt.

"You're going to Rebecka's girls' do the day after tomorrow. Let's go into town tomorrow and buy you a dress. Come on, Mum. When was the last time you bought something for yourself?"

After dinner Sven-Erik called Simon and asked if he would mind looking at some photos, to see if he recognised the men who had driven the camper van with the sex workers.

"I don't remember," said Simon. "I was much too drunk."

That was obviously a lie. He didn't want to. Sven-Erik made one more attempt. Simon could just look at the photos anyway. It couldn't hurt. After all, he had seen them on more than one occasion. And now Galina Kireevskaya had been found dead. It wasn't at all clear it was an accident. Who knew she was working up at Riksgränsen?

But Simon remained adamant, verging on angry.

"I said I didn't want to get involved," he said. "I've no idea what those blokes looked like." Then he said: "It's a high-risk job, being a prostitute. They knew that."

Sven-Erik was filled with so much loathing he could barely breathe. He realised Simon was scared. But that couldn't be helped.

People are just so bloody spineless, he thought.

Anna-Maria Mella got off the sofa and did something useful with her life. She wiped down the sink, emptied the dishwasher and called Kristoffer Westman, the man who had got Galina Kireevskaya the job up in Riksgränsen. She already knew he worked as an electrician at LKAB and lived in a detached house in Lombola with a wife and two teenage children.

"Who the hell gave you my number?" he wanted to know when she had introduced herself. "Was it Mange Eriksson?"

"Yes," Anna-Maria said. "So if you could just answer a few questions about Galina Kireevskaya—"

"Listen," Kristoffer Westman almost screamed in her ear. "I don't know anything about her. I never met her. I don't know who she is."

"So how come she rang you and you got her a job?"

"Don't ask me!" Westman was yelling so loud she had to lower the volume on her phone. "She got my number off someone. And no, she didn't say who. But it must have been someone who knew that I know people in the area. This is what you get for being a nice guy and trying to do someone a good turn. The boys in blue turn up and put you in handcuffs."

"No-one's going to put you in handcuffs, but if you'd prefer to have this conversation at the station that would be fine. What I need to know is, who knew she was up there?"

"Fine by me. Take me down to the station. You can turn the fucking blender on. You'll get exactly the same answer. And nothing more. I didn't know her. I don't know who she got my number from. I don't know who knew she was working in Riksgränsen. I was just trying to be nice. Too nice. That a crime in your rulebook, is it?"

All of a sudden Anna-Maria felt convinced that Kristoffer Westman knew more than he was willing to admit, but protracting this call was pointless and she gave up. The bloody public. They called the police the moment anything went wrong but they never wanted to get involved themselves. Too worried about their health and their marriage and scared of what the neighbours would say, and sometimes they simply didn't want to.

We're the enemy until there's a crisis, she thought despondently.

Sven-Erik and Airi were sitting outside on the steps with a glass of wine. The evening sun was low in the sky. They were pleased to see the first patches of bare earth. They would be able to make their way through the woods before long. They talked about hiking to the cabin in Satmalajärvi, about the potatoes sprouting in the food cellar, waiting to be planted, about Airi's job: two years left and then she would be a pensioner too.

"That was the best posho bucco I've ever eaten," Sven-Erik said contentedly.

"Poor Rebecka," Airi suddenly said. "She needs her job. Not like me just counting the days."

Sven-Erik nodded.

"Maybe we should ask her round to dinner," Airi said. "Do you think she'd want to spend time with us old folk?"

At that moment a car came along the main road. It slowed at their house and the window was rolled down. A woman wearing sunglasses stuck her head out.

"Sven-Erik Stålnacke," she asked. "Where does he live?"

"Here," Airi answered. "And he's home."

Like a cartoon figure she pointed exaggeratedly at Sven-Erik, who raised a hand in greeting.

The woman in the car waved as well, steered the car round and drove into their front yard. Airi and Sven-Erik were now able to see there was an old man in the back. The woman jumped out and opened the rear door.

"Hi there," she said to Sven-Erik and Airi. "Sorry to disturb you. Hang on, Dad, just wait a bit."

She helped the old man find solid ground beneath his feet and took his weight as he stood up. He put his cane down and shook her off.

He may have tottered but he was smartly dressed. A pressed shirt and coat. His chin was shaved smooth, his silver hair neatly trimmed. His daughter stayed by his side, ready to catch him if he fell as he slowly approached the steps.

"Sven-Erik Stålnacke?" he asked in a voice that was twenty years younger than he appeared. "I read in the paper that you were investigating the murder of Raimo Koskela, Börje Ström's father. I have a confession to make."

His name was Karl Andersson, a native of Piilijärvi. His daughter's name was Emma, her married surname Lindskog. Karl said yes to half a glass of wine while Emma had to assure them three times that she just wanted water. Airi put an alcohol-free beer on the table in case she changed her mind.

They admired the view and Sven-Erik's home-made smoker in the front yard. Then Karl began to speak.

"From what I've read, Börje Ström's father disappeared on June 16th 1962," he began. "And he was recently discovered in a freezer on Palosaari. Shot dead. With ammunition from a handgun."

"That's correct," Sven-Erik said.

"I was an army officer at that time," Karl Andersson said. "On June 16th that year some friends and I were practising our marksmanship at the regimental shooting range. I then drove to my parents' home in Piilijärvi. We always spent our summers there. In any case, I had my gun with me. I didn't go home and lock it up. I left it in the car on the passenger side. That sounds like madness, but . . ."

He took a sip of wine, pulled a handkerchief out of his pocket and wiped his mouth. He was shaking his head as if the memory were something he needed to shake off, get rid of.

". . . those were very different times, Dad," Emma Lindskog said, and put her hand over her father's.

He jerked his hand away.

"I wasn't born in the Dark Ages," he yelled. "There were rules, for heaven's sake, even then, whatever you young people may think. As an officer you kept your gun at home in three pieces. The pistol, the magazine and the ammunition had to be kept separate. There can be no excuses."

He took a break to allow his breathing to calm down.

"That evening I went out to the car to get the cigarettes I'd left in the glove compartment. And discovered the gun was gone."

Airi and Emma exchanged surreptitious maternal glances. Just the thought that a child might have got hold of it.

"The car wasn't locked, I take it?" Sven-Erik asked.

Karl Andersson came out with a joyless laugh.

"Lock the car? In your own parents' yard? People don't even do that nowadays. Obviously I was terrified. I asked my wife, but she hadn't seen it. Our eldest child, Ville, had just begun to crawl. Emma here wasn't even born yet, so it couldn't have been them. I knew I had to report the theft to my superiors. But I put it off. Heavens above, I could barely sleep. I kept cursing my own stupidity. Only, who would have thought—"

"May I ask—" Sven-Erik began.

"Just let me finish telling you," Karl Andersson said. "In the morning the gun was back in the car. On the passenger seat."

"You're certain this was June 16th?" Sven-Erik asked.

"Absolutely. Brazil won the World Cup final against Czechoslovakia on the 17th. The entire family was gathered in the kitchen listening to the commentary. All I could think about was the gun. I thought someone might have stolen it and then changed their mind. Or some kids had borrowed the weapon to play with. Only, wouldn't they have emptied the magazine? In any case I decided not to report the incident. I believed that nothing serious had occurred. I just thanked my lucky stars and I was never careless with it again. You have to understand there was nothing in the paper about Raimo Koskela having disappeared, or anything about a murder. As far as I knew, no-one had used the gun for any funny business."

"And then Raimo Koskela turned up," Airi said. "Murdered."

"What sort of handgun was it?" Sven-Erik asked.

"A Kamrat 40," Karl Andersson said. "Pistol model 40, to be precise."

"It no longer exists?"

"Oh no, it was destroyed long ago. It just seemed to me like a really unfortunate coincidence."

"Looking back, was there anyone in the village you think might have been involved in this business? Someone with a link to Koskela or the boxing club?"

"No, they were ordinary decent people. I've made a list of everyone who lived nearby."

He took from his pocket a handwritten lined A4 sheet of paper, folded in four. Sven-Erik skimmed through the list of names. They told him nothing.

"I knew them all," Andersson said with a glance at the list. "You won't find a murderer among them."

"Thanks for coming to let me know," Sven-Erik said. "Thanks to both of you. Though prosecuting the murder is barred by statute, it's important to find out what happened, for Börje Ström's sake. And everyone makes mistakes."

Karl Andersson got to his feet with some effort.

"I made two mistakes," he said. "The first was not to drive home with the gun, take it apart and lock it away. The other was to decide on a version of the truth that provided me with an illusory sense of being at peace. I persuaded myself that the gun had not been used for anything bad while it was missing. In order to spare myself having to report the incident."

They thanked their hosts for the drinks and drove away. Sven-Erik read the names on the list once again: Lindmark, Olsson, Nilsson, Nutti, Järvinen. Not one of them rang any kind of bell. And all the same, there was something there he couldn't quite dredge up, couldn't put his finger on.

Rebecka Martinsson ended her day in bed with her phone. The Brat was already dreaming in his. His tongue was hanging outside his mouth. His tail was thumping as his paws jerked.

She went onto Krister's sister's Facebook page. A film showed Tintin and Roy running around Krister as though he had been off to war, presumed dead, and had now returned. She was looking at his legs, the dogs wove in and out of the image, she could hear him telling them to calm down, laughter in his voice. Krister's sister was egging them on: "Who's happy then? Who's happy then?"

Then she went onto Marit Törmä's Instagram. No photo of a ring, at least.

She dropped onto her back and stared at the ceiling. It was perfectly empty and white.

WEDNESDAY 4TH MAY

Pohjanen rang just as Anna-Maria got out of the car in front of the police building.

"I'm sorry," he croaked without further ado. "There is nothing to indicate that Galina Kireevskaya was subjected to violence. Everything suggests that she fell or jumped out of that hotel window."

"Bugger," Anna-Maria said and felt depression digging in its claws. "No defensive wounds? No bruising? Nothing under her nails?"

She ran her key card over the lock and opened the door.

"Would I have said there is no evidence to suggest anything other than an accident or suicide if I had found defensive wounds on her body?" Pohjanen snapped. "Don't waste a dying man's time, Mella."

He cleared his throat and changed his tone.

"It would have been quick in any case," he said, sounding almost gentle. "She ... hgrrrr ... cracked her temporal bone in the fall. Haemorrhage between the cranium and the meninges. The bleeding spread and compressed the brain against the opposite wall of the skull. Ultimately the flow was forced down towards the back of the neck where the brain turns into the spinal cord. That's where ..."

He had to stop and catch his breath.

"Unfortunately that's where the respiration centre is located, and when it became compressed, death was instantaneous," he concluded.

"That's a comfort, I suppose."

Anna-Maria was thinking about the two Russians. It would have been easy for them to chuck a woman with the body of a twelve-year-old out of a window without her being able to put up any resistance.

"Is it impossible she was thrown out?" she asked.

"Of course not," Pohjanen said. "I said there were no indications that she had been subjected to violence. But there's one thing you should know about bruises, Mella. They can take their time. I had a woman on my table once. Her bastard bloke had kicked apart every organ in her body. But she didn't have a single bruise, even though she was torn up inside. She died so quickly there wasn't time for any haematomas to form. Have you heard anything from Martinsson?"

"Uh, no. You do know that—"

"Yeah, yeah, I read about it on the Internet. She's been booted off the investigation. I'm guessing the Pest threw a party. Tell her to ring me if you see her. She's not answering her phone. She's got time now to devote herself to Börje Ström's father. I want to get a much clearer idea of what happened to him. You're going to a party over there tomorrow, aren't you? You can tell her then!"

"Uh, not sure I want to . . ." Anna-Maria began.

But by then Pohjanen had ended the call.

". . . be your secretary," she said to thin air.

She looked up at the sky. It had clouded over. A heavy grey gloom overhead.

Nyrkin-Jussi said hello to the staff at Indian Summer Court as he made his way along the corridor to Sisu-Sikke's room. It was so peaceful here in the mornings. The scent of freshly brewed coffee, the staff getting things ready in the kitchen.

"I just took in his breakfast," Hiba told him. "He said he wasn't hungry."

"I'll make sure he eats something," Nyrkin-Jussi said.

Hiba patted his arm as he went into the room.

Sisu-Sikke was sitting in the wheelchair, his breakfast in front of him. It had already been cut up into small pieces; he was wearing a clean shirt and his hair had been combed. The potted plants had been watered.

As ever Nyrkin-Jussi was moved by how well looked after Sikke was in this care home.

"*Rakastan*, darling," he said. "You've got to eat something. Or else you'll go down in the first round."

Sisu-Sikke smiled. But there was a glint of sadness in his eyes.

"I've been thinking," Nyrkin-Jussi said as he moved around the room turning the lights on; the room got so gloomy otherwise when it was overcast outside. "Why don't we ask Börje Ström to dinner at home with us?"

Sisu-Sikke shook his head.

"I'd deal with everything," Nyrkin-Jussi insisted. "We'll arrange transport for you. And you could sleep at home for one night; that bed gets so lonely. And it would be nice to reminisce. He's never told us, has he . . . I'd really like to hear him tell us in person about the Olympic gold. Stop shaking your head. You'll lose your hair if you keep doing that. What's the matter with you?

8 SEPTEMBER 1972

Nyrkin-Jussi has gone with Sisu-Sikke to his parents' home in Kuoksu. It's time to dig up the potatoes. He was over there at the end of June to help with the haymaking. Sisu-Sikke's family like him. Sikke's brothers say they've ended up with an extra brother and pretend to complain about their mother making him her favourite.

The understanding is that Jussi and Sikke are best friends as well as coaches at the North Pole boxing club. The family may know more. They probably do. Sikke's parents have stopped going on about him needing to meet someone. And his mother makes up a bed on the pull-out couch and another on a mattress on the floor in the box room, while the rest of the adult children get squeezed in here and there around the house. What Jussi and Sikke get up to at night is their business as long as nothing beyond a close friendship is openly displayed.

The family appreciate Nyrkin-Jussi's strength; he can do the work of three men, even though he's "on the small side". He is cheerful and full of team spirit, and eats like a whole company of soldiers. The latter may be the best quality of all in the eyes of Sisu-Sikke's mother, who never stops trying to coax him to eat even more. "Dig in if you like it," she says, and serves him another round. "You just peck at your food like a bird."

The potato tops have frozen, and it is hard work having to hunch over to chop away the leaves and then tug the cold withered plants out of the soil before digging up and sorting the potatoes. The large ones go into a separate pile, while the small ones are kept for the animals. It's the sort of job that really makes your back ache. It's also all hands on deck so the kids have got Thursday and Friday off school. They light the sauna in the evenings so they can sweat out the day's exertions.

On this particular day, though, they are going to stop work early. Börje Ström has reached the Olympic final, and coverage starts at 5 p.m. Sweden already has four golds: Ulrika Knape in diving, two for Gunnar Larsson in the pool and one for Ragnar Skanåker at the shooting range. But the light heavyweight final, that beats everything else. The whole country is seething with excitement. Norrbotten has almost boiled dry. An assassination took place in the Olympic Village just as Börje was securing the silver medal. On September 5, the Palestinian terrorist group Black September stormed the village in Munich, killing two Israeli athletes and taking nine hostage. The games were stopped, and on September 6 West German police and army troops fired on the terrorists. Black September executed their hostages and a West German policeman. Five members of Black September were killed. Cancelling the remainder of the Games was seriously discussed. In the end it was announced they would continue, and that any other outcome would be a victory for terrorism. The boxing final would go ahead. The headlines could not have been any bigger: "Börje Ström's Going to Win – Not Terrorism."

They abandon the potato field and clean off in the sauna at two. And at four they eat fried perch and potatoes. Finally it is five o'clock, the time has come.

Everyone squeezes into the living room, some of them find seats on the sofa bed, chairs are brought in from the kitchen, the youngsters spread out on rag rugs. The television is placed on the folding table. Sisu-Sikke's brothers spent a good deal of yesterday messing around with the aerial on the roof to get the best reception.

Sisu-Sikke's eldest brother hands out beers to the adults, the kids get Trocadero after promising not to spill a drop. The children have been infected by the excitement and keep reading aloud the Danish joke on the Tuborg cans. They giggle and roll around, repeating the comical slogan until Sikke's eldest brother starts yelling and threatens them with being sent out of the living room.

"We should have been there," Nyrkin-Jussi says for the hundredth time when Börje Ström comes on screen.

As a rule, coaches accompany their Olympic competitors. But the Swedish Boxing Association decided a coach from Stockholm would go with Börje instead, because the Stockholmers had some useless welterweight going and one coach was enough in their view. There was

343

nothing to be done about it. Börje called them just before the semi-final and told them that he had hardly seen the coach at all. Which was just as well as he was completely clueless about the way Börje boxed, all he did was call out a lot of pointless comments during the match and get in the way. Only after the last victory, once Börje had got the silver, the same man had his arm around him, grinning at the cameras. What a bloody prat.

The bell rings.

Emilio Martinez, the Cuban, comes out all guns blazing. He's six foot one and eighty-one kilos of muscle. His right is devastating; first he lashes out with his left and then his right slams into you like a piston. Börje is driven back, unable to counter-attack. Being forced to back away leaves him feeling stressed and just inside the second minute he lowers his guard to block a left hook. That creates exactly the opening Martinez needs, and the Cuban's razor-sharp right cross hits the mark perfectly. There's a howl in the Munich stadium as Börje Ström hits the floor.

There's a howl too in the living room in Kuoksu. The referee has started counting. Börje Ström gets to his feet at three, and Martinez is on him like a hailstorm. The rest of the round Börje keeps his forearms raised to block the other man's punches. The Cuban manages to get in a few blows. One lands above the left eye.

Two of the sisters-in-law leave the room, it's too ghastly to watch; they can't bear it. They call out from the kitchen: "Is he bleeding?" "What's happening?" Their husbands are threatening divorce if they don't shut up.

Börje comes out in the second round with ointment on his eyebrow. Now he has a feel for that right piston. It never stops coming at him, but Börje is moving in slowly, blocking and throwing his opponent off balance, landing some apparently ineffective jabs on the other

344

man's right shoulder. Nyrkin-Jussi and Sisu-Sikke exchange glances. That's a good move, smart. It doesn't lead to any points, but that right has got to be disarmed. Towards the end of the round both of them start forcing the pace. Along with the one in Kuoksu, the audience in Munich get to their feet and cheer them on. Börje is pummelling him with uppercuts, slamming in hooks, aiming for the kidneys. Martinez is clearly targeting Börje's already damaged eyebrow. He knows Börje is a bleeder, and his second is bound to have told him to pepper that cut.

The audience in the living room are screaming so loud it drowns out the commentator.

What happens then should never have been allowed to happen. Martinez lands a punch that splits Börje's eyebrow open. A gush of blood pours into his left eye. Börje pulls back. Martinez is alternating blows to the head and the gut. Börje is crouching, backing off. Peering out of his single eye.

Nyrkin-Jussi yells at the set that the ref should be cautioning him about blows below the belt. Then he shouts at Sisu-Sikke:

"Do you see that? Look at the Cuban's shoulder."

"I'm looking."

Martinez's shoulder muscle twitches before each right-hander.

Nyrkin-Jussi is tearing at his hair and calling out impotently:

"His shoulder, his shoulder!"

Only there's no point expecting that pathetic excuse for a coach to see it and help Börje to do so as well.

The seconds keep dragging until the gong finally sounds. Börje finds his way to his corner. He is bleeding like a stuck pig; the white towels go to work. Sisu-Sikke usually uses red ones, so the opponent is unsure of the lie of the land. But he isn't there. He's thousands of kilometres away. The cutman is on hand and the doctor is examining him. Is it all over? Will there even be a final round?

Sisu-Sikke gets up and moves over to the television. He stands to one side so as not to be in the way of the others. He looks at Börje, only at Börje. And when Börje is no longer on screen, he can see Börje in his mind's eye. His lips form words the others cannot make out.

Sisu-Sikke's mother gets up as well. Her eyes are huge with worry. She is the first person in the room to understand what he is up to. Being able to stop bleeding goes back a long way in their family. It is said that her great-grandfather on her mother's side, a settler in Sockenträsk, looked after a war horse following the 1808–9 Russian occupation. The horse had twenty-eight sabre cuts and was headed for a painful death but he stopped the flow of blood and cared for the animal all winter long following the surrender. The settler was never himself after that incident, though. He became the queer fellow people took their sick animals to while his wife had to manage the forestry and the farm and the household. He was mostly to be found brooding in the stables. He died there of anaemia the same year their fourth child, Sisu-Sikke's grandmother, was born. The horse lived to well over thirty and helped the widow to transport timber and do the spring ploughing. It grazed freely in the woods during the summers. While the man was alive it always came back to the farm during its summer holiday to say hello to the person who had saved its life. Her own mother had always had difficulty refusing the villagers who came to her with their ailments. She would sleep for several hours afterwards; the children had to manage the evening milking. Though the gift has never been particularly strong inside her, she used it on the children when they were small, that was the extent of it. But she's perfectly aware that Sigvard possesses it too.

"*Varota*," she says now to her son standing beside the television, trying to stop the flow of blood from Börje Ström. Be careful.

Then the bell sounds for the final round. Börje comes back into the ring with a face that is as good as new. A plaster and some sticky stuff appear to have stopped the bleeding. He looks composed. Everyone realises he's behind on points. He's got three minutes left.

Delivered from his blindness he goes on the attack. He hammers home a short left and then his right at the other man's head, following it up with a left punch to the temple and then a right at the body. Martinez dances away, blocking with his right, all he has to do is keep out of the way and victory is his. Only then he gets Börje on the ropes. He steps in close.

"He's expecting the right, he's expecting the right," Nyrkin-Jussi shouts.

And it comes. But Börje noticed that twitch of the shoulder that immediately precedes it.

Lightning fast, at almost the same moment that Martinez launches his piston, Börje slams in his short right and lands a perfect blow on Martinez's chin. Martinez's legs give way beneath him like in a slow-motion film; his right arm is still extended when Börje hammers him with an extra hook as a bon voyage. Then the Cuban is down. Not like a fir tree; he collapses like a little flower. The floor receives him mercifully. The ref is counting. The roar of the crowd in the Munich stadium reaches the rafters. In the living room in Kuokso everyone is holding their breath until the ref has counted to ten.

And the match is over. The referee raises Börje's hand towards the sky. The commentators are yelling about a miracle for Sweden.

Nyrkin-Jussi is grinning shamelessly for all to see. The women pour back in from the kitchen.

Sisu-Sikke is still standing by the set, white as a sheet. He doesn't say much and goes to bed early.

*

Nyrkin-Jussi wakes in the night. Sisu-Sikke is not lying beside him.

The clock shows twenty past two. Jussi pulls on his clothes and steps into the darkness of an autumn night.

"Sikke," he calls quietly.

The barn door is open. He weighs up for a moment whether to go back inside and put some shoes on, but he is too worried. The ground is freezing cold beneath his feet.

He finds Sisu-Sikke among the cows. He has turned a plastic bucket upside down and is sitting on it beside Omena. All the cows are chewing away in the darkness, they've been given a stack of hay, presumably to stop them lowing during the night. Sisu-Sikke is leaning his head against Omena's side and when Nyrkin-Jussi says his name he does not respond.

He understands in some way that he mustn't disturb him and that Sisu-Sikke is getting energy from that bellweather cow Omena; that he is healing himself.

Nyrkin-Jussi fetches a bale of hay to sit on. He puts it on the floor so he can lean against one of the calf pens. He is exactly far enough away that he can still make out Sikke's shape in the darkness. The chewing of the cows and the sound of their breathing are rocking him to rest.

It occurs to him that Sikke isn't in any danger. And that Omena is looking after him now.

When he wakes at dawn, Sisu-Sikke is gone. He gets up on stiff legs. He cracks his neck and steals back inside the box room. Sisu-Sikke is asleep on the pull-out sofa.

It is only later during that autumn that Nyrkin-Jussi discovers Sisu-Sikke has changed. Sikke has always been an ambidextrous boxer. Just as fast and strong with both hands. This has proved very useful when preparing one of the lads to face a southpaw. But after the Olympic finals he has become orthodox, right-handed. They never discuss it.

Not even thirty years later when Sikke suffers his first stroke and loses control of his left side to such an extent that he has to teach himself to manage simple tasks using only his right hand. He swears when he fumbles with his shirt buttons and stops having cheese on his breakfast round of bread because he can't slice it; he ties his laces and opens screw caps uttering oaths that would make a cooper blench. And woe betide Nyrkin-Jussi if he tries to help.

"Why don't you want us to have Börje round for dinner?" Nyrkin-Jussi asked as he poured out a cup of coffee for himself as well. "Are you cross with him? Listen, you've got to eat something."

"Not . . . not . . ."

Sisu-Sikke shook his head again and rolled over to the counter-top where his pointing board lay, a basic wooden board with the letters of the alphabet burned into it. A little pointer was attached by a cord, so it wouldn't go missing. Sisu-Sikke put the board on the kitchen table and pointed out his message letter by letter.

NOT ANGRY IT WAS MY FAULT BS DAD DIED YOU WILL LEAVE ME

As soon as Rebecka Martinsson woke on Wednesday morning, she found herself reflecting on her decision not to return to her job at the prosecutor's office. How was it that other people seemed to just plough straight ahead through life without continually finding themselves in dead ends, their relationships abruptly cut off?

The Brat laid his head on the edge of her bed and stared. Are we going out? Are you getting up? Is something going to happen?

"I'm coming," she said, wishing for a life in which there was no-one wanting things from her, not even a potted plant.

She had missed calls from two journalists who still wanted her comments on being removed from the investigation.

"Up you get," she said to herself.

She was going to make coffee and then she would do the cleaning. Maria Taube and her friends were supposed to be arriving tomorrow. The house looked like a tip.

She put a load of laundry on and gathered all the empty bottles. There were quite a few. She put half of them in a black rubbish bag and chucked it in the back of the car. She took the rest out to the old barn. She couldn't face driving the entire crop to the recycling depot. There were so many people keeping an eye on her.

They all know who the monkey is, she was thinking. The monkey in the cage is suffering from depression and is chewing on its tail.

The Brat was running around, sticking his muzzle into the deep snow.

She was debating whether she should shut him in. God knows what he might find to consume now it was thawing. Dead mice and other little treats Nature chose to offer.

She shook out the rag rugs and threw them outside onto the snow, then dusted the place with a damp cloth, Grandma's voice in her head: "A feather duster, huh, all you're doing is whirling the stuff around." She vacuumed herself into a sweat, the sofa and cushions were covered in dog hair.

When the washing machine beeped, she put on her skis and tied the washing line between the trees. She picked up the laundry basket and, skiing across the soft snow, hung it up. It was hard going and she broke through several times. But at least she had got the place properly clean.

"I'll soon be boiling up my own soap out of birch ash and fat," she said to the Brat, who kept standing on her skis so as not to sink in the snow as well.

She peered up at the sky. Just as long as it didn't start snowing.

She was thinking about her grandmother. How did she manage to keep the place so clean and so cosy? Why did she not spare herself the bother of the potted plants? How had she managed to sow seeds every year, not just for the vegetables but for the decorative stuff? How did she keep the barns tidy, along with the space under the sink while also ironing the pillowcases and changing the curtains?

Rebecka had always been behind with everything, the bills and the cleaning and buying new tights. The job had always come first.

She thought about her mother, wondering what she had been like. Stuck up, according to people in Kurravaara, that much was obvious. And, of course, they thought that about Rebecka too. Some of them still called her the lawyer, just as they had ever since she moved away to study.

Don't think about that now, Grandma said in her head. *Ei se kanatte,* what's the point?

Her grandmother had lived her whole life based on strategies like that. No point harping on the past. Sufficient unto the day . . . Time will show the way. Sayings and Bible quotes one after the other.

And it worked, too, Rebecka thought. Maybe it was a better way.

Grandma's life had been a succession of losses. Her siblings, her husband and son, they'd all gone before her. And things were different in those days. No-one did therapy, or mindfulness or yoga. You went into the woods and cried, pulled yourself together and went back to work. There was none of the current faith in the healing power of talk.

And aren't I just like that myself? Rebecka was thinking while she scrubbed the kitchen floor on her knees.

When I stopped going to therapy, she added in her mind, and dipped the brush in the hot soapy water. Stopped, though? I barely started. Wasn't that exactly how I felt about it? What's the point of rooting around in all this? The past is the past. Mum and Dad were two people who suffered losses and had shortcomings of their own. They reached for each other as though they were drowning, and neither of them could save the other.

And soon everyone will be gone who could tell me anything. Sivving. And Ragnhild Pekkari.

She shoved away any thought of Ragnhild Pekkari while pushing aside the boxes of evidence from the Pekkaris' firm. That creep von Pest would have to send someone round to collect them once they'd decided to cancel the search warrant.

Now you don't have to open all the boxes and go through the contents, she thought. You can just not give a toss about that either.

The house was starting to smell freshly cleaned. She was going to pick some birch branches to put in the big vase.

The Brat had retired to the kitchen sofa. He sighed forlornly and gave her long looks. How long are you going to go on being this boring, he was asking.

Grandma used to sing while she cleaned. And take coffee breaks.

The washing machine beeped again. She would hang up the next load and then take a coffee break, ring Sivving and ask if he wanted to come round.

"I hate this so much!"

Anna-Maria Mella was trying to pull off the dress inside the changing room. It had got stuck half-way. She was bent forward with the dress over her head. She couldn't see. It felt like she was suffocating. Sweat was making the fabric stick to her body.

If I pull any harder it will split, she thought. That could be expensive.

"Let's just forget this," she said to Jenny, who was standing outside. "Let's go and have lunch."

Jenny pulled the curtain open and came in.

"Close it, close it," Anna-Maria yelled from inside the dress.

"Oh Mum!" Jenny laughed. "I have closed it. Hang on and I'll help. Just wait, I said. Stop moving."

"Get me out of this bloody dress," Anna-Maria screamed.

"Is everything alright?" the shop assistant asked in a high voice. "Would you like a different size?"

"No, but a crowbar would be nice," Anna-Maria groaned.

She got out of the dress with Jenny's help. She stared at it with loathing as Jenny put it back on its hanger.

"You were supposed to show me when you'd put it on," Jenny said. "Wasn't it any good?"

"No, it was," Anna-Maria said. "On the hanger it looked really good."

"Try this one then. You've got gorgeous shoulders."

Jenny held up a flowery evening dress with a halter neck.

"It's too long," Anna-Maria muttered apprehensively.

"I'll help you hem it. Come on, Mum, trying on clothes is fun."

"No, it's not," Anna-Maria said, pointing her index finger at her daughter. "It may be fun when you're twenty. But when your arse has dropped to the back of your knees . . ."

"Oh, stop it," Jenny said severely. "No body hatred."

Anna-Maria pulled the dress on obediently. A madwoman stared back at her from the mirror.

"Shh!" Anna-Maria said. "Now I'm in touch with my inner goddess. Quick, we need to burn some incense."

"Yeah, yeah, take it off," Jenny said. "And stop whining."

"I'm putting a little heart around your attitude," Anna-Maria continued, wrenching herself out of dress number two.

Dress number three turned her into a cake trying to escape from the patisserie. Dress number four puffed out at the back because she was too short.

"The bells! The bells!" she said, limping around the changing room.

Anna-Maria refused to try dress number five.

"I've got pants that are longer," she complained.

"I give up," Jenny said. "Forget the party. You don't have to go if it's going to be this much of a problem."

"I do have to go," Anna-Maria said despondently. "Especially now Rebecka's been taken off the investigation. Not going would look so pointed. You've got to help me."

"Pull yourself together then. This one."

"That's just a sleeve. OK, OK."

The dress was as blue as twilight. And it fitted like a glove.

"That is so lovely it's sick," Jenny decided.

354

Anna-Maria agreed. She inspected it from behind as well. Then she examined the price tag.

"Nineteen hundred! Has it got jewels sewn inside or what?"

Jenny initiated Operation Persuasion. When had Anna-Maria last bought a dress? Since they had the same shoe size, Jenny might consider lending her best pair.

In the end Jenny called Robert who said yes.

"Alright then," Anna-Maria said finally, hoping she had enough in her account. This was going to be a very expensive party.

Half the cost of the dress could be written off just by the kiss Jenny pressed against her cheek. They laughed and found they had time for lunch before Jenny had to go back to school.

The Lingonberry King's son Spike Mäki had aged in a way that made Börje Ström feel bad. Huge but no muscles. Pale as unbaked dough, with rings under his eyes. He had been losing his hair; the little that was left was too long. If Spike hadn't been the person he had come to see, Börje would never have recognised him.

"The old stream in the flesh! It's me, Spike!"

Three men were working in the factory where they produced portable cabins for construction sites. They were standing by their machines wearing ear protectors. Spike had to shout over the noise:

"It's gotta be ages. Absolute ages. Lads! Lads!"

The machines were turned off one by one; the ear protectors were pulled down around their necks or shoved further up their heads.

"Let me introduce you to a real celebrity," Spike called and shook Börje's upper arm with his left hand while shaking Börje's hand with his right. "Börje Ström, Olympic gold medallist 1972, three national championships."

The others came over to say hello. Someone told him his cousin's kids were training at the North Pole Club and took a selfie. Spike squeezed into the frame, putting his arm around Börje, so they got a photo of him as well.

"And let me tell you I got some good ones in on this legend back in the day." He aimed some shadow blows at Börje who counter-attacked in similar fashion.

Börje said nothing about that. Spike had not been much of a boxer. He had been physically fit at the time but his reach was poor. Incapable of reading his opponents. It was like that with a lot of people. Everyone could have been a star if they'd just buckled down, if they hadn't been hindered by parents who had no interest, or one thing or the other. Börje had long ago stopped getting irritated by that kind of gibberish.

"So maybe you could fight a match then?" one of the lads suggested.

The others were grinning behind their hands.

"Right." Spike laughed. "I'm a true heavyweight now."

"Really terrible about your dad," one of the men said.

Börje grunted something grateful in response.

"Anyway, I'm off for lunch," Spike announced. "We're going to talk over old times so I might not be back before midnight."

Spike had booked a table at Ripan, he insisted on treating Börje. He was on first-name terms with the waitress.

"So you've got famous company today, have you?" she said.

They sat at one of the tables by the window.

"The best table," Spike said with a wide gesture. "They know me here, so I get a bit of special treatment."

Börje looked around; he couldn't see anything to distinguish this table from any of the others.

This was his first real opportunity to get a proper look at Spike. It was an old habit: assessing his opponent in the ring, getting his measure. Spike was a talker, Börje couldn't remember if he had been before. Their eyes would meet every now and then, and Börje felt he could sense something sly, untrustworthy, in them.

Though not just in relation to him, Börje. Something untrustworthy in relation to Spike as well. Börje found himself thinking about who this man really was under all the gibberish, all the jokes about his weight. None of it fit, it was all disconnected. As far as Spike was concerned as well.

"If you're moving back to Kiruna, just say the word," Spike said reaching for the bread basket. "I can arrange a job and a flat. The business is going great guns."

Börje listened with half an ear. Spike told him they sold portable cabins, construction-site barracks and tiny homes to the whole of northern Europe. They had more orders than they could meet. And in Kiruna more and more workers were commuting and not living in town, so the areas of barrack housing were expanding. Not that Spike was complaining. That was the future calling. A highly mobile labour force. With their families parked in one place. True, they paid their local taxes elsewhere, but the local authority didn't have to pay to educate their kids and so forth. Everyone was a winner. Not the environmentalists and the Left, of course, they were always opposed to everything anyway.

"Adapt or die, isn't it?" Spike said, his mouth full of bread. "Change with the times or go under."

Some people, Börje Ström was thinking, they seemed to be put together out of sayings like that, stock phrases. They were cars held together by their bumper stickers.

It had turned overcast and the shadows had disappeared. Spindly birches were attempting to stick out against the milk-white countryside.

The waitress took their order.

"The elk-mince steak," Spike decided. "And—"

"—generous helpings of the sauce and potatoes," the waitress filled in with a smile. "I know."

"I was going to say 'and your phone number'."

"My phone battery is flat," the waitress said with a wink and moved away.

"I'm a catch, you know," Spike called after her and patted his stomach. "You get two for one."

Spike went on talking, he was telling the story of Ripan. This happened to be the site of the washing lake in old Kiruna, did Börje know that? The women used to rinse their winter laundry here. After that it had been an outdoor swimming pool for several years, and then they rebuilt the camping site as a hotel.

"Kiruna is growing by leaps and bounds. And that is one train you definitely do not want to miss."

Spike had finished off the rolls and was now shovelling down crispbread he'd buttered while they were waiting for their food. He reached for the butter dish on the neighbouring table. Börje was waiting for a gap to appear. It felt like the stand-off between Ingo Johansson and the giant Ed Sanders from Los Angeles in the heavyweight final of 1952. Ingo kept out of reach. Backing off, sidestepping, dancing. In the hope Sanders would tire. Sanders had reached the final by knockouts, but he could never get at him. They kept moving around the ring but after two rounds neither had landed a punch.

The elk steak came and was devoured; lunch was approaching its end. A natural opportunity just never arose. In the middle of a sentence about the deposits in the new ore body that ran from Luossa to Nukutsjärvi, Börje said:

"Listen, my dad . . ."

Spike appeared distracted as he checked his mobile.

". . . you were older than me after all," Börje went on, "you'd been boxing at the club for a while. Did you know him? I mean, he did do some work for your dad, didn't he?"

Spike wiped his face with his hand.

"Your dad was like thirty something then, I guess," he said. "We didn't exactly know the old guys. I just don't remember."

"I was talking to this guy called Lars Grahn; he's at the same home as Sisu-Sikke. He said that Dad was involved in some kind of fiddle with a bloke called Forsling. And they were selling fake currency to the Russian mafia and Dad was shot by them, the Russian mafia. It's true I get a bit punchy, you know, from all the blows I've taken, but that doesn't make any sense."

"I couldn't say, only there's a load of stuff we don't know about our dads," Spike said.

He pushed his plate away and started moving his glass, the low-alcohol beer bottle and the salt cellar around.

"Believe me, when you're the son of the Lingonberry King, you've heard things you really don't want to know. There's been many a time I thought I should have moved away from this town and . . . made a fresh start, I suppose. It was pretty much the Wild West in those days though. All the older guys at the club were involved in some shady stuff now and then. That's just the way things were."

"So you think Grahn was telling the truth?"

Spike shrugged.

"I was fourteen, you know, when your dad disappeared."

"I'd really like to talk to your dad," Börje Ström said. "Only he seems to have a small army guarding him."

Spike shook his head slowly.

"He's almost ninety. And not in the best of health. When I see him, he can only manage ten minutes at a time. And it's really no army."

He laughed.

"Just his wife and some people who look after the place. That's essential. There are people who go round robbing old people whose houses are out of the way like that."

"Get me five minutes with him."

"I can't get you anything. Wouldn't it be best just to forget all that?"

Spike nodded at Börje's tattooed arm and produced a hollow laugh.

"I mean, what are you going to do if you find out he was involved in something dirty? Have every single tattoo removed with a laser?"

"Is that what you've done? With your dad? Not given a shit?"

"As much as I could."

The salt cellar switched places with the beer bottle once again.

The waitress was back with the bill. Spike gave her a good tip and she exclaimed in surprise:

"Thank you so much."

The moment she had turned away Spike got to his feet.

"Well, I suppose if I'm going to get anything done today."

He reached for his jacket that was hanging over the back of his chair.

"You don't mind making your own way back to the hotel, do you?" he said. "It's not that far."

"No, that's fine. Thank you for lunch."

"Don't mention it, let's do this again," Spike said, avoiding his eyes.

"You could ask him in any case," Börje insisted while they walked towards the exit. "Ask if he'd be willing to see me. Five minutes. I could always just drive out there and knock on the door."

They had reached Spike's car.

"You just don't get it," Spike said. "Do not drive to my dad's house. Promise me that!"

Börje stayed in the car park watching Spike's car drive away.

The gloom overhead appeared to be getting darker. Maybe it was going to snow.

He was thinking once again about Ingo's title fight in Helsinki. After two rounds the ref had raised Sanders' fist in the air. Ingo was disqualified, and he didn't even get the silver medal despite coming second. Börje was racked by a sense of powerlessness.

You want to believe in matches that aren't dirty, he was thinking. And you believe in straight talking and cards on the table. But the real power is so far away, so far outside the ring. It remains inaccessible. Which is why we keep pummelling each other.

He called Ragnhild. She answered immediately.

"Come over," she said. "You can have a coffee after your meal."

"Even though I'm a curse?" he felt brave enough to joke.

"What's one curse more or less," she said. "You just get over here."

Anna-Maria Mella was sitting at her desk when her eye was caught by the cloth-handled bag next to the door. She closed the door and unwrapped the dress from its tissue paper. Was it really as gorgeous as she remembered? Or had she paid nineteen hundred just for the thrill of going shopping with Jenny?"

She undid her trousers and let them fall to her ankles. She shrugged off her top and pulled on the dress, turning towards the mirror.

Just then there was a knock on the door and Sonja the receptionist popped her head in.

"Oh my god, Anna-Maria!" she exclaimed. "Don't you look lovely! What a dress!"

"Cost a fortune," Anna-Maria said, pulling on her trousers and buttoning them up. "When am I ever going to wear it?"

"At Rebecka's dinner tomorrow?"

"Yeah, but after that? You'll have to remind Robert to bury me in it. So it gets put to some damn use."

"I've got a call to put through to you," Sonja said. "I just wanted to tell you that you need to take it."

"OK, what . . .?" Anna-Maria began, but Sonja was already clattering down the stairs.

Her phone blinked and rang at the same time and she picked up the receiver.

"Inspector Mella."

"Hello," a man said in English with a pronounced Russian accent. "I have information about Galina Kireevskaya. Am I speaking to the right person?"

"Yes, you are," Anna-Maria said, grabbing her Post-it notes and a useless black pen that just left blots on the paper. She finally found one that worked in the upper drawer.

"Her family have been informed she has been found dead," the man said. "An accidental fall."

"That's right, I was one of the first people on the scene. Who am I talking to?"

"I'm a friend of hers. Just listen, please. When I heard the family had been notified of her death, I had to . . . I just want you to know that she called me before she died. She told me that she had been a sex worker in Kiruna, am I pronouncing that correctly? Kiroona?"

"Correctly enough."

"She said she had been working with two other women in a camper van. And that the pimps who drove the van were very bad men. That was how she put it. Russians."

Anna-Maria's heartrate ratcheted up a notch inside her expensive dress.

"Go on."

"One evening two, maybe three weeks ago, the plans were changed. They were supposed to be working, but instead the pimps drove off with them to an island somewhere. They were installed on the upper floor of a house owned by an old man, an alcoholic. She told me that the women stayed on the upper floor, surfing the Internet and eating. A row broke out on the ground floor. One of the women crept down the stairs to see what was going on. And she came back up and said "They're killing him, they're killing him. They're going to kill us as well.""

"Who was killing whom?"

"The pimps were killing the old man. They suffocated him on the sofa."

That's it, Anna-Maria was thinking. We've got them now.

"Why did they think the pimps would kill them as well? They would never have gone to the police, would they?"

There was silence for several seconds.

"Why would they never have gone to the police? Even though they'd witnessed a murder . . . because they were sex workers? That makes them completely lacking in morals, does it? Calling you was a mistake."

"Sorry," Anna-Maria exclaimed. "I didn't mean it like that."

"They were terrified, you realise. They believed the pimps were the kind of people who do away with any witnesses. Galina said they got in a panic. They put their shoes on, opened the window and jumped out into the snow. Then the other two ran off. Galina got stuck in the snow. She said the other two ran off in one direction, towards land, but when Galina freed herself she ran towards the other side of the water because the forest was closer there. Once she reached the edge of the trees she could hear a snowmobile start up. She didn't turn to look but made her way through the woods and finally reached the main road. She walked along it until she got a lift. She called one of her clients. He

363

got her a job at a restaurant. I don't know where. Somewhere nearby, I think. She wanted to earn enough money to get to Germany."

"I've got a lot of questions," Anna-Maria said. "What is your name?"

"I can't tell you my name," the man at the other end said. "But believe me, she wasn't about to take her own life."

"I need to get an interview recorded with you. This information is important, as you must realise."

"I'm sorry, I can't help you. The police here are a great danger to us."

"Us?"

"I'm gay. Galina was too. And I don't know any more than I just told you. She never told me what the men were called or anything. I told her to be careful, that she had to get away. But she had left her bag with all her money in that house. She was only going to work until she had enough to move on. We were supposed to speak, only—"

"The police in your country don't have to be involved," Anna-Maria appealed to him. "We could—"

"I'm sorry," the man said. "She was a good friend to me. I am very sorry."

"Hello?" Anna-Maria said. "Hello?"

But the call had been cut off.

"No, oh no, no," Anna-Maria yelled at her phone.

Then she galloped through the building to Carl von Post's office in the Prosecution Service.

"Wow," he said when he saw her. "Sit down, Mella."

"I can't sit," she said. Then she told him about the conversation she had just had. "Let's bring them in."

Carl von Post put his elbows on his desk and rested his chin on his folded hands.

"And then?"

Anna-Maria said nothing.

364

"But they did it," she said. "They murdered Henry Pekkari and Galina Kireevskaya, and Adriana Mohr and the woman who has still not been identified. Four people."

"I'm convinced you're right. But we don't have anything on them. If we bring them in now they won't say a word, they never do. And when we release them, that'll be the last we see of them. They'll have left the country for good."

"Aren't we going to do anything?" Anna-Maria said.

Von Post ran a hand over his face. "We'll have to try and trace the call," he said. "Only your informant can't identify the men, can he? We've got to come up with a witness who can connect these men to the camper van. How's it going, knocking on doors in the barracks housing?"

"Badly," Anna-Maria said resignedly. "No-one knows anything. Odd that, isn't it?"

This isn't good enough, Anna-Maria was thinking as she left the Prosecution Service. I cannot bear the thought of them still living in this town, expanding their criminal territory, while I arrest pickpockets and speeding drivers.

And why did they kill Henry Pekkari? What the hell happened out on that island?

It wasn't until she got back to her office that she realised she was still wearing her new dress over her jeans. Von Post hadn't said a word.

He really must think I'm potty, Anna-Maria thought.

"This won't do," Sven-Erik said, glancing out of the kitchen window. "I've got to clear the snow off the potato field. Or we won't have any potatoes for your birthday."

"It's been a snowy winter, no doubt about that," Airi agreed. "I'll put some potatoes in tubs, so we'll get a first crop a bit earlier. Though I agree the field does need clearing. I'll help."

They tidied the kitchen after their snack. Airi did the washing-up and he dried and put the crockery away. The cats each got a rolled-up slice of cheese. As usual Boxer dug her claws into his sleeve to make sure she didn't go without. Sven-Erik kept feeding them the cheese bit by bit. This was a moment of pure pleasure in the course of the daily round, and it could happily last a bit longer.

"One each!" Airi urged him as she went into the hall to put on her work boots. "You shouldn't give her extra, that's not fair."

He lumbered after her into the hall. Behind him Boxer miaowed, accusing him of breach of contract; she was used to getting a bit extra after all.

They cleared the field. It was hard work. The snow was heavy and wet. Sven-Erik raised the issue of a snow blower once more, and once more Airi asked him whether or not he wanted to go on living with her.

"Physical labour can help us stay fit," she said. "Feel that. I've always cleared the yard and turned the earth by hand."

He squeezed her powerful upper arms.

"I want to live with you for another hundred years," he said. "At the very least."

"In that case, all you've got to do is keep clearing this stuff." She laughed and drove her spade into the snow. "Don't try for those big spadefuls. Smaller ones and more of them are better. I don't want to have to look after an old man with a slipped disc."

That's the way of it, Sven-Erik was thinking as he dug his spade into the snow and lifted just the right amount. If you work the way women do, you get more done. He was remembering his grandfather, the haulier. Besides working on his own farm, he transported both timber and water with the same horse, brought the kids up and became a village alderman. "When life has been at its best it was hard work and a lot of effort," he used to say in jest, but he would go on: "Luckily life hasn't always been at its best." Though everyone understood there was a serious truth beneath the joke.

Even so, it was his grandmother who got everything done. The animals and children and the house and the old people. She got up first so when his grandfather came in from a day of hard work he could sit at a table that had been laid and then stretch his aching body out on the kitchen sofa. While his grandmother had cleared away and done the washing-up, gutted and cleaned the fish for the following day and done the evening milking. Every gap was filled with a little piece of work, even if it were just running to the edge of the woods and filling a coffee cup with blueberries or knitting another row.

"And she was brilliant at putting us kids to work," Sven-Erik said aloud. "Jobs that were just the right size so we didn't get worn out. Along with a great deal of praise. Mum was the same. When Granddad took you with him to work, you'd pull a face because you'd be so exhausted come the evening."

"Where have you gone off to in that head of yours?" Airi asked with a laugh.

"Never you mind," Sven-Erik said and laughed as well. Christ Almighty, I've reached the age where I don't even know I'm thinking aloud.

Though he told her what he'd been thinking about as they cleared the snow. And they talked about their grandparents on both sides. Sven-Erik thanked his lucky stars for Airi. Who'd had the same kind of upbringing he had. You never had to explain anything to her.

"So how's the investigation going then?" she asked.

"It's beginning to feel like there aren't any more rocks to turn over," Sven-Erik said, leaning on his spade and shoving his cap further up his head. "We're not getting anywhere with that handgun someone 'borrowed' and then put back in Piilijärvi. As for the Lingonberry King, after what Rebecka and Anna-Maria had to contend with I'm not even going to try and get an audience. Börje talked to his son, Spike Mäki, but he was so young in 1962 there wasn't much he could tell him. And as for that idiot Lars Grahn who kept babbling about the Russian mafia and fake dollar bills. No, not a chance."

"And what about the police investigation at the time? Can you really not get hold of the records?"

"Destroyed long ago. It was only a missing person after all. And he wasn't declared dead until ten years later. The same year Börje won the gold at the Olympics."

"But there was a police officer looking into the disappearance, what was his name, was it Fjäder? Isn't that what he said, Lars Grahn, that his name was Fjäder?"

"Yup, Stålnacke's better though, isn't it? If you were thinking of swapping?"

She trudged over to him in her heavy boots and wrapped her arms around him.

"Would you like to see me in a veil and a tiara?"

That too, Sven-Erik was thinking. The fact that she's always touching me and not just in the bedroom. Hjördis and he had never cuddled like that in the middle of the day. Airi might even come and sit on his lap when he was on the loo having a pee. The first time he had been really alarmed, but then he had welcomed it. Everything to do with the body felt natural to her. She was like her cats, their cats. They jumped up into his lap as well when he was on the loo, lay down across the paper when he was reading it. While that wasn't something Airi did, it was the same thing. She would often stop in the middle of doing something and say: "Now you've got to put your arms around me for a moment."

"That's gone and made us hungry again," she said. "Supposing I grated some of the old potatoes, we could turn them into pancakes."

"With lingonberry jam and bacon," he said.

At the bottom of the steps Airi stamped the snow off her boots. She looked back at Sven-Erik who was still wielding the spade on the potato field. This murder investigation that couldn't be officially investigated had turned into a real blessing. Sven-Erik was back to being his old self again. He was sleeping well. During the enforced idleness of winter he had slept like a person in a rage, with clenched fists that he kept raising in his sleep, lurching around so much she and the cats got bounced about in the bed. As if the way he slept was a protest that life no longer gave him enough to make him need to rest.

And now there's Fjäder, she thought. Definitely worth checking into.

Sven-Erik stopped work when a third of the field had been cleared. The soil would be exposed as soon as they got a few warm days. He peered at the mountain range. Unfortunately it looked like there was more snow coming. If more than ten centimetres fell he was going to borrow the neighbour's snow blower, Airi and her biceps could say what they liked about that.

She was in the kitchen with Boxer on her shoulder and had just finished grating the potatoes when he came inside.

"Just look at this," she said, and dried her hands on the kitchen towel. "I asked a question on Facebook. And guess what, that police officer Fjäder is still alive."

"What?"

"Lucid too, according to one of his great-nephews. He lives in Parkalombolo."

Sven-Erik rubbed his moustache.

"Parkalombolo," he said. "They've got a football team, or had one. They came eleventh in the fourth division of northern Norrland in 2006 before slipping down to the fifth."

"There you go. Worth a visit, then. Shall we take a trip there tomorrow? I'm working in the evening, but as long as we get away early."

"What about the potato field?"

"Hopefully it will still be here when we get home. You should join Facebook."

"Not for a million kronor."

Carl von Post was squeezing an avocado without much enthusiasm when his phone rang. He was pining for Stockholm and the indoor market at Östermalm, just to be able to wander around its stands and not have any firm plans for dinner, maybe start with a piece of fish or meat and go from there, salad, sauce, side dishes. To sit and have a glass of something or an espresso before coming home with bags full of goodies.

Anders Pekkari was on the other end of the line.

"Well done," he began. "Must be a relief to get Rebecka Martinsson put in her place, isn't it? So, when are we going to get back the company accounts, do you think?"

Carl von Post's mood got even worse. First, he didn't like being praised as though he were one of Anders Pekkari's labourers.

You say "Well done" to your employees, you idiot, he was thinking.

Second, he didn't like Anders Pekkari saying it was a relief to get Rebecka Martinsson put in her place. What did he mean a relief? As if it was common knowledge that he was the underdog in relation to Martinsson. As though he needed to assert himself.

And third, Anders Pekkari could kindly refrain from interfering in Prosecution Service matters, calling to get him to hurry up as though he were the one in charge.

No, he was going to have to put his foot down when it came to being ordered around by Kiruna's other Rotarians. Barely educated flatheads who had struggled to get through secondary school and were now earning four times as much as he did, eating out and going on holidays to Thailand on company money. And then talking openly about their tax evasion!

He never said anything, but they had another thing coming if they were going to try snapping their fingers and telling him how to do his job.

He chucked the avocado into the shopping basket and retreated to an empty aisle.

"We'll very probably be cancelling the decision to issue a search warrant."

"Very probably?" Anders Pekkari repeated shrilly at the other end. "It was fucking illegal and has to be cancelled. Now!"

Carl von Post smiled. It was almost touching to be lectured on the law by someone of Anders' limited intellectual gifts.

"Well, the CSIP hasn't announced its verdict yet. When and – nota bene – *if* they rule against Martinsson, the decision to issue the warrant must be cancelled swiftly, but only then. You can ask your lawyer about the details of the process. I'll try and have a look at this next week. But we've got a number of murders to deal with, as you know."

"What the fuck, Calle?" Anders Pekkari appealed.

That's the ticket, von Post thought cheerfully. Really not that difficult, was it?

"Listen, I've got to . . ." von Post said in conclusion, deliberately not specifying what he might or might not have to do. "See you at the indoor bandy match on Monday."

He ended the call. Just like that! For a few seconds he could feel his good mood returning. But the sight of the avocado brought him back to reality. His wife had asked him to shop for dinner and to eat at home that evening. They needed to talk, she had said. The boys were away at their mates. To study, they said. Though they would be playing computer games behind closed curtains. A sense of loathing was twisting him in its washer-woman's hands.

The snow arrived at dinner time on Wednesday. Huge woolly tufts falling thickly.

Ragnild Pekkari was looking out of her kitchen window. The cars on the road were crawling along on their summer tyres. Windscreen wipers going at top speed.

Villa got up on her paws and slipped into the bedroom.

Ragnhild could see a shadowy figure running across the road down below. It was Börje Ström heading for her front door.

He had not been deterred by her crying in his arms.

She was remembering the snow bridge.

A week had passed since she was supposed to have skied onto it and ended her life.

It wasn't cowardice that had driven her to the snow bridge, and it wasn't cowardice that had driven her away from it. Something else had just happened to intervene.

She had had a meaningful career. She had actually saved people, from pain and illness, from death.

Then, when she retired, all that was left was the other thing. And that wasn't something she could bear.

Inside her, loss had stamped out a hard and unyielding foundation and she had been left alone to face it.

I've been so angry, she thought. Almost every waking minute. Angry and unforgiving.

At *Äiti* and *Isä* and Henry and Olle. At Virpi.

At all the doctors she had heartily despised over the years, for their lack of empathy for their patients, for their incompetence and their smugness, for their inability to recognise the value of the nursing staff.

At Paula's father. She thought about all the revenge fantasies she had entertained about him, how she would play them over in her mind on the nights she couldn't sleep. Like arriving in an ambulance at the scene of an accident. And Todde and his new wife were stuck fast in a burning car wreck. The rescue services hadn't arrived. She could look into his staring eyes and hear the crackling sounds from the burning vehicle. The seconds that elapsed before the explosion.

Todde had got sober. When Paula was thirteen, one of his white-water-rafting mates had dragged him along to AA.

He had said to Ragnhild she should go to the support-group meetings. She had refused. Everything that had once revolved around his drunkenness now revolved around his sobriety. His meetings, the writing down of his life story, which was one of the steps, his self-examination.

His sponsor got him a job. And he left Ragnhild. She suspected he had met someone in the group. That turned out later to be true. Paula shared her time between Ragnhild and her new family.

Paula attended the support group. She thought Ragnhild ought to go as well. She was young. She knew everything there was to know. "You were the one who enabled his drinking," she said. "You kept it going."

"I thought I was paying the bills, doing the shopping and the cleaning," Ragnhild had replied.

It was so profoundly unfair. And then Paula chose to live with him full-time. She came to see Ragnhild less and less. Ragnhild's friends said that was to do with the age she was at. "She'll come back," they said. But she never did. She slipped away. She became silent and hostile. Ragnhild always felt she was being judged and criticised. That drove

373

her to mention all the things she had done as a mother over the years: "Do you remember when you wanted to have new wallpaper in your room? I worked extra night shifts, and then we went and bought it one Saturday?"

Paula turned eighteen and moved to Luleå. She never called. Whenever Ragnhild got in touch she felt like she was disturbing her. So she stopped trying. She thought she was bound to miss her eventually, but in vain.

Paula did accept Ragnhild's friend request on Facebook. And Ragnhild got to see photos of the grandchildren. Todde and his new wife were in the pictures from time to time. Ragnhild had tapped Like. Which felt like being stabbed with a poison needle every time.

How had it turned out like that? she thought. How did he become an out-and-out saint while she was transformed into a demon? She had even fallen so low as to ring him one time. When she hadn't been invited to celebrate Paula's birthday. "You'd have to sort that out with Paula," he had said. And then he had encouraged her to go to the meetings again. "You were a lot more use when you were fucking drinking," she had replied.

She was so tired of being angry. Bored with the same bitter old taste. The same trite song. The same heaviness, the same worn-out boat engine sinking down and further down.

The snow bridge was bound to still be there across the *jokk*.

There was a great deal of strength to be found in that knowledge. That she could still do it. That it was still there. One way or another.

I don't have to bear it more than one second at a time, she was thinking.

The flakes outside the window were whirling, twisting, dancing, making the most of their tiny journey. Tomorrow they would be water. The day after that a blade of grass.

A knock at the door. Börje.

She moved towards the door. There was no liberation in being a couple. She had no faith in the modern cult of love. But it soothed the pain of being alone. You could live by your convictions some other day, when you were feeling strong.

Anna-Maria Mella was blitzing her kitchen. She chucked the fish in the oven and put a pan of potatoes on the stove, cleared the kitchen table, threw the newspapers in the recycling bin and put the post in the growing deal-with-later pile.

She emptied and then filled the dishwasher, picked up the rubbish bag and shook the contents towards the bottom so it could be tied. Her fingers got sticky.

Is it that much harder having to tie the rubbish bag, she was thinking, compared with shifting the rubbish around at the top in the expectation that someone else will tie it and put a new bag in? And how hard can it be, having to carry out the rubbish bag to the bin? Is it really any harder than having to step over it on your way out the front door, pretending it doesn't exist? Why do people put empty yoghurt containers back in the fridge instead of crushing them and chucking them in the rubbish? So many questions. Someone really ought to be doing some research into that.

She called Tommy Rantakyrö, put the bud in her ear, stepped into her clogs and slid through the newly fallen snow across the yard to chuck the rubbish bag in the bin.

Tommy failed to answer and she left a message. She had told him to stay home for the rest of the week, but he could at least answer when she called him.

Once back inside she forgot about cleaning the kitchen and started to sort out the chaos of shoes in the hall. No point taking the winter shoes up to the attic now it was snowing outside. God, what a filthy month May could be.

She was going to drive past Tommy's tomorrow, she decided. Knock on his door and see how he was doing.

She wrenched the hoover out of the cleaning cupboard and the long-handled scrubbing brush fell on top of her. There was never any space with all the mess inside.

Or maybe I shouldn't drive past tomorrow, she thought. I'm behaving like a mother. We've all done it. It really is the bloody limit for him to be hungover while on the job though. And to have to take days off because of all the partying. And wasn't that a dreadful word? As if there was anything to celebrate about that kind of drinking.

Maybe it was time to stop coddling him. Then again, why was it considered coddling when all you wanted to do was help? Why was it considered more professional not to care? Shifting the responsibility for one's fellows to the organisation you work for?

She got her phone out again and texted Tommy: Please ring me. Now. I just want to check how you're doing.

Jenny came down the stairs listening to music. Anna-Maria pursued her into the kitchen.

"Could you do the hoovering?" she asked.

Jenny moved one of her headphone cushions aside.

"What?"

"The hoovering," Anna-Maria said. "Just down here. The kitchen and the hall. I've tidied the shoes and—"

"Christ, Mum, the moment I turn up I get given work to do. Why don't you ever ask Petter or Gustaf?"

"Of course I do. Just stop."

"No, you don't, you only ask me. You're always ordering me

376

around. You're raising us to be proper members of the patriarchy. Congratulations."

She turned on her heels and marched up the stairs.

"Is that all you've got to say?" Anna-Maria said. "So I'm left with the hoovering, am I? What kind of equality is that?"

"I'll do it," Jenny called out. "I'll do it later. Not everything has to happen when you say. You're getting hysterical."

I'm going to run away from home, Anna-Maria was thinking. I just have to water the plants and take the supper out of the oven first.

Rebecka Martinsson shovelled fresh snow onto her rag rugs and then gave them a going-over with the piassava broom. She laid them out on her newly scrubbed floor and lit the stove to draw the moisture out of them.

The phone rang. She was considering whether to check who it was. Bound to be a journalist.

Dear God, let them have something else to write about soon, she thought.

It was Måns Wenngren.

"You asked for the name of someone who knows about organised crime," he began without further ado. "She'll be ringing you in the next hour and the number will be withheld. Answer your phone. She wasn't very keen, if you know what I mean."

"Thanks," Rebecka said and lowered herself onto the edge of the kitchen sofa so as not to compress the neatly puffed-up cushions. "Although I've been removed from the investigation now."

"Yeah yeah, it's not like you could miss that bit of news," he said with a laugh. "Though that's never stopped you before."

They talked a bit more. He was going sailing with his mates at the weekend. She told him you couldn't see your hand in front of your face in the current snowstorm.

"I can imagine – only too well," he said with feeling, and she could hear he really wasn't missing the time he had been forced to spend with her in Kurravaara.

Once the call was over she reheated the coffee that was left in the pot, thinking that she ought to eat something resembling a proper meal. She leafed through the papers while inhaling the smell of coffee and freshly scrubbed home. The Brat was moving anxiously about and refusing to settle.

"What is the matter with you?" she asked. "Go and lie down."

The telephone rang again. Number withheld.

"Rebecka," Rebecka said and grabbed the Brat's collar, forcing him to lie down.

"Hello, this is Eva Johansson. Måns asked me to ring you."

"Thank you for doing so. I'm a prosecutor in Kiruna and—"

"He told me what it was about. And I've been reading about you. About the murders up there."

Rebecka could hear Eva Johansson lighting a cigarette and taking her first drag.

"So, how can I help you? We can talk for half an hour but there won't be any more calls after that."

Rebecka told her about the Lingonberry King, Frans Mäki.

"And he'll soon be ninety," she said, wrapping up. "Newly married to a woman in her thirties, from Russia. A facial-recognition program suggests she may have been involved in a massive corporate hijacking a few years ago. One vast tangled web of corrupt police, prosecutors, judges, civil servants at the taxation authority. There are also two men providing the muscle at the house they live in, plus a young woman who looks like . . . bum, breasts, fake nails, fake hair, Botoxed lips. We're as certain as we can be that the muscles have been driving a camper van around with three sex workers plying their trade inside. And selling drugs."

She told her about Bengt, the dog the two fighting dogs had killed.

"And they haven't vanished now the murders have been discovered?"

"No."

"Kiruna is a town being transformed, right?" Eva Johansson said. "I mean they're going to move the entire town because of the expansion of the mine. A town like that is low-hanging fruit for the criminal element. What kind of companies does the Lingonberry King own?"

"Phew, a whole load. Construction, wood products, excavation, that kind of thing . . ."

"There's a lot of organised crime in the building sector. The Housing Agency has calculated that construction fraud costs our society 83 to 111 billion kronor every year. That's money that should be going to social care, education and the health service. If, as you suspect, the wife has got links to organised crime, then . . . and I'm only speculating here . . ."

Another deep drag on a cigarette could be heard at the other end. Rebecka got up and looked for tobacco in the junk drawer in the kitchen. The Brat immediately got to his feet and took up position by the door to the stairs. He whined but Rebecka ignored him.

"If she has contacts of that kind, then she'll have access to a highly effective network for channelling money," Eva Johansson went on, "through banking connections, shell companies in Cyprus, companies in tax havens. Getting their claws into towns like Kiruna is a hugely attractive proposition. A great many lucrative contracts. A lot of major projects that have to be completed swiftly. Added to which she's managed to marry into a local company through this Lingonberry King. So she doesn't have to start an operation from the ground up. She's got hired muscle, two professionals who help her with everything from her own security to the persuasion of key individuals, decision makers in the local authority and the commissioning companies. It can be tedious being stationed for a long time in some little dump, so a girl of their own for the guys and maybe the Lingonberry King, depending on what he enjoys in the autumn of his years, and a bit of dog-fighting into the bargain."

Rebecka found her tobacco and her roller and the papers.

"It seems they've already taken over prostitution and narcotics," she said. "There's a good market for that here. Men who don't live in Kiruna, whose families and family life are elsewhere, but have to live in dismal barracks housing in some depressing area and do demanding shift work."

"I see," Eva Johansson said. "But this alliance with the Lingonberry King. All of that points to the building sector. They aim to rake money in off potentially highly lucrative construction projects. They secure those through bribes and threats. Then they put up shoddy work, you know, using an unskilled labour force through sub-contractors they actually run themselves. Cheap, poor-quality cement in load-bearing areas, no damp courses. I could list you a hundred tricks like that. There was a construction project in Spånga a couple of years ago, eleven hundred apartments. There was no electricity, heating or water when the tenants were supposed to move in."

"You're kidding!"

"I'm really not. One of the project leaders in that particular affair was shot in Lidingö. It was a contract killing, they arrested the guy who did the shooting and he had no links of any kind to the victim. He refused to talk. So no-one was prosecuted for the incitement of the murder because it was impossible to prove who had ordered it. This goes on all the time, but there's very little about it in the press because, well, it's always complicated and difficult to untangle. People prefer to read about celebrities who've made a fool of themselves or are expecting children out of wedlock."

"You work for an insurance company, though, don't you? What is it you actually do?"

"Mhmm, when work on building a tunnel comes to a halt or a bridge has collapsed and is going to cost two hundred million to fix all of a sudden, and the company responsible has gone bankrupt and the money has moved a very long way away. Well, that's when the commissioning body turns to their insurance company, right? My job is to find the decision makers who are a contributory cause. The ones who signed a contract with a shady operator, the ones who looked away and failed to pull the handbrake despite warning flags about irregularities being raised. So then the insurance company comes onto the scene and says: 'We have evidence, or indications at least, that you and a network of people around you have been taking bribes. We can hand our evidence over to the Prosecution Service, or we can decide not to. You can withdraw your loss report to the insurance company, or not.' And then it all gets buried in silence. No politician or official wants to be mired in a scandal. And my employer, the insurance company, doesn't have to pay out huge sums."

"The tax-payers have to do it instead," Rebecka said curtly.

"Correct, if it's the government or the local authority that did the commissioning. And it frequently is."

A noise forced Rebecka to turn around. It sounded like someone had stepped on a plastic ketchup bottle. The Brat was hunched over by the door. Diarrhoea was spraying from his rear. He waddled like a canine Charlie Chaplin, squirting poo across the floor and the rag rugs.

"Bastard dog," Rebecka exclaimed. "Stop that, don't move."

"What's going on?" Eva Johansson asked.

"My dog just got the runs," Rebecka said. "Hang on, don't hang up."

She grabbed the Brat by the collar and hauled him, still shitting, down the stairs and out the door.

"Oh God," Rebecka groaned into the phone. "And I'd just finished cleaning the place."

"The Labrador I had before found a pile of human shit and rolled in it two years ago," Eva Johansson said. "We'd stopped for a break, we were in the car on our way to . . . doesn't matter. I managed to wipe her down with two lemon-scented wet wipes I happened to have in the car. That helped a bit. Then I had to drive another two hundred kilometres. I still can't bear the smell of lemon-scented wet wipes."

"But you can still bear dogs?"

"Can't live without them."

"Why can't we love aquarium fish instead," Rebecka said, watching the Brat who was still waddling like Charlie Chaplin across the fresh snow.

"Go and deal with your dog," Eva Johansson said. "And if you ever want to change jobs, let me know through Måns. He's told me about you."

"Has he now," Rebecka said.

"Much better paid than a prosecutor. And you can live wherever you like. Though there's a lot of travelling involved. And, as you'll understand, it's a job with a high level of threat built in so you need to keep a low profile. You haven't got a black belt in that, I've heard. Though maybe you could change."

"OK," Rebecka said. "Can I call you again if I—"

"No, I'm sorry. I've got enough tangles of my own to unpick."

"Is your name really Eva Johansson?"

The woman at the other end laughed.

"Of course not. But Måns and I are old mates so if you're interested in the job you can let me know that way. Good luck with your dog, and one other thing . . ."

She seemed to be hesitating for a moment.

"There have been three, maybe four murders these individuals can be linked to. They're people who can vanish with ten minutes' notice. And yet they haven't. What do you make of that?"

"They've made a considerable investment here and have a lot to lose."

"Mmm, I'd keep pondering if I were you. I don't like to speculate about other people's cases."

Then she ended the call. Abruptly. Just like Måns used to.

They've got to be related, Rebecka was thinking. Or they've gone to the same private school. Been taught how to make people feel condescended to.

She felt a bit more cheerful, though, at the offer of a job.

Why not? she thought.

Then she scrubbed the dog shit off the kitchen floor and the stairs. Two of the rugs had another go in the washing machine.

She was thinking about Krister a lot. About the fact that she would have rung and told him about the diarrhoea. He would have laughed. And got in his car and driven over and helped her with the cleaning.

THURSDAY 5TH MAY

The walloping of snow the weather gods had dished out continued during the night and kept on throughout Thursday morning. The roads were covered in slush that hardened into ruts. Drivers who had recklessly changed to summer tyres could only crawl along. Seeing anything in front of you was virtually impossible, like fumbling through thick fog; snow kept collecting on the windscreen from the bottom up.

The snow drifts were a pain for the owners of detached houses. Those with north-facing front doors could barely get them open because so much of it had piled up. Homeowners whose front doors were out of the wind faced a similar problem, with no wind to clear the accumulation. On social media people were posting photos of snow-covered bicycles, cars, prams. There was even an item about it on the television news.

Sven-Erik Stålnacke and Airi Bylund were laughing at the sheer futility of yesterday's attempts to clear the potato field. They cancelled their planned trip to Parkalompolo. Sven-Erik put in a call instead to the long-since-retired police officer Adrian Fjäder.

They introduced themselves, shared a sigh over "Oh welcome back, lovely May" – and how! It was snowing in Parkalombolo as well. They brought up a few of the historic snowy winters and then spent three quarters of an hour digressing on the history of the local police force.

"I liked living in Kiruna," Fjäder said. "Only now I think I'm never going to visit the town again. It's too painful, what with all your memories being torn down."

"There's a lot that's going to look really good as well though," said Sven-Erik and surprised himself by defending the changes. "The new combined town hall and art museum will be lovely, and so will the Bleckhorns once they've moved them up Luossa."

He changed the subject and got down to business.

"I remember Raimo Koskela going missing," Fjäder said. "I actually did quite a bit of work on it, I was young and ambitious then. I remember his ex was an attractive woman. She said that Koskela must have simply left the boy unattended, got drunk and gone back to Finland. He was one of those odd-jobs guys, doing casual work here and there. He rode a motorbike and had tattoos over more than half his body. I mean, that was pretty unusual at the time. Though I read all the details in the paper when you found him. In a freezer. Have you found out anything more?"

"Not really, though the weapon was most probably a Kamrat 40 that vanished from an army officer's car. It was returned and never reported as missing. One shot had been fired."

"Well, I'll be damned."

"Did you ever find out if he'd been up to something?" Sven-Erik asked.

"As it happens I did. There was this person who sought me out to say he was involved in some kind of fake currency business that went wrong. They'd been selling dollar bills to the Russian mafia."

"Who told you that?" Sven-Erik asked.

"If only I could remember," Fjäder said.

"Lars Grahn?" Sven-Erik was guessing.

"You know what, that's right," Fjäder said. "Odd the way the brain works. I saw a forest in my mind when you asked. Grahn. That sounds like *gran*, a fir tree. Only I didn't take it any further. It was just a missing person. Though many years later, it must have been '82 or '83, I was talking to this villain who was being pursued by the police in Gävle for stealing two hundred kilos of turmeric from Kockums."

"What?"

"Yeah, it was one of our own boyos who'd been trying his wings down south, Kjell-Fredrik Esko, he's long since dead. Anyway, it seems you feed turmeric to trotters, so they worked out they could make a bundle on it. In any case he'd been one of the Lingonberry King's lads back in Kiruna. And he told me that around the time Raimo Koskela disappeared, a shopping bag full of cash belonging to the Lingonberry King had gone missing. Esko thought Koskela had taken the money and scarpered, only now he's been found shot dead you've got to wonder."

"A shopping bag filled with cash?"

"Well, they were never much for accountants, those guys."

Once the call was over, Sven-Erik got out the folder with his case notes on Raimo Koskela. It felt hopeless. Little dots you ought to be able to draw lines between until a picture emerged. But there were too few dots.

I've got to talk to the Lingonberry King, he thought. What are those Russians going to do about it? If they show me the door and won't let me see him, at least I'll have tried.

Anna-Maria Mella skidded onto her garage forecourt at around four on Thursday afternoon. She was transformed into a snowman during the seven seconds it took to get from the car to the house.

"It's actually spewing down," she said to Robert and Jenny who were sitting at the kitchen table. "Come and put a carrot nose on me."

They were both absorbed in their mobiles and neither replied. Jenny had an empty glass in front of her, you could tell it had contained Oboy.

She was always downing sugar and snacks before dinner and then picking at her food, as if she wasn't hungry. And every now and then she'd go on a health kick and make nutritious smoothies or bake seed cakes.

They're turning into adults who behave like little kids, though you're not allowed to treat them like children all the same, Anna-Maria was thinking.

She stamped the snow off on the rag rug in the hall and hung her wet jacket on the radiator knob.

"I'm going to ring Rebecka and tell her I'm not coming tonight," she said. "I'm not driving to Kurra in this weather. She'll understand."

Jenny and Robert were jerked out of their self-absorption as if they were one and the same person.

"What are you on about?" Robert said. "I'll drive you there and come and fetch you later, obviously."

"Course you should go, Mum. I'm going to do your make-up and fix your hair. And the dress!"

"No, really," Anna-Maria objected, opening the fridge to see what could be turned into dinner. "No-one will miss me."

"I forbid you to be that dull," Jenny said.

She aimed her phone at Anna-Maria and took a picture.

"There you are," she said. "A 'before' photo."

Anna-Maria looked at the picture.

"Christ Almighty. A stray cat some idiot put through the washing machine."

"You're going," Robert said firmly. "Even if I have to drive you there on my brother's snowmobile."

And so it was decided. Anna-Maria was feeling so much reluctance at the thought of the evening ahead there wasn't room to feel anything else.

"What am I even going to talk about?"

*

"You've got to be very good now," Rebecka said to the Brat as the guests' taxi slowly turned into the yard. She was already feeling a bit fuzzy; she'd only had two beers but hadn't had time to eat a proper meal.

The plane had been delayed because of the snowstorm. Maria Taube had taken photos of her gang at Arlanda airport and posted them on Instagram.

Rebecka had looked up the three girlfriends Maria had tagged in the photo and kept repeating their names to herself. Sofi, Clara and another Sophie, although spelled differently.

The Brat took his duties as a host seriously and greeted them as though they had saved him from the animal shelter. They had their hands full paying for the taxi and removing their luggage, so in the end Rebecka had to grab him by his collar.

There was nothing stiff about the introductions at least, so it didn't matter that it was a bit chaotic. Rebecka was sober enough not to overgreet them the way the Brat had. Maria kissed her hastily on the mouth, and Rebecka said her hellos and welcomes and nice to meet yous and I hope the awful weather stops so you get some decent skiing. Then she herded them inside the flat on the ground floor where they would be sleeping.

It was where she had lived with Dad when he had been alive. Grandma had lived on the upper floor, which was where Rebecka was now.

"It's lovely," Sophie exclaimed.

Rebecka already liked her the best. Sophie was large and rather boisterous, taking up space in a way that allowed other people to relax because they didn't need to do their bit.

The guest flat did look really nice. She thought so too. Old kitchen cupboards from the fifties, furniture from the same period. The only thing she had bought from IKEA were new beds. She had got carried away when she was with Krister, though, and repainted everything so it felt less depressing, in a mixture of pink, turquoise, yellow, red and pale blue. Her aim had been to make it feel like you were stepping inside a picture book and that had worked. You felt happy in here. And she didn't see Dad sitting round the kitchen table every time she came in.

They had a sauna. The Brat lay in front of the open fire in the sauna room. Rebecka had spent all afternoon firing it up. There were beer bottles outside in the snow and she had carved some lightly smoked, marinated reindeer meat. She forgot she had made up her mind earlier not to have any more to drink before dinner.

They poured water onto the stones, groaning as the first wave of steam rose from the hearth. They toasted each other and rolled around screaming in the fresh snow between sessions.

They were easy to get to know. Sophie worked in management, and it turned out it was her family's wealth she was managing.

"Though I don't get why they insisted on my studying law," she said. "What my family needs are more trained medics to prescribe their drugs."

And then she entertained them with stories about her half-mad relatives on both her father's and mother's sides.

The other Sofi was a tax lawyer, just like Rebecka. She specialised in international VAT ("the old VAT lady"), was recently divorced as well, so there was some talk about that. Maria brought up the latest gossip from her and Rebecka's former workplace. Clara and her husband were building a holiday home in Åre.

"I want it to look exactly like this," Clara said with a gesture that encompassed the sauna and the main house.

Rebecka zipped her lips on the comment. Mountain chalet in Åre vs. Eternit-clad hovel in Kurravaara she thought, weighing one against the other.

She poured a hefty scoop of water onto the hot rocks, which meant both Clara and Sofi shifted down to the lower shelf.

Didn't they always go on like this, she thought gloomily. Posh people, the upper classes. They talked about their crazy relatives, brought up some impoverished ancestor who didn't come from Stockholm in an attempt to tone down their poshness, or talked about dogs, all for, well, what?

"Who wants another?" she said and went out into the falling snow.

In order to try and conceal the gulf between us, she was thinking as she stepped barefoot onto the snow and grabbed five beers. So I don't have to be embarrassed and feel inferior. So they can talk with the peasants in their own language.

Then she thought: Fuck off the lot of you. At the same time she was telling herself: Stop, don't do this now. They're nice and kind and they haven't done you any harm.

"Another half hour," she announced when she went back into the sauna. "Then we can wash and wrap things up. Anna-Maria will be here soon."

They had time to sit for a while in front of the fire in the sauna room. Then they leaped half naked into their boots and ran up to the house. Maria tripped over. Rebecka scooped up snow with her hands and pressed it against her face in an attempt to sober up.

She rang Sivving and said the sauna was hot and free of any females if he wanted to make the most of the opportunity.

"God, I just can't believe this much snow is falling," Anna-Maria said in the car on the way down to Kurravaara. "What if you can't pick me up later on?"

"Shit, you look so gorgeous," Robert said, peeking at her.

"Keep your eyes on the road!"

"You're not making it easy for me, if you know what I mean," he said and looked obediently at the road ahead with a determined expression, as though it required huge effort.

Anna-Maria checked herself out in the sun-visor mirror. She actually was pretty. Jenny had done her make-up and hair, painted her nails and lent her her best shoes against a sacred vow they would come back in perfect condition. "Not one step outside, no letting Rebecka's dog step on them . . . or worse."

Robert turned cautiously into Rebecka's yard and stopped close to the steps. Anna-Maria reached for the gold-wrapped present on the back seat, stopped in mid-motion and all of a sudden leaned against Robert's shoulder.

He stroked her head warily so as not to ruin the hairdo.

"Listen, *knaso*," he said tenderly. "This is a party. It's going to be fun."

"But I want to be home under a blanket watching 'Call the Midwife'."

"Off you go," he said. "Ring when you want a lift home."

She kissed him gently because her lipstick needed to stay on. Then she got resolutely out of the car and took Rebecka's outside steps in two strides.

She got out of her boots and stepped into Jenny's posh shoes in the entrance hall on the lower floor. Music and a lot of chatter could be heard from upstairs. The Brat began to bark. The upstairs door opened and she could hear Rebecka's voice.

"Is that you, Anna-Maria? Come on up."

She held on to the banister, the stairs were wet and slippery with melted snow. The shiny present was clutched firmly in her other hand.

She was hit by a feeling very like playground anxiety as she stepped into the room. None of the others were dressed for a party. Even worse, they were barely dressed at all.

Their undergarments were hanging on racks on the radiators and on the clothes horse above the wood-fired stove. They were wearing thermal pants and bras, two of them had aprons on. A bit of mascara left under the eyes, their hair wet.

It took considerable effort for her to register what their names were when they introduced themselves. Everyone was involved in preparing dinner.

"Did I miss something about the dress code?" Anna-Maria said, and could feel the joke fall flat.

"My God, don't you look gorgeous!" Rebecka exclaimed drunkenly.

"So you're the one who stole Rebecka from me," Maria Taube said. "She doesn't love me anymore. Just talks about you, all the time."

Anna-Maria managed another smile. Maria was lying, that was obvious. Rebecka would never talk about her to these particular friends.

"Does she now. Like what?"

"Only good things."

Yeah right, Anna-Maria thought and put the bag with the present on the draining board. She hoped Rebecka wouldn't get the bottle out. It was much too expensive, just like the dress.

No risk of that. Rebecka was hanging around Maria's neck, assuring her that she still loved her a little.

"And you're wearing make-up," Rebecka went on, turning to face Anna-Maria. "You look really lovely."

Anna-Maria was suddenly filled with a desire to pat her. Couldn't she just stop messing about?

"Thanks," she said instead. "Is there anything I can do to help?"

"Eh, have a seat and a beer," the large woman said – was her name

Sophie? "You'll have to catch up in the drinking stakes if you're going to last."

"I can drink and carve at the same time," Anna-Maria grinned gratefully. "A Kiruna girl, you know. Just as long as I look after the shoes, they're my daughter's best pair, she'll kill me – slowly and inventively – if there's even the tiniest mark on them when I get home."

"How old is your daughter?"

That was Clara asking. Anna-Maria wondered if she took amphetamines to keep her appetite under control. She was as thin as an envelope. Anna-Maria didn't like her; there was something cold and toffee-nosed about her.

"She'll be twenty this summer."

Scattered exclamations.

"Twenty? So how old were you when you had her? Twelve?"

Anna-Maria had heard that one before and gave the standard reply:

"My father had to petition the king for permission for us to marry."

"Anna-Maria's got five children," Rebecka said. "Five!"

She spread out all the fingers of one hand.

And the next second they were all told that Anna-Maria and Robert had been together since secondary school.

They said "Wow!" and "That's great!" and "Three cheers for love!"

Anna-Maria felt like an animal in a cage. A small grey nocturnal animal who had put on a dress and high heels.

They ate char from a mountain lake with shiitake mushrooms and green peas. Sophie whisked up a *beurre blanc* that she topped with trout roe.

"To think they're going to move the entire town," Clara said to Anna-Maria. "How do you feel about that?"

Anna-Maria began to answer, but in the middle of her second

sentence Clara threw herself into a conversation with the other side of the table, which made Anna-Maria lose her thread and fall silent. It bloody well isn't women are from Venus and men from Mars, Anna-Maria was thinking as she followed the conversations around the table. Robert is from the same planet as me.

These people on the other hand. They never went back to their villages. They drove 'to the country'. To the places their families had owned for generations, where they had an old retainer to serve as a tractor and where they put on rubber boots and worn old oilskin jackets, they had three children and not two. And definitely not five. And if they got a dog it was a terrier or a Labrador. They bought their coffee beans from micro-roasters. They ate at restaurants where the staff wore long rough aprons made of linen. They had all lived abroad but they would never go on a charter flight. They put their children's names down for the best schools when they were still tadpoles swimming in the womb and on their walls they had portraits of their relatives painted in oils. They ate ecologically, with sourdough bread, apart from envelope-Clara that is, who was definitely, with one hundred per cent certainty, gluten intolerant. Though they knew how to sail and to ski, finding your bearings on a map or lighting a fire in the forest didn't score many points.

Anna-Maria was remembering a school graduation ceremony she had attended with her family in Tromsö a couple of years ago. One of Robert's cousins had married a Norwegian and moved over there. At the ceremony the children had gone up to receive their certificates dressed in folk costume. It had looked so lovely she started to cry but Robert's cousin had whispered to her that those hand-embroidered costumes with the silver detailing cost more than six thousand kronor. And then there were the ball gowns and everything else on top. Then one of the pupils had appeared on stage wearing jeans and a T-shirt. Anna-Maria had immediately stopped crying. She had a stomach ache instead. She had been wondering if that boy got to go to the ball and all the other parties during the exam period. Not likely. Later on she had seen him leaving the hall first accompanied by his mother.

She looked at Rebecka on the other side of the table. Was this what she really wanted? To spend time with people like this? How did she think they saw her? Did she think she could belong to this little group? Did she want that? Was this the kind of life she wanted? Privileged and blissfully unaware of her privilege.

Anna-Maria was thinking about the boy who had gone onstage to collect his certificate in jeans and a T-shirt. She was thinking about all the people who couldn't afford to buy nice clothes for their children, who couldn't afford to support them doing sport, riding, going away to camp. And then there were these women's children who would eventually be getting on with their own lives while telling people they had been given nothing for free. That they had been the architects of their own good fortune.

She is embarrassed by me, Anna-Maria thought, and felt wounded that Rebecka had introduced her as a "colleague". Not a mate, not a friend.

The main course was cleared away and dessert was put on the table. Cloudberry preserve and vanilla ice cream.

The other women tried to involve Anna-Maria in the conversation. They asked about the dark winters, wasn't it awful not to see the sun for so long? Only then they said they wanted to see the northern lights and the midnight sun. And reindeer! They would get to see some in Riksgränsen, wouldn't they? They asked about the mosquitoes and how cold the winters were. They asked her if being a police officer was exciting, and Sofi knew a policeman she could tell them a bit about.

"It's an important job," Anna-Maria said. "And I'm proud to be one of the girls in blue."

The others agreed. A really important job, a lot more important than theirs, of course.

Anna-Maria became monosyllabic and quiet. Why am I bothering? she thought.

And one of the things she had learned on the job: the reality behind those lovely facades was often far from pretty. Abuse, suicide attempts and addiction could all be found in their circles as well.

They've got their troubles, she thought. They're just people. I'm the one being unfair.

But she didn't have the energy to dig herself out of the hole she had fallen into. She ate too quickly; she had finished both the main course and the dessert long before the others. It was all those years when the kids were little that had ruined her.

Rebecka was being too loud and waving her arms about as she got more drunk. Sophie wanted to drink moonshine, so a plastic bottle appeared on the table after the food. Rebecka taught them a Finnish schnapps song that went: "Nyt" – Now. They learned to say "Kippis". And then they showed off their knowledge of Finnish. "Ei saa peittää" – Do not cover – was a phrase they'd all read off a radiator at some point.

Anna-Maria could barely look at Rebecka. She was pretending to be coarse, unrefined. She was actually being affected and fawning. She would bet that was ordinary vodka in the plastic bottle.

Various cheeses the guests had brought with them were placed on the table. And there was talk of cheese and wine and French villages. Anna-Maria went to the loo just to see what the time was. She peed against the porcelain so it couldn't be heard in the kitchen. Another indignity to put up with when you'd given birth to five children. You peed like a cow.

"Will it clear up, do you think?" Envelope-Clara asked when Anna-Maria got back to the table. "It's so lovely here, it makes you want to see the mountains as well."

They checked the forecast on their phones and Rebecka said the weather was changeable. But at this time of year the snow wouldn't keep falling, would it?

They looked at Anna-Maria as if she could read the future from a reindeer's belly. Anna-Maria shrugged.

"It really is lovely here," Clara said. She had been skiing in Riksgränsen before. "I'm happy to pay my taxes to keep Norrland going."

"What do you mean?" Anna-Maria said. It came out more forcefully than she had intended. Everyone's ears pricked up.

"Having thriving rural communities is something everyone in Sweden ought to value, shouldn't they?" Clara said. "And that goes for us asphalt kids too."

Asphalt kids, Anna-Maria thought. Well, howdy do.

Clara knocked back her arctic starflower before topping up everyone's glasses. Rebecka appeared to sober up for a second. Anna-Maria avoided her eyes and tipped her own glass back and forth while having a think.

"I don't know what you mean about rural communities," she said. "Norrland accounts for sixty per cent of Sweden's surface area. Personally I have difficulty distinguishing between Stockholm, Malmö and Västerås. What I would say about Kiruna is that while we have a housing shortage, we also have almost zero unemployment. The mine is owned by the state and in the last ten years the dividend from LKAB has been roughly thirty billion kronor. But all the dividends and all the tax go to central government, which is in Stockholm. So the people paying to keep all of Sweden going aren't you lot. We're glad to have the work opportunities, it's not that. But it sucks when all we get back are the dregs, along with being branded 'welfare recipients'. The same goes for forestry and hydro-electric. There's no God-given law that it has to be the way it is. In some countries part of corporation tax goes to the areas where the companies operate. So you can't just pump out the resources there without giving anything back. Isn't that right, Rebecka? You're the tax lawyer after all."

Three extraordinarily long seconds went by.

"I'm not an expert on international corporate taxation," Rebecka finally replied.

Anna-Maria was so disappointed by Rebecka's spinelessness she had to close her eyes for a moment and press her fingers against her eyelids.

I've had enough of these girlfriends of hers, she thought.

"Thanks for dinner," she said. "I should go now, otherwise I'll end up snowed in here in Kurra."

She got up and headed for the door.

"Don't go," Rebecka said and got to her feet. The chair tipped over behind her.

The others called out cheerful goodbyes.

Anna-Maria grabbed her jacket. But then she turned in the doorway.

"You know what," she barked, "all the government departments and official bodies should be situated in small towns. Us tax payers would save billions just on the rents the authorities have to pay to their landlords. Though maybe not, because then all those young people who managed to get an education could move back home to get jobs. And in that case how could the value of all your villas and housing co-ops keep shooting up – like that!"

Her hand flew up vertically.

She stomped down the stairs. Rebecka rattled after her.

"Come back," Rebecka appealed. "What the hell happened?"

Anna-Maria threw open the front door and walked down the steps straddle-legged so as not to slip on the snow. Rebecka tried to grab her.

"Stop! You can't just leave. How are you even going to get home?"

"I'll call Robert," Anna-Maria said. "He'll pick me up."

She got out her phone. Rebecka reached over and grabbed it.

"You can get a taxi later. I'll pay."

"Stop it," Anna-Maria hissed. "Give me my phone."

She reached for her phone. Rebecka put it in her pocket and knocked Anna-Maria's hand away.

Rage exploded in Anna-Maria like an airbag. She punched Rebecka with both hands. Rebecka landed on her backside in the snow. Anna-Maria bent over and reached for her pocket. Rebecka grabbed her hand and yanked her onto her back.

"Are you out of . . . give me the phone!"

They wrestled. Rebecka resisted like a kid in nursery school refusing to put on its overall, but she was drunk and clumsy. Anna-Maria got her onto her belly and twisted her arm behind her back.

The door opened and the other four women tumbled out into the yard with cries of "Stop" and "What are you doing?"

But by then Anna-Maria had got her phone. She left the dinner guests behind her; they could help Rebecka get back up. She glanced over her shoulder to make sure Rebecka wasn't following. When she reached the main road she rang Robert.

"You can pick me up now," she said. "I'm walking towards Kiruna."

"What?" Robert said. "Why . . . I mean, can't you wait indoors?"

"I'll explain later. Can you get off the sofa right now, do you think? My legs are freezing."

She rang off and looked down at her frozen legs in their nylon stockings. Only to discover that she still had Jenny's best shoes on.

"Oh fuck it, no," she yelled. "Goddamn it to hell, no!"

But her voice failed to travel, drowned out by the thickly falling snow.

"I've got to ring her," Rebecka said.

She was soaked through after rolling around in the snow with Anna-Maria.

Maria Taube took the mobile away from her.

"There's no point trying to resolve conflicts when you're drunk," she said firmly. "And never after ten at night."

"We've got a rule in my family that we don't resolve conflicts at all," Sophie laughed. "We just . . ."

She finished her sentence by pretending to blow dust off an imaginary object.

"You'll have to sort all that out tomorrow," Maria Taube said.

"Or the day after tomorrow," Sophie said and smiled kindly. "Cheers everyone, Kurravaara is where it all happens. The last time I went out to dinner people argued about which was the best stove: LaCanche or AGA. No-one wrestled in the snow."

"I'm going to call her tomorrow too," Clara promised, putting her hand on her chest. "I didn't mean to . . ."

"Tomorrow," Maria Taube commanded. "Now let's get dancing!"

Oh fuck it, Rebecka thought, only to discover that every object in the room had a ghostly double. All my relationships are fucked in any case. I'm going to move. Or something.

While she was getting out all the bottles she had in the corner cupboard, the others were lifting the chairs onto the table and kicking away the rag rugs. Maria got up her dance playlist and connected her phone to the speaker. The Brat was getting comfortable on the pile of rag rugs under the table. As if they had arranged it just for him.

Rebecka was drinking straight from the bottle. Alcohol was lining all her thoughts and feelings with cotton wool. Being drunk was so wonderful. Her intoxication felt like a warm embrace. All the sub-personalities that were constantly on the rampage inside her – with razor-sharp splinters in their paws and long claws – had been defeated. They were huddled in on themselves nose to tail while she was dancing herself into a feeling of warmth with her guests.

"I told you it would be a disaster," Anna-Maria said to Robert.

They were in the car on the way back to town.

"She got too drunk," Robert said. "That's the kind of thing that happens."

"Could you just take my side for once?" Anna-Maria hissed. "Do you know what she is? She's a fucking class traitor."

"She was probably feeling inferior as well," Robert said.

"What do you mean 'as well'? I don't feel inferior. I'm pissed off because they feel superior. There's a difference."

Anna-Maria leaned forward to wipe the condensation off the inside of the windscreen. Her wet clothes and the heat from the AC were turning the car into a steam bath.

"And then there's Jenny's shoes," she whined. "They must have cost over a thousand. Rebecka could have written that on the invite. Dress: thermal underwear and bras! Buying this dress was completely pointless. I've never felt more out of place in my entire life. Only they're the kind of people who say: 'Putting a knife in one's mouth is perfectly acceptable as long as one actually knows how to use the cutlery.' Just what the hell is that supposed to even mean? The upper classes can behave how they like while the rest of us have to toe the line. Is my make-up running down my cheeks? I think I've got mascara under my breasts."

Robert glanced at her.

"No . . . you look incredibly sexy!"

"Oh stop it, just stop. Wait, where are we going, you're going in completely the wrong direction."

Robert shushed her as he turned left at the roundabout, leaving old Kiruna behind. "I want to show you something."

"What? What do you mean, show me something? Some construction project beside the new town hall? I don't think so. Can't we do that some other time? You can't see anything in any case."

He shushed her again, smiled and winked. She tried twice to ask where they were going and to tell him all she really wanted was to go home. But he kept silencing her with "uh-uh . . . uh- uh."

They went through the village of Kauppinen, even though motor traffic wasn't allowed.

"Do you remember?" he said.

"You're out of your tiny mind!" she said.

She had to smile though, she couldn't help it.

How could she forget! He was eighteen and she was sixteen. They were both living with their parents but Robert had a car. That first summer before he moved into his studio flat on Timmermansgatan they used to drive down to the gravel pit at Poikkijärvivägen, park out of view of the road, and have sex.

"First I got you all hot and bothered through Kauppinen, and then it was: action!"

"What a windbag you are." Anna-Maria laughed. "Do you remember our first time?"

The very first time had been one warm bright summer night. He had the windows wound down as they drove through the village. Then they had snogged like crazy, folded back the rear seat and wriggled out of their jeans. But they had forgotten to wind the windows up, or she had forgotten. He had thought about it, he told her afterwards, but didn't want to spoil the mood, he'd been nervous getting the condom on. The car had filled with furious mosquitoes in next to no time. Robert must have got a hundred bites on his backside.

"Between the buttocks even," was all he had to say now, they knew the story and didn't need to repeat the details.

Anna-Maria laughed and wiped her eyes.

"My mother had an elkhound cross that got worms one time," Robert said. "It dragged its arse across the kitchen floor to scratch the itch. I felt like that dog for three whole days."

"I can't believe it," Anna-Maria whimpered. "When is that ever going to stop being so funny."

He steered in behind the gravel pit. Kept the engine running.

"Are you being serious?" she said. "Shouldn't we go home? The bed in our room has been feeling so neglected."

"Not a chance," he said and undid both their seat belts.

He leaned in and kissed her the way he knew she liked to be kissed, tenderly on the temple and under her jawbone. He took the lobe of her ear between his lips and laved it with his tongue.

He pinched her nipples through the fabric of her dress. She opened her legs and raised her bottom so she could pull the dress up and the stockings down to her knees.

"How are we . . ." she said and glanced back. "It's going to be difficult with the car being a rubbish tip."

The whole of the back seat was cluttered with stuff for the recycling depot.

"Shh . . ." Robert whispered. "Sit still."

He knew his girl. In his eyes she was still that cool girl in the first year of the upper second and he couldn't believe his incredible luck in having her. Her breasts were heavy and hot in his hands, he squeezed them tenderly. She opened her mouth and began to gasp. He was

404

looking at her face without blinking. He wanted to see her being pleasured, tortured almost, see her come. He never tired of that.

His hand moved between her legs, his fingers finding their way.

"You didn't take off your panties," he said, checking her rolled-down stockings.

"No, because I just bought these posh new ones," she said.

She smiled into his eyes. The snow had formed a blanket over the car. There was just the two of them in all the world. Her teeth glistened in the dark. As if they belonged to a cunning little animal.

His fingers stole under the edge of her panties. She uttered a squeak. They were used to being quiet with five children in the house. But this time he wanted to hear her. He found her places, she was getting wet, he rubbed her where she liked, kissing her all the time, her fantastic soft mouth, her gorgeous tongue. He hoped he wasn't going to pull a muscle; his twisted position in the driver's seat would definitely not have been approved by an ergonomist.

She tensed, he worked her harder, she braced herself with her feet, making those noises of hers, the best in the world.

She slammed her hand against the side window when she came. He could feel her pulsing against his fingers as she yelled: "Now, oh yes, now!"

He was so moved he began to weep. He blinked away the tears. How could she possibly have chosen him? And then stayed with him? All those years, the kids, all the nights he had got to sleep beside her. Her face right now, the genuine pleasure on it, the expressions only he got to see.

Anna-Maria slid into an indolent relaxed state.

"Oh my giddy aunt," she gasped, and he laughed at the quaintness of the phrase.

"What about you?" she asked.

"I'll take a rain check," he said and got out of the car to clear the windscreen.

Then he drove out of their old hideaway and took her home and got her into a hot bath. He found a bottle of bath foam. It was covered in dust but there was nothing wrong with the contents.

"I'm going to keep you for a bit longer," Anna-Maria said as she sank back into the hot water.

"Lucky me," he said.

FRIDAY 6TH MAY

Rebecka stumbled into the kitchen at around ten in the morning. Her guests were already up and her arrival was met with applause.

"Ow . . . ow," she said, waving them away. She crashed into a chair. Maria placed a cup of black coffee in front of her.

"Bad?" Sophie asked.

Rebecka grunted.

"I've got such a pain in my neck. Must have slept in a weird position."

"Oh no, not the neck," Sophie said grinning.

"Ah, the neck," Clara said. "Maybe your pillow's what's wrong. You should get one from Tempur."

"You fuckers," Rebecka said. "Wasn't I the one who treated you to a wonderful dinner last night? And now you're mocking me in my own home."

Sivving was at the stove, cooking pancakes. Bella was under the table with her mitten. The Brat was sitting some way off staring at her. He wasn't going to be allowed under the table and that spot had now become the only place he wanted to be. He wanted the mitten as well. More than anything else in the world. Sivving gave Rebecka a look, half amused and half reproachful.

"Huh, good thing your grandmother can't see you now."

"She can see me," Rebecka groaned. "She's watching me from that heaven of hers and judging me. What have you been up to?"

Through a half-open eye she could see that the table, the kitchen sofa and the floor were covered in pieces of paper and open files. The accounts of the Pekkari family.

"We thought we'd help you go through these," Sofi said and took a swig of her coffee. "You were telling us about your case yesterday, remember? And we can't go skiing anyway. Apparently it's going to snow all day. We made a start and then Sivving, the one and only Sivving, turned up and began cooking breakfast."

"It's not my case anymore," Rebecka said. "And how are you up to doing any work? If I read even one letter of the alphabet I'm going to be sick."

Sophie appeared at her side and put a champagne glass in front of her. It was hissing with bubbles that popped up to the surface and burst. At the bottom of the glass a thick yellow juice was slowly swimming. Sophie put a white pill beside it.

"Put that in your mouth and down the glass in one go," Sophie said quietly. "You'll feel better in a flash. I promise."

"What is it?"

"A Valium. And champagne and mango juice. I packed it for Riksgränsen, only we needed it now."

"I don't know if pick-me-ups are my thing," Rebecka protested.

"Oh, come on," Sophie said. "It's not like we're alkies necking hand sanitiser at A & E, is it? You're not going to die. Quite the reverse. Trust Nurse Sophie."

Rebecka tossed the pill into her mouth and downed what was in the glass.

Sophie went to the stove and threw her arms around Sivving and kissed him on the cheek.

"Why don't we settle down and get married?" she said. "You're going to have to get over that Maj-Lis at some point?"

"Huh!" Sivving said, looking pleased.

Rebecka found herself feeling better more or less immediately. She regarded her empty glass as if it had contained a magic elixir.

"Did you find anything?" she asked with a nod at all the bits of paper that had been spread out.

"Actually, we did," Maria said. "Have a bit of pancake and we'll tell you."

Raimo Koskela, Börje's father, was buried on Friday morning. Snow was still falling thickly, falling through the sky as if God were sitting up there making notes on tiny bits of paper and dropping them.

Börje and Ragnhild arrived at the church. They sat in the car for a while, waiting for the hearse. The coffin was unloaded to wait for the bearers.

That could have been me, it occurred to Ragnhild.

Would Paula have come to the funeral? What sort of life have you led if no-one sheds a tear when you're gone?

There were six coffin-bearers: Ragnhild, Börje, Sven-Erik Stålnacke, Spike, Nyrkin-Jussi and a man from the boxing club.

The sexton had gritted extra so no-one would slip and kill themselves.

The priest was standing at the very front of the church to receive them as they marched inside.

The bearers took their seats. The roses for the coffin had been placed on the seats, waiting for them. Ragnhild put hers in her lap.

She spoke well, that priest, the one who looked like a twelve-year-old, Ragnhild thought. To provide the eulogy for a man who went missing in 1962 and bring him to life was like making bricks without straw. But she spoke about what he had meant to Börje Ström as a child. How Börje had managed to keep his father such a visible presence throughout his life, in those tattoos on the outside, but tattooed inside him as well. How his father had lived on in him. Then of course came the association, a bit like a crossword clue, to everlasting life and the eternal presence of Our Father in heaven. But overall a really good funeral oration. Ashes to ashes and dust to dust. What would the priest have said about her, about Ragnhild? That she was a good casualty nurse. That she cared about her patients and showed them respect and treated them with dedication.

She was looking at the altarpiece. It has been painted by Prince Eugen. A landscape in Södermanland with the kind of large deciduous trees you would never find in Norrland. Was it supposed to represent the eternal meadows of heaven?

What contempt, she thought. The homeland of the rich in central Sweden is supposed to provide us with an image of paradise.

When the church was built at the beginning of the twentieth century the vicar had complained there was no cross. In the end the diocese had to have one made. One of the church commissioners had his artist friend Christian Eriksson produce a small statue that was placed on the altar. A group of Sami in front of a cross. Some of them kneeling, others standing with their arms crossed. The church was enraged. The statue had to be reworked several times. More and more of them on their knees, fewer and fewer with their arms crossed.

Obviously the cross had held no interest for the commissioner and his well-off friends. They could manage without a god who suffered, the working-class boy who sweated blood in terror and was crucified.

The ordinary people though, the common people, they really needed it. To give them hope. To keep them in their place.

Echoing churches with that faint odour of dust had never held any real attraction for her. She had never been able to understand people who said they found peace in them. It was a different matter in the woods. And the mountains.

And just as she was thinking that, a microscopically tiny spider floated down from above on a single thread of silk.

Well, hello there you little rascal, Ragnhild thought and let the spider land on the back of her hand. Where did you come from? How on earth can you survive in here?

God as a spider, she thought the next moment. Not a lion. A little lord spinning a secret web of goodness that manages to stick to life's most painful spots.

I'm going to talk to Rebecka, she thought. I'm going to tell her about Virpi.

And as soon as she had that thought, she was filled with peace.

We'll all be dead soon anyway, she was thinking. The entire existence of this planet is just the merest blink of an eye. Pain, fear. Let it come.

The spider, little rascal that it was, was moving across the back of her hand. She put the hand on the backrest of the pew in front to let it move across.

They sang "Narrow is the Gate that leads to Eternal Peace" and then they went up in line to the coffin to put their roses on it and say goodbye.

The Ragnhild who got to her feet was a different person to the woman who had sat down on the pew. She moved carefully towards the coffin so as not to scare this feeling of hers away.

A bit longer, she prayed to God. Stay a bit longer.

Börje's hand reached for hers when they went back to their places and she let him take it. The organist played the Pilgrim hymn and they started to leave. Ragnhild was still bathing in her inner lake of peace. Bottle-brown but pure humus water. To live, just for a short while. And then be cremated and return to the earth. Dust to dust.

The Old Testament never rabbits on about eternal life, she thought.

The verse from Isaiah came to her: All flesh is grass, and all its loveliness is as the flower of the field. The grass withers, the flower fades.

There is true consolation in that, she thought. There's nothing to be anxious about in our being the blink of an eye, just a speck of dust. Here I am sitting in a church pew. I am grass. There is withered dead grass in that coffin. Börje may be driving back to Älvsbyn when the funeral is over but right now he is holding my hand.

Maybe what is completely meaningless and what is profoundly meaningful are one and the same?

She and Börje went out of the church without letting go of each other's hand.

She raised the tailgate. Villa was sitting there tapping her tail.

Ragnhild gave her a treat and put on her leash.

"Good girl," Börje said when she let the dog hop out.

"That's right," Ragnhild said. "She's such a good girl. She's starting to feel confident we don't mean her any harm."

"Are you our little girl?" Börje said to the dog.

Our. Ragnhild smiled at Börje. And the bells started ringing.

Nyrkin-Jussi came out wheeling Sisu-Sikke. Their taxi was already waiting.

Sven-Erik's partner Airi reached up on tiptoe to give Börje a hug. He found Ragnhild's hand again when they finished hugging. Everyone saw that. No-one said anything. That was nice.

Sven-Erik said they were welcome to come to their house and help clear the snow from the potato field.

As if we were a long-established couple already, Ragnhild thought.

She was expecting her inner self to buck against that, but her hand remained in Börje's. Those feelings of resentment were taking a long holiday, or so it seemed.

"You're joining us for coffee and cake, aren't you?" Börje asked the others, seeking reassurance before they all started walking towards their cars.

"How are you doing?" Ragnhild asked when they were in the car on their way to the parish hall.

"It was nice seeing so many people there at any rate," Börje said. "And Nyrkin-Jussi carrying the coffin as well, not bad for a guy over eighty."

The snow was sticking to the windscreen and Ragnhild put the wipers on.

"What would my life have been like if he hadn't gone missing?" Börje asked. "I'd never have become a boxer. For the dead person death is an ending. For those around him it's the start of a new chapter."

SEPTEMBER 1972

"And the devil, taking him up into an high mountain, shewed unto him all the kingdoms of the world in a moment of time."

Despite his nickname Big Ben, the boxing manager Ben O'Shaughnessy is a short fellow. There are patches of sweat on his shirt, his braces have been left dangling and his trousers are baggy at the knees. He must be slightly vain nonetheless because he obviously dyes his hair, what little remains of it. He leans back exaggeratedly when Börje steps inside his hotel suite. He gazes up at Börje as if he were standing beneath a lighthouse.

"Fetch me a ladder, I can climb up to say hello to this star," he calls out jokily to some men in suits and attractive women in short dresses who are seated in armchairs. They are drinking whisky in the middle of the day and laughing heartily. They get up as if on command.

Mr O'Shaughnessy offers a Cuban cigar, and Börje makes a joke someone told last night when the celebratory cigars were going. He makes it his own now in his halting English.

"No thanks. I smoked a Cuban yesterday. That's enough for me."

The suits laugh and Big Ben O'Shaughnessy pounds him on the back.

"Funny," he calls out and points with his thumb at Börje Ström. "I love a funny guy. If he hits like a grizzly. And takes gold at the Olympics."

And speaking of big. Börje has seen plenty of hotel rooms before, but this one is something else. It is as large as a three-bedroom apartment. Wall-to-wall carpet, dark wood polished to a shine, and brass. Heavy fabrics and a thick fog of tobacco smoke shroud the room. Börje shakes hands with the suits, a promoter from Miami, the president of a sponsorship group whose name he didn't catch, an assistant, a representative of the WBA, who was only here to congratulate him on the gold medal, and a lawyer. The gorgeous women do little waves when they are introduced by their first names.

Big Ben may look like a villain but he is one of the most important boxing impresarios in the United States. He has led boxers to world championship titles in the lightweight, featherweight and welterweight divisions. What he wants passionately is a heavyweight world champion. But light heavyweight isn't bad either. Not bad at all.

"Besides," he puffs when they are sitting on the three-piece suite to have a talk and the beautiful ladies have departed. "You're still young. You're going to put on more muscle. I'm going to make you a world champion at light heavyweight first, and then at heavyweight. Marciano was just a little bastard, that didn't stop him. The public are going to love you. We could do with a white guy right now."

That's right, the white American man on the street is longing for a white heavyweight world champ. Bill O'Shaughnessy sucks furiously at his cigar and calls Muhammad Ali a clay pigeon. The era of the clay pigeon is over, he says. After the loss to Frazier, Ali has been travelling round the world giving boxing demonstrations. Which is right up his street. All he can do is jump and dance backwards. That fucking Mohammedan, conscientious objector and agitator. And as for Frazier! Mr O'Shaughnessy shrugs resignedly. The World Championship match seems to have finished him off.

Börje is trying to get his head round this naming business. Ali has rejected his Cassius Clay name. He says it was his slave name. Börje's thoughts turned to his mother who, like many of the inhabitants of the Torne valley, translated her Finnish name to Swedish because Finnish was considered inferior. People who talked Finnish were considered inferior. From the beginning of the twentieth century until after the First World War it was impossible to get work in the mine if you were *lantalaiset;* the jobs all went to "real Swedes". Börje and his mother are called Ström, while the surname used by the rest of the family is *Niva,* which actually means stream. And at some point Börje had heard that the Swedish authorities used to give the Sami new names. The names were often to do with some kind of defect they had; if you were blind then *Blind* became your surname. You could get given slave names. Or you could be subjected to so much contempt you came to hate your own name.

He has to return from his musings, though, because there is a contract on the table. Big Ben is puffing out small clouds of smoke and explaining what is in it. No-one will be offering Börje better terms than these. The contract is for five years. Forty per cent of his earnings. That's a lot, but then Börje is an Olympic medallist. A gold medallist, even though it was by the skin of his teeth. Amateurs rarely make a go of the transition to a professional career, it has to be said. Professional boxing is an entirely different discipline as everyone knows. But Big Ben O'Shaughnessy is going to take a chance on Börje, he says. He believes in him.

Börje is thinking that that agitator and clay pigeon started out as an amateur boxer. Frazier and Foreman too. That is why Mr O'Shaughnessy has come all the way to Germany from New York, to sit in the crowd at the Olympics.

Big Ben O'Shaughnessy says that Börje mustn't tell his wife about this deal because then she would make Big Ben's life hell. The contract is much too generous. Being married is bloody expensive. Is Börje married? Right, not anymore. Big Ben knows how that is, doesn't he just. He is on his fifth. There's only one thing more expensive than a wife and that's an ex. But what are you supposed to do? You should see the new one. She has a backside like the fruit on the tree of paradise.

The suits yap in chorus. Ha ha.

"My coaches," Börje says, sitting there with the pen in his hand. "What about them?"

"Not gonna happen, my boy," Mr O'Shaughnessy says.

Mr O'Shaughnessy works with professional boxers, he explains. He has his own gym and his own coaches.

"Besides," he says and looks lovingly at his cigar, "I don't have any time for fruitcakes."

Börje Ström doesn't have to think too hard to work out that Big Ben, or one of the suits, must have spoken to the coach from Stockholm. People are just so full of shit.

He signs the contract. He came here to sign it. It still seems like an incredible dream, all of it. For a moment he feels a pang that there is no-one for him to ring, no-one to tell. No wife, no mother, and not Nyrkin-Jussi or Sisu-Sikke. They are going to be deeply disappointed about him turning professional and his leaving them now he is a success.

"Take the boy with you and buy him some snazzy clothes," Mr O'Shaughnessy orders one of the gorgeous women. "And a gold watch. If you're not married then you've got to make an impression on the ladies, right? You don't want to look like me, do you? Off with you, my boy, we'll celebrate tonight."

Airi and Sven-Erik sang the hymn "Narrow is the Gate" all the way home in the car.

He still had a good voice. He could see Airi smiling appreciatively at his side as he sang louder. She was better at remembering all the words.

The insight hit him like snow sliding off a roof. He fell silent.

"What is it?" she asked, trying to see through the curtain of snow. "Reindeer?"

Good thing he was driving so calmly and cautiously.

"No," he said. "It was just something that occurred to me."

"What?"

"I'll have to tell you later. I'll drive you home and then I'm driving back into town."

"Alright then, as long as you drive carefully."

She asked him if she could put on the local radio and he nodded. He dropped her off and waited until she was properly inside. You never knew with locks. They could freeze up or have any number of other problems, but once she had opened the door, he turned the car and drove back.

Perfectly fine, Airi thought. This is the way I want him.

One hour later Sven-Erik was standing at the entrance to Indian Summer Court. A piassava broom was leaning against the wall, and he took the opportunity to brush the snow away from the door while he gathered his thoughts, brushing and humming words from the same

Revivalist hymn about overcoming obstacles as you force a way through the narrow gate to heaven: "you have to force your way through to everlasting peace". That was what had brought him up short. The idea of having to force a way through.

He brushed off his trousers and shoes. Stamped the snow off the soles and went inside.

Sisu-Sikke and Nyrkin-Jussi had just had lunch. They asked if he'd like some coffee. There was something in the air, though, a kind of alertness on their part, or certainty maybe. They knew that something was about to happen.

They took their time. There was no hurry. They talked about the snow, the funeral and about the fact that Börje appeared to have got together with Ragnhild Pekkari, which was one hell of a surprise.

"Listen," said Sven-Erik finally, stroking his moustache. "There's this thing I've been wondering about."

Nyrkin-Jussi nodded. Sisu-Sikke's eyes were wide open. It was the look of a lathered horse. One that is rearing at a fire, a barrier that is terrifying it.

"Eighteen months ago the Pekkaris' main company, Berksäk AB, issued new shares and gained a new partner," Maria Taube said. "MOGI Capital Group, which appears to be a foreign investment company. If you look them up you get some babble about global growth, but not even a mention in any real economic forum or financial newspaper."

Sivving was at the sink doing the brunch washing-up by hand. The other women had started packing. The weather forecast said the snow was going to stop. So they were off to Riksgränsen. Sophie had her phone on speaker and was ordering a helicopter pick-up.

"Tell me more," Rebecka said, sprinkling sugar and cinnamon on her third pancake.

"One month later the company did a lease-back sale, basically selling its entire inventory to another foreign company and then leasing their machinery from them. They invested the purchase sum and the share premium following the new issue in a mining project in Uganda, but I can find very little information about that mining project online. The quarterly profits for the first quarter of this year were eighty per cent lower than in the preceding year."

Rebecka tried to catch her breath and then let it out in a loud exhale.

"You sound just like your grandmother now," Sivving commented from the sink. "She could sigh. By the way, you've got your vehicle inspection booked in today. Don't forget!"

"What?" Rebecka exclaimed. "I can't get behind the wheel today. You've got to check with me before you book that kind of thing."

"You'll end up losing your licence," Sivving said. "You haven't got a choice. I texted Krister. He said he'd come over and drive you there."

Maria looked pointedly at Rebecka.

"No," Rebecka mumbled. "This is a catastrophe."

"No, it isn't," Maria said. "Just do it. It's got to be a good thing if you can finally get together as friends. In any case, Bergsäk AB has acquired two of the major operators in the mining industry here in Kiruna, a drilling company and one that does tunnelling, demolition and disassembly. I can't tell you if they paid what they were worth. But I looked up the former owners on Facebook. None of them stayed on at the company to work as employees."

Rebecka wrote the names of both companies and their executives into her phone.

"People with skill and experience usually stay on in the job, for the transitional period at least. But they both left on the day of the sale," Maria continued. "And both of them moved away from the town afterwards. This is just guesswork, but if you get forced to sell then you tend to leave."

"So the profits diminish dramatically and you avoid Swedish taxes," Rebecka said. "And you buy companies from owners who flee the town after the sale."

"Three years ago Bergsäk was a family firm that reinvested its profits in the company and just kept beavering away," Maria said. "They've obviously changed tack."

"The make-the-money-and-responsibility-disappear tack," Rebecka said. "Only there's nothing to take them to court with. Or even to launch an investigation."

"Bergsäk was very definitely in trouble before the new issue. Liquidity was in the toilet. Two more things. Well, hello!"

The last was said to the Brat who had quite shamelessly leaped onto the kitchen sofa beside her. Bella gurgled a warning. He wasn't to get near her or her mitten glove.

"No, get down!" Rebecka said in a strict voice. "No dog of mine is going to sit at the dinner table."

"He's allowed to sit with me at the dinner table," Maria said. "You should come and stay with me in Stockholm, Bratty, and we'll go to the pub and eat shellfish."

The Brat buried his head in Maria's lap and avoided eye contact with his owner.

"I give up," Rebecka said. "Two more things?"

"One odd acquisition. A small printing firm. Why would they buy that? And, something that may interest you, the company owns a white camper van, wasn't that—"

"Yes," Rebecka exclaimed so forcefully that the Brat jumped back onto the floor. "The Russians drove around in a white camper van. With the sex workers."

"It's a diesel van, but there isn't a single diesel receipt in the company accounts."

"Would you bloody believe it," Rebecka said. "So what was the van being used for? And where is it?"

Then she leaned back in her chair.

"Only this isn't my case anymore. I'll have to give this to von Post. Not that he'll do a fucking thing. He won't want to go up against this corporate gang, not likely. Not even the camper van, that won't make any . . . all they've got to say is they lent it out, or failed to check on who was using it without permission. I think I've had enough of this town. I'm tired of working myself to death for nothing."

Maria Taube glanced over at Sivving, who was drying the plates and glasses and putting them away in the cupboards.

"Come outside with me for a bit," she said to Rebecka. "And we'll have a smoke."

They stood under the porch roof and looked at the falling snow. It was floating down in thin drifts.

"Didn't think you smoked," Rebecka said, offering her packet tentatively to Maria.

Maria waved it away.

"I'm going to resign from Meijer & Ditzinger," she said without preamble. "We . . ."

She tilted her neck towards the upstairs of Rebecka's house so as to include Sofi, Sophie and Clara.

". . . we're going to start our own firm."

"You're kidding!"

"No, Sofi and I are bound to be quarantined but that's not going to stop us. Sophie's brother is as rich as a troll and he's going to finance us to start with. Offices on Kommendörsgatan."

"Congratulations. Have you told—"

"God, no. You can't breathe a word about this to Måns. He's going to kill me. Sixty seconds after I resign I will be out on my ear for good. Do you want to join us?"

"Join you, as an employee?"

"As a partner. You didn't really think we went through those boxes for you to pass the time, did you? We were trying to cosy up to you, as you must have realised."

"And you managed to cosy up to Carl von Post by mistake," Rebecka said, smiling joylessly.

"Never mind. So what do you say? Måns will get over it. You can still sleep together. And you can fly up here every other weekend if you like. Even work from here every so often, we're flexible."

Rebecka took a deep drag. So that was why Maria had stopped going on at her about coming back to Meijer & Ditzinger. And that's why they had decided to fly up and say hello.

"They like you. And they know you're an absolute demon when it comes to corporate taxation."

"How long have you been planning this?"

Maria Taube shrugged.

"We started talking about it a year ago. You know how it is, you keep complaining. You're working yourself to death and you're always exhausted."

"Only you're already a partner, you must be earning—"

"I know, but that doesn't really help. So, what do you say?"

Rebecka put out her cigarette in the thick snake of snow that had accumulated on the handrail.

"I'm going to think about it. I don't want to stay on in the Prosecution Service. It wasn't as if I tried to get a job with them to begin with, I just had nowhere else to go when they let me out of the psychiatric ward."

"Please consider it carefully," Maria said and clasped her hands as if in prayer. "And one more thing. Don't get angry, OK?"

"Are you worried I'm going to start wrestling with you in the snow?"

"Yes."

They laughed out loud.

"I'm your friend," Maria said. "I love you. I think you should go and talk to someone."

Rebecka could feel her insides knotting. She concentrated on trying to keep her face relaxed.

"Am I difficult to be friends with, do you think?" she said in a tone that was nowhere near as light and jokey as she intended.

"Oh, Rebecka, not at all. Didn't I just get on my knees and beg you to come and work with us? Don't you remember what fun we had when we were working together?"

No, Rebecka thought. I don't remember. I've got a film crew in my head compiling a record of my worst moments, all my shortcomings and all the times I've embarrassed myself. Then they run the film over and over again. Even things I did when I was fourteen.

"You just seem so down to me. I'm worried."

"Sorry," Rebecka said. "I don't want you to worry about me."

Gentle on the surface, dismissive inside. And it worked. An end to the serious conversation. Being someone other people worried about felt loathsome.

"OK," Maria said, looking sad despite her smile. "Thank you for a really lovely evening and breakfast. Let's go back up before Sophie gets engaged to Sivving."

"There'd be wrestling in the snow for real if that happens," Rebecka said with a grin.

"What occurred to me, you see," said Sven-Erik, who could feel his stomach aching from all the coffee, "is this business of the cottage that Raimo Koskela went to with Börje."

They were onto their third cup. Sisu-Sikke had a sipping cup in front of him, but wasn't drinking. An untouched packet of biscuits was on the table.

"Raimo drove a motorbike," Sven-Erik went on. "Börje rode pillion. Only, Börje told us there was a car that drove up that evening, when Raimo went missing. He could hear the engine and then it drove off and Raimo was gone."

"That's right," Nyrkin-Jussi said.

"It's just that," Sven-Erik went on, rubbing at his moustache, "the aunt who was renting it out, a relative of yours, Sikke. She'd put up a barrier across the forest road at that point. According to . . ."

He took his phone out of his pocket and checked the notes Rebecka had sent him. God bless that girl for being so thorough and methodical.

". . . Mervi Johansson, who Rebecka Martinsson talked to when we were over there."

Nyrkin-Jussi stirred his coffee. The spoon clinked against the china. Like a little bell. Like the heart of an anxious animal.

"You can drive round a barrier on a motorbike. But not with a car. They must have had a key. Did you have a key, Sikke?"

Sikke shook his head.

"But you knew where she lived . . ."

He looked at his notes again.

". . . this woman, Olga Palo, your aunt's sister-in-law, who let the cottage."

Sisu-Sikke reached for Nyrkin-Jussi's hand.

"Do you want me to tell him?" Nyrkin-Jussi said.

Sisu-Sikke shook his head. They sat there like that for a little while. Sven-Erik waited. Being in a hurry was rarely useful. Sometimes you had to give silence its due.

Then Sisu-Sikke said, "Poi . . . poi . . ."

Nyrkin-Jussi got the pointing board that had been placed to one side. Letter by letter Sisu-Sikke pointed out his account:

"Lingonking asked after Raimo
where he'd gone with the boy
I told him the truth
that he'd rented off Olga in Kurkkio
he asked where she lived
then Raimo went missing
a week later and the King wanted to see Raimo's locker at the club
there was nothing special in it
he said
tell me if you hear from Raimo
I knew
he said that to trick me
I got the feeling we would never hear from Raimo again
but then I said to myself
I was imagining things
though
I knew really."

"We didn't ask questions, you know," Nyrkin-Jussi said, looking anguished. "The Lingonberry King owned the gym, he still owns the property, but at the time he provided most of the equipment as well. Some of the lads worked for him at one thing or another, that was common knowledge. But we tried to keep out of it and focus on doing our jobs . . ."

He broke off.

"Here I am trying to make excuses for us."

"For me," Sisu-Sikke pointed. "I never told Jussi what the King asked me."

"True, but obviously I couldn't help wondering as well," Nyrkin-Jussi said. "There was the talk about the money."

"What talk?" Sven-Erik asked.

"Raimo wasn't one of the King's henchmen, not at all. Even though he did do jobs for him. The usual things, carpentry and the like, but a lot of driving as well. The King knew he was a decent guy, that you could trust him. He collected money for him quite a bit. From people who owed money for all kinds of things, alcohol and drugs, but rents as well along with payments for stolen goods, for his various services, you might say. He would be given the money in a plastic bag and then drive on to the next one."

"OK?"

"Two of the lads at the club, they turned up with bruised knuckles the day before Raimo disappeared. We didn't ask about it, but we heard talk anyway. A bag of money had gone missing apparently, a luxury car that had been driven down to Germany and sold over there. They had beaten up the guy who did the driving and who was given the payment. Gave him a proper going over, though in the end they were convinced he hadn't in fact handed over a bag filled with toilet paper but one with real money in."

"And it was after that Frans Mäki asked if you'd seen Raimo?" Sven-Erik said. "And once Raimo had gone missing, he checked his locker and asked about him again. And then the rumour spread that he'd been involved in a fake currency deal and been shot by the Soviet mafia."

"Yeah," said Nyrkin-Jussi, breathing in.

"It sounds like the Lingonberry King might have been checking to see if there was a bag of cash in Raimo's locker."

"Yeah."

"It sounds like he was asking if you'd seen Raimo after he disappeared,

426

while spreading the rumour that it was the Soviet mafia that knocked Raimo off to divert attention from himself."

"Yeah."

"It sounds like Frans Mäki shot Raimo Koskela. The island where they found Raimo is only a kilometre away from the cottage where he was staying with Börje. And Frans Mäki knew Henry Pekkari."

"Only we didn't know," Nyrkin-Jussi exclaimed. "The way we saw it Raimo had gone missing. He could have turned tail and run for it, couldn't he? It's not like we were mates or anything – he used to box at the club, that was it."

There was a note of appeal in his voice. Then he waved dismissively with both hands. As though to signal that the words he had uttered in his own defence were worthless.

"Olga Palo has been dead for years in any case," Sven-Erik said. "There's no knowing if she handed over the keys and kept that quiet when Raimo went missing."

"Or they just went in and got the keys, borrowed them. People never locked their houses in those days. It was late. She might have been asleep."

"Thank you for being honest with me," Sven-Erik said as he got to his feet.

"Are you going to tell Börje?" Nyrkin-Jussi asked.

"Yes, I've got to, don't I?"

"How can you ask forgiveness for something like that?"

Sven-Erik was thinking about the time he had been furious at Anna-Maria. After the shooting at Regla.

"We're all old men, the lot of us," he said. "And life passes by so incredibly fast."

*

Nyrkin-Jussi was sitting with Sisu-Sikke's right hand clasped between his own. Börje Ström looked down at them from the newspaper cuttings on the walls.

"We did look after him," Nyrkin-Jussi said. "He got to be world champion. If we'd gone to the police, what would that have achieved? Nothing apart from our getting kicked out of the club. And who would have looked after Börje then? What were we supposed to do?"

"Th . . . e . . . r . . . ri . . . right . . . thi . . . thing," Sisu-Sikke said.

Krister texted Rebecka soon after lunchtime. Her guests had left. Sivving and Bella had gone home and she had pulled herself together and gone for a walk with the Brat. She was lying on the kitchen sofa, slow-surfing on the Internet.

Hi there Krister wrote. Sivving called and said you had your car inspection today, only you're in no condition to drive after yesterday's party. Do you want me to come over and drive you?

She sat herself up and began to tap an answer.

That would be so . . .

At first she wrote "lovely" but then deleted it. Good God, she had begun to sound just like Maria Taube's friends. Then she tried out a load of other adjectives. In the end it was "great".

On my way Krister wrote. Your appointment's at half one

She had another shower, as her body was sweating out yesterday's sins like a steam engine. She chose a sweater, one of her father's old ones, it wouldn't do for Krister to think she'd made an effort. She let her freshly washed hair hang free. She looked at herself in the mirror several times. She had butterflies in her stomach.

When he arrived it was all she could do to stop the Brat from running into the yard to say hello. She locked the door and the barking from inside was loud and unhappy.

He didn't have the dogs with him. Before, when everything was the way it was supposed to be, the Brat, Tintin and Roy would have been allowed to run a few crazy circles around the yard. They would have left them all together in the house. And made dinner together.

He looked at her front door. She looked at the empty dog cage in his car.

"So shall we go then?" he asked.

He had already cleared the snow off her car. An odd sense of calm settled over her when she got into the passenger seat beside him and handed over the car keys. At least he wasn't at home with Marit.

He pushed back the seat and adjusted the rear-view mirror.

Sivving had sat in the passenger seat most recently. A good thing because he always shoved it as far back as it would go. From where she sat she could keep looking at Krister without him noticing.

It was a shame he had his jacket on, she liked his forearms. But she could at least gaze at his wrists and hands.

His lovely hands around the wheel. All the parts of her body those fingers had touched, there wasn't a spot they had not visited. Just the way he used to kiss her and pinch her earlobe at the same time, his other hand moving down towards her breasts.

"What a snowfall," he said. "I really hope no-one's going to be stupid enough to head out and powder-ski when it stops. There's a real risk of avalanches all over."

Her thoughts leaped immediately to mountain rescue and from there it was only a ridiculously short hop to Marit.

What did he do with Marit? Did he pinch her ear as well while he was kissing her and fumbling for her breast. Did he do the same things with her?

It was impossible to think about, while being entirely possible to imagine. Unbearable.

She realised that she thought about him all the time. She really did, all the little habits of daily life reminded her of him, walking the dog in the woods, putting on her skis, folding the milk container his way so it would take up as little room as possible in the rubbish, brushing her teeth. The toothbrush that never moved into his bathroom cupboard. The one she always took with her when she left.

If only she hadn't slept with Måns.

She couldn't even remember why she had, how Måns and she had decided to get together over dinner.

Why? And why did she tell Krister? The way she did. Her mind got fuzzy; she couldn't see herself in the story.

She drove directly to Krister's house from the airport. Told him, straight out, in the doorway. She didn't even take off her shoes. She knew what would happen. Perhaps she wanted it to happen. He showed her the door without saying a word. And after that it was over.

They were coming up to the town. Krister was driving carefully in the loose snow. The fan was running at top speed; the windows were misted on the inside from the soaking their clothes had got from the snow. She ought to say something about the weather. Only, the words were stuck.

When it was over, the moment the door closed behind her she had wanted him again. Though, no, that wasn't true. At first it had been easy. She got the Brat to jump into the car and she drove down to Kurravaara alone with the dog and felt free. It hurt, but in a good way. That sense of ease must have lasted a good week.

Then she started thinking about him. The longing for him crept up on her. She didn't do anything about it though, and then all of a sudden Marit and he were a couple. Quicker than you could say attachment issues. Everyone was talking about it at work; they were all so happy, they didn't realise how much she cared, did they, that it hurt, every single word.

So she had put on a smile and uttered the kind of meaningless phrases that made her feel like she should rinse out her mouth with bleach. "She seems to be good for him." "He's such a lovely guy."

They didn't have to wait for the vehicle inspection. Her registration number came up on the display so they could just drive straight in.

Rebecka got a coffee from the machine, but Krister waved the offer away. He went out into the falling snow, pulled up his hood and made a call.

To her, of course.

Rebecka felt so dejected it was a miracle she stayed in her chair. She kept tipping it back and forth; it was dirty white plastic, a garden chair in fact.

What am I going to do with myself? she was thinking. I can't be with Måns, I couldn't be with Krister, I can't bear being alone, I can't stay on at work. There's something fundamentally wrong with me. Everything turns to shit.

She was watching the vehicle inspection team; she could see them testing the brakes while the car was in the air. She checked her phone. No messages.

She looked at Krister's back outside in the falling snow.

What were they talking about? What do you fancy for dinner? You. And I fancy you. Was Marit in bed rubbing herself off while he talked filth in her ear? While she sat there with a brown plastic cup of terrible coffee, looking on.

Then the car was ready and she paid.

Krister put his phone away when she rapped on the windowpane.

"Did it go OK?" he asked as he steered out onto the main road.

"Yes," she said. "So . . . was that Marit you were talking to? Do you have to report in?"

She could have bitten off her tongue.

He glanced over at her, his face hard.

"Sorry," she said quickly. "I was just joking. So bloody clumsy."

It was a while before he replied.

"It was Marit who persuaded me to help you with the MOT," he said. "When Sivving asked me. She feels sorry for you. And so do I."

That's the problem with lovers, Rebecka thought as the flickering snow made her eyes swim. They find out which particular words are deadly. And then before you know it they've said them.

The entire way home she was calculating how much paid leave and holiday she could take. Almost enough to last through her notice.

Börje Ström called Spike Mäki. He had been sitting at Ragnhild's kitchen table, deciding there was no point thinking about it. He was just going to climb straight into the ring.

Ragnhild was lying on the sofa in the living room, reading a book.

"I've really got to see your father now," Börje said. "If he didn't shoot my dad, he knows who did."

Spike at the other end, backing away while he parried.

"That's a terrible accusation," he said. "I know Dad's no angel, I really do, but how do you know he—"

"That doesn't matter. I've got to talk to him. So either I drive out there on my own and sit outside the house until they let me in. Or you can help me, help me get to see him. I just want to know what the fuck happened. I'm not out for revenge; I'm not going to create problems."

Spike was silent. Börje could hear him chewing something and then swallowing.

Ragnhild turned the page in the living room.

"I'll arrange a meeting," Spike said finally. "He's not a well man. But do not drive out there on your own."

Then he hung up. Börje went in to Ragnhild.

"How did it go?" she asked quietly. Villa's muzzle was visible from her spot behind the sofa and she didn't want to scare her. "What did he say?"

"He said he would arrange a meeting."

"Do you think Frans Mäki is going to confess? Even if it was him?"

"Dunno, but you've got to keep at it if you want to get anywhere."

"Hum. And what are you going to do if it was him? If you do find out? Burn his house down?"

"No," Börje replied laughing. "What good would that do?"

"I'd like to burn Henry's house down. Only the problem is it's my house too, my childhood home."

That's the thing about revenge, Börje was thinking. You have to be really careful about what you set fire to.

1972–1974

Börje Ström's New York is not that big. He lives on the west side of Hell's Kitchen in one of the Irish neighbourhoods. The people here are as poor as church mice and the street is crawling with kids. There's no escaping the smell of cooked cabbage and rotting rubbish.

Every morning he takes the narrow stairs down to the front door in a few cat-like jumps. He does his run early and afterwards has breakfast a couple of blocks away at the Sunshine Diner, fried egg and sausage, two cups of coffee, even though the coffee is a pathetic excuse for the real thing, rusty water from a ditch.

Big Ben's gym is located in a six-storey brick building in Brooklyn. There's a warehouse on the ground floor and the gym is on the third. The place is airy with large windows that can be opened; nice and clean, all the equipment is new.

Börje still stops outside every now and then just to listen to the sounds coming from the open windows. The clatter of boxing balls and skipping ropes, the quiet rhythm of leather gloves meeting sandbags. The gym is his home.

In the evenings, if the apartment is too hot, he sits on the tarred roof of the building. The residents refer to it as Tar Beach. When the wind is in the right direction he can hear the sounds from Madison Square Garden as people gather. The tooting of taxis and sirens, never-ending sirens, the noise of the crowds making their way inside. Some day he's going to box there.

In the ring he's still being matched against palookas and veteran journeymen on their way down.

His coach is a mild-mannered older man from Paris, Texas, so everyone calls him Paris. His boxing career was ended prematurely by some form of retinal detachment, just like Dad's. He keeps telling Börje he has to be patient.

"They've got to build up your rep," he says right from the start, scratching at one of the dry patches that constantly bloom on his arms and the back of his hands. "You were an amateur until very recently. Everyone knows you won the Olympics, they've got their eyes on you, but professional boxing is a different ball game. You've got to have a track record before the big matches are going to come your way."

Paris is pleased that Börje doesn't laze around, that he is hard-working and disciplined, that he lives to train and can skip rope like a breeze.

"Keep it up," he says. "You're going to be needing that fitness soon enough."

Börje is winning all the matches he fights. The strength of his opponents starts to increase before too long. Börje still wins. He is relentless in the ring and he punches hard. All the papers are writing about him. They start calling him The Swedish Viking, The White Polar Bear; they compete with each other to see who can come up with a nickname that sticks.

Börje isn't particularly funny, he can't do the patter and show off like many other boxers but he has pale skin and is blond and blue-eyed. Swedish Bond-girl Britt Ekland tells the paper: "So no, he doesn't talk a lot. But Börje Ström doesn't need to talk to knock a girl out."

On October 13th, 1974, Börje Ström fights a match against Jim Jones. He's an old boxer, over thirty-five.

"Don't underestimate him, though," Paris says. "He's still got a vicious right uppercut. And he's stayed on his feet in all his matches."

There are a lot of people in the audience. Big Ben and his entourage are sitting in the front row. The press has gathered and a film camera has been rigged up just outside the ring.

Jim Jones's wife is also sitting in the front row with their eldest son.

Börje immediately goes in hard. He knows that Jones can take a lot of punishment but he keeps pushing him, keeping him off balance. He's not going to allow Jones to root himself to the floor to gain the energy for that right of his.

They both land a good few punches but these are mostly on the arms and hands. Börje Ström is focused on the sixth round. He is not going to miss his opportunity. By the sixth Jones will be tired. Börje is going to keep him constantly working. He drives Jones between the corners, giving him no breaks.

When the pin-up girl totters through the footlights around the ring, dressed only in a few threads and carrying the sign for round six, he can hear Big Ben saying to his entourage:

"If he can't knock that poor guy down, how's he going to beat the big guys?"

The audience is getting impatient too. The bell rings for round six. Börje knows he is ahead on points but that won't be enough today.

Börje ramps up the pressure. He's aiming for the knockout and Jones is running out of fuel. Jones tries to get at Börje's vulnerable eyebrow. Börje, for his part, is focused on keeping Jones off balance so he'll be forced to move with his legs wide apart and lose his reach.

Börje steps left, launches a right uppercut, following it with a hook while simultaneously predicting the path of Jones's right punch so it just glances off his ear. Before Jones has time to regain his balance Börje has landed a vicious combination of punches to the body.

He's got Jones on the ropes now. Börje is launching missiles, Jones is bravely holding on, turning, twisting, and managing to avoid the final blow but he is snorting like a bull. Börje feels like a firework going off. The audience is on their feet, howling. He is worried the bell will ring just as much as Jones must be hoping it will. There's not going to be another round. He lands two good blows on his opponent's jaw. He can see that Jones's legs want to give way; the guy is standing on two strands of boiled spaghetti, his guard is down and Börje clouts him on the head.

Jones thuds to the floor like a horse that has been shot. The referee starts counting.

The ref is lifting Börje's hand. It is only now he realises how out of breath he is. And that his ear is bleeding. The audience is roaring.

Jones is still on the floor. His legs keep jerking and twisting like two fish that have just been caught. Someone hangs the cape over Börje's shoulders and he leaves the arena. The medical team are already in the ring.

Big Ben arrives in the locker room with his escort to congratulate him even before Paris has finished untying Börje's gloves.

"How is Jones doing?" Börje asks.

"You're my white guy," Big Ben laughs. "And my white guy sent that black guy to the hospital. That's what I wanna see. That's what I wanna fucking see."

In the break room Anna-Maria Mella was scraping the last of yesterday's leftovers from her plate. The family had eaten chicken and rice while she was at Rebecka's and there was enough left for her lunch box, though it was mostly rice and sauce. She shouldn't have microwaved the salad as well.

She felt a twinge of pain in her side as she got up, but made an effort not to let it show. She had pulled something when she was wrestling with Rebecka. Fuck her as well. She looked out of the window, but Rebecka's car wasn't there.

Good thing, she thought. Or I'd have forced her to clear the hell off.

"Hi there. Have you hurt yourself," asked Magda Vidarsdotter, who had just been reheating her noodles.

"Slipped on the snow yesterday."

Which wasn't entirely untrue.

"Oh god, you poor thing."

"Not to worry, just bruised."

"So what do you make of this weather?" Vidarsdotter said. "The forecast said it was going to stop snowing today."

Anna-Maria shrugged. She turned on the coffee machine which woke up and started humming. She stared at the bright-red slogan on the display with hatred.

Karzan Tigris came in. He had just taken a "Look it's snowing" photo for Instagram. He'd been holding up today's cop-coffee and let snow fall into the cup. In the rest of Sweden it was already spring.

"Lucky for us the trouble is staying indoors," he said. "Where is everyone today?"

Anna-Maria shrugged. Tommy Rantakyrö was at home. She'd told him to stay at home until next week, hadn't she. At least there hadn't been a complaint about the phone he had smashed in Riksgränsen.

Her phone rang at that very moment and his name came up on the screen.

"Hello," she said, making an effort to sound warm and cheerful.

"Is that you . . . Anna-Maria . . .?"

Tommy's voice was hoarse, high-pitched. Like a cry.

She immediately became concerned.

"Tommy, how are you?"

"I just can't hack it anymore, Anna-Maria, I can't deal with this."

"What, hang on. Hang on a moment."

She grabbed her coffee cup and rushed out of the room and into her office.

"I'm going to end it," he said. "I've got my service weapon out and I . . . I . . ."

An alarm went off inside Anna-Maria. What a God-awful mess, he's at rock bottom. He must have been for months. And all she'd done . . . she hadn't done anything.

She took a deep breath.

"Tommy," she said calmly. "You're an adult and you can do what you like. Only you and I are going to have a talk first, do you hear me?"

Her phone rang. Rebecka Martinsson. She rejected the call.

"Tommy?"

What the hell, had they been cut off?

"Tommy, are you still there?"

He was whimpering like a child who's been stung.

"I'm still here."

"Where are you? I'm on my way. Don't do anything, OK? I'm coming."

*

Krister parked in the driveway to his house. He had put the knife into Rebecka. He had known what he was doing when he said Marit and he felt sorry for her and that was the reason he had driven her to the inspection.

"For fuck's sake," he said aloud.

Being capable of that kind of cruelty, wanting to inflict it, had left him feeling deeply disturbed. He wondered what his sister would say. Definitely something he wouldn't want to hear.

Through the kitchen window he could see Marit sitting at the table with her head in her hands. He got out of the car and inside the house he could hear the dogs hurling themselves against the door and barking. Marit usually let them out to greet him. Otherwise the shoe pile would be a mess. But this time she was staying where she was. He went to the door, a warning bell ringing inside him.

He said hello to the dogs in the hall. Then he stuck his head into the kitchen before hanging up his jacket and taking off his shoes.

"How did it go?" she asked.

"Alright, the car passed," he said. "How are you?"

"Not that great," she said. "We need to talk. Do you want tea? I've been baking."

There was a crack in her voice as she said the last bit.

He told the dogs to go and lie down. He sat opposite her. He said nothing, waiting.

She poured out tea. He thought about all the times she had got irritated over his teapot, tea always ran down the spout when you stopped pouring. You had to hold a piece of kitchen paper beneath it.

She passed him a slice of banana cake. He broke a bit off and put it in his mouth, nodding to indicate it tasted good. But he left the rest on the plate.

"I don't want this anymore," she said.

"You don't want what?"

"Us."

He had to take a deep breath. Tintin got up on his paws and put his head in his lap.

"Is this because I drove Rebecka—" he said, but she stopped him with a gesture.

"Of course not," she said. "But . . ."

She looked him in the eye. And he was wondering what face he was supposed to adopt, what she wanted from him.

". . . it's just so unfair," she added. "I think I'm better than her."

"You *are* better than her."

He tried to grasp her hand but she let it slip down into her lap. Tintin lifted his head and scratched him with her paw.

"I'm happy," Marit said. "Almost all the time. I'm an orderly person. I've got friends. I come up with things to do. The sex is good . . ."

"Very good," he whispered.

". . . When it happens. So, this isn't about her. Forget about her. This is about me. I don't feel loved. I think I deserve to feel loved."

"I do love you," he said, repressing with all his strength a feeling close to rage at her forcing those words out of him.

"You say you love me," she said. "But that word is so . . ."

She gestured with her hands, as though trying to grasp something that refused to be grasped. Sand running through your fingers.

"The dogs like her better than me," she said.

And then she started laughing. At herself, for saying something so childish. He failed to join in. Her tears were so close. His too.

"It's true," she said then and stirred her teacup so the spoon clinked against the china. "Why shouldn't I say it when it's true?"

"I'm not my dogs."

She didn't reply to that, slicing her cake with the spoon, slicing it again but not eating any of it.

"I deserve better," she said again and nodded at her own words. "I deserve to be loved. Whatever that means."

"You do deserve that."

"Maybe what's wrong is just in here."

She tapped the handle of the spoon against her head.

"Only what difference does that make?"

"Oh God," he said unhappily.

He grasped her hands. Quickly, before they could vanish again. He squeezed them so hard she made a little grimace of pain, and he loosened his grip.

"I don't understand," he said. "Do you love me? I love you. You've got to give me another chance. I will be a better boyfriend."

She shook her head. He was wondering whether this counted as cruelty too. If she took comfort in the fact that he was being tortured.

He wanted to say that she was too good for him. He had said it many times. But he bit back the words. He had always felt grateful. She was too pretty for him. Too, not well liked maybe, but popular. Everyone agreed he was a lucky dog.

It's really not that great, he was thinking. Being a lucky dog. Always having to be grateful. It puts you in a subordinate position and that wears away at you. You end up feeling guilty. You try and compensate. And then love mutates and becomes something else. Dependence maybe.

He was thinking about how hard the dogs had to work who were the lowest ranked in the pack. He was thinking about Rebecka. He had loved her for such a long time before they became a couple. But he'd never put her on a pedestal.

"I'm dissatisfied," Marit said. "And I hate being this dissatisfied person. I can't stand her."

She freed herself from his hands. Got to her feet.

His hands stayed where they were in the middle of the table.

"I'm off," she said. "Markus is at Isak's; he wanted to be picked up at seven. I'll have to have a talk with him. Just not now."

He nodded.

"Drive carefully," he said in a hoarse voice.

She looked out at the falling snow.

"I'll text you when I get home. But don't respond. I'm turning off the phone after that."

She had already put her things in an IKEA-bag in the bedroom. She fetched it and put on her outdoor clothes. He was stroking Tintin's head, caressing her ears, scratching her chest. Tintin's tail was thumping gently against the floor.

Marit Törmä drove through the snowstorm; she could feel the tyres skidding on the slippery surface of the road; she could hear the frantic squeaking and thumping of the windscreen wipers.

Almost the worst thing about ending it was the risk Krister and Rebecka would get together again. How would she ever bear that?

She couldn't understand Rebecka. On the outside she seemed to be a rather integrated person, smart, a prosecutor, and cool. Dutiful and hard-working, with some form of social conscience. And she liked the natural world and dogs. But Marit also got the sense that she was made up of a load of contradictions. Clever, almost wise, like an oracle or an ancient crone, but mad at the same time, reckless. Kind and yet thoughtless and selfish. Controlled and calm, but sometimes furious. High-functioning, but broken. There was something disillusioned about her that Marit was vaguely aware of, a sense of something wasted.

Whenever they had met, the encounters had been brief and

superficial – they had definitely not become friends, not even acquaintances – she got the feeling that Rebecka could see through her, listening attentively, while pretending to be distracted, to everything Marit said. And then dismissed her. Weighed her on the scales and found her too lightweight.

That notion made Marit angry. And she felt angry with Krister as well. Why would anyone want all those complications. It was incomprehensible.

She was embarrassed when she thought about all the times she had tried to steer conversations between Krister and herself towards his former girlfriend.

Why do I think about her so much? Marit wondered. It's toxic.

At home she changed into soft comfortable clothes and put the tea on. She took a selfie and wrote a post for her Instagram account saying she was feeling very, very sad and finishing with the words: "In a world where you can be anything, be kind."

Then she turned her phone off. She couldn't cope with all the hearts.

"All those bastards who got the snow-clearing outsourced to them are having to go back to work," Spike said with some satisfaction. "They'll have put the machines away for this year."

They were in the car on the way down to Esrangevägen. Spike had rung Börje to tell him the Lingonberry King had agreed to see him. Börje had called Sven-Erik who got in his car and drove through the snow into town.

Sven-Erik was sitting in the back, not saying much. He hadn't told Rebecka they were going to see the Lingonberry King. Henry Pekkari had called his brother Olle before he was murdered. In turn Olle had called Frans Mäki.

And now he was on his way to speak to the Lingonberry King

about the murder of Raimo Koskela, a case that could no longer even be prosecuted. Raimo, who had been stuck in Henry Pekkari's freezer. None of it made any sense.

Rebecka and his former colleagues were not going to be happy when they discovered he had been out this way. They just didn't have enough to bring the Russians in for questioning. Not for the murder of Henry Pekkari, nor for those two poor girls who were run over by a snowmobile, nor for Galina whatever-her-name-was up at Riksgränsen.

And here he was, coming at it from the side, his private sleuthing interfering with the investigation. The Russians would be put on their guard, and that was not what anyone wanted.

Only, I don't work there anymore, he thought, running a finger over his moustache. I've accepted a job as a private detective, and that's where my loyalty lies.

In a way, though, it was lucky Rebecka wasn't leading the investigation any longer; he'd much rather clash with von Post.

He was jerked out of his musings when Spike slammed on the brakes and they were all thrown forward.

"Sorry, guys," Spike said.

They had arrived. An earless fighting dog was hurling himself at the fence of the dog run, biting at it like crazy.

It was the two thugs who opened the door. Even though Sven-Erik had not met them before, he could understand what had scared Rebecka and Anna-Maria. There was some serious muscle under all that flesh, that much was immediately obvious. They patted down Sven-Erik's and Börje's clothes so rapidly it wasn't until a second or so later he realised they had been frisked. They had to hand over their mobiles. They were in no position to protest.

The wife of the Lingonberry King was nowhere to be seen. They were led through the hall to Frans Mäki's bedroom. There wasn't enough room inside to swing a cat, so Sven-Erik had to sidle in and stand along one of the short walls on which a large television was mounted.

A young woman, a girl really, was reclining in an armchair in one corner. She was engrossed in her phone. Her glossy black skirt was short. A semi-transparent blouse with little pink puffed sleeves revealed her lacy black bra. She was made up with those heavy fake eyelashes young people wore nowadays. Sven-Erik felt a pang. How old could she be? And what the hell was she doing in this place?

The Lingonberry King was propped up with several large pillows on a hospital bed. The grey control switch that regulated its height and reclining position hung at one side. There was a wheelchair by the bed.

"Would you look at that, a visit from a VIP!" the Lingonberry King said to Börje Ström. "Come closer, no need to stand there like a tinker!"

Börje would not have recognised him. The dark Walloon hair was gone, grey wisps crossed his scalp instead. His arms stuck out of his T-shirt like toothpicks. Though his cheeks had fallen in, they were neatly shaved. His ribcage rose and fell in time with his rapid shallow breathing. Like some wretched plant being kept alive with a UV light and extra nutrients.

Warily, Börje grasped the frail hand extended towards him.

Sven-Erik introduced himself as well and shook hands.

Spike said hello from his corner, although the Lingonberry King barely glanced at him. The corners of his mouth turned down in an expression of displeasure.

"You look almost the same as you did back then," the Lingonberry King said to Börje. "Do you still box?"

"I do a bit of group training at home in Älvsbyn. Because you've got to try and keep in shape."

The whole time Börje was thinking about his question. He should have asked Ragnhild to help him with it. With how to put it. The right sequence of words. He should have prepared.

They talked a bit about boxing, but neither Spike nor his father really followed it anymore. They talked about old fighters and about amateur boxing being better before, about mixed men's and women's competitions being boring and how there were no real stars in boxing now and no-one ever wrote about it in the papers. Börje felt a sudden weariness, always the same old.

How old we've all got, he thought.

"You know there ought to be a few more guys like we were then," Spike said to Börje. "Do you remember when we crossed the border and went up against the Finns?"

"Come off it, for fuck's sake," the Lingonberry King huffed at Spike. "Why don't you just shut up, you mountain of flesh: 'Like we were then!' It's not as if you've amounted to anything, have you? Who the fuck is ever going to remember you? Soft-skinned and lily-livered."

Silence reigned.

"There was a reason you came here?" the Lingonberry King said to Börje Ström.

He was getting tired. The audience would soon be over.

"Right," Börje said. "I don't know how to sugar-coat it. As you know my dad was found in Henry Pekkari's freezer, he'd been shot. Did you have anything to do with that, Frans? Were you the one who . . .?"

"Your father stole from me," the Lingonberry King said. "Over forty thousand kronor. That was a lot in those days. That couldn't go unpunished."

"It is what it is," Sven-Erik said very calmly. "Can you tell us how it happened? Just so Börje can get some closure. This is no longer a legal matter, after all: the murder is way past the statute of limitations."

The Lingonberry King stroked the blanket with his withered hand.

"Raimo had done a collection round for me. In our Ford Taunus transit, do you remember it?"

The last question was aimed at Spike.

"Of course," Spike said. "It—"

"That's how it was back then," the Lingonberry King continued. "Simple. The money in a plastic bag with a little piece of paper and the name of the person it came from written on it. But when I was sorting through them, doing the count, one of the bags only had toilet paper in it. So then we did the usual. Had a chat with the guy who delivered the bag. And he wasn't in any doubt he'd handed over the money. It was just your dad and me who had keys to the car. And it was your dad did the round. So . . ."

He broke off and cleared his throat.

"Tonya!"

The girl in the chair looked up. He pointed to a juice pack beside the bed. She stuck her feet into the high-heeled shoes beside her seat and minced over; she picked up the pack, freed the straw, stuck it in, holding it for him to drink. Her face remained expressionless as he stroked her backside. She went back to the chair and her phone.

Sven-Erik could only look on, feeling a combination of powerless and revulsion. How old was she? Fifteen? Twenty? And what was she doing here?

". . . so we picked him up," the Lingonberry King said.

"We?" Sven-Erik asked.

He wanted to grab the young woman by the arm and drag her away from here.

"Me and two of my lads. Mauri Kaatari and Toivo Lahti. They've been gone a long time now. We drove over to Henry Pekkari's to have a private talk. He was living nearby on that island, you see. Henry

Pekkari used to hang around the club when he was in Kiruna, so we were acquainted."

"What happened?"

"Well, Raimo denied it. Then he turned to threats and I bumped him off."

Sven-Erik stroked his moustache.

"Where did you get the gun from?" he asked.

"Fuck if I remember," the Lingonberry King said. "Must have been one of my guys who brought it with him. It wasn't mine. I hadn't been planning to get rid of him. You can go now. I've got something else to do."

He gave Tonya a long look, from top to toe.

The two Russians nodded towards the hall. The visit was over.

"How old is she, Tonya?" Sven-Erik asked on the way to the front door.

"Nineteen," one of the men said in English. "She has passport. Nothing illegal here."

"Fucking hell," Sven-Erik said once they were in the car on their way back to town.

It was like a parallel universe, he was thinking. While he was clearing snow and reading the paper and stroking the cats, other people were living in a completely different world, one filled with guns and assaults on women, where crime was a profession.

Spike and Börje were silent.

Börje was watching the snowflakes landing and melting on the windscreen. So that was it. Now he knew.

There wasn't any point in killing the Lingonberry King. There was hardly any of him left. And even if there was . . . he had killed a man once. That was more than enough.

OCTOBER 1974

Jim Jones remains in hospital for three days. Then he dies of a cerebral haemorrhage. Börje hears from one of the other boxers at the gym that the widow does not have the money to pay the hospital bill. She's got three kids, no job and no husband.

The hacks keep referring to "the death match". While boxing may be a dangerous sport, they write, it is more dangerous for the average American to get into his car and drive to work than it is to box, and no-one is going to prohibit driving because of that. And every boxer knows what he's getting into when he steps into the ring. They all say they hope Börje Ström will keep going after the accident and fight all the way to the light heavyweight world championship.

Börje refuses to do interviews. He searches out Big Ben and asks him to pay the hospital bill for Jim Jones.

Big Ben almost loses his cigar.

"Are you out of your mind?" he roars. "Why would I do that?"

He turns to one of his suits, who shrugs.

"Because you can," Börje says. "You can afford it. The family don't have the money to pay."

"Never ever! What kind of a signal would that send out? That we're responsible for his death? That you are? You won! You did your job in the ring and you won."

"In that case," Börje said, "I'm going to pay the bill. I've pulled in a load of money the last twelve months, and now I'd like some of that."

Big Ben sinks back behind his enormous desk. Börje thinks he looks so ridiculously small that it almost makes him want to laugh. But Big Ben's face has turned to concrete. He snaps his fingers and his secretary, who seems able to read his mind, marches off as quickly as she can in that narrow skirt. She is back inside a minute with a folder. It is stamped with Börje's name.

"Here," Big Ben says and opens the folder with a bang. "Here's your account right up to today. Your share of the winnings in one column and what I've spent on you in the other."

Börje glances through the figures; they include costs for training, clothes, use of the gym, a lot of match expenses he has never heard mentioned before now, travel, meals, the rent of the apartment, the cost of a car . . .

"I don't have a car, though . . ." he says feebly.

"Of course you do," Big Ben says and puffs life back into his cigar. "If you decided not to go and get it, that's your problem."

He points to the column in question. It says that Börje Ström rents a Rambler American. That's a lot of money for a crap car with a sewing-machine engine, it strikes him.

"You're not telling me I'm expected to . . ."

"Not expected to do what? Pay for what you cost? It's all in the contract. I own you, do you get that?"

Börje isn't one for perusing information on paper but the columns lay it all out clearly. He owes Ben O'Shaughnessy almost ten thousand dollars.

Only then Big Ben laughs and shuts the folder.

"Don't worry about it, boy. You'll have earned that back soon enough. And a lot more on top. You've got two matches in December, one in January, and before June next year you'll be in a championship match. Then you can buy a house with a swimming pool. Get yourself a girl and put a proper jewel on her finger. The press will love that."

The suits laugh as well, as if they had an on–off switch on their backs.

"You've got a good heart," Big Ben says. "There's nothing wrong with that. But I'm all business. Which is how I made my way to the top and how I am going to get you there as well."

In the nights that follow, Börje Ström dreams he is taking part in a Battle Royale. The plantation owners in the southern states started this brutal form of entertainment by bringing slaves together and forcing them to fight each other until only one man was still standing. Between four and thirty men, almost all of them Black, would beat each other unconscious, often with blindfolds on so they couldn't see. The money would then rain down on the last man standing.

He dreams he is being dragged into the ring even though he's yelling: "It's a mistake". He wakes up in a cold sweat, with images in his mind of men lying across one another, their legs twitching and jerking. In the dream his mouth is full of blood. There is an iron collar around his throat, like you'd find on a chained-up dog.

Battle Royale continued up until the 1930s, he knows that.

And it's still going on, he thinks.

One of the neighbours thumps on the wall and yells "Quiet!" A child starts bawling. He must have cried out in his dream.

Anna-Maria Mella was driving towards Tommy Rantakyrö's cottage. Although the wipers were going at top speed, snow was sticking to the windscreen. At one point she was forced to get out of the car to wipe it off with her bare hands. She had to crawl along the last bit of the journey, terrified of crashing into one of the lorries coming over from Narvik. Tommy's Toyota was parked in a snow-ploughed patch, just like he'd said. She squeezed in behind it, parking just a bit too close to the verge maybe, but then she wasn't going to be staying that long. So long as no-one drove into the car because they couldn't see properly. It was already covered in snow.

She tried ringing Tommy but there was no answer.

The cottage wasn't that far from the road. His footprints could still be made out as faint impressions in the snow.

Anna-Maria locked the car and wrapped her scarf around her head, covering her face up to her eyes. She followed the tracks, which were gradually disappearing as they filled with snow. Her shoes were soaked. She decided to buy a pair of good boots that would always stay in the car.

The wind got fiercer as she crossed some peatland without any sheltering trees. There was snow in her eyes, a white crust had formed on her cap. Not that she was feeling chilled, it was hard work making any headway at all.

It wasn't far. Barely a kilometre, if that. But it took her more than twenty minutes.

The cottage was one of those brown sporty models from the sixties, more of a cabin. A drift had formed along one wall all the way up to the windowsill. She looked behind her; there shouldn't be a problem finding her way back even if a real snowstorm blew up. Just as long as she could get the car out.

"Tommy!" she shouted as she got closer, but her words were swept away by the wind.

As she reached for the handle he opened the door from inside. She gave a start.

"You scared the shit out of me," she gasped. "What's the matter, tell me."

He was crying. She had never seen him cry. He looked completely done in. His greasy hair all over the place. Snot was dripping from his nose like a small child. A synthetic blanket around his shoulders even though he had his jacket on.

"Anna-Maria," he said.

He raised his arms to give her a hug, but then they dropped. The blanket fell to the ground in the doorway.

She shoved him inside, picked up the blanket and shut the door.

It was sparsely furnished inside. A bunk bed. Two chairs at a folding table. The wind was pummelling the thin walls.

"Why haven't you got a fire going?" she said. "What's happened? Has this got something to do with Milla? Is she having a kid with her new guy?"

"No, not that."

He slumped onto the lower bunk, his elbows resting heavily on his knees.

"I've screwed up, Anna-Maria. I've fucking screwed up."

And then the sobbing started. He was half crying, half yelling. You couldn't make out a word he said.

Anna-Maria opened the cupboard under the sink. She found a bottle of Jägermeister and poured a big glass. He was already drunk, she could see. But one more would hardly make any difference. Just as long as he could get to the car.

"Drink," she said authoritatively. "Then I'm going to drive you home. You drink that up while I get a fire going."

She opened the damper; the wind was howling in the chimney. She set light to some balls of newspaper and a muesli box in order to get rid of the plug of cold air in the flue; she split some thin birch wood and added the kindling. It caught straight away.

She sat down in one of the chairs.

"You're going to tell me everything now. I can't sit here guessing. Are you addicted to gambling?"

He shook his head.

"I'm so screwed. You know when Milla left me, I went out partying pretty hard."

She did know that. She thought about all the times he had turned up for work green in the face and sweating like a bag of rotting scraps.

"I was at the Ferrum. There was some band playing. I was pretty drunk and the others had gone home. So there was this girl who picked me up. She had a room at the hotel. I thought she was a flight attendant or something because she was so fucking pretty."

He emptied his glass. The tears were still there in the jerky way he was breathing, but his voice was steady as he went on with his story.

"I didn't think I'd be able, I was that drunk. Only, well, you don't need to know the details. But then she wanted to be paid. I said no, of course. That wasn't something we'd . . . I would never. But when I tried

454

to leave there were these two blokes in the corridor. The same ones. That you and Rebecka . . ."

Anna-Maria could feel herself turning to ice inside.

She put two more bits of wood on the fire; it was drawing really well with the wind blowing this hard.

"Shit," she said.

"Too right. Shit. They weren't planning to let me leave without paying. I said I didn't have any money. And they said 'Swish.' That was all. 'Swish.' And pointed inside the room. She stood there and just said: "You fuck, you pay." Pretty loud. Then she started screaming that she was going to call the police. And I just . . . you know, like I couldn't think straight. But then it occurred to me that you or Fredde, or someone else I knew, would turn up. I couldn't have that. So I paid by Swish."

"What the hell, Tommy?"

"I know."

He covered his face with his hands.

"You know I'm not the brightest penny, Mella."

An idea began to form in Anna-Maria's mind. It started growing like a black tree.

"Was it one of them? One of the dead women in Kurkkio?"

"Maybe. Maybe the one with her face sliced off. She was blond in any case. And it's my fault."

Anna-Maria tried to come up with something that would sound sympathetic and encouraging. But she couldn't get anything out. She wanted to scream and had to clench her teeth so hard they ached.

"One week later," Tommy went on, "those blokes turned up again. They rang my doorbell. They'd filmed it. There must have been cameras rigged in the bathroom and by the bed. I took a look at the film. You could see me stagger into the room with her. Vomit into the bathtub, which I don't remember. And we fucked. You could see me walk out after I refused to pay. Then me coming back inside and paying. Once they'd shown me the film they said: 'Maybe we show this to your boss?' They said I had to let them know if the police were planning a raid of some kind. For both sex and drugs."

Anna-Maria couldn't look at him. Her eyes wandered from one insignificant object in the room to another, tiny bits of bark and dust on the floor in front of the stove, a rolled-up reindeer skin in the corner.

Oh God, she thought. No, please no.

"They were deadly serious," Tommy went on. "They came to see me again. Forced me to carry a phone with me."

"You've had a phone on you? Their phone?"

Anna-Maria knew exactly what he was referring to. Expensive mobiles from specialist producers that used encryption the NFC could not crack.

"They called me up, piling on the pressure. They said they were losing patience, that kind of thing. And then a month ago I was out for the evening and the vice squad from Luleå were eating at Momma's. Anja Häggroth, you know. She and I have ended up in bed from time to time."

"She's married though," Anna-Maria said, and immediately felt like an idiot.

"I know that. But we met up later for a drink and one thing led to another. Then she told me they were going to do a raid on these people selling sex from a camper van. They'd had their eyes on them."

"Right," Anna-Maria said quietly. "Sven-Erik's source said the van didn't turn up when it was supposed to. In the car park at the barracks housing in the industrial zone."

"I thought, I'll do this," Tommy said. "Just this one thing. It wouldn't be working against you, after all, just the Luleå squad. And I thought the police would just have to get them the next time. I couldn't have known they were going to take them out to Palosaari. And that someone was going to drive over them with a snowmobile. What were they doing all the way out there? What the hell do you think really happened?"

"I don't know," Anna-Maria said.

She wasn't going to tell him about the anonymous conversation with Galina Kireevskaya's friend. Not now.

"And they didn't say anything to you?"

"No. They never tell me anything, do they? Only, of course, they asked me about the investigation and then . . ."

"What did you tell them?"

"Nothing really. Nothing important. About Rebecka getting Pohjanen to check the autopsy report again, and that Henry Pekkari had been murdered. It's my fault. If I hadn't . . . they would still be alive now."

"Where's that phone?"

"I left it at home. I've stopped answering it. After her, Galina, in Riksgränsen."

"Oh Tommy, did you tell them about her? Did you tell them she was up there?"

He looked at her, appalled.

"No, I didn't. I never would, not ever!"

She nodded. He was telling the truth. She knew him. Someone else had tipped them off. Someone who had then gone home to his wife and children at the end of the working day. Krister Westman who had yelled at her over the phone. Or someone else.

"You must be so disappointed."

He burst into tears again.

Anna-Maria looked out of the window. The weather wasn't getting any better. There wasn't much wood left and it was burning like tinder.

457

"We've got to get out of here while we can," she said. "We'll drive to the station. I'll record your statement and we'll take it from there. One step at a time."

She edged up to him and drew him into a hug.

"You've got yourself in the shit but we're going to sort it out. And I'll be with you all the way, OK?"

There are other jobs, she was thinking. There are other lives to live. He's young. He could land on his feet.

His lips found their way to her face and he pressed them against her mouth in a clumsy attempt at a kiss. She pushed him away.

"Get a grip, for Christ's sake," she hissed.

"Sorry," he bleated. "I'm completely . . ."

She took out her phone and rang Robert. He failed to answer. Then she rang Jenny. You could rely on teenagers. They always kept an eye on their phones. She didn't answer either.

Answer NOW IMPORTANT Anna-Maria texted and called again. Jenny answered on the fifth ring.

"Hello, love," Anna-Maria said. "I don't want you to worry but can you get hold of Dad and tell him I'm in Tommy Rantakyrö's cabin at Tiansbäcken. I've parked on the road. If I don't come home it'll be because I can't dig the car out. In that case we'll just sit in the car and wait for him. And he'll have to come and get me. I'm with Tommy, so it's no big deal. But tell Dad, OK? Hang on . . ."

Anna-Maria pricked up her ears. Had she heard something? No, it was just the wind. The cottage creaking and cracking.

The handle turned at that very moment and the door opened.

The two men Rebecka and she had encountered at the Lingonberry King's place stepped inside. The wind brought the snow eddying in with them. They were covered in it, but she recognised them immediately.

They looked at Tommy. They looked at Anna-Maria. They recognised her too. In a fraction of a second they realised Tommy had told her.

One of them took two quick steps forward. And all of a sudden there was a gun in his hand. Her brain couldn't work out how it got there.

Tommy yelled. She didn't even have time to draw breath. A bang. And Tommy falling backwards onto the bed.

She did have time to think: What if they autopsy me and find Tommy's saliva on my mouth. What's Robert going to think?

She got no further. The other bullet went straight through her skull.

Jenny had gone into the corridor to talk to her mother. When she heard the yell and the two shots, she was so startled she dropped her phone. It bounced on the hard floor and vanished beneath one of the radiators.

She lunged after it and hit her head on the radiator as she tried to grab it. The screen had broken. It was black.

The corridor was empty, most people had finished for the day. Still on all fours she tried to get the phone to work again, but it just buzzed and the screen stayed black.

"Mum!" she yelled. "Mum!"

Her maths teacher opened the classroom door.

"Jenny . . ." she said.

That was when Jenny felt blood running from her eyebrow to the tip of her nose. She had cut herself on the forehead. She held out the phone to her teacher as if it were a lethal object, a time bomb. And something began to disintegrate inside her, collapsing like an earthquake.

"My mum," she whispered, barely audible.

She got up on wobbly legs; she had to keep her wits about her. Keep the fear at bay. One thing at a time. Calm now, panic later.

"Something's happened . . . You've got to . . . help me . . . ring . . . 112."

*

"Have you had anything to eat today?"

Anna Granlund, the forensic technician, had found Lars Pohjanen sitting on the shabby sofa in the break room looking dejectedly at his phone.

"Yes," he croaked and waved her away.

"No, you haven't," she said firmly. "I thought I'd close the shop. Everything's been put away and it looks nice and tidy in there. Unlike you! Either you eat something or I'm going to ring your wife."

"Fetch me something then," Pohjanen said angrily. "Don't ring the wife. She just tried to get me to look at fabric samples for new curtains."

"And that would be good for you," Anna Granlund said, opening the little fridge. "You can't just look at tumours and crushed skulls."

She put a chocolate biscuit bar and a carton of juice on the table in front of him.

"Please go home," she implored. "Shall I ring for a taxi?"

"Look," Pohjanen said, clearing his throat. "I'm eating, aren't I? Sit down. Keep me company."

He unwrapped the chocolate biscuit, broke off a piece and shoved it in his mouth.

Anna Granlund sat down and shrugged out of her jacket.

"I just talked to Börje Ström," Pohjanen said. "They've been out to see the Lingonberry King, Frans Mäki. And he told them straight out he was the one who shot Börje's father."

"Oh, good Lord!" Anna Granlund said. "Because . . .?"

"He suspected Börje's father had stolen money from him. Maybe he had."

Pohjanen leaned back on the sofa. Saying all those words and nibbling at the biscuit meant he had to gasp for breath, and then he had a coughing fit. Anna Granlund waited it out patiently.

"That was good, though," she said. "He found out. You did well."

Pohjanen gave her a tormented look.

"It was the very least I could do," he said. "My father and Börje's mother were cousins, you know. And Börje's maternal uncles, Erkki, Daniel and Hilding, were right bastards. God in their mouths and Satan in their hearts. Hilding was even a priest, for Christ's sake. He took Börje into his home when he was fourteen, to straighten him out, as they used to say. That didn't turn out so well. Something must have happened because that summer . . ."

Pohjanen exploded into his handkerchief and then drank some juice before continuing:

"Börje's mother had a cottage. The brothers had divided up the woodland and the house among themselves. All she inherited was the cottage. Nice place. Not the cottage itself, but the woods around it. But in the summer of '66, the uncles chopped down all the trees. All of them, there wasn't a twig left. A wasteland. Börje's mother, she never went there again. Every time she came to visit my parents, she just cried the whole time."

"How awful," Anna Granlund said with feeling.

"And my father never said a word about it. He didn't want any bother with Hilding, Erkki and Daniel. I never said anything either."

"You were just a child . . ."

"I was seventeen! I was perfectly capable of speaking out. That's the thing I've found hardest to deal with in this job, when they bring in women and kids and you know the neighbours, their workmates . . . adults . . . knew what was going on. But kept quiet. Lickspittles, determined to keep in with other people and never take a stand. There's nothing worse in my book."

"Listen to me," Anna Granlund said in a strict voice. "You're an incredibly difficult person in many ways. But a lickspittle you are not."

He gave her a tired smile.

"Thank you," he said. "Thank you, Anna."

"Now you're making me nervous," she tried to joke. "Please bark at me so I know you're you. Come on, I'll drive you home."

"Nah," he said. "Order a taxi in an hour. I need to recover for a bit."

She did as he asked. And then she drove home. Anna Granlund was single and had no children, her workplace was full of death, but her small flat was full of life. It was like a jungle of potted plants. She had two large aquariums, two rabbits in a spacious cage and four budgerigars."

Pohjanen lay down on the sofa.

"I got what I wanted," he was thinking. "I wanted to help Börje find out what happened. And now that's done. Time to let it go."

He reached for his phone. Thinking he would listen to some music. But the mobile and his headphones remained on his stomach.

He could hear noises in his head. The sound of oars on water. He's a little boy, maybe six. Dad is rowing them out into the river so they can haul the nets up. The evening sun is glittering like fish scales across the water. The mosquitoes are buzzing. The splash as the oar hits the surface. The squeak from the rowlocks. The water running off the blades as they lift out. The gurgle against the gunwale. On the other side of the river the cows on the neighbouring farm are lowing. They want the evening milking to happen now.

Pohjanen drew one last gasping breath. And then he went to his eternal rest.

Ambulance staff and officers Fred Olsson and Karzan Tigris reached Tommy Rantakyrö's cabin at 17.32 on Friday. Snow was falling thickly and the wind speed was 24 metres per second. Karzan took the lead and started investigating the evidence.

Both Anna-Maria Mella and Tommy Rantakyrö had been shot in

the head. Tommy's body was lying on the floor, the rag rug beneath him was red with blood. He was holding a gun in one hand.

The doctor who arrived with the ambulance confirmed that Tommy Rantakyrö was deceased.

"This is impossible," Fred Olsson said. "He couldn't have done this. It's impossible."

"She's alive," the paramedic said, taking Anna-Maria Mella's pulse.

Though Anna-Maria had been shot in the head and was unconscious, unbelievably she was still alive. The paramedic took her blood pressure. They laid her on a tarpaulin and using their combined strength managed to carry and drag her through the snowstorm to the ambulance by the roadside.

She needed to be transported to Umeå, but that hospital was six hundred kilometres away and no plane or helicopter could take off in weather like this. They plumped for the hospital in Gällivare instead, only one hundred and thirty kilometres away.

The accompanying doctor intubated her in the ambulance before they drove away and then connected her up to the mobile respirator.

The paramedic was a skilled driver. She knew the road and was able to keep driving at ninety kilometres an hour despite the loose snow on the road and the fact that it was impossible to see anything ahead of them.

Eight kilometres south of Skaulo they came to a stop. There was a five-car traffic jam ahead.

The ambulance nurse jumped out into the snow and rapped on the windscreen of the car in front. He was told a timber truck had skidded some way ahead. The truck had turned over, the timber had come loose and was blocking the road.

Five minutes later an ambulance left Gällivare to meet them on the other side of the accident.

Meanwhile, Anna-Maria's heart rate was dropping, and her blood pressure was going up.

The doctor checked her pupils. One of them was enlarged.

"Swelling on the brain," he said. "We need to give her Mannitol."

At 20.34 Anna-Maria was wheeled into Gällivare hospital. Using images from a CT-scan, a surgical diamond drill was employed to relieve the pressure on her brain.

One hour later and the snowstorm vanished eastwards and everything was still.

Börje came home to Ragnhild. He told her about his visit to the Lingonberry King. And about the King admitting to being guilty of the long-ago murder. And about the dog without ears.

Villa was lying in front of the balcony door in the living room. It was slightly ajar and snow came in through the gap to melt on the parquet floor.

"It's too hot for her in the flat," Ragnhild said. "She's used to being outside whenever she wants. How are you feeling?"

His elbows were on the table. He put his hands over his eyes.

"I don't know," he said. "Mostly I feel . . ."

He tried to find the words, wishing he had more to choose from. For this combination of emptiness and a deep weariness at everything.

She pulled her chair closer and threw her arms around him. His arms closed around her. She kissed him on the temple.

He felt desire for her then. Kissed her back. Touched her that way.

"Now?" she asked. "Are you sure?"

He nodded gravely.

So then she got to her feet and led him into the bedroom.

They got undressed, he was ready first. He had no underpants on. She laughed at that.

464

"A lot of martial artists and boxers don't wear them," he said.

"Men," she said.

Whatever she meant by that.

He was standing very close behind her and helped her off with the last of her clothes. He got to his knees to remove her panties, kissed her behind. Then he got up. Undid her buttons. He peered over her shoulder to see her breasts when he undid the catches on her bra. She shivered.

They weren't in a hurry. She remained standing while he pulled off the red rubber bands from her braids and undid them. He lifted her hair. Kissed her in the little hollow beneath her ears, on the nape of her neck.

He kissed her shoulder blades, squeezed her muscles, the teres minor and major along the lateral border of the scapula, and the serratus anterior. Her back was broad, her shoulders powerful. From behind you might almost mistake her for a man.

"How can you be so bloody lovely?" he whispered. "So strong?"

"Skiing with a heavy load," she said.

There was a smile in her voice he liked a lot. It made him feel good inside.

Skiing had given her a well-developed gluteus maximus.

"Nice arse," he said aloud and let the rough inside of his hand caress her buttocks. All those years with wrappings on his hands. It wore away at the skin. They ended up almost like sandpaper. He alternated between the rough inside of his hand and the softness of his fingertips. Letting them slide along the groove between her buttocks down towards her curly bush.

They lay on their sides facing one another. He was glad she didn't want to crawl under the blanket.

"Just let me look at you," he said.

She looked back. He was proud of his erection. As large and as hard as in his youth. He didn't need medication to ensure that.

It came almost as a surprise how much woman she was once he could see her properly from in front: the bulge of her belly, her soft breasts; he wanted to feel the weight of them in his hand. The long tuft on the mound, more grey than dark brown. Like beard moss. As if she had freed herself from a mighty and ancient pine tree and been waiting for him like a creature of the forest.

He was grateful she was so free, without any shame, no questions from her about parts of her body that ought to be smaller, bigger, firmer. Her profession would have accustomed her to everything to do with the body, after all. Like his.

They reached for each other. Kissing, stroking. He wanted to touch all her places.

She slowly became wet.

"Not like we're fifty anymore," she said softly.

Her breathing was lovely and heavy. He was listening attentively; those breaths occasionally became shallow and fierce, when he touched some part of her that gave her extra pleasure.

Thank God they weren't fifty, was what he felt. Thank God he hadn't met her before now. They were like two scarred old lynxes. Still supple and strong. They had the energy to play. Knew better than to rush to orgasm.

He took his time with all of her. Her nipples, the crook of her arms.

She took him in her mouth but he felt he had to pull away. Otherwise he would come like a schoolboy.

He turned her onto her stomach. And lay all of his weight on top of her. He realised she liked that, feeling small and enclosed beneath him. His cock lay against the crack of her arse. She arched up towards it. It jerked as though it were a blind animal, sniffing, nudging, wanting in.

Supporting herself on her lower arms she used her strength to twist round so she ended on her back.

His cock was sliding towards her mound.

He raised himself above her on hands and knees. She grasped his cock gently but firmly. Her hand was just as rough as his. She parted her legs. Guided him inside her.

"Be careful," she said. "I bite."

"Bite away," he said. "You don't think I'm scared of a kitten like you?"

Their eyes locked onto each other. Her legs like strong birch saplings around his waist. One of her hands around his balls, the fingers of her other were feeling their way between his buttocks.

He was being welcomed inside her, something trembled inside him. He was so moved by her sexual energy. Even though he had long ago lost count of all the women he had had. When he reached all the way in, it felt like he was on the verge of tears. She was a river flowing with pleasure. It washed over him like a blessing. He wasn't damned, not completely. Not beyond saving.

Then those philosophical reflections went the way of all flesh.

She wasn't the quiet kind. Nor was he.

Afterwards they crept under the duvet. Lying there looking into each other's eyes, they caressed each other more casually. He was looking at her weathered, sunburned face with all its lines and marks. She was tracing the scars on his face, those mauled eyebrows, the deviated septum of his nose.

"Why did you stop boxing?" she asked. "If you don't mind me asking?"

"You can ask anything you want to," he said.

He told her about the death match with Jim Jones.

"And then there was the match in the Catskills. After that it was over whether I wanted it to be or not."

Börje is changed after the death match.

Big Ben said he owned Börje, but he is no slave, not in the ring at least. Muhammad Ali has just taken Foreman down in Zaire. Though he said to the papers he was going to "dance, dance", he secretly trained to keep his guard up while standing still. Ali had taken a name of his own and he fought in his own way too.

"I'm not 'The Swedish Viking'", Börje says to Paris, his coach. "The papers, they give us all these names: 'The Bomber', 'The Little Murderer', 'Mad Dog', they want you to be a 'killer', a 'beast', a 'hitman'."

Paris hums in agreement. It is early morning; Börje has skipped both breakfast and his run. The gym is empty, apart from his coach and him and two young boxers sparring in the ring.

"I had Jones on the ropes," Börje says. "He couldn't get away."

"We're all on the ropes," Paris says, scratching his hands and forearms. "In one way or another. I love this . . ."

His hand waves across to the two lads sparring.

". . . but it's the Devil himself who's in charge of everything that happens outside the ring. The money, the contracts, the promoters and the managers who have always managed to suppress any attempt by the boxers to form a union, the cheating."

"How does anyone live with that?" Börje says.

"What else are you supposed to do? What else am I supposed to do? Queue down there in the port and hope for a temporary job? I did that for three years after my eye got bust. Then they let me in here. I thank God for every day I get to spend in this place, for every boxer I get to train. Every day my back holds out so I can let my boxers drill blows

468

against my gloves. All that other stuff, there's no point thinking about it. I think about boxing, I breathe boxing."

In the ring the taller man is moving around the shorter one. It is obvious that the shorter boxer is the better of the two. He maintains his centre, lets his opponent strike, but slides away, meeting the punches with his guard, then strikes back, putting the other man off balance.

"Boxing?" Börje asks. "Morning, afternoon, and evening?"

"Yup," Paris says and clasps his hands in a gesture that looks pious, but whose sole aim is to stop him scratching. "And you're allowed to think about women a bit as well. In the breaks."

Börje does think about boxing. He goes back to the gym and trains as usual, but he has started thinking about boxing in a different way. And he only has to fight a single match for the press and the spectators to realise he has changed.

He boxes more gently than before. As if the opponent were his brother and he didn't want to do him any serious harm.

It's a more dangerous way to box, not going in for the kill, and giving the opponent a sort of pause for reflection instead, as though Börje were asking: "What have you learned from this?" The audience boos throughout the final rounds. Annoyed, they yell that they paid to see boxing.

Though Börje wins the match on points, he is still the loser.

The press discuss Börje Ström's mental health in the following weeks. The commentators write that he was broken by Jim Jones's death, that though he may be strong on the outside, he's obviously weak inside; they speculate as to whether he has fallen prey to religious doubts, or maybe he despises the crowd. They ask whether he has what it takes and answer that question themselves with a "no".

And Big Ben O'Shaughnessy is furious. He's not going to let some old woman fight a title match; Börje should be in no doubt about that.

What Börje is thinking, though, is that in the ring he is on his own. And he is the one who makes the decisions there. Between the ropes it's just him and another boxer. Big Ben's place is behind a damn desk.

Börje fights another two matches. Unperturbed he continues to box in his newly acquired style.

"You've pissed off the boss," Paris says to Börje. "He's used to people doing what he says."

"Am I getting it wrong? Is that what you think? I'm still winning."

"Oh, my boy," Paris says. "Those three matches. You boxed so beautifully it made me want to cry. But the crowd doesn't get it. They want to see brutal combat and blood."

In March 1975 the match in the Catskills is announced.

Börje suspects nothing. Not before they get there. And by then it is too late.

Afterwards Börje will think he should have realised something bad was brewing. When Big Ben stopped raising hell and appeared to accept Börje's new style of boxing. When Paris disappeared two weeks before the match because of "pressing family matters" and was replaced by a different coach. He should have realised from the name of the place – the Catskills are mountains – that it was somewhere high up, that you can't just turn up at a place like that the night before, that you have to acclimatise.

His opponent is a southpaw from Mexico, José Luis Pérez. He is lower ranked than Börje and just a year older. He is tall with a monstrous reach. He is also the kind of guy who could build himself up and move up to a different weight.

Börje thinks this shouldn't be much of a problem. He doesn't know that Big Ben has already agreed with Pérez's manager to take him on.

"Tire him out," says the new coach. "He drops his guard when he gets tired."

Börje knows that already. He doesn't like having to listen to someone who doesn't know him. All the people around him are strangers. There's a new cutman he doesn't know either. They come across as sycophantic and much too convinced he's going to walk away with it. He tries to shut all that out.

He can sense something is wrong even in the first round. He can't seem to catch his breath. When the bell sounds he sits in his corner trying to regulate it. Inhaling and exhaling. Deep breath in, relax and breathe out. But as soon as the match restarts he is out of breath again.

He's unable to keep Pérez in front of him; he can't seem to hold the centre. It is Börje who has to circle round the Mexican instead. It's making him incredibly tired. His brain slows down, he steps to the right instead of the left and Pérez follows up with a left hook that slams into his eyebrow, which immediately splits and starts bleeding. He can't keep track of his opponent's punches like he should and they're getting harder.

His cutman fixes the split on his eyebrow, but the adrenaline is a faint piss-yellow colour and it fails to stop the bleeding. The bottle was opened some time ago and the contents must have passed their expiry date. Börje understands all this afterwards when he also realises it must have been deliberate, but how could he prove anything?

In the sixth round Börje is finding it hard to keep up his guard. The Mexican is going all out. Börje tries to counter but his breath refuses to work for him, he's got no more fuel. His left eyebrow is bleeding and making it hard to see, he has to turn his head at the wrong angle.

He doesn't see the blow that knocks him down. He can't remember it afterwards. Suddenly his legs go and he only manages to get up on nine.

Pérez wins on points.

*

"It's important not to let yourself get down," the new coach tells him afterwards. "Sometimes you lose."

"Rotten luck, that's all," someone else says and tells him that the Mexican was having a good day.

Börje says nothing. The masseur's fingers are pushing deep into his badly bruised muscles.

All he says to the press waiting outside is that he was not as good as his opponent today. Which is no more than the truth.

They go out to eat that night. Girls appear in dresses with plunging necklines. Someone persuades him to have a beer and he has two.

Then everything around him goes fuzzy. He has no memory of leaving the restaurant or where they went after that.

Later he will remember fragments of what might have been a nightclub. Cigar smoke in the air, women dancing on a stage, skimpily dressed girls coming round with drinks.

He wakes up in the afternoon of the next day. It takes a while for him to realise he's in his own bed in Hell's Kitchen. He feels like he died in the night. His body is so sore from yesterday's fight it's as though it's trying to turn itself inside out.

He doesn't see the newspaper reports until the evening. The images of him with girls on his lap and a Champagne bottle in his hands.

"FIGHT WAS FIXED!"

"Here he is celebrating his loss!"

"The drinks are on cheat Börje Ström after scandal match!"

"I was finished," Börje tells Ragnhild, stroking her lips with his fingertips. "I had two years left on my contract with Big Ben, but he dropped me right there and then. When I woke up the next morning I was a ghost. I didn't have a gym, I couldn't get any matches, I got chucked out of my apartment without a penny to my name. They cut me off for cheating, saying the match was fixed. Big Ben had contacts everywhere."

"I remember the newspaper reports here in Sweden," Ragnhild said. "Though I'm not that interested in sports. What happened then?"

"I was saved by a woman. One of the waitresses at my breakfast place let me move in. I got temporary work in the port, laid asphalt, worked on construction sites."

Ragnhild's eyelids closed briefly, and then again.

"Sleep," he said to her softly. "We've got plenty of time to tell our stories."

They drifted slowly off to sleep. She dropped off first. He was awake a few minutes longer. Looking at her pale eyelashes, those wide eyebrows. She was fantastically beautiful.

When Ragnhild woke an hour later, Börje was deeply asleep beside her. She was pleased he didn't snore.

Villa was lying on the floor beside her head of the bed.

"Well, hello there," Ragnhild said as softly as she could.

The bitch pricked up her ears, not in a vigilant and anxious way, but simply paying attention. And stayed where she was, feeling secure, her nose on her paws.

It had stopped snowing outside. The whole town was silent, resting under a duvet just like Börje and her.

Ragnhild closed her eyes and was surprised by how calm she felt.

That's the oxytocin and the endorphins, of course. Heavy duty. And no prescription required.

She turned on her side towards Börje. Grasped his index finger. Like a baby. And went back to sleep.

*

The story that two police officers had been found shot in a cabin ten kilometres north of Kiruna had leaked onto the news even before Anna-Maria Mella was wheeled into the hospital in Gällivare.

Five of their colleagues from the Norrbotten police district got into their cars and drove to Kiruna. Von Post issued an arrest warrant for the Russian men, and a patrol was sent to the home of the Lingonberry King. There was no-one there apart from the King himself and his wife, whose name, according to both her passport and the local authority's register, was Maria Mäki. There was another woman there as well whose name was Tonya Litvinovitch.

The wife and Tonya were brought in for questioning.

The wife told the investigators that the two Russian men who lived in the house were tenants. She showed them the contract, which she had on her phone. The contract was signed with the names Yegor Babitsky and Yury Yusenkov. What did they do for a living? She had no idea. She thought they might be working on some road-building project south of the town.

The police executed a search warrant. Yegor Babitsky and Yury Yusenkov lived in one of the buildings next to the main residence. Or *had* lived, rather. There was nothing there anymore, apart from two bed frames without mattresses, a little table on which a microwave had been placed, two chairs. The place was otherwise completely empty. And lacked windows as well. Karzan Tigris and a fellow officer from Kalix found themselves wondering what sort of person could live like that.

Footprints led from the house to what looked like a bonfire some way off; the fire had gone out. The forensic technicians who were still at Tommy Rantakyrö's cabin were called in and after a preliminary examination could confirm that the burnt objects were two mattresses, various fabrics and the body of a dog. The dog had been shot.

At the police station Maria Mäki went on to say that she would need a lawyer present if she was to answer any further questions. She wanted to go home. She had a sick husband who was currently alone in the house and required constant care.

They had no cause to detain her and she left the police station together with Tonya who had proved just as ignorant under questioning about Yegor Babitsky and Yury Yusenkov. When asked if either of them had been her boyfriend or if she had had sex with them or worked for them in any way, she replied they were two old guys and not her type. The old guys present in the interview room weren't her type either.

Two officers from Gällivare were posted to keep watch on the road from the house. A close eye would be kept on the whereabouts of the two women in any case.

The police station was besieged by reporters. At half past nine that night Carl von Post held a very brief press conference. He confirmed that two police officers had been shot, one of whom was dead, while the other was in a critical condition. He did not reply to any questions.

At 11.10 on Friday night the Brat got up on his paws and started barking frantically. This was followed by a knocking on Rebecka's front door.

When she drew aside the kitchen curtain to look out of the window she could see Carl von Post's car.

I really can't deal with this, she thought. What does he want?

She stomped down the stairs. This wasn't the first time he had appeared in person to argue with her. Maybe all he wanted was the Pekkaris' accounts.

An errand boy, that's all, she thought contemptuously. He was just going to have to jog up and down these stairs and carry the boxes himself.

But when she opened the door she was met by a Carl von Post she had never seen before. He looked miserable. Bags under his eyes, pale as rotten ice. Frail almost. His eyes told her he was exhausted, defenceless. It made Rebecka feel very apprehensive.

"May I come in?" he asked.

"Why?"

"You haven't heard? I've been trying to call you. Fred Olsson has too. You turned off your phone."

"I did, yes, because I . . ." she began.

She had turned it off because she didn't want to look up Marit Törmä's Instagram account. Because she didn't want to text Krister and tell him he was a bastard.

"It doesn't matter," she said. "What's happened?"

He told her. He stood there in the spring light reflected off the new snow and the story that came out of those pale lips was as inconceivable as it was horrifying.

"They tried to get it to look like Tommy had shot her first and then turned the gun on himself," he went on to explain. "He had the gun in his hand. They had no idea she was talking to her daughter on her mobile when they arrived. Anna-Maria must have dropped the phone when they came in and then fallen backwards on top of it. They never saw it."

"Jenny," Rebecka said.

"Yes. It must have been awful, but it was a stroke of luck for us. Jenny told us Anna-Maria said, 'Hang on a moment,' as if something had attracted her attention."

"Like someone coming," Rebecka said. "When you hear someone outside the door."

"That kind of thing. Then she heard Tommy yell, 'Please no' or just 'No', sort of. Then two shots. Jenny dropped her phone on the floor at that point and it smashed. She turned out to be the kind of person you can rely on, if you know what I mean. Her mother's daughter."

476

Rebecka must have raised an eyebrow or tilted her head. It was the first time she had ever heard him say anything in praise of Anna-Maria Mella. He noticed the movement.

"I know," he said. "Erika, my wife, says I'm a swine. And she's right. She . . ."

He cleared his throat to get his voice back.

"Uh, she wants a divorce. I've had a couple of really shitty days, Martinsson."

His face crumpled, his lips twitched.

"Only fuck that. Mella's all that matters now. And Tommy . . . of course."

"Anna-Maria. How . . .?"

Rebecka's voice failed; there was a lump in her throat.

"We really don't know. They've drilled into her skull to relieve the pressure but she's still unconscious. No-one can say how serious the damage is or whether she'll survive. They're flying her to Umeå, right now I think."

"What about Tommy though?"

"He died on the spot."

"I don't get it," she said. "Why?"

"I've got to tell you something about Tommy," he said. "I hardly know where to begin."

Rebecka wiped her face with the back of her hand.

"Come upstairs," she said. "You look awful. When did you last eat?"

She reheated the char from the day before. She let the cold, boiled potatoes roll around in the cast-iron pan and poured over the last of Sophie's sauce. Von Post ate as if he had been starving. The Brat parked himself under the table and fell asleep like the dead. There had been a lot going on in the worlds of both the two- and four-legged creatures lately. Von Post interrupted his meal every now and then to look at him as his paws twitched in his sleep and he came close to barking out loud from the dream world where he was the King of Kurravaara, terror of the hares and darling of the bitches.

"The police liaison for prostitution and human trafficking in Luleå contacted me on Wednesday 27th," von Post said and took a swig of the alcohol-free beer Rebecka had placed in front of him. "This was in connection with a raid they were planning in Kiruna, and about Tommy Rantakyrö. An extremely sensitive matter. They had been tipped off that sex was being sold from a camper van at the barracks housing in the industrial zone. They knew they were due to be there on the evening of April 7th. But the camper van never turned up that evening. And no trace of it since."

"OK . . . so where does Tommy Rantakyrö fit into all that?"

"It was a watertight operation, that's how they work, with complete autonomy. Inspector Anja Häggroth informed her squad leader she had met up with Tommy and told him about the planned raid. Apparently she and Tommy got together from time to time and . . ."

He finished with a pointed nod.

"You're kidding."

"Sadly not. And because the camper van and the girls had disappeared, the squad suspected they'd been tipped off. The surveillance team and the investigators had been working together on this for a long time. Anja Häggroth believed it was Tommy. She said he seemed a bit batty to her. That was the phrase she used. So they wanted a warrant to tap his phone. To monitor the traffic."

"Thin."

"Yup, but extremely serious."

"Thursday 28th I took one of your cases at short notice," Rebecka said. "Was this why?"

478

"Uh-huh, I drove to Luleå and issued a covert warrant for the phone tap. Like I said, sensitive doesn't begin to cover it. Then those sex workers were found dead."

Rebecka felt she had to stand up for a bit. She cleared the table and ran water into the sink. She immersed her frozen hands in the hot foamy water. Her brain worked better if her hands were busy. The Brat woke up and helped with the pre-wash.

"I was so pissed off at you for dumping that case on me," she said. "I thought you'd bunked off to Riksgränsen to go skiing."

"You've got a load of other reasons to be pissed off at me," von Post said. "They had no choice but to involve me. If Tommy—"

"Yeah, yeah," Rebecka said. "I get it. If he was the leak, it was vital to find out what he knew and what he didn't."

"If only I'd had the Russians brought in when Anna-Maria asked me to," von Post said.

At least the last thing you did with her wasn't a punch-up, Rebecka thought.

"What about Tommy?" she asked. "Did he ring anyone after speaking to Anna-Maria? Who knew he was in his cabin?"

Von Post shook his head.

"Olsson's checking with his family and friends. To see if anyone's been asking for him."

"He's been off sick a lot lately," Rebecka wondered aloud. "And there was something shaky, something off about him somehow, but his girl-friend ended it so everyone thought that was why. Presumably he was feeling like shit. There must have been something going on between him and those Russians. And in the end he rang Anna-Maria to tell her. She's like a mother to all of them."

"I'm guessing they knew Tommy was there, but they hadn't counted on Anna-Maria," von Post said.

"Have you brought them in?"

"No. We drove out to the house on the Esrange road but they weren't there anymore. It was just Frans Mäki, that young girl and his wife Maria . . . Maria Berberova before she was married, according to the civil register."

"Or Elena Litova."

"Uhm, I sent over an information request about Elena Litova, but all we got back was that she had emigrated. Not even a passport photo."

"Sounds like someone might have paid to have any trace of their past removed."

"Only how are we going to prove any of this? I've issued arrest warrants for the men. We were given two names when we questioned Frans Mäki's wife, whoever she actually turns out to be."

Carl von Post looked at his phone.

"Yegor Babitsky and Yury Yusenkov. Might just as well be called Humpty and Dumpty. They've vanished."

"And forensics?"

"Going over the cabin with tweezers. And we've got surveillance on Maria Mäki. Officers from Gällivare are sitting in a car at the end of her road and will follow her if she drives past them. It's the only way out of the place, so . . ."

Von Post scratched the Brat behind his ears, laughing out loud when the dog could no longer stand up straight because it felt so lovely.

"I was determined to get control of the investigation," von Post said. "Because of this business with Tommy, of course. Though I would have been anyway. I don't like you very much."

"I don't like you either," Rebecka said. "Do you want some dessert?"

Rebecka dug out her father's boots from whatever nook they were in and they went for walk through the village with the Brat. It was past midnight.

480

The clouds had cleared away. Carl von Post commented on the low shimmering pink light, the pale-blue shadows and the fresh snow that shrouded the village in a virginal beauty. He got out his mobile and tried to capture the moment as a puff of wind sent a flurry glittering into the air.

"It's all going to melt before you know it and then it'll be a sea of mud," Rebecka said.

"You really are the life and soul of the party," von Post said. "What do you think about the connection between the Lingonberry King and Olle and Anders Pekkari? If I know you, you've already had a look at their accounts."

"Eighteen months ago Bergsäk AB, Olle and Anders Pekkari's company, took on a foreign partner," Rebecka said, deciding on the spur of the moment not to reveal she had help with the accounts. "They were having liquidity problems. And the nature of the business changed as a result. A lease-back sale of the investment-heavy machinery. They bought up a couple of firms operating inside the mining industry. Both of the vendors left town after the transfers of ownership. A great deal of the capital in the company has disappeared overseas; investments in a foreign mining company that could be anything at all. One acquisition I just don't get though: a printing firm. And! There's a white camper van in the company inventory."

"What a surprise."

"Not that that proves anything."

"No, I know," von Post said. "But tell me what you believe, whether or not it can be proved."

"I think Elena Litova was sitting on a pile of money that represented her share of the proceeds from a corporate hijacking. She has access to a network that can set up financial transactions passing through several stages, so they end up outside the reach of the legal system. She marries into a quasi-criminal company that has been losing its way."

481

"The Lingonberry King Frans Mäki."

"Exactly. So now she's got one foot in Kiruna. Step two is to gain control of an established company with a good reputation."

"The Pekkaris' Bergsäk AB," von Post said.

"Correct. In buying into it you also acquire several more companies. You make sure you've got violence on tap for enforcement, i.e. those Russian blokes. And then you start working the market. Through blackmail and threats you gain control of key players in the commissioning bodies, the mining company LKAB and the local authority, that is. After that, landing construction and works contracts is child's play. In ten, twenty years, when the bridges collapse and tunnels have to be reinforced, the roads repaired, when roofs fall in and buildings begin to suffer from damp, the companies will already have been liquidated or made bankrupt and the money will have been transferred overseas in so many different steps that it is impossible to trace or recover. The people who made money from the operation will also be long gone. Taxpayers will have to foot the bill."

"You might just possibly be able to haul the civil servants and individuals on the commissioning bodies before the law."

"Though that hardly ever happens. In Sweden, construction-related fraud costs society over a hundred billion kronor a year. It rarely features in the press as the decision-makers responsible are afraid for their jobs. No-one probes any deeper. There isn't even a police report or criminal investigation. And if there *is* a report, or a case is opened, it gets shut down. These matters are so hard to investigate. I think that's what's about to happen. Humpty and Dumpty got to take over the drugs and prostitution racket as a bonus. And they were unwilling to let go of that once they had a firm grip on the town. Do you remember Ohlsson Maskin & Entreprenad AB?"

"Not really, no."

"The company value of just over ten million kronor consisted essentially of machinery, trucks, loaders, things like that. The new owner was an investment company. The entire inventory was sold off and shipped out of the country. The company paid no capital gains tax. Once the mills had done grinding at the tax authority, the money had gone. The Dutch investment company had been liquidated, the owner was a goalkeeper. The Tax Agency handed the case over to us for prosecution, but I shut it down. There were thirty or so other companies registered at the Amsterdam address of the parent company, but there was nothing there, just an abandoned factory building. According to the Dutch police, the goalkeeper was some poor wretch living on a park bench. The former CEO and owner in Kiruna said he had acted in good faith when he sold the company, and he may well have. There was nothing to take before the court. But I kept getting the feeling that he . . ."

She broke off, looking for the right phrase.

". . . that he was scared. People get like that of course when the boys in blue knock on the door, but he wasn't just scared of us. That was the feeling I got."

"What are you getting at? Was there a connection to Bergsäk or Litova in there?"

"No, but it really makes you want to check it out, doesn't it?"

They were back at Rebecka's grey Eternit-clad house. Rebecka looked on as von Post wound the Brat up. The dog dived into the loose snow, turned on a farthing and ran back like a lunatic. Von Post called "I'm going to get you now" and threw snow into the air that the Brat snapped at.

"I checked into Bergsäk AB on the company register," Rebecka said. "They've got a new member on the board, one John Berg whose home address is Fortaleza, Brazil."

"What does that make you think?" von Post asked.

"Nothing positive," Rebecka said. "Why don't we have a whisky? I can't stop thinking about Anna-Maria, and it's driving me crazy."

"No, I've got to drive," von Post said, checking his watch. "I'm going to stay at a hotel tonight."

"You can sleep here if you want," Rebecka said to her own astonishment. "In my father's old flat on the ground floor. It's empty."

"What's going on, Martinsson. You're supposed to loathe me, remember?"

"I know," she said. "It must be Anna-Maria. What does all that crap matter?"

Rebecka lit a fire in the kitchen stove and poured them each a whisky. They clinked glasses and downed the first round, and she poured out another.

"There's no doubt in my mind that Bergsäk AB was the victim of a corporate hijack," Rebecka said. "Things tend to happen very quickly in that kind of situation. The hijackers ensure the company borrows a hell of a lot of money and then they empty all the assets and vanish. You can get that done in six months. But I think, given Kiruna's particular situation, they have a more long-term plan."

"Old Kiruna is due to be torn down, the new Kiruna has to be built, as many projects and commissions as you could want," von Post said.

"Exactly. We're talking billions. And the construction projects need to be completed in a hurry. Kiruna is the perfect host, just waiting for a really fat parasite."

"And then there's mining on top of that," von Post said.

"Yup. If LKAB outsources the dangerous jobs to subcontractors in order to avoid the responsibility. And if the subcontractors are then run by second-rate operators with poorly maintained equipment and not much in the way of safety checks . . ."

Carl von Post was thinking about his Rotary brethren and how over the years they had become increasingly open about their cheating: tax evasion, payments under the table, unregistered workers. Backs were pounded and holidays were taken in the Seychelles. He felt faintly nauseated at himself. All the times he pretended not to hear, pretended not to get the joke.

"It's on the back of widespread dishonesty," he said. "You begin by excusing yourself with 'Everyone does it, after all' and 'There are people who are worse', and then when you become the target for blackmail and threats, it escalates into financial crimes, corruption, construction fraud, drugs and sexual procurement."

"And violence," Rebecka said. "There's always someone willing to try and con the con man, someone who doesn't pay up, refuses to sell, and tries to take over the drug trade for instance. Then you get shootings, contract killings, arson. And no-one dares testify."

"Especially not now," von Post said. "The fact that they shot Rantakyrö and Mella is a quite extraordinary show of strength. They've demonstrated beyond any doubt that they're willing to kill anyone, and not just a few prostitutes."

Von Post shook his head to another round. Rebecka also felt she'd had enough.

"If this is what is going on, then Kiruna is suffering from cancer."

"And we're so slow to react," Rebecka said.

"What can we . . . we've got to do something," von Post said.

Rebecka looked into her empty glass.

Not going to be me, she thought. We're never going to be given the resources needed to hack off all the tentacles on this monster. He doesn't realise how difficult it is. How many hours it takes. I've got job offers, I'm going to sell up and move. I'm not planning on staying here to watch it happen.

She was vaguely aware of a guilty feeling of relief. It wasn't her investigation any longer. The whole thing was appalling, revolting. But not her problem.

"It's after one o'clock," she said. "You've got a long day tomorrow."

Von Post got to his feet and rolled his shoulders back. He tried to catch her eye.

"Let's not lose hope for Mella," he said. "If anyone can survive being shot through the skull, it's her."

Robert Mella woke abruptly and briefly experienced an intense sense of relief before surfacing fully and remembering where he was and the turn their lives had taken.

He was lying on a hospital bed beside Anna-Maria. She was no longer intubated. The monitor was displaying an even green curve.

It was 3.15 a.m. The room was dark. Footsteps and the quiet voices of the night shift could be heard outside in the corridor.

He reached a hand towards her and grasped her fingers. They were warm but lax and lifeless, there was no answering pressure from them. He had asked if he was allowed to touch her. As much as you like, one of the nurses had said. They told him that talking to her was good, too. Research showed that unconscious patients often responded to the voices of their relatives.

And talk to her he did. Until his throat was sore and his mouth was dry. He was keeping the fear at bay that there was nothing left of her capable of registering his presence. That she was gone for good.

Not like this, he thought. Not like this.

They had to have time to say goodbye. Time for the kids to have grown up.

486

The kids were with his sister. He didn't want them here and had argued with Jenny about it. She had shouted loudly, shrieked at him; "She's my mum!"

It had been resolved in the end. Only a single member of the family could go with her in the helicopter. They had only just made it; Robert's brother-in-law had driven like a bat out of hell through the freshly fallen snow all eighty-two of the kilometres separating Kiruna from Gällivare.

A logging truck had overturned across the road and it had only just been cleared as they passed the site.

When the phone call came he had cried. For five minutes maybe. He was dried out after, that was how it felt. He was completely dried out. Like a desert.

He didn't dare cry now. He had no idea where that might lead.

That time at Regla, when she almost got shot and Sven-Erik Stålnacke had been forced to shoot a man. That time, he had been so bloody scared after the event. Scared and so angry. In the end he couldn't go on working. He was off sick for a month.

You had to keep holding that fear at bay, all the time. That she might find herself in a life-threatening situation. Some drugged-up idiot might have a knife. Some crazy man who abused women might have a gun. And at the same time you thought that just doesn't happen. The risk was non-existent, statistically speaking. Even more non-existent in Kiruna.

Then the unthinkable happens and your whole world falls apart.

He tried to change his position on the bed. Every part of his body was aching.

He stroked her arms. Felt the silky-smooth hairs under his fingertips.

There were so many memories coursing through him. When she had Petter in her womb and ate paper. Absently tearing bits off the ragged edge that remained along the spiral in her notebooks and chewing away. How he had said you never knew what that contained, just think if it could harm the baby. When they were young before the kids came and lived in that one-room flat on Timmermansgatan. It was freezing cold in winter, and they hung their washing in the attic and it took for ever to dry because it froze into stiff pieces of cloth. The happiness on her face when she got into the police academy and he was terrified the entire time she would meet someone else. When they got married and everyone realised she was pregnant because she wasn't drinking. And she was so happy and danced like a lunatic, she could barely get out of bed the next day. And Robert's father got more drunk than he had ever seen him before and said, "You make sure you take care of that one."

Robert drew her floppy hand towards his lips.

"You've got to come back to me," he whispered. "My lovely Anna-Maria, please come back. I've got to have a chance to tell you I love you. I've got to be able to say that over and over again. That I love you."

SATURDAY 7TH MAY

Carl von Post woke Rebecka Martinsson shortly after 3 a.m. He was standing in the doorway to the kitchen like a shadow, rapping gently on the door frame. The Brat was whirring around him, expressing the canine version of delight along with a humble enquiry as to whether it might already be time for breakfast.

Rebecka sat up in bed. Immediately wide awake although behind her eyes and in the muscles of her body she could feel she was severely sleep deprived.

"Sorry, Rebecka, it's just me," von Post said. "Something occurred to me . . ."

"Let the dog out to pee, I'll put the coffee on."

She pulled on yesterday's clothes, put the percolator on and lit the kitchen stove, leaving the grate open for the cosy feeling of warmth it gave.

When she opened the roller blinds, spring light came flooding in even though it was still the middle of the night.

The Brat and von Post came back upstairs ten minutes later. He had snow on his sweater and trousers.

"I slipped when we were playing," he confessed.

You little therapist, Rebecka was thinking as she scratched the Brat between his ears.

They sat down with a cup of coffee each, the fire got going and the Brat was given his breakfast even though it was really much too early.

489

"I couldn't sleep," von Post said. "And while I was lying down there, I started thinking about this training course the NFC arranged last year on drug-related crime. You said the Pekkaris' company had purchased a printing firm and you couldn't work out why."

"That's right."

"Cocaine sometimes gets smuggled in paper. It's highly soluble in water and alcohol. So they dissolve the cocaine, place paper in the bath to absorb the solution and then hang the paper to dry. Once it's been delivered, the paper is shredded and the cocaine gets leached out; it's simple, you don't need a lab or anything, you can use ordinary windscreen-washer fluid and then you just let it evaporate. And you're left with the cocaine."

"Cocaine is produced in Colombia," Rebecka said, thinking aloud. "It usually gets smuggled into Europe on container vessels and then comes into Sweden by road from the Balkans, right?"

"Yes, only with climate change, the Arctic Ocean has become a transport route to reckon with as well."

"So you could unload it in northern Norway or a Russian port city?"

"And that would give you a fantastic distribution set-up for Sweden, Scandinavia, Europe. There's not much in the way of border controls between Sweden and Norway, Finland or on the Öresund Bridge. And paper, who checks paper?"

"If that's the case," Rebecka said, "you can understand why those two were reluctant to give up this territory. It would have been worth shooting two police officers for."

She went over to the boxes on the floor with the accounts and got out the binder of receipts.

She leafed through it quickly.

"I was just thinking they might have been planning to use the printing works for money laundering," she said. "And they might be doing that anyway. Just overseas customers, or that's what it looks like. They print the manuals for coffee machines, that kind of thing. Only there isn't much on the revenue side . . . I'm starting to feel really curious about this print shop."

"How curious?" von Post asked. "I've issued a search warrant. And Benny's Locks & Alarms are going to be there in . . ."

He looked at his watch.

". . . twenty minutes. Do you want to tag along?"

"Is a frog's arse watertight?" Rebecka said, getting up.

At last a proper thread to pull. She gave von Post an appreciative look.

The Brat got up expectantly as well.

"Not you, old boy," Rebecka said. "What grounds did you cite on the search warrant?"

"We're not bothering with any of that, Martinsson," von Post said tiredly. "Our only goal now is to try and put those men behind bars. Let them find me guilty of professional misconduct. I don't give a toss."

Von Post gave Rebecka Martinsson the keys to his car. He sat in the passenger seat. She understood that, sleepless and alone during the night, he had had more to drink. He must have had a bottle with him in his overnight bag. But she didn't ask about his wife.

Because we haven't become mates, that wasn't bloody happening, she told herself.

It was 4.15 a.m. when they arrived at the printing firm. A single-storey building in the industrial zone with corrugated green-metal sidings.

Rebecka braced herself and drove at high speed into the snowed-in car park. The white stuff sprayed all over the windscreen, and though she turned the wipers on, it was completely pointless. Carl von Post cried out and reached for something to grab on to when Rebecka stepped on the brakes. The car skidded and spun in a semi-circle before coming to a stop. He swore and she laughed out loud. They got out of the car. The snow reached almost to their knees.

"How did you see us getting out of here?" he asked, looking at the snowdrift in front of the bonnet.

"You've got a spade in your car, haven't you?"

When she saw the expression in his eyes, she said:

"Seriously, how long have you been living in Kiruna?"

It was Benny himself from Benny's Locks & Alarms who turned up just a minute later. Wisely he parked on the side of the road and trudged cautiously towards the two prosecutors in his high-top rubber boots. His legs seemed stiff and every now and then he had to put his toolbox down even though it risked disappearing into the snow.

"How are you?" Rebecka asked as he came up to them.

"Eh, you might as well send me to the bloody knacker's yard right now. I tipped over on the snowmobile last winter. Trying to get over a snow ridge. And you just put your foot down, you know, like on reflex to brace yourself. And – snap – that was my ACL gone."

He waved away the prosecutors' expressions of sympathy.

"Eh, it's fine really, you've just got to take it a bit slower."

While he was picking the lock he talked about the news. He had been reading about Tommy Rantakyrö and Anna-Maria Mella online.

"Who'd have thought something like that could happen in our town," he said shoving back his trapper hat.

After all these years he knew better than to ask if the job he had just carried out had anything to do with that business.

"Hope you get them," he said with feeling.

And not a word about paying extra for calling on his services outside normal hours. He nodded a goodbye and, following the deep footprints he had made, trudged back through the snow to his car.

Rebecka and von Post found the switch and turned on the lights. The fluorescent tubes hummed as they cast their chilly light over the premises. The place was open-plan and had no windows. A door that looked like it could lead to a toilet and an office with glass walls so you could see inside. There were no binders in there or anything else to suggest a business was being operated here.

"And no printing equipment," Rebecka observed. "Isn't that odd?"

"Very odd," von Post said.

Against one of the walls were bales of paper loaded onto pallets.

"I'll contact the NFC," von Post said. "They've got to come and see this. Should we call in one of the drug dogs?"

"Yes," Rebecka said. "Only we're going to check the place out as well."

"For what?"

Rebecka shrugged and got out a penknife to slit open the plastic wrapping around the paper bales. She climbed onto the edge of the pallet and wiggled one of the packages out.

"I'm not sure," Rebecka said, swinging the package experimentally up and down. "Does this feel a bit heavy to you?"

Carl von Post took it from her.

"Maybe it does," he said.

There were perfectly ordinary A4 sheets in the pack. Rebecka ran her thumb along the edges and between the sheets.

"Look at this," she said. "There's a difference between . . . can you make out that tint?"

The top ten sheets in the pack were pure white. The rest of them had a faint lilac sheen.

"Fishy," von Post said.

They tested the weight of the differently coloured paper sheets, holding one in each hand.

"I think the lilac-coloured ones are a bit heavier," von Post said. "But that could be because I want them to be a bit heavier."

Rebecka was staring at the pallets with the paper bales. She tried to do a quick tally in her head.

"How much paper is that? Half a ton?"

"Thirty to forty per cent of the weight could be cocaine," von Post said. "So roughly 200 kilos. And on the street a gram fetches . . ."

"Over a thousand kronor. Two hundred million. Even after the costs of the distribution chain that's a very tidy sum."

"How big was the load they seized in the free port in Gothenburg a couple of years ago?" von Post asked.

"A whole ton," Rebecka said. "Only this is still an incredible amount if—"

Suddenly they heard the sound of an engine outside. A large vehicle. There was the sound of braking and the ignition being turned off.

Rebecka and von Post looked at one another. They didn't need to say anything.

It's them, Rebecka thought. They've come to get their stuff. And we . . .

Von Post looked round for a way out that didn't exist. No windows. No back door. The large gates you could drive trucks in and out through would open in the same direction as the front door.

In her mind Rebecka was seeing two men jumping out of a lorry and approaching the entrance. They looked at one another when they saw the car parked outside, the footprints in the snow that led into the workshop, and got out the guns they kept concealed inside their clothes.

There was no time to ring for help. Her legs were trembling with terror. She looked at Carl von Post. He stared back at her, pale as a corpse, almost bluish under the fluorescent tubes. His breathing had become ragged and he was panting like a wounded elk.

Paralysed, they watched the handle as it started to turn.

Kerstin Simma had been driving the snowplough since 2 a.m. It was much simpler if it all got cleared before the morning traffic started, and she had to be home at seven to wake her husband so he got off to work. Then she would sit on her own with a cup of tea while the kids enjoyed a lie-in. Saturday mornings were the best.

She was listening to a documentary about a religious cult and feeling reasonably alert. She was meticulous in her work. No drifts were allowed to obscure the crossroads, and no pedestrian was going to have to face clambering over mountainous ridges of snow to cross to the other side of the road.

When she reached one of the car parks in the industrial zone she swore out loud. A car was parked at an angle right in the middle of it. How could anyone call that parking?

There was no snow on the roof of the car though, and fresh footprints led to the front of the building. She raised the blade, drove into the car park and stopped. She was going to ask the person who'd just been given a driving licence for Christmas to move their car. Not because she thought she might scrape the vehicle, but because leaving the car park with an unploughed spot in the middle would trouble her sense of order.

She trudged over to the front door and tried the handle. It was unlocked.

"Hello," she called into the echoing premises, kicking her shoes against the outer wall to get the snow off them. "Hello, is anyone here? I'm going to plough the car park and it would be helpful if someone could move the car – it's in my way."

The toilet door opened and two individuals peered out. She recognised one of them straight away. That was Rebecka Martinsson, the local prosecutor. Her face had been in the papers and on TV. The other person was a man of the same age, dressed like a snob in a long coat that looked like it cost a month's wages. Both were staring at Kerstin Simma as if she were a ghost.

"Snow ploughing?" Rebecka Martinsson said.

Kerstin Simma pulled off her cap. What was all this? Had they been having it off in the loo?

That was when Rebecka Martinsson started laughing. The man alongside her started laughing as well. They were laughing so hard they could barely draw breath. The man in the expensive coat couldn't keep himself upright but sat down on the floor laughing so much he ended up sobbing.

"Oh my God, oh my God," was all he could get out.

Rebecka Martinsson leaned against the wall with her arms around her stomach. The tears kept flowing.

"I can move the car," she said, and staggered over to the front door.

"You can park it on the road beyond the forecourt," Kerstin Simma said. "Are you sure you're in any state to drive?"

Rebecka Martinsson got a cigarette pack out of her bag. She and von Post leaned against the outer wall and smoked with trembling hands. They watched the snowplough clear the car park and waved as the woman in the driver's cabin raised the blade and drove away.

"Honestly, I have never been so scared in my entire life," von Post said. "We'll have to put a watch on the place."

What does he mean "we"? Rebecka thought gloomily.

They drove back to Kurravaara and just as they were almost there both their phones pinged.

Rebecka grabbed the steering wheel so hard her fingers turned white. Carl von Post managed to dredge his phone out of his coat pocket.

"Anna-Maria?" she asked while he was reading.

It was half past five in the morning. It was too early for it to be anything else. Just not that, though. Not that.

Von Post shook his head.

"No," he said. "It's from Anna Granlund. Pohjanen died last night. Or yesterday evening. He passed away on his sofa at the hospital."

Rebecka's mind had nowhere to go. It kept spinning round in circles, witless like a white ptarmigan on white snow.

The sun was high in the sky, lighting up the day to come with all its terrors. Fresh snow weighed down the branches of the trees. A white casing had frozen onto the birches.

She had to take her foot off the accelerator. She was scared she would stamp down on it by mistake and drive them off the road. The car crawled along the long bend that led down towards the village.

"I'm going to bring Anders and Olle Pekkari in for questioning about the printing firm and that camper van," von Post said once they were back in Rebecka's yard in Kurravaara. "Thanks for the overnight stay and the dinner."

And for the printing shop, Rebecka thought darkly. Only he's already forgotten I'm the one who found it.

Carl von Post was watching Rebecka Martinsson. It struck him he'd often wanted to see her like this. Burned out almost, from within. What he really wanted now, though, was to have the difficult bitch back, the one who used to irritate him to death. The way she talked when she got worked up. When her eyes moved fast and her mouth turned hard. That enviable ability of hers to just keep on working, angry and tired and stubborn.

"Are you coming to work today?" he asked.

She shook her head.

Their old discord caught light again, like when you blow on a fire that has almost died.

Two police officers shot, von Post was thinking. And she chooses to stay home and play the victim.

I'm not his little assistant, Rebecka Martinsson was thinking.

Von Post shrugged. He didn't want to argue. Not with Rebecka. Not with anyone. He looked at his phone. No sign of life from Erika. She was going to leave him.

They could do what they liked, the two of them. He was just going to try and survive this day.

Anders Pekkari and his father Olle Pekkari were brought in for questioning at 7.15 a.m. Carl von Post and Sergeant Fred Olsson handled the whole business.

When Anders Pekkari opened his front door, Carl von Post was standing outside. He asked him to accompany him to the station. Another car had stopped at the side of the road. Anders' father, Olle, was sitting in the back. He was staring in fury at the driver's headrest in front of him. Not looking at Anders.

Carl von Post asked for Anders' phone.

After Anders Pekkari handed it over, he found himself standing in front of the jackets in the hall. He didn't recognise them. Couldn't understand which one was his.

In the end Carl von Post had to reach for the other man's jacket, asking: "This one?"

Anders Pekkari nodded absently.

Carl von Post laid one hand lightly on his back as they walked to the car.

Anders Pekkari was so frightened he got hiccoughs. He had been fearing this moment for so long. Incredibly vivid mental images of it had been keeping him awake at night. Now and then, as he lay beside his sleeping wife, he had even wanted it to happen, just so it was all over.

He had even toyed with the idea of losing everything: respect, friends, the business, his family. Having to serve a prison term – and then being able to start again. Get a studio flat and an ordinary job, whatever that might be. Or take to the bottle, should it come to that.

But there was no relief to be found in what was currently happening. It was just another stage in the ongoing nightmare his life had become.

He was grateful he and his father were travelling in separate vehicles.

The reception was not manned and there was no-one in the waiting room. He didn't care. That business of caring what people thought about you. Thinking all that was important was what someone with the same name as him did, someone who lived in a different solar system to this one, though. His hiccoughs had become quite loud. A police officer fetched him some water in a plastic cup.

Chance is the pseudonym God uses when He is unwilling to sign on the dotted line. Börje woke up in Ragnhild Pekkari's bed. They were spooning and his nose was in the back of her neck. She woke up as well and turned towards him; they made love again. Taking your time like this was new to him.

She wanted scrambled eggs afterwards. And juice. But the fridge was bare. Börje got dressed to go out to the shops. He headed towards the petrol station down at the crossroads between Adolf Hedinsvägen and Malmvägen.

The town looked like a picture postcard in the morning sunshine. White snow covering everything that had been dissolving into grey slush. The trees sparkled and he could see the tracks of a hare in the snow. He liked the fact that there was light and air between the buildings in Kiruna. So much space.

He went into the shop at the petrol station. Put a bunch of squeaky tulips in the basket as well. By the refrigerated display he was tapped on the shoulder by another customer who began with the usual:

"Aren't you Börje Ström?"

There was no denying it. The guy, who was a bit older than him, introduced himself as Harry Svonni and told him he used to box for the North Pole Club as well. They stood there tugging at their memories, trying to recall the ones that had to do with people and matches they had in common. Once more Börje was able to enjoy a quiet feeling of pleasure at being back in Kiruna. Ragnhild, that was like a miracle all on its own. And then this as well, it just felt so nice coming across people like this.

"Oh, good Lord, I remember when you turned up at the club as a little lad and Jussi and Sikke took you under their wings. They must have been able to see what an incredible talent you had."

They had a laugh about the matches in Finland. And about all the lickings they'd come in for over there.

"It's really good the club still exists," Harry Svonni said. "Though I've no idea who owns it nowadays, would that be the King? Is he still alive?"

"Yes, he's alive," Börje Ström said. "Lives out on the Esrange road."

"There you go. His son wasn't much of a boxer, Spike Mäki. We were the same age," Harry Svonni said. "You didn't dare punch him too hard or you could end up on the wrong side of his dad. Things can't have been easy for him, though. We were neighbours, you know, in Piilijärvi."

"In Piilijärvi?" Börje Ström asked as something stirred inside him, like when you get the sense there's a fish on your hook.

"Yeah, his mum got divorced from the King early on, didn't she. Got remarried to a fitter from Piilijärvi. He still owned his parents' home in the village along with his brothers and sisters. They spent the summers there. And my family are from round there as well. So Spike and I actually played together when we were six or seven. Cowboys and Indians. Only after that he turned a bit dodgy. Kept getting up to no good."

Harry Svonni let a concerned shake of the head finish his sentence for him.

"He's done well for himself all the same," he said. "Apart from all that weight. Have you seen him? Must weigh two hundred kilos at least. Not like you, you look like you've kept in shape. Do you still do any boxing?"

Börje could hear himself answering but could only follow the conversation in disjointed fragments as though a storm had brewed up between the shelves of merchandise that was blowing the other man's words away. He hoped in some distant part of himself that he was saying something sensible. In the end Harry Svonni must have noticed he was distracted.

"Well, I won't keep you," he said in a friendly voice. "Only it was really, really great to see you. I've been boasting about the fact that we belonged to the same club for years."

They said goodbye and Börje headed towards the exit.

Harry Svonni called after him:

"Your shopping. Don't you want your shopping?"

But Börje Ström left his basket behind and walked straight past the tills and out of the shop.

Piilijärvi, he was thinking. Sven-Erik Stålnacke had told him a man had had his gun stolen, or "borrowed", by someone from Piilijärvi.

Von Post ended up in the kitchen at home. Erika wasn't there. Her car wasn't in the garage. There was bread on the counter beside a piece of sweating cheese, while the gooey contents of a margarine tub suggested she wasn't just out for a bit.

He tried calling her again but got her voicemail. Again.

He could hear wild yelling and laughter from the boys playing their games upstairs. He opened the door a crack; they said hello without taking their eyes off the massacre going on between heavily armed men on the screen.

"Why aren't you at school?" he asked.

"It's Saturday," his sons told him.

He left them alone. He realised they hadn't got up early but hadn't been to bed at all. He assumed Erika hadn't told them. He wondered if she had spent the night at one of her girlfriends, drinking wine and rubbishing him into the wee hours.

He took a quick shower. He was hoping Erika would come home. And hoping she wouldn't.

After he had put on some clean clothes his phone rang, but the screen said it was Fred Olsson. That must be the Pekkaris making problems for him.

"Has something happened?" he asked, and went down the basement steps to the laundry so as not to have to hear the yells and sounds of butchery from the floor above.

"It's Olle and Anders Pekkari," Fred Olsson said. "They say they're prepared to talk. Anders in any case."

"Are you kidding me?"

"No, Anders is completely out of it."

"Have they asked for a lawyer?"

"They haven't actually, should I ask if . . ."

"No, for Christ's sake, don't. I'm on my way.

*

Börje called Ragnhild and explained he was going to be a bit late. Though she wasn't aware of it, he could tell that the way he was acting was indicative of a major change. He didn't usually tell his women what he was doing. Once, when one of them had complained, he had said: "What kind of relationship do you want? One where you're the government?" It had ended shortly afterwards.

He told her about his encounter in the shop. And in the middle of doing so realised he hadn't brought the food with him. While they had a laugh about that, matters soon turned serious.

"I've got to talk to Spike," he said. "I'll have to go shopping again afterwards. And remember to pay and take it with me."

"I'll go out with Villa meanwhile," she said.

Even when they were discussing everyday matters his thoughts would linger on their physical intimacy. He was thinking about kissing the back of her neck, the way he'd woken in the night only to notice that they were holding hands under the duvet. His mind kept finding ways of coming back to her. Often those little things. Her hair sometimes, the down on her arms, the rough rather crispy stuff on her sex, the barely perceptible down on the tips of her ears.

And like just now when Harry Svonni had started talking to him in the shop – he'd been standing at the refrigerated counter trying to work out what sort of juice she liked. That was new, too.

"So have you made up your mind she's going to be called that?" he asked. "Villa?"

"Kind of," she said. "No other name seems to stick."

Börje took the lift in the block of flats Spike lived in and was regretting it even before the door closed.

It ascended slowly, stinking of piss; the walls were covered in old graffiti that had been only partially scrubbed off, making it fade rather than disappear.

Spike opened the door. His eyes kept wandering. The huge white T-shirt had a stain in the middle of his chest. Börje had to stop himself looking at it.

"Börje!" Spike exclaimed. "Well, what a . . . yeah?"

He checked his watch, peering over his shoulder. The flat really wasn't in a state to receive visitors.

"May I come in?"

Spike backed away. Börje took a step into the hall and pulled the door shut behind him.

In the living room the television cast its cold gleam over two over-stuffed leather armchairs. There were two empty crisp packets and a plastic bottle of some soft drink on the floor beside one of the chairs. No carpet. No curtains. Lowered blinds. Börje realised Spike had not just been watching television: the set was on all the time.

A sense of loneliness, awful and somehow dull at the same time, pervaded the flat and Börje declined the invitation to have a seat in the kitchen. It smelled cramped and stuffy and of old pizza, crisps, farts and the gases given off by the body in sleep.

"This will be quick," he said.

"As the actress said to the bishop," Spike joked, but the humour fell flat.

"You used to be in Piilijärvi a lot in the summers when you were a kid." Börje got straight to the point. "And the gun Dad was shot with belonged to a guy in Piilijärvi. Disappeared from his car right at the time of the murder and was then returned. You were the one who took it, weren't you? You gave the gun to your dad. That was why he refused to answer where he got it from."

When Spike failed to say anything he continued:

504

"I'm not going to tell people, you can trust me on that. I just want to know."

"That was all so long ago now," Spike said in entreaty.

Only then Börje yelled: "No, it was today, yesterday. All the days I lived without my dad. Never knowing. Always wondering."

The yelling could be heard outside in the stairwell. He couldn't give a damn.

Spike ran the back of his hand across the sweat breaking out on his forehead, small drops that were running down into his eyes.

"It's true," he said despondently. "I was the one who took the pistol. You know what my dad was like. You were supposed to get toughened up. And then you got to be part of that kind of thing every now and then. Putting people in their place, making people toe the line. He called me and told me to drive the moped to the crossroads leading towards Vittangi. I took the gun with me."

"What happened then?"

"Christ, he took the gun off me straight away and gave me a slap. Only then it came in handy, so to speak, didn't it?"

"You were there when it happened?"

Spike nodded. Then he shook his head.

"But I'm not going to talk about that. It happened like Dad said it did."

His eyes turned hard.

"It turned out alright for you though, didn't it? Just look at yourself. And then look at me. My dad is alive. What good has that ever done me? You can fuck off now. Kill me if you want. Put an ad in the local paper for Christ's sake, if that makes you feel better. It's all the fucking same to me."

Spike broke off and gasped as though he had been running.

"I've got to sit down," he said and staggered into the kitchen where he thumped onto a chair, grimacing. That would have to be hard on his knees with his build.

Börje looked at Spike bent over the kitchen table, gasping for breath and overweight. What if he died of a heart attack right now?

He turned towards the door to go.

"I was fourteen," Spike said behind him. "I was only fourteen."

Börje slammed the door shut behind him. Spike could hear him walking down the stairs. His upper body started folding forward towards the kitchen table so he could lay his forehead on it. His stomach got in the way so he straightened up again.

"I didn't say anything," he whispered to the empty air. "I didn't tell."

Börje ran down the flights of stairs as though he were escaping a house on fire. Then he strode off towards the petrol station. His basket was still where he had left it.

It turned out alright for you though, didn't it? Just look at yourself . . .

Did it turn out alright for me? he thought. The only thing I ever aspired to was boxing.

MARCH 1977

Börje's girlfriend Nancy straightens up as the doorbell tinkles in the diner where she works. Börje is eating breakfast at one of the tables before going off to work for the day: hauling concrete in a wheelbarrow on a construction site between Broadway and Mercer. It's the perfect day for a job like that, good weather, warm but not scorching the way it can get in summer.

Paris, Börje's former coach, comes in the door. Nancy comes out with her usual:

"Hello handsome, take a seat. I'll bring you a menu."

She's twenty-one. So pretty her customers often ask her if she's really an actress. She usually laughs at that. As if they had said something crazy. She is saving up to study, though she doesn't tell the diners that. "I'm happy right here," is what she says, putting their tips into her savings account.

Börje gets up. Paris catches sight of him and bursts into a smile.

"There's my boy," he says.

It's true he calls everyone his boy apart from Big Ben who he always refers to as "the boss". But he appears to be genuinely touched to see Börje.

He orders coffee, orange juice and eggs over-easy on toast.

Almost immediately he announces that he's stopped working as a coach at the gym.

"I'd had enough."

He tells them that the last four years he's been coaching a promising young black boxer. Hot-tempered, not in the ring, but when he couldn't get things right he was always wanting to give up and leave. Like when he couldn't get the twist right when he punched.

"Damn, you wouldn't believe the rows we had. But the moment I discovered it was his back foot that was slightly misplaced, that meant he was able to keep at it, and then he'd be grinding away, sweating buckets. Do you remember him? He trained at the gym the same time as you."

Börje says he doesn't remember. Paris looks a bit disappointed.

"It was a good thing for me when I got given you," Paris says. "A white boy. That let me help my own boys. If you get my meaning."

Börje nods.

"He was still young," Paris goes on. "I told Big Ben that boy wasn't ready for big matches. But you know how it works. It's easy to bullshit a boy who's barely dry behind the ears and still lives with his mom. 'You've got to fight fifty, sixty matches just to have a prospect of a title fight, so when are you actually going to start? Paris will think you're ready by the time you get your first grandchild . . .'"

He goes on about the same young man, who is currently fighting match after match against guys whose rep has already been built. He keeps getting beaten time and again.

"He's stopped boxing," Paris says. "Now he just rushes head-first into the ring like a bull, with his head up, and simply accepts all the blows that land and he'll be hanging up his gloves before he's twenty-five."

Nancy arrives with the breakfast and Paris carefully places his paper serviette in his lap so it covers his thighs.

"He used to be able to read his opponents," Paris says. "Supple, he was. Needed more technique, we were working on his punch. Damn fast when he got inside. But now . . . he's just a punching bag. He's finished. Twenty-one years old. I asked Big Ben to spare him. I went up to his office and begged him."

Paris blinks several times and looks up at the ceiling.

"So I quit. I couldn't stand by and watch it happen. Every coaching session, every match. Like a funeral that never ended. And what Big Ben did to you . . . Only that's actually why I'm here. Your contract with him has run out now, hasn't it?"

Börje says that's the case, but there is no manager who would be willing to take him on. No promoter would set up a match for him. No-one dares cross Big Ben. Börje is blacklisted, and his fingernails are black under the edges besides.

He shows Paris his workman's hands with a smile.

"You could box in Europe," Paris says and leans back in his chair.

Nancy comes over and tops up their coffee. She asks Paris if everything is to his satisfaction.

"I'm just fine where I am," Börje says to him.

"I can see that, son," Paris says with a glance at the departing Nancy. "Only let me tell you something. José Luis Pérez . . ."

Börje can feel the muscles in his face tensing. The match against Pérez in the Catskills comes back to him. The day after, when his life was over. Pérez signed on with Big Ben after that match and in November he won the belt in the light heavyweight world championship.

"Pérez is touring Europe," Paris is saying. "It's absolutely vital to Big Ben that he keeps that belt. He won't let him come home to face any real opposition. It's all about the money. The more matches he fights as 'the undefeated champion', the more . . ."

Paris rubs his thumb against the tips of his index and middle fingers.

". . . is to be made from gala events and sponsors. Pérez is a good boxer, but you know as well as I do: a good boxer has to be pitted against other good boxers. He's fighting matches where all he basically has to do is stick his arm out. Before you know it he'll start believing he really is immortal."

Paris pauses to let his words sink in.

Börje checks his watch, a cheaper one, he had to sell the gold one. It's time for him to head off for work.

"And!" Paris says, giving him a crafty look. "Pérez is due to fight in Hamburg in July. I've got contacts there. And you look like you're in pretty good shape at any rate, you haven't put weight on. Are you still training?"

"No gym to go to. But I run every morning. I'd go crazy otherwise."

"What about your speed? Do you think you've still got your reaction time? Can you box as beautifully as when you stopped?"

Börje laughs.

"No idea. I play ping-pong with some Irish guys three evenings a week. They've got a table in the basement of a bar. No-one can beat me right now."

Paris makes a slightly surprised sound, evidently trying to work out whether this is what he really needed to hear. He's got something on his mind and Börje realises he is actually curious to know what it is.

Paris stirs his coffee and says:

"If I can arrange for you to fight that match in Hamburg, would you do it? Would you be up for training so hard you'll be sweating blood by then? Would you be up for beating Pérez?"

Paris looks at him over the rim of his coffee cup. There is something about his eyes Börje has always liked. You can see he's been doing this for a long time. He's a wily old fox. Börje has no idea whether Paris can actually arrange for him to fight the match in Hamburg, but one thing he does know: Paris is no bullshitter.

Börje is aware of something he has not felt in ages. That unique combination of pleasure, expectation, killer instinct and rage: the desire for revenge.

So Pohjanen is dead, Rebecka Martinsson was thinking.

She longed to be able to cry but could feel no grief.

She was sitting at her kitchen table looking out at the lovely weather, sunshine and snow. The Brat was lying at her feet.

I haven't always been like this, she thought. When I was little, when Grandma was alive, I was brim-full of feelings and sensations. My nose was always filled with scents: sun-warmed pine forest and wet dog and old barn. I know how birch catkins smell when you crumble them between the tips of your fingers, only when did I do that last? As I child I was constantly aware of the way things smelled. I never think about that nowadays.

My feet used to get so hard at the end of summer that I could run over pine cones without it hurting. I used to go swimming and diving in the river, I was never bothered it might be cold. If I found an old fishing lure on the bottom it was like finding treasure. I used to creep like a cat through the high grass among the midsummer flowers and the buttercups. I picked cudweed and was amazed by it. I climbed trees, my knees were always scraped, there was dirt under my fingernails, my body was covered in mosquito bites and I had tangled knots in my hair.

In winter my Lovika mittens were covered in lumps of snow. I used to eat the lumps and get the woollen fibres in my mouth. My nose ran. I licked a piece of iron and my tongue got stuck: you only do that once. My tears were always so cold they hurt.

I was totally and utterly alive, she thought. How did I end up feeling so empty?

Those words of Krister's like knives: "Marit feels sorry for you. So do I."

It occurred to her that she hadn't been on a skiing trip since she and Krister split up. Not a real one.

She got to her feet and opened the kitchen window. You could hear a circular saw from somewhere on the other side of the inlet.

The air smelled of snow. Empty and clean. She could feel her nostrils widening, her lips were twitching like an animal's. She was assailed by such a violent longing for the mountains there was barely room for it in her chest.

It felt like a call. Come.

She knew she had to get out. Away. She had to get on her skis and travel into that great silence.

It was nine in the morning when Rebecka parked her car in a gap at the Låktatjåkka bus stop. She locked the car, put on her backpack and pressed her ski boots into the bindings. The sun was burning white. Glittering across the mountains and over the fresh snow. She had to squint even though she had sunglasses on. She ought to get proper ones that covered the sides as well.

She skied for a hundred metres and stopped, turned the pole over and stuck it experimentally into the snow. It went easily through the crackly thin crust that had already formed over the new snow and the thick layer of downy snow beneath. Then the pole came to a halt where a gritty frozen layer of late winter snow had formed. Beautiful snow. Dangerous too.

There were no ski tracks ahead. No snowmobile tracks. Just her.

She set off. The soft sound of skis against the surface. Into the world of the mountains. At one time these mountains were pointed, high and rugged. After four hundred million years their shape had softened. They rose all around her like vast creatures, indolent female wolves half-asleep, white fluffy pelts, enormous paws, one ear pricked. They were watching her out of the corners of their eyes as she came skiing along.

Halfway up to Laktå she stopped and drank water from a blue Nalgene water bottle. Krister had given it to her. She ought to buy a new one.

Their trips into the forests and the mountains. She had always felt she could be herself with him. The way they could deal with practical matters without having to speak. One of them would make a fire while the other chopped the frozen dog food into pieces. When they pitched the tent or cooked the food there were four hands and one mind. The sex. Waking in the night and edging towards him before going back to sleep.

She put a bit more effort into the poles. She hadn't meant to hurt him. She had hurt him. She wanted to be someone you could trust. You couldn't trust her. She ruined everything she touched and there was something wrong with her. Something that was broken, jagged, that other people cut themselves on.

She would wake him in the middle of the night sometimes. Talk to me. And he had talked. About dogs and the forest and the fishing trips he had been on as a child. He had stroked her hair and she had grown calm.

It was slower going than she would have liked in the pass between Låktakåkka and Kärketjärro. She had to force the pace when she began the last steep ascent towards the Låkta chalet. A lot more snow had collected on the slope.

Don't stop now, don't shorten the forward movement as you go up, just tense the muscles of your thighs, shift your hips forward and put the pressure on the middle of the ski to get the maximum benefit from the sealskins. Ignore the lactic acid build-up. Pain is just weakness leaving the body, as old Kiruna residents used to say.

Panting, she reached the top of the slope and the Låkta chalet came into view. It was closed for the season. New snow had drifted up its walls; just the upper half of the red window frames was visible. Finally. She had been in the open air for almost two hours.

Right leg forward. Left leg forward. She was panting and sweat was running into her eyes. There was an unpleasant scraping sensation in her right eye, bound to be an eyelash.

She stopped when she reached the chalet and drank more water.

To her left she could see the old geared wheel that was part of the long since disused lift that used to run up what was known as Pumping House Hill.

She gulped down some handfuls of trail mix – chocolate, raisins and nuts. Chewing and swallowing with a bit of water. She had to get fuel inside her.

Low blood sugar and dehydration would mean she wouldn't be able to manage the rest of the trip.

The rest of the trip? asked one of the great wolves. Where were you planning on going?

She looked towards the summer trail.

Fear was flapping its wings inside her. An avalanche danger zone, she knew that.

You wouldn't dare, the she-wolves said. Turn around, little girl.

Which was when she knew that was the path she had to follow.

Come and get me then, she thought. I don't care. I stopped caring long ago.

She kept going. The important thing was to hold a steady course, following the unmarked summer trail so you got to the two small lakes at the beginning of the glen between Kuoblatjårro and Latnjatjåkka. You had to get the trail right on the pass over Kuobla.

Here and there she saw the traces of ptarmigan in the snow. Little criss-cross tracks and the tiny indentations where they had holed up.

She was worried about missing the two small lakes because of the major snowfall of the last few days. In deep snow it was harder than expected to work out where the lakes began and ended. She remembered a fly-fishing trip with her father when he had drilled all the way down to the soil thinking they were on a lake. The ruined bits of that ice drill and his wounded pride. "We're not going to tell anyone about this. I was planning on buying a new one anyway."

The blazing sun and the light like a swarm of arrows flashing at her off the snow made her eyes tear up. Only to her relief she could now see the first oblong lake. Someone long ago had taught her the mnemonic: if you follow the inner curve of the banana and the upper edge of the pea you can find the right way through the pass that leads to the higher of the two lakes and then you'll be facing the slopes of Biran. As it happened she had always found it irritating that someone so lacking in imagination could have referred to beautiful mountain lakes as bananas and peas, but now that the snowfall had erased their contours the mnemonic was doing the trick. She followed the bend of the first lake so as not to miss its end and the hissing of her skis got louder. Right foot forward, left foot forward.

She was almost about to pass the point where the banana gave way to the pea, but an abrupt rise in the level of the land indicated solid ground. These were not lakes people fished in, so it couldn't be an abandoned fishing hut. More like a large block of stone. She had the two peaks of Kuoblatjårro to one side of her and was going to head for the one on the right.

She got out the bottle and drank a bit more water. She should have brought more with her she realised, it would soon be empty.

She stood perfectly still and listened for any sounds but the silence between the mountain slopes was a presence, the quiet space inside a church. During the period Måns had gone with her on trips and she had managed to guide them to a place like this in the forests or the mountains, it had always seemed to frighten him somehow. He became incredibly talkative, almost chatty. It had the opposite effect on her, the silence made her grow still. She was moving more softly, putting her feet down more gingerly.

She had reached the ascent up the pass. The muscles in her thighs were protesting. She was no longer skiing properly but leaning forward towards the tips, putting her body weight on the poles to take it off her legs. That backfired, the sealskins lost contact with the snow and the skis started slipping back with every step; the rhythm of the motion was being lost and her skiing was becoming ragged and even more tiring.

She urged herself on. Pull back the upper body, accept that it hurts, that it feels as though someone were twisting the muscles around your thigh bone in different directions, roll your shoulders back so you can fill your lungs with air. Forward, upwards. Keep to the right.

Once she had the two peaks behind her at last, she was sweating so hard it ran down her back, she could feel the sting of the droplets collecting at the base of her spine and along the back of her thighs. Her eyes were burning; it started to feel as though she had been rubbing them with gravel.

She got the water bottle out and it was empty. Her tongue immediately started swelling. She grabbed a handful of snow, shoved it in her mouth and took a look round. She was high up. She had reached the upper lake. Biran lay to the south-east. And it was here, between Biran and one of the peaks of Kuobla, that the descent to Kårsavagge she had been aiming for opened up. Both slopes were steep. In favourable conditions off-piste skiers or young snowmobile drivers with high treads on their sports models could put down tracks between them, the only problem was conditions were almost never favourable here. There was almost always a risk of avalanche. So this was complete madness. She understood that in some distant part of herself.

She made her way over the first flat area. She wanted to reach the side of Biran; westerlies had been blowing as usual, which had led to a huge fall of snow collecting there. Once she reached the steep section that she needed to descend, she hesitated.

The she-wolves had got up onto their paws. They were looking at her. Their hot breath was licking the snow. So show us then. How you're getting out of this.

She brought her skis together and jumped up and down on the spot. Listened to the noise the snow made. No warning sounds. With a firm push of her poles she glided forward and down. There was more snow than expected and it was difficult to turn, the right ski slid out to the side and she thought she might fall. A combination of the volume of snow and her exhausted thigh muscles. That awful feeling of losing control when your body couldn't catch up with the changes to the surface. She stayed on her feet but it was a close-run thing. She stopped to catch her breath.

When her pulse had slowed again, she took another look all around her; she had to shield her eyes with one hand. Blinking hurt, squinting was painful. These pathetic sunglasses.

How stupid, she thought. Just how crazily stupid can you be?

She was going to follow the edge below the steepest part of Biran where the slope grew flatter and spread out more gently than the sheer drop above. Most of the snow had collected on the slope below because it was in the lee when the wind blew. But the snowfall had been so powerful that even at 250 metres above sea level a great deal had fallen. The sun had melted the topmost layer to a thin crust that would hold. She was grateful she still had the sealskins on her skis; those and the steel edges provided her with a firm base which meant she didn't have to press the skis hard into that delicate crust.

After three hundred metres or so she heard the sound. It was as if one of her watchers had uttered a deep sigh. A second later the snow shifted beneath her skis. It was only a minor shift, but she could feel it very clearly and came to a stop.

This was not good. The snow this high up should be stable enough for a single skier.

She looked up at Biran. Three lemmings were darting upwards across the crust in the sunlight. She remembered something she'd heard before: the more lemmings run upwards over snow, the more you should worry about what lies beneath it.

And what about that crack in the snow cover up on the ridge. Had it really been there the whole time? Or had it just split open?

Danger! Only then she gave herself a strict talking to:

"Figments of your imagination. There's no danger at all. And that business about the lemmings is a complete myth; the crack's just a thin little line. You can barely see with these useless sunglasses on and you're not thinking clearly."

She continued on. Without her wanting or deciding to alter them, her movements had become more cautious. Light, light pushes with the poles. She was listening intently. Then she heard it again, it wasn't a figment. The sound was more powerful this time and no longer a sigh but more a muffled rumble.

The snow was shifting perceptibly beneath her. She froze and her heart started pounding. Slowly she turned her head while trying to keep the rest of her body still. Despite the brilliant sunshine she could clearly see the crack in the snow cover that had opened up where the steep section began.

It's about to slide, she thought. The whole slope is about to collapse in one huge avalanche.

She stood there completely motionless, like a wild animal snared by the headlights of a car. Her poles in mid-air, terrified that two tiny holes in the snow cover might become the trigger for several tons of snow to sweep her away before burying her.

It was not the idea of dying but how she would die that filled her with terror.

Arms and legs stuck fast in the snow like cement. Buried alive, conscious and slowly dying. Snow in her mouth, snow in her nostrils. Suffocating slowly while trying to scream.

She had been taught that it was vital to keep your hands in front of your face so as to create an air pocket if you were caught in an avalanche. Until rescuers arrived. There were skiers who had survived for several hours under the snow just as long as they had air in front of their faces, while the cold slowed their bodily functions and that meant your chances of survival increased. Krister had saved some people in that state with Zack, the dog he used to have.

But Krister and his dogs were not going to come and rescue her. No-one would be coming. No-one knew she was here.

518

She was breathing so shallowly the air barely reached the back of her mouth, her chest hardly moving. With her poles still in mid-air she tried to collect her thoughts.

Turning back was not an option. It would mean moving beneath the area where a crack had already formed.

She felt a powerful impulse just to turn her skis slightly and head straight downhill. In reality, though, trying to escape from the slope that way was a trap: she would risk being right in the line of fire if the avalanche was triggered. Besides, snow had a tendency to spread out in a cone. That would make for a larger and larger zone in which she risked being dragged down. The chance she could escape sideways was still there. She would only have a very narrow window to move out of its path to one side and then ski down on the diagonal. Only how was she going to be able to move forwards when she hardly dared breathe as it was, even less push off with a pole.

Extremely warily she began to move one of her skis forward without putting too much weight on it. And then the other. Just as gingerly. Moving felt terribly dangerous, all she wanted was to keep everything as still as possible. And for the mountains and the great she-wolves to calm down, lie down, drift off to sleep. But there was only one way out. Away from where she was. One step at a time.

The sealskins beneath her skis went from being a help to a hindrance. They damped down her speed. The friction against the surface made it difficult to glide while moving lightly.

After skiing for five hundred metres, moving with all the slowness of a t'ai-chi practitioner, she dared to prod the snow with her poles. Next time she would do something more like a proper push-off.

She stopped. Had a listen. Stuck her fingers inside her sunglasses and wiped the tears out of her aching eyes. She squinted at the crack. Any bigger? She wasn't sure.

She was terrified of the moment when the surface would start to move. And be pulled away from under her like a carpet.

Warily forward again. Her senses were continually alert for any movement in the snow.

Sweat ran into her armpits. Not from exertion, but from fear. The sour smell of adrenaline sweat reached her nose.

After an endless period of crawling along on her skis she judged she was out of danger. The terrain below had evened out and she was a long way from the steep sides of Kuoblatjårro and Latnjatjåkka.

The death trap was behind her.

Her legs gave way and she thumped onto her backside with her boots still in their bindings. From sitting she fell onto her back in the snow, her knees to the side, the boots still locked onto the skis. She pulled off her sunglasses, laid her hand over her eyes and felt the tears against her palm.

The wolves settled down. She was no longer their concern.

During the course of a day and a night, Elena Litova, now known as Maria Mäki in both the civil register and on her passport, had cleaned the house with Tonya. They had not slept, their hands were red, the skin flaking. But now they were done. They had followed a list. Everything they had touched had to be wiped with water mixed with washing up liquid and bleach: door handles, door posts, light bulbs, lamp switches, household utensils, frying pans, saucepans, cutlery, glasses, shelves, table surfaces, counters, the toilet brush. Everything. They were bound to have missed something, but it would be hard to find. She had burned their clothes in several loads in the grate. Today she had burned their sheets.

She looked at her watch. She could hear the rat-like scratching of Tonya scraping the varnish off her nails. She paid extraordinary sums for those claws of hers, only to gnaw and scratch the thick layer of colour away until her nails looked like the paint peeling off houses in a town where all the industry had been shut down.

"When?" Tonya asked, her nail still between her teeth.

Tonya already had her gold-coloured down jacket on. The package from Net-a-Porter arrived once a week. Saving for a rainy day wasn't Tonya's thing. She had wept as though grieving for a dead child once her trendy clothes were crackling in the flames.

"Fifteen minutes," Elena responded. "How many pairs of trousers have you got on?"

"Three, you can't see that. I'm thin."

She ought to tell Tonya to remove the extra layers. Order her to do it. But Elena was so utterly exhausted she could barely put one foot in front of the other. Two years ago she had a million Euros. Now she had nothing.

When the British lawyer had contacted her following the corporate hijacking in Novosibirsk the deal had sounded too good to be true. Four years, five max. Married to a Swede. Buy up some local operators. Reel in a load of contracts in just a few years. Drain the projects of money, empty a few companies. And then disappear with at least ten million Euros in her pocket. He had said she was a valuable resource. He knew she had studied economics at the state university even if she hadn't had the money to graduate. He had praised the grades she had obtained. He had said what she had been thinking, that a million Euros was a lot of money but not a sum you could live off for the rest of your life. Particularly if the security services were after you for swindling money from the Russian tax authorities. He promised her a new identity. Both before and after Kiruna.

"I was like you," he had said, "smart but alone in the world." He had shown her pictures of his horses. A house in the background that looked almost like a castle. He had known she would look at the castle. Just at the castle. "I've got to be able to take my sister with me," she had declared.

He had replied that that wouldn't be a problem. He told her what to do. Told her she could contact him at any time. Told her to bring in some muscle, some security. Provided her with a contact at a company that dealt with that kind of thing.

"They believe in you upstairs," he had said in his perfect English.

The Upstairs. The very idea of it made her sick with fear. Inhabited by powerful and terrifying shadows who, though they were beyond reach themselves, could get at anyone else.

If only Zory and Dima hadn't taken the whores to that island. If only she hadn't relied on them from the start. If only, if only . . . She is exhausted by all the second-guessing and trying to think of what she should have done differently and when.

Olle Pekkari had rung her that evening. "Can you explain what the hell my son is doing with your henchmen and a bunch of whores at my brother's house?" She couldn't. He was furious and not particularly coherent. But she had gathered there was this Henry person who was his brother, who'd been threatening to call in the police and the media. She rang Zory. He was a professional, he always answered when she called. She had told him curtly that this was their mess and it was up to them to clean it up. Immediately. She needed Anders Pekkari. Did they understand what would happen if he was involved in a police investigation into procuring?

Then Henry Pekkari had been found dead. And the women in the snow. She had tried to sack Zory and Dima then. But they had refused to accept it.

"You don't really think we're your employees, do you?" they had said. "You buy our services, that's not the same thing."

They had already cleaned out most of the competitors in their market. They were earning a lot of money. They refused to move out. The balance of power started slipping. They began to come into the house. Sit down at the kitchen table. Look at Tonya.

She had contacted the security company. They had explained they were just the middlemen between the client and potential service providers. She had turned to the men upstairs. Rung the lawyer. But he was glacial. Your employees, your problem.

She had no idea where Zory and Dima were right now. And she had to be grateful she was being helped to get out. She had settled huge bills from four companies in Kiruna in the last twelve hours. And it was only a matter of time before that was discovered.

Frans was calling from the bedroom.

"Hello, hello, hellooo!"

She pulled the sleeve of her sweater over her hand and turned on the tap. Let the ice-cold water run and then gulped it down. The sedatives made her mouth dry.

He needed to piss. He had knocked over the things on the bedside table in a rage at no-one turning up when he was forced to call for help. What a revolting little man he was. In a kind voice she said she would fetch the urine bottle. She asked if there was anything else he needed. She smiled.

There was not one phone in the entire house. He wouldn't be able to contact anyone. Tonya wanted to kill him of course, not that either of them were up to it. There wasn't any good reason either. He knew nothing. And besides, he wasn't someone who would spill the beans unless he had to, you'd have to give him that. She had no desire to be wanted for murder.

She went and got her jacket and handbag. Let the old man wet the bed.

Tonya kept peering in the rear-view mirror on the straight part of the road to Jukkasjärvi.

The grey Volvo V60 that had been parked in a pocket on the Esrange road was following them. Plain-clothes police. Elena stuck to the speed limit but kept a careful eye on the speedometer to make sure she wasn't driving too slowly either.

The whole time she kept expecting them to put the flashing-blue light on the roof of the unmarked car. After every turn she thought she would find the road blocked. She was afraid of crashing, afraid of running into someone.

But none of that happened. She turned onto Österleden towards the shopping centre and parked outside the Co-op superstore. The unmarked police car parked some way behind them.

Elena and Tonya got out of their car and walked towards the entrance. They did not turn round.

"I am a valuable resource," Elena Litova was telling herself. "I studied at the university. I don't do drugs." She was hoping to be relocated somewhere where the climate was kinder to humans. She was longing for the sea. To be able to drink pastis at an outdoor cafe at sundown with the soft murmur of waves in the background.

But she was well aware that Upstairs had invested money in a project that had now been lost. And she had managed to turn the spotlight onto their financial highways.

She hoped she would still be alive in forty-eight hours.

Police officers Gunnar Paulsson and Petter Autio were following Maria Mäki, the wife of the Lingonberry King, and the other woman as they drove into the town. They were on loan from the force in Gällivare and had been sitting in their car keeping watch on the house until their backs were aching and their bottoms felt like cement. This trip had taken them to the huge customer car park outside the shopping centre on Österleden.

"Are we supposed to follow them inside?" asked Constable Gunnar Paulsson as he watched the women get out of the car and disappear into the Co-op.

Petter Autio, who was twenty years his junior, was having a stretch while emitting a series of groans. "There's a Frasse's here," he said. "Why don't we grab a bite to eat? Two Frasse meals, with onion rings? We'll be in a better position to keep an eye on the car."

"Frasse's, you've got to be kidding," Gunnar Paulsson said. "Do you know how many calories are in that rubbish?"

"Time you gave up on that New Year's promise. I've got to have lunch in any case. You could go into the Co-op and buy a bit of celery. One hamburger isn't really much to go on. And you're as skinny as a rake. How much weight have you lost?"

"Twenty-five kilos. I can see my dick again after all these years."

"Not that there was ever much to see," Petter said, and they had a laugh. Gunnar gave in.

"Alright then."

Petter Autio got out of the car and headed towards Frasse's. It took nineteen minutes of standing in the queue to get his order served. They ate their hamburgers and drank their large soft drinks; that took another fifteen minutes. Then there was this bloke from Oinakkajärvi, a former soccer coach who knew Petter from when he played as a young-ster, who stopped to rake over old memories. He was an entertaining old man and the officers had been bored for so long they didn't really pay attention to how much time had passed.

Von Post took a seat opposite Anders Pekkari in the interview room.

"Sorry to keep you waiting," he said.

He'd had to attend a meeting with two officers from the NOA. Their investigators were preoccupied right now on the terrorism front, following the explosions in Brussels. They were overworked and tended to ramble on. The murder of a police officer was, however, a high priority. They had found a phone in a rubbish bin in Tommy Rantakyrö's flat. It had been impounded but the guys from the NOA were not particularly hopeful it would lead anywhere. It looked like a Vietnamese V-smart, they said, but they were convinced its Android system was fake. You couldn't make ordinary calls from a phone like that or get onto WiFi. It probably had a program concealed in the software to hard-encrypt the transmission of texts, sounds and images. No GPS either.

"We can never trace or put a tap on organised crime nowadays," one of them had observed with a resigned shrug.

On the underneath of Tommy Rantakyrö's car they had found a tracking device. A basic model that people used on boats and on snowmobiles that were worth stealing. They were assuming that was how the Russians had found him. His car on the roadside first, and then they would have followed his tracks to the cabin.

The NOA investigators had declined an invitation to be present during the questioning of Anders Pekkari, although they wanted a copy of the recording afterwards. If it led anywhere.

Anders Pekkari had said he wanted to talk. Carl von Post hoped he hadn't had time to change his mind.

Fred Olsson was setting up the camera, checking the batteries, the recording level and the memory card. Von Post did not become irritated by his meticulous attention to detail. He tried chatting for a bit to Anders Pekkari, about all the snow, and whether the coffee from the dispenser was drinkable, but the latter was reluctant to respond and they fell silent.

After a while Anders Pekkari said:

"Is it on? Can we start?"

He had an untouched plastic-wrapped sandwich in front of him. The skin between the corners of his eyes and the bridge of his nose was a bluish black.

Fred Olsson gave a quick thumbs up.

"It's Saturday May 7th, the time is eleven twenty-three," von Post said as informally as he could. "Interview with Anders Pekkari. Those present include Sergeant Fred Olsson and myself, acting Chief Prosecutor Carl von Post."

Anders Pekkari took a deep breath.

"Since you've stated your willingness to help the police and work with us, why don't you start talking and we can take it from there," von Post said.

"Right; God, I just don't know where to begin," Anders Pekkari said, running his hand over his face. "Our liquidity was at rock bottom."

"Our? And when was this?"

"The company's. Bergsäk AB. Two years ago. I won't deny there was some friction between Dad and me. He'd built up the company from scratch, you've got to give him that, but he's not expansive. Whereas I think money should be made to work. So I'd staked our capital, taken out a loan and invested in a Norwegian drilling company. Our turnover was going up, only then the Finnish mining company that was our major client suffered financial problems and stopped the payments. It just . . ."

He made a nose-diving gesture.

"We were in deep shit as a result of that company acquisition, what with owing money on the machinery and then there were the wages and the interest that had to be paid. Things like that. We'd bought portable cabins from Spike Mäki before so he was someone we'd known for ages. He said he could put us in touch with an investor who wanted access to the Scandinavian market. It wasn't like we could ever have hoped for that kind of opportunity. That's the difference between construction and mining. But the first contacts were overwhelmingly positive. It required some persuasion on my part and Dad wasn't exactly enthusiastic to begin with. But there weren't any real alternatives in our situation."

"I understand," von Post said. "Would you like something to drink? We've got plenty of time."

He was feeling tied and dejected: Tommy Rantakyrö, Anna-Maria Mella and his wife were all grinding away inside him.

But all that was making him better at leading the questioning, not that he understood why. He looked dishevelled. There was nothing forceful or threatening about him. No particular ambition. He wasn't on the other side, the winning team. He was just sitting there like a priest holding out the vague hope that confession might lead to some form of release.

Fred Olsson went out of the room to get drinks. He stood at the automatic dispenser in the break room, trying to get his head round this new Carl von Post.

Who would ever bloody believe it?

"It was a simple set-up," Anders Pekkari went on. "A loan of 10.3 million. Plus a new share issue. They would get forty per cent of the company. We just couldn't turn that down. Too good to be true."

"What kind of company was this . . . that you'd been in touch with?"

"William Ainsworth, that was his name. Senior legal adviser at some law firm. I never met the management of the company. He sounded like the kind of Englishman who'd been to private school. Incredibly pleasant. As long as you did what he wanted. He said we should continue operating as usual. The investors wanted to keep a low profile. Their role would be 'advisory'. Frans Mäki's Russian wife Maria attended our meetings. They knew one another from before and they trusted her. She trusted us. Blah blah."

"What happened then?" von Post said, trying to sound supportive.

Anders Pekkari snorted air through his nose.

"They started giving orders immediately. Two major items straight away. First up was all the machinery. It had to be sold off, and we were supposed to lease it instead. That would free up capital for investment. We agreed to that, I got a repurchase option agreed, mostly for Dad's sake. They wanted us to grow the business, they said. That was what I wanted too. There are a lot of business opportunities in Kiruna at the moment. The new town has got to be built. LKAB is going great guns. They're prospecting for new mining sites. But then all of a sudden we were supposed to invest in an African mining project. That was when I tried to dig my heels in. They began issuing threats right away. The lawyer turned up accompanied by two Russian men. They threatened us with a demand for repayment of the corporate loan. There was some covenant that the loan capital was not allowed to be greater than the company's resources, and since we had sold off all the inventory . . . it wasn't like I'd kept track of all those technicalities. I'm no accounting nerd. And our bloody accountant didn't have a clue about any of it until we were standing there with our trousers round our ankles. Our only option was to let them do what they wanted. I started trying to convince myself that the investment on their part had been legit. Because I wanted to believe that. I *had* to believe that."

Fred Olsson came back into the room with three colas.

Anders Pekkari pressed the can against his forehead before going on:

"Frans Mäki's wife began popping up at the office along with the Russians. There were various papers I was obliged to sign. I rang the English lawyer and he recommended that I cooperate. The piano wire was round my throat by this point. She, Maria Mäki, told me that the

529

Economic Crime Authority would be very interested in that investment in the foreign mining project. I was the one in deep shit. I was the one who signed for the company, my name was on everything. It was like this nature programme I'd seen on television. Those ants that carry fungal spores inside them. The fungus changes their brains and makes them climb up to a sunny spot. Where they die and the fungus grows right out of their skulls. I was that fucking ant. Bloody hell, Calle, I've barely slept for more than a year. I've just been so fucking scared the whole time."

"Can we fast-forward to the evening Henry Pekkari made a phone call to—" von Post began.

"Yes, of course," Anders Pekkari said. "Can I pop to the bathroom?"

They let him. Fred Olsson was kind enough to tell him you couldn't lock the door. The toilet had no windows and the mirror was unbreakable. Both Carl von Post and Fred Olsson waited outside the door. They could hear the contents of Anders Pekkari's guts spraying onto the porcelain and they both looked away from one another as though neither were really there. Then they could hear the toilet paper unrolling. It sounded like a hundred metres of it were being used. Two flushes and then the brush, he was the neat and tidy kind. The tap ran for what seemed like an eternity.

Then he came out. His face and scalp were wet.

"Can we continue?" von Post asked.

Anders Pekkari nodded.

"They turned up at my house on the evening of April 8th," Anders Pekkari said once they were back in the interview room. "Those Russians. They said the police were watching their girls. I got it straight away: they'd bought a camper van through the company, after all. So now they wanted me to hide them. Just for a night or two."

He was wiping away the drops of condensation from the unopened cola can with his index finger.

"They could have done it on their own. They didn't need me really. They did it just to . . . to demonstrate their power . . . maybe to pull me in more deeply, but most of all it was to show me my place. So I just obeyed, attached the trailer to the snowmobile and then the snowmobile sledge to the car. They followed behind in the camper van. I was thinking it would be quiet at Uncle Henry's. No-one coming and going. Far way from the police. But Henry, he . . ."

There was a fizzle as Anders Pekkari opened his cola. He took a big swig and put it down with a bang.

"We drove the snowmobile over the river to the island. Sent the girls to the upper floor with their bags and the smallest mattresses from the camper van. But Henry, like I said, he went crazy. Yelling this wasn't some hotel for whores. Started going on about Grandma and Granddad like he was . . ."

He uttered a joyless laugh and shook his head.

"Like he was some defender of the family honour. He rang Dad. Yelling and screaming. He said he was going to ring the papers and the police. Tell them his ever-so-proper nephew was driving whores around at night. Then Dad called Frans Mäki."

Von Post took a peek at his mobile. Nothing new on Mella. And nothing from Erika.

"And Dad asked in no uncertain terms what the hell they were up to," Anders Pekkari went on. "Though obviously he had to do it in English, because he was talking to Maria. You'll have to ask him how that conversation went. But Dad didn't tell them to kill Henry. He didn't. Henry was his brother, after all."

"Tell us in the order it happened," von Post said calmly, thinking that particular matter was not something Anders Pekkari could know about. "Tell us what you saw; after all, you had no idea your father was calling Frans Mäki. So then Henry rang your father. Those Russians, do you know their names?"

"No, Dad and I just call them the bulldogs. I did ask once, as it happens. 'You can call us Sven and Sven,' they said."

Sven and Sven, Carl von Post was thinking. No more unlikely than their real names are Yegor Babitsky and Yury Yusenkov.

"What happened when Henry rang Olle?"

"One of the Svens asked me what the call was about. I told him he was ringing my father. My nerves were pretty frayed by then. After all, I'd been trying to keep Dad out of it as much as possible. One of the bulldogs took the receiver from Henry's hand and hung up. After a while one of their phones started to ring. A short call. The bulldog who answered barely said anything. Though . . ."

Von Post straightened up a little. Fred Olsson took his eyes off the video screen and, without moving his head, looked over at Anders Pekkari, who was trying to remember.

"He said a Russian word when he finished speaking, only I don't know Russian."

"Try to remember. Close your eyes if that helps."

Anders Pekkari closed his eyes. Von Post and Fred Olsson opened their mouths to breathe without making a sound.

"He put the phone in his pocket. Looked at the other one. And said: 'Litova'. As if he was relaying an order. Then he shoved Henry onto the sofa. He, shit, oh fuck it, he sat on him. High up, just below his head. He grabbed a cushion and held it against his face. Henry struggled a bit and his arms were flailing around, but it all happened so unbelievably quickly. And then he was still. I could barely take in what had happened. And then . . ."

He fell silent.

"Litova, you're certain that is what he said?"

"Yes, I am."

"You're doing well," von Post mumbled while tapping out a text to the effect that Elena Litova, aka Maria Mäki, should be arrested immediately. They had her now. Not for incitement to murder obviously, the evidence was too thin for that. But for the corporate hijacking of Bergsäk AB, blackmail, threats. That was something at least.

"You're doing the right thing," he said. "Keep going. We'll take a break in a bit."

"Then one of the whores appeared in the doorway," Anders Pekkari went on. "She came out with a little shriek because she'd seen Henry and, well, the bulldog was still sitting on him. She rushed back up the stairs. I could hear the girls yelling at one another up there. The bulldogs exchanged a few words in Russian. I was sitting on the floor at that point. I couldn't get up. One of them was still sitting on Henry with the cushion. The other one, he went upstairs. Then he came straight back down again. He went out into the hall. I could hear him looking through the keys that were hanging out there. He went outside. I heard him starting Henry's snowmobile and then he drove off. The other one told me to get up. But I couldn't. He fetched the girls' things and carried them outside. He took the cushion with him as well, the one he had held over Henry's face. He wiped down the phone receiver and maybe some other things. After a while the other one returned. We drove back to the mainland on my snowmobile. All they said to me was that I shouldn't say a word about any of this. It was supposed to look like Henry had died of natural causes. They laughed and said it was lucky for me they'd told me to leave my phone at home. Their phones were the kind that couldn't be traced."

Von Post's thoughts went to the mobile in Tommy's rubbish bin.

"I was so scared my teeth were chattering," Anders Pekkari said. "I've never experienced anything like that. I had no idea you could be that terrified. And it didn't pass. I haven't even told Carina about it. Though she realises something must have happened. And I didn't tell Dad about it either. Only then he found out that Henry had been murdered. When Rebecka Martinsson came round to his house . . . I'm completely shattered. I just sit in my office and move papers around. I can't even think."

"Let's take a break for a bit at this point," von Post said. "And we'll be talking to your father later."

"You've got to bring in Carina and the boys," Anders Pekkari yelled. "And my mother. So they don't . . . Because I talked to you."

"We will," von Post said. "Though we're pretty certain they've left the country."

Von Post was thinking: Somewhere. Somewhere in the world there are people searching for places like Kiruna. They've got the maps and the information in front of them. They find the places to go in and suck dry. They find the right people and send them in with resources.

He felt like a metronome swinging between sheer terror and feeling like some hysterical conspiracy theorist.

Constables Petter Autio and Gunnar Paulsson had a long talk with the guy from Oinakkajärvi. Esrange got mentioned as well. Not that they told him what they were doing in Kiruna, or that they had been sitting in a parked car keeping watch on Maria Mäki and Tonya Litvinovitch. It was more general stuff about the town, the tourist industry, the mine and Esrange.

"What do they actually do out there anyway?" Gunnar Paulsson asked.

"They shoot retired sled dogs into space," was Petter Autio's suggestion.

The guy from Oinakkajärvi, who was a former physics teacher, had found out enough to share some of his knowledge with them. His sister's sister-in-law actually worked over there. Kiruna was apparently best in the world at building instruments that measured ions and energy-rich neutrons.

"Things like that, right," Petter Autio grinned.

The guy from Oinakkajärvi said it involved fundamental research, the kind of research that wasn't aimed at developing anything, an invention or a medicine, but at working out how the world was formed. Research for the sake of curiosity.

"It's pretty cool that they're doing that kind of thing in Kiruna, isn't it?" he said.

Autio and Paulsson laughed at that and said they'd definitely chosen the wrong career path. Research for the sake of curiosity! That's what they should have been doing. Could you be curious about anything at all? They came up with some jokey and off-colour suggestions.

The guy from Oinakkajärvi asked if they'd heard of the Ig Nobel prize. The prize was awarded to the kind of research that might appear ridiculous but often turned out to be much more significant than you would have thought. He told them about the mathematicians who had won for calculating how many group photographs you had to take to end up with one in which no-one was blinking. The answer was at least seven if there were less than twenty individuals in the photograph. The 2006 Peace Prize had gone to a Welshman for inventing teenager repellent, a high-pitched noise only teenagers could perceive.

The police officers agreed that this last prize was real, socially relevant and highly useful research. Maybe a gadget they could put on top of the car instead of the flashing-blue light.

Petter Autio gathered up the take-away boxes, cups, bags and paper napkins covering the floor of the car and went off to bin them.

His telephone beeped: it was the text message from Prosecutor Carl von Post.

Bring in Maria Mäki was all it said: short and sweet.

He forced the rubbish into the already over-filled bin and returned to the car.

"Time to go to work," he said to his colleague. "It was really good to have a chat," he said to the guy from Oinakkajärvi. "But now we've got to do our bit for society."

He nodded in the direction of the Co-op and Gunnar Paulsson got out and blipped the car locked. The man said a quick goodbye, impressed that the importance of their work could so abruptly cut off the conversation.

On their way into the shopping centre Petter Autio explained the situation.

They forced their way through the Kiruna residents doing their Saturday shopping and all the people from the surrounding villages wheeling overflowing trolleys, then did a circuit of every aisle in the supermarket, checked out the pharmacy and the restaurant and did another circuit of the supermarket.

Petter Autio ran out to the car park. Maria Mäki's car was still parked in the same spot.

After just over fifty minutes they gave up the search and reported in.

Elena Litova and Tonya Litvinovitch had disappeared.

Rebecka Martinsson was half-lying, half-sitting on the snow. She spread out the backpack and the seat pad beneath her as best she could. She was so unbelievably tired, her arms and legs felt like jelly. The sun was a furnace.

She realised she had gone snow blind. It felt like someone had been rubbing away at her corneas with gravel.

I'm going to rest for a bit, she thought. Then I'll ski through Kårsavagge to Abisko. That's a safe route. You can't get lost. Nice and calm. I'll get there when I get there.

The dehydration caused by the rivers of sweat she had produced during her skiing trip, and because the sun was shining and she hadn't had enough water with her, had brought on an almost unbearable headache. Her tongue felt like a huge lump in her mouth. It felt rough as well, the taste buds had risen and gone stiff, she couldn't stop pulling it towards her palate, which only made the sensation more unpleasant.

She ate snow and more snow, vaguely aware that it didn't contain any salts and it was the lack of sodium that was making her feel sick.

The shadow of a rough-legged hawk moved across the snow, but she didn't have the energy to look up. Its cry sliced through her skull like a jigsaw.

It was past two. She really ought to . . .

She tried to get to her feet and immediately felt unsteady. Her blood pressure had dropped.

This is bad, she thought and lay down again, uncertain as to whether she was referring to her condition or this whole stupid idea.

Though it wasn't a stupid idea.

I made myself go on a skiing trip, she thought defiantly. On my own. I made it. I found a way to slip between Biran and Kuobla.

Madness. She might have skied between those huge paws, the wolf-paws of death. But . . . she had been terrified of dying in an avalanche, stuck fast as if in a vice, her mouth filled with snow.

Only, living like this is worse, she thought. Constantly holding a beggar's cup. And what was she expecting people to put in it?

She could feel that something had come loose inside her. That she had been . . . set free.

It doesn't matter, she thought. None of it.

It wasn't really something you could capture in words and pin on the noticeboard like an affirmation.

That feeling got her back on her feet.

She shrugged into her backpack and fixed her boots to her skis.

The crust on the snow had softened. She broke through it with every move forward across the trackless waste. She hung on the poles which sank deep every time.

She hadn't gone two hundred metres when she gave up. She was too ill. Too weak. She couldn't do it.

That was when she heard the sound of a snowmobile.

"Rebecka Martinsson," the man said when he had stopped. "Is that really you? Out here to do some skiing?"

She squinted.

"Nisse?"

As usual he was dressed in Ski-Doo overalls with yellow edging, a knife belt with rivets in white, blue and red cinched tight around his waist. Jörn brand beak boots and the same old reindeer-skin cap pulled far down his face, which was sunburned and as wrinkled as a tobacco leaf.

They knew one another from before. Niilas Skarpa was the middle son in a family of reindeer herders. The eldest brother, Anden-Heikka, had been destined from the moment of birth to take over the family's earmark, so he could coast through life on a reindeer pelt, as Nisse would often say.

But Niilas had not managed to find his place in the world. He did get a reindeer earmark from his mother's father, but his grandfather was an unhappy soul with such a penchant for the bottle and female tourists from Stockholm that all he possessed was a few animals who were herded by a cousin. And for some peculiar reason the cousin's herd kept getting larger and eventually all that Niilas's grandfather had left were two pitiful reindeer. When the new Reindeer Husbandry Act came into force, that was the end of his earmark along with the grazing rights, the county council saw to that.

Nisse had nursed some hopes as a young man because Risten Poidnakk, from Dellik, had taken a shine to him. She was the eldest daughter of a herding family with only daughters and a lot of reindeer. She was raven-haired and lovely. One time he had helped her fasten a shoelace that had come loose. And her hand had rested on his shoulder. That autumn he turned up to the Sami dance in Giron wearing shiny silver on his traditional costume and a smile that reached from ear to ear. Only Risten had gone off arm in arm with his older brother. What's better than a large herd of reindeer, after all? An enormous herd of reindeer of course.

His brother and Risten had got married. Nisse had to endure seeing his big brother with everything he had ever dreamed of. Risten, children and reindeer. Though they would meet at the calf branding and the separations of the herds, he rarely saw them otherwise.

There was no need for Rebecka to say how happy and grateful she was to see him. He understood. He got out a thermos of blackcurrant juice, a chocolate bar and a green apple that he divided into slices.

"Eat," he said, waving her hand away when she tried to give him half the chocolate. "And drink up. All of it. No point saving any."

For many years Nisse had been scraping by with odd jobs in the tourist industry, repairing footbridges for the county council and driving gas and wood out to the holiday cabins. Everything he needed for everyday life fit into two packing cases. Some checked shirts, bandanas he fastened around his neck with a reindeer-antler ring, woollen undergarments, a pair of jeans and a pair of leather trousers. He bought his underpants in a twelve-pack at the Co-op and chucked them as necessary.

Rebecka saw Nisse looking for the tracks of her skis as they vanished northwards.

"Did you ski from Låkta?"

She nodded – not something you could lie about, and she didn't want to either. If he had any comments to make about that he kept them to himself.

Instead, he looked at the knife hanging from her belt and immediately guessed which craftsman had made it.

"Listen, let me see your hand, would you?" he asked when she had emptied the thermos, licked the chocolate crumbs off the wrapper and devoured the apple slices.

She held out her hand. He wrapped it in his rough fist, checked the back of it and pinched the skin. The folds stayed up.

She felt silly: dehydrated and snow blind in the heart of the mountains. She was still so thirsty but didn't dare ask for more.

He was a thoroughly good sort. They had got to know one another when she attended the staff party for the Norrbotten prosecution service at Nutti Sámi Siida, a Sami camp open to tourists in Jukkasjärvi.

When she had tired of all the moaning about bad lawyers, both on her part and that of her colleagues (it was just incredible how some people actually got paid taxpayers' money for their court appearances: the accused would actually stand a better chance without any of the interventions and objections made by the defence attorney in question), and bad judges (some of whom simply swallowed the most ludicrous objections, there was no point the prosecution going ahead once you'd seen who was wielding the gavel; holiday plans that had to be shelved because of appeal court cases and the impossible workload, bad pay and a useless local police force), she had crept out to the pen for the reindeer bulls. That was where she had met Nisse who was about to feed them their evening meal of pellets and moss. She had asked if she could go in with him. Sure, that would be fine, he had said.

He had explained how to approach the reindeer, taught her that you should talk to them in a quiet voice the whole time so they knew where you were. She had asked if any of them were bad-tempered and had to be watched out for, but he had said as long as you treated them properly almost all the bulls could be handled.

They stayed sitting round Nisse's fire afterwards. Drinking coffee and eating slices of green apple, which was his only vice.

They had both expressed their appreciation of solitude and Nisse had told her he tended to live from place to place, only now he was obliged to work with the tourists for Nutti, because he had acquired a huge tax debt. Over fifteen thousand. He had written off his old Ski-Doo Elan, even though it might have had some value as an antique, at least, and bought a Ski-Doo Tundra. The problem was that he had used up all his money on the new snowmobile and there was nothing left to pay the tax he owed. He found all the letters from the Tax Office so exhausting he had stopped opening them. And now the taxman was after him.

In the end Nisse had gone to fetch a paper bag filled with papers and receipts. Rebecka had quickly glanced through it all and asked if she could take the whole lot with her along with an authorisation to act on his behalf, which they wrote on the back of one of the menus.

One week later she returned with a binder that contained all the papers sorted into order. She had requested a reassessment of his tax demand. Once she had deducted various expenses, the debt had gone down by half. She had asked for a grace period and presented a payment plan.

He didn't say thank you, just "Righto". But now he would pop by Rebecka's house from time to time with smoked fish or some lovely dried game.

She bought green apples from time to time as well, even though she didn't eat them herself. They reminded her of Nisse, sitting there on the fruit counter.

"What are you doing here?" Rebecka asked.

She couldn't keep her eyes open. She could feel the tears forcing their way out between her lashes.

He said he was checking the ptarmigan tracks.

"Not that you're allowed to hunt them at this time," he said in that soft voice that always sounded as if he was about to launch into a *vuolle*, one of the quieter forms of the traditional Sami *joik*. "Or drive snowmobiles for that matter, so I'd better be heading back. And I think I should give you a lift. Though we're going to take a different route."

He nodded in the direction she had come.

Then she admitted that her car was parked near the Låkta bus stop.

Rebecka sat behind him, her arms around him. He was the same age her father would have been. There was only three months between them.

When they got to the car he insisted on driving her home. She got into the passenger seat. She was in no condition to drive, as she realised.

He stopped at Björkliden, took her card and bought water and a small bag of crisps.

The pleasure he took in driving her posh car was obvious. He asked how much it cost and switched over to P4 Norrbotten radio.

She answered the question about the price of the car honestly and fell asleep. When she woke up they were in her yard.

"So now how are you going to get home?" she asked.

"No problem," Nisse said. "I've already rung my cousin, she's coming to pick me up."

Anna-Maria Mella came out of her coma at 5.15 on the afternoon of May 7th. Robert had nodded off at her side.

He was saying her name in his dream and woke up to the sound of her voice.

"Did you take Jenny's shoes in for repair?"

Robert opened his eyes, thinking his brain was playing a cruel trick on him.

But she was looking at him with her one eye. And that was Anna-Maria behind it. She said his name.

"Robert." And then: "God, look at you! Just like after your stag night!"

She grinned. And then her face crumpled in an abrupt grimace. Her hands reached up to the patched-together part of her face.

His head had been so filled with catastrophes the last twenty-four hours that the word "stroke" had immediately gone off in his skull like a siren at full blast. He pressed the button and rushed into the corridor.

"She's dying. She's dying," he yelled.

He heard her voice behind him then.

"What are you on about? Have you lost your mind?"

And then. With fear in her voice:

"Where am I?"

A nurse came hurrying in, with an assistant one step behind. A doctor came racing along the corridor. Robert tried to get back into the room but was refused entry.

He stood outside like a pillar of salt. He kept mouthing over and over: "Dear Lord, dear Lord, dear Lord, dear Lord, dear Lord . . .", as though her chances would improve the more times he could say it in a minute.

Elena Litova had disappeared. So had Tonya Litvinovitch. The police force in the Norwegian town of Narvik had sent a squad to check the border. The force in Gällivare had a unit in place on the E10 north of Svappavaara after the crossroads with the E45, where it turned to the east. The Kiruna police even felt obliged to set up a roadblock to the west, though that route led only into the mountains and not out of the country. The Finnish border police had been informed and were calling in backup.

The CCTV at the Co-op showed that Elena Litova and Tonya Litvinovitch had walked through the shop, and then into the staff area behind the deli before entering the warehouse. There were no cameras there, but it was assumed they had gone out through a staff entrance. You only needed a code to get in, not to get out.

The previous evening someone had thrown stones at the CCTV camera in the loading bay at the back. So it wasn't working. The ground behind the store had been completely churned up by cars, so it was impossible to discern what kind of vehicle might have picked them up.

Where had they gone? They could only guess. After consultations with colleagues from the NOA, it was agreed to overfly the area in a helicopter. It was known that the Russians had been driving a Kabe camper van. Could they have used it to pick up Elena Litova and Tonya Litvinovitch? That was one obvious possibility, though hardly likely.

A white camper van was stopped at the Norwegian border. In it was a Dutch family on their way to Lofoten, where they were due to go on a whale safari. The make of the van was indeed Kabe, but it was the wrong model and the number plates didn't match. The officers searched it thoroughly anyway and the children were scared by their harsh tone. The Dutch holidaymakers were allowed to continue their journey after forty-five minutes.

An arrest warrant was issued through Interpol and Europol for Maria Mäki aka Elena Litova. And for Tonya Litvinovitch as well.

Hospital staff were sent to bring in Frans Mäki, the Lingonberry King. A place was arranged for him at a local care home.

He was astonishingly ignorant about the two missing women.

Tonya Litvinovitch had been employed as an untrained nurse to look after him. What did he know about her? She used to make his bed neatly and empty his bedpan. Anything more? She couldn't even boil an egg. And the two Russian men? Tenants, they were working on some construction site as far as he knew.

As for his wife, he had never heard the name Elena Litova.

Her name is Maria Berberova, he explained to investigators from the NOA.

She had been interested in buying one of his companies; he was a successful businessman, just in case they weren't aware of that fact. One thing had led to another.

Spike Mäki was interviewed as well. He explained that contact between him and his father was very sporadic, not to say non-existent.

He hadn't even been invited to the wedding. Maria Berberova had got in touch in connection with the acquisition of a company. This was a timber products firm that mainly produced portable cabins. Although he, Spike, ran the operation, it was his father who was the owner. So Spike had put them in touch with each other.

"You'd have to say she entrapped him," he said.

They got nowhere. Just like Carl von Post and all the police officers involved, the investigators from the NOA had long since learned the difference between what one knew and what one could prove. There were no grounds for detaining them. Nevertheless Carl von Post ordered the accounts of the portable cabin company seized.

They released photos of the Russian men and women to the media. They had nothing to lose.

Sivving took his time scraping the snow off the soles of his shoes on the doormat before going up Rebecka Martinsson's staircase. It was steep, and he was well aware that a fall could be the beginning of the end.

This could be the death of me, he thought, and grabbed the handrail more tightly as Bella and the Brat pushed past him in their eagerness to get upstairs.

He noted with irritation that each step was wet with melted snow. If only that young lady could also take her time on the doormat. For his sake at least.

Her car was in the yard, but she hadn't come in to fetch the Brat and when he took the dogs out to pee he had noticed that the blinds were drawn at every window. That was unusual. And made him uneasy.

He entered the house without knocking. He was ready with a sermon about bringing snow onto the stairs, but he lost the thread. No lamps had been lit. In the faint but sharp spring light that came in at the side of the roller blind he could see Rebecka. She was on her back on the kitchen sofa, a tea towel folded over her eyes. She still had her anorak on. And her shoes.

The dogs fawned around her, jostling each other to get to lick the bits of her face they could reach and the hands that were folded on her belly. Bella's hard pointer tail kept rapping like a drumstick against the legs of the kitchen table.

"How are you, little lass?" he asked.

He was about to say something about having tried to get hold of her all day, but decided not to.

"I'm OK, I'm OK," she said.

He could hear from her voice that she was lying.

His foot got stuck in a rag rug as he moved towards the table. His hand shot out and grabbed the back of one of the wooden chairs. When he finally got the chair pulled out and could sit on it, he let out a sigh, as if he had only just managed to struggle onto a life raft.

"Lie down," he said to the dogs.

But they completely ignored him. They kept sniffing around as though these were new hunting grounds. Then they went back to Rebecka. The Brat laid his head on her stomach. She unclasped her fingers and patted him on his head and ears. Bella was staring at him in the dark.

"What's going on?" she seemed to be asking.

He ran his hand over the surface of the table. It was a gate-leg model Theresia's brother-in-law had made. He was wondering how many times he had sat at it. All those times that were gone for good.

When he was a boy and both his parents were friends with Rebecka's paternal grandparents. When Mikko, Rebecka's father, was just a little fellow and there were cows in the barn and they were worried about the summer weather, especially when the hay had been put out on the racks; it had to dry before it could go into the barn.

When Theresia and Mikko lived here and they had barely any money because things were going so badly for Mikko's company. He could do the work, but there were always problems with payments and contracts.

When Virpi moved in with Mikko on the ground floor. The firm started doing better then. She was the one who made the calls and had the energy to argue that Mikko should get paid. And not with old "all that needs doing is to change the gearbox" cars, but hard cash, thank you very much.

When Virpi packed her things and left. And Mikko was drinking too much and there wasn't much money again.

All the tears shed at this table. When Albert died, when Mikko died, when Virpi died. When his Maj-Lis got sick and died.

Theresia never said a word about him moving down into the basement at the time and staying there. Though the villagers talked. He couldn't have cared less.

He remembered when Rebecka came home for Theresia's funeral. Black clothes that looked expensive. He had been sitting in this very chair and told her: "Don't sell. You never know."

He had been so worried about her. When she came home from Stockholm, listless, overworked, dark rings under her eyes.

And then when she ended up on the psychiatric ward and lost it completely. They gave her ECT. He had had no idea they still did that.

His joy when she moved back home. His secret joy when she got a dog; that was a kind of anchor, she couldn't move back to Stockholm with a dog. Dogs plural, too, the short while she had Vera. Good Lord, poor Vera. That too.

He had spent time with Rebecka, talked to her, worried about her, taken pains with her. More than with his own children. They managed fine.

It's a blessing to be needed, he thought philosophically.

And in a locked and bolted room inside him he was aware that

Rebecka was dearer to him than anyone else alive. His own children and grandchildren included. Though he always told himself it was just different. In various ways.

The dogs were lying under the table. The only thing you could hear in the kitchen was their snuffles, the clock on the wall and the faint creaking of the chair he was sitting on.

"It's hard getting old," he said. "Your body doesn't have the strength and you can't rely on it. This arm of mine. And you get a bit forgetful and start mixing things up. But the worst thing is when people discount you. You notice that they stop listening or get irritated because you tell them something you've told them before, or they think you're too demanding. Though they won't even tell you that anymore. Shall I put some coffee on?"

He was convinced she would say no. But she said:

"A cup of tea would be nice. And three lumps of sugar. I've got a bit of dried game in the fridge. If you wouldn't mind getting it out?"

He felt absurdly glad to hear her say that. As he was making a clatter with the pot of water he could hear her groaning faintly and realised she must have a splitting headache. He was more careful after that and let the water run into the pot in a thin stream. He tried to pull open the packet with the tea bags as gently as he could.

He stood there in silence, watching the water beginning to boil as small bubbles burst against the surface, and took the pan off the moment it reached boiling point and filled their mugs. He had to make three trips to the table, he only had one hand he could trust, one mug at a time and then a Perspex bowl they could put the used bags in.

"Talk to me," he said. "Otherwise I might just as well be dead."

He wanted to ring Krister but realised that was out of the question.

"I spent the whole day skiing," she said. "Completely useless sunglasses. I went snow blind."

He was no dummy. As a young man he went away to study and

qualified as a civil engineer. That's how he got his nickname, from the abbreviation of his title in the phone book: civ.eng. Which the villagers pronounced as Sivving. A reminder not to get too big for his boots.

He knew she was telling the truth but also that it wasn't the whole truth. Why had she been out for a whole day skiing when Anna-Maria Mella and Tommy Rantakyrö had been shot and it was all hands, hers too, on deck?

"Was it because of Pohjanen?" he asked.

Sven-Erik had texted earlier to tell him Pohjanen had bitten the dust. Not much of a surprise. Still, it was sad when people you knew died.

Rebecka was breathing rapidly and shallowly. Like Maj-Lis towards the end. She was pressing her hands against her belly as if something were eating her from inside.

He stayed where he was at the kitchen table and endured the feeling of powerlessness.

But he was scared. He was thinking about when she was given the shock treatment. It had happened once. It could happen again. This wasn't one of her usual low moods.

He wished he could touch her. Or tell her he loved her. But that wasn't something they did and it would feel awkward. He was deeply grateful when the Brat got up, jumped onto the sofa and squeezed in so his head was on Rebecka's leg.

Half an hour later he texted Sven-Erik Stålnacke from the loo. He wrote that Rebecka had gone snow blind. What he thought she needed was some kind of cream and eye drops, but how were you supposed to find those on a Saturday evening?

Ragnhild and Börje turned off the news and took a break from the police murders and the hunt for the suspects that seemed hopeless in any case.

They cooked dinner together. Börje chopped onions and praised the sharpness of her knives. She put breadcrumbs to soak and heated lingonberry jam while waiting for the breadcrumbs to swell. They talked about meatballs. She told him about her mother's and the way she used boiled potato, not bread, and how fast she could roll them, perfectly round and small.

"They could do anything, the women in those days," she said.

"Not my mum," he said. "She could cut hair. She used to make meat loaf because that took less time. And she didn't change the curtains at Christmas and Easter. That was near enough a scandal. The other kids used to tease me about it. No dad and no Christmas curtains."

"Sounds like a pretty awful childhood."

Villa couldn't resist the smells. She was sitting by the kitchen counter, tracking every movement the two-legs made. Ragnhild took a pinch of raw beef mince and gave it to her with one hand while stroking her head with the other.

"I'm teaching her to beg," she said.

"Er, you're teaching her we're kind and that she belongs."

Ragnhild kissed him on the cheek. He put down the knife and wrapped his arms around her.

"You haven't finished," she reproached him.

"Breaks are essential," he mumbled into her hair.

She caught sight of the pink dry-cleaning ticket next to the kettle. She realised she needed to pick up her winter jacket.

Her phone rang and Börje released her from his embrace and went back to the onions.

It was Sven-Erik Stålnacke. They exchanged a few words about the terrible events of the last few days. Sven-Erik wanted a favour. He knew Ragnhild was currently retired, just like him. Only, Rebecka

Martinsson had gone snow blind and he wondered if Ragnhild could help get her the right kind of medication.

Ragnhild glanced at the Bible on the kitchen table.

"You never give up," she said to God.

Though it wasn't until Sven-Erik said "What?" on the other end of the line that she realised she had said it aloud, and she had to come up with a quick fib about talking to the dog.

She promised to sort something out. And she had to reassure Sven-Erik it wasn't a bother.

The dogs began barking when Ragnhild drove her car into Rebecka's front yard in Kurravaara. She had been there before. When Rebecka was six and Virpi was celebrating her twenty-fifth birthday. Ragnhild had plucked up her courage and driven to Kurra with a present. While she remembered the bag, she could no longer recall what she had bought. A plant, perhaps.

Virpi had been dismissive and abrupt. If Theresia hadn't been there to say, "You should have a bite to eat at least," she wouldn't even have got coffee. So she had spent half an hour talking to Theresia while Virpi sat beside them, smoking, her face a hard shell.

She was afraid Rebecka would be the same. New feelings being nourished by old ones.

You'll just have to do your bit to help, she said to God as she went up the steps.

An old man opened the door. She could see straight away that he must have had a stroke. One side of his body refused to obey. She automatically took an imperceptible step towards the weaker side as they shook hands. To check whether his sight was affected, but he didn't need to turn his head to keep her in his field of vision. That was good. He introduced himself as Sivving, the nearest neighbour.

Rebecka was lying on her back on the kitchen sofa. The blinds were drawn. The dogs greeted Ragnhild as though she were Father Christmas.

She could feel Sivving changing his view of her. The hint of hostility was dispelled when she took time to greet the dogs and when she praised the rag rug that lay in the hall as she undid her boots.

"They end up being a lot thicker and steadier with a four-shaft weave", she said. "Did Theresia make it?"

Sivving said he thought she did. And that was all that was needed for the hostility to vanish. She was no longer a Pekkari. Not only one in any case.

"Right," Sivving said, and extended his good arm towards Rebecka. "So here's the patient."

"Sivving was the one who rang Sven-Erik," Rebecka said from under the tea towel. "You didn't need to come. It's not serious."

"Anyway," Ragnhild said in her nurse's voice. "I'm here now and I've brought Viscotears, so I might just as well have a look."

She put some drops into Rebecka's red eyes.

"You can put the bottle in the fridge," she said. "It feels nicer when it's cold."

Rebecka thanked her. Ragnhild could hear the snow bridge in the other woman's voice. She was overwhelmed by a desire to help her that she was afraid wasn't healthy.

In her head, Paula said, "Florence Nightingale."

Then she thought, No, it's not wrong to care about your fellow human beings. That's not wicked. It isn't a sickness or a sign, a bad sign, of a co-dependent personality. You're allowed to be a good nurse.

"It'll feel better in the morning," she said.

"Would you like some tea?" Sivving asked. "Or coffee? If you drink coffee in the evening? Some people say they can't sleep if they . . ."

He went on for a bit about caffeine and how notions like that could change over the years and someone he knew who could drink three cups before going to bed.

She said yes, please. She needed an excuse to stay on.

"Thanks," Rebecka said again. "I feel like a bit of a drama queen."

"You're not well," Ragnhild said. "And I'm glad to have a reason to come over. I'd been planning to get in touch. Because I wanted to talk to you about your mother."

There it was. It had been said.

Ragnhild could hear Sivving stopping what he was doing at the stove.

"Why?" Rebecka asked.

It was only then that Ragnhild understood why. She looked at Rebecka's hands, clasped over her belly once more. The same hand had batted against Virpi's breast as she was breastfeeding her that time at the hospital. That little hand filled with the urge to survive. The instinctive ability to get the milk to flow.

The first sentence of the Confession in the Swedish Hymnal came back to her: *I poor sinner who shares our human inheritance of sin and death* . . . She had always felt those words to be oppressive.

Though they're actually liberating, she thought. A religion for those of us who feel like shit. Who know that what we've done is crap. As for all the others with haloes round their heads, they can bugger off to some hill and meditate.

"Because I want to ask for forgiveness," she said.

She hastened to add:

"And you really don't have to forgive me. It's not like that. I just need to say it."

"I don't begin to understand that," Rebecka said. "You've never done me any harm. We don't even know one another."

"No," Ragnhild agreed. "But . . ."

But it lives so strongly inside us, she thought. The family inheritance. The sins of our fathers.

She turned her head and met Sivving's eyes. He nodded almost imperceptibly.

"The dogs need a walk," he said. "I'll take them for a turn round the village."

The stroke had not affected him cognitively, Ragnhild thought gratefully.

He took the dogs with him and left. She heard him admonishing them on the stairs.

"Just go easy now. On the old man."

It was better in a way that Rebecka wasn't sitting up and looking her straight in the eye. She lay there unmoving and listened to the whole of Ragnhild's story with the tea towel over her eyes.

"Virpi came to live with us on the island when she was three," she began. "I was eight then. The life we led was carefree, wild. Right from the start we used to play together all the time even though she was so little. Dad said I had a tail, a windtail though, a *tuiskusapara*, because she didn't always let me be the one to decide. We basically only went indoors to eat and sleep. We climbed trees, I was allowed to row the dinghy so we could go on all kinds of expeditions and *Äiti* used to sigh when we came home with resin stains all over and our trousers ripped, or when our sweaters had hay stuck to them because we'd been playing in the barn. 'Do you have to drag half of God's creation with you into the kitchen?' Though she mended and washed and we would just go off again."

Ragnhild stopped for a moment and remembered Virpi in the clothes she herself had grown out of, and boots that were too big. The way Virpi used to shove the boat out with all her strength, the effort making her turn red in the face. The strength in that little girl's body. Ragnhild sitting there like a female captain at the oars: "Jump in!" and Virpi just managing by the skin of her teeth to pull herself into the boat before it slid too far out, and without losing her boots. If she failed, Ragnhild might just row away without her. Leave Virpi on the shore. That had happened.

"I remember Mum saying you had a dog," Rebecka said. "Was her name Villa?"

"Yes, it was," Ragnhild said. "Villa."

The past and present swirled together inside Ragnhild. And it was making her chest hurt.

"Anyway," she went on. "We moved to town when I was twelve and Virpi was seven. The idea was that Henry would take over the farm and have the chance to straighten himself out. That didn't turn out well for any of us."

She touched a finger to the edge of the tea towel. You could see from the selvedge that it was home-sewn. And beautifully ironed. It touched her that Rebecka was living in her grandmother's house and caring for her things.

"My mother became, I suppose you'd say that she became depressed," she went on. "Though no-one used that word at the time. Not among us, in any case. She kept our home scarily clean. She didn't know anyone, she didn't even dare speak to the woman at the till when she went shopping, her Swedish was so bad. If someone came home with me from school, I'd say to *Äiti*: 'Don't say anything.' I didn't want my classmates to hear her asking: 'Halvaks leipää', would you like a sandwich."

Äiti's insecure smile, Ragnhild was thinking. That will of hers that had distorted into a desire to please. She turned see-through in that flat, like grease-proof paper.

"I just wanted to fit in," Ragnhild said. "I was so quiet that first year.

Practising my Swedish pronunciation so you couldn't hear the Finnish behind it. Virpi, though. She got into fights. The moment anyone called her a Finnish brat, that set her off. So they did it often."

Something like a laugh came out of Rebecka.

"Then I started hanging round boys. In the middle of the night. We lived on the lower-ground floor, so it was easy to slip out. Virpi used to wake up and follow me if I wasn't quiet enough. I didn't want her hanging on my heels but it made no difference whatever I said. She would have been nine then, when that started. And she got in with the older kids by telling jokes."

Get to the point, Ragnhild thought. I don't need to tell her how young we were, how drunk we got, that Virpi was just a child.

"Every other weekend *Äiti* drove back to the village and cleaned for Henry. She cooked food and put it in the freezer. In the spring and summer of 1967 *Äiti* was ill: she had stomach ulcers. Olle came over to our flat to talk it through. Henry needed help. I'd got a job as an auxiliary at the hospital, so I wasn't in the running. Virpi was fourteen. Olle said it was time she did her bit. She should spend the summer at Henry's and keep house for him. She tried to refuse, but Olle had made up his mind. And none of us said no. I was relieved it wasn't me. On the first day of the summer holidays we put her on the bus.

"The smell of diesel and dusty seats in that bus. Bags of bread and food *Äiti* had prepared beside Virpi's little bag of clothes. Virpi's pale clenched face staring straight ahead, not looking at us as we waved goodbye from the bus stop.

"Two weeks later and she rang in the middle of the night. Crying and whispering over the phone. 'I'm not staying,' she said. 'You've got to come and get me.' *Äiti* and *Isä* had been woken by the ringing and *Isä* took the receiver from me. The conversation wasn't a long one. 'What's happened?' *Äiti* asked when he had hung up, but *Isä* said he didn't know.

He rang Olle, who came over first thing the next morning. We were in the kitchen and Olle said it was time Virpi learned to take responsibility. And that she was spoiled because she'd always been the youngest. He reminded *Äiti* and *Isä* that they'd started working when they were twelve. If they gave in now and let her come home the moment things started getting tough, or boring or whatever the problem was – Virpi hadn't made that clear, just repeated we had to come and get her – she'd end up a slacker who would never be able to make her way in the world. We didn't say no that time either. Olle rang and spoke with Henry and Virpi, giving them both a talking to over the phone. He reminded them *Äiti* was ill. All this was making her worried and that had to stop. That evening Henry rang. Virpi was missing. She's bound to turn up, Olle said and asked Henry if he really had searched everywhere. Henry was furious. He'd been left alone to handle the responsibility for the farm and everything. Virpi was just one more problem. Was he supposed to be her babysitter on top of everything else? She hadn't taken one of the boats because he had removed the cable from the spark plug, disconnected the fuel hose and locked the oars away. The thaw had been late arriving, the water hadn't reached ten degrees yet."

Ragnhild had to take a breather. Telling the story brought with it a shift to a new perspective. When you turned round, all the familiar landmarks looked different. Olle had always been the villain of this piece. He was the one who had told them what to do. Only now she was seeing herself, *Äiti* and *Isä*. Dark, forbidding rocks that stopped you finding your way on land.

"Virpi turned up two days later. She had swum across to the mainland. It was absolutely astonishing she hadn't drowned in the cold water. Then she had hitch-hiked into town. Olle yelled at her, the rest of us said nothing. She was . . . 'obstinate', that was Olle's word. She said almost nothing herself. But she wasn't going back. 'You can't make me,' she said. That was when Olle made the consequences clear. If she thought she would get free board and lodging in our family while behaving entirely selfishly, she had another thing coming. In this family we did our bit. She started packing some clothes."

"She was fourteen then," Rebecka said quietly.

"She hadn't even finished year nine," Ragnhild said. "She lived with various blokes. Whoring for board and lodging, as Olle put it."

Unbearable, Ragnhild was thinking. "People expressed their sympathy for our family. Who had done everything for Virpi. And whenever the subject of Virpi came up, Olle would talk about her background. Who knew anything about her biological parents? 'Shit sinks to the bottom,' he used to say. And I managed to pull myself together the last year of secondary school. I didn't want to see Virpi, so I stopped going out and I stopped partying. Dad drove out to the island that autumn and put the cows down."

"She ended up meeting Mikko. Had you."

"And left us," Rebecka said. "New husband, new child."

"She rang me a month before she died," Ragnhild said. "She said she was going to leave her husband and move back to Kiruna with her kid. She asked if we had room for her. She talked about you as well. But my life was so . . ."

She thought about Todde and Paula. About him staying awake all night, which meant she couldn't sleep. He spent the day snoring on the sofa.

"No," she said. "I shouldn't blame my life. The reason she couldn't stay with me was that I was still angry at her."

There was a slight movement of Rebecka's hands while she continued to lie where she was.

"Why were you angry with her?"

"Because I should have been ashamed. Me, *Äiti*, *Isä*, Olle. And

Henry, obviously, only he doesn't really count as a human being. We should all have been ashamed. Instead we chose to scorn and reject her."

"Do you think Henry . . ."

Ragnhild waited, but Rebecka did not finish putting her question.

"Yes, I do. She swam across the river, for heaven's sake. She was fourteen. Girls at that age. They are like flowers just come into bloom."

Ragnhild was intent on remaining on her chair so as not to leap up and wash the dishes in the sink, put the bottle of Viscotears in the fridge, maybe clean the windows and scrub the ceiling.

She forced herself to stay with the realisation of the pain she had caused Virpi, her betrayal.

"Forgive me," she said to Rebecka. "I should have stood up to Olle for your mother. I should have let her live with me."

"I'm not my mother though," Rebecka said. "I never even think about her."

Ragnhild said nothing to that. After a while she said she ought to go. She would have liked to ask if she should give Rebecka another round of drops. But she couldn't bear the idea of her saying no. She plucked up her courage though, and said:

"Can I ring you tomorrow? To find out how you are?"

Rebecka managed to shrug though she was lying down. And it struck Ragnhild that this gesture probably caused mothers more heartache than any other.

In the car on the way home the thought of Börje waiting for her kept her warm. She was thinking about the photos of Paula in the drawer of her desk where she'd put them when she did the death-cleaning.

I'm going to get them out, she thought. I'm going to show them to Börje. I'll go through them all one by one. If I start crying like I'm never going to stop, then so be it.

*

Lying on the sofa, Rebecka heard Ragnhild's car start and drive out of the yard. Sivving turned up only five minutes later. He was going to let her sleep. Did she want him to take both dogs with him?

She said yes, though she would have liked to have the Brat stay. But she thought he should have the chance to be away from her.

The whole idea of having a dog suddenly seemed absurd. People were just apes. Apes that took other animals prisoner. Kept them as slaves and treated them as they saw fit. It was revolting.

She asked Sivving to put the eye drops in the fridge and promised to use them. She also promised to ring him the moment she woke up. And she promised to get undressed and get into bed under the duvet.

When he left she stayed where she was.

She tried thinking through what had happened. Anna Granlund had texted her and von Post as they were on their way to Kurravaara. To tell them Pohjanen was dead. And she had come up with the ludicrous idea of going skiing in an avalanche area.

So much to deal with and all at the same time. Insufferably childish. Foolish. Dangerous.

She thought about Pohjanen.

Why am I not in tears, she wondered.

She also thought about the time she flew down to Stockholm and slept with Måns, which led to the break-up with Krister.

It frightened her that she did things on impulses she didn't understand. Without even making up her mind to do them.

She didn't want to die. Did she?

The captain in charge of this boat was unreliable and utterly reckless.

The captain was steering for the rocks and everything below decks had come loose and was sliding helplessly from one side of the vessel to the other and crashing into the hull. She was almost grateful for the pain pounding in her eyes.

But the skiing trip wasn't that simple. She wasn't going to reduce it to little more than a moment of madness.

I've looked death in the white of its eye, she thought. And now I can do anything.

She reached for the phone to call Krister, but when she squinted at the screen it hurt so much her eyes filled with tears and she managed to stop herself.

No, she thought. Not doing that.

Because that's broken, she thought. I broke that too. And I can't repair it yet. Maybe not ever.

She was feeling so much contempt for herself she had to laugh when she realised she was actually capable of feeling self-pity as well; a laugh that was more of a croak.

An image of her therapist popped into her mind. After Lars-Gunnar Vinsa had shot himself and Nalle, and she had come home from the psychiatric ward, she had been to see her a few times but then stopped going.

Her name was Agnes Stoor. Rebecka had looked at her shoes and her clothes and found things to despise, her saffron-yellow blouse, the bird brooch. She had never said anything about herself, but Rebecka had been convinced she was unbearably respectable in private.

She still had Agnes's telephone number. She wrote her a brief text. That took its own sweet time. She turned down the brightness of the mobile's screen. Her eyes were aching and kept weeping tears.

Hi, this is Rebecka Martinsson. I came to see you for a few sessions several years ago. I don't know if you remember me. I'd like to start again. If you're still working. And have time for me

She hesitated. It was Saturday evening. But then she pressed send.

She put her mobile on her chest and thought she'd get an answer at the start of the working week. On Monday maybe. Or Tuesday.

I've got to do this, Rebecka thought. Because I can't bear it anymore. And it was the only thing she could think of doing that seemed right.

Twenty minutes later her phone hummed.

Hi Rebecka. Of course I remember you. Let's speak on Monday and arrange a time

Rebecka put the phone on the table. She put the tea towel back over her eyes.

She felt so grateful. Grateful for that woman replying at once even though it was a Saturday evening.

JUNE

Early summer had arrived in its soft green dress. The ice on the Torne river began to crack on the same day Tommy Rantakyrö was buried. The floes rose and climbed up the banks in a rage, displacing a summer cottage by seven metres and bringing down trees. The rumbling was so loud at Poikkijärvi cemetery that the priest had to raise his voice.

Anna-Maria Mella wept out of her one eye with Robert and Jenny supporting her on either side.

"For technical reasons to do with the nature of the case", the lid had been firmly closed on any suspicion of criminal activity on Tommy's part. As far as the media and his parents and the witch-hunting general public were concerned, he and Anna-Maria had been shot because they were key figures in a police investigation into murder, drug crime and prostitution. At a formal photo array, Anna-Maria had identified her assailants as the two Russians known to the investigators as Yegor Babitsky and Yury Yusenkov.

Those names had been found on the rental agreement Elena Litova had signed, but it was assumed their identities were false. They could not be prosecuted as they were still missing. In all likelihood they had left the country. Wanted by both Interpol and Europol, they might be imprisoned for something else one fine day. At some point, in some place. Elena Litova's identity had not been corroborated. While the authorities in her home town were able to confirm that she had left the country, they could not provide any photographs of her. There was no record in any Russian civil register of a Maria Berberova who was married to Frans Mäki. A warrant for her arrest on charges of blackmail, threats and tax evasion had been issued nonetheless.

While the formal investigation into the murders of Tommy Rantakyrö, Henry Pekkari, Galina Kireevskaya, Adriana Mohr and the third woman who had still not been identified remained open, the case was no longer being actively pursued. The facts were known. As far as the police themselves were concerned, the matter was now closed.

Rebecka had not seen Anna-Maria since she came home from hospital. Once the funeral service was finished, she went over to her.

She was feeling extremely nervous. Because of the disastrous dinner and their wrestling match in the snow. Because the woman who looked like she was Anna-Maria might not really be Anna-Maria on the inside anymore.

"Hello," she said. "It's good to see you."

"Rebecka," Anna-Maria said, and gave her a fleeting and slightly guilty smile, as though it wasn't quite right to be happy in the midst of grief.

Anna-Maria opened her arms and Rebecka stepped inside them. They hugged one another hard and for a rather long time. Speaking very quietly into each other's ears.

"I'm alive," Anna-Maria said. "I'm so grateful for that."

"Me too, me too," Rebecka chorused.

"You know what," Anna-Maria said. "I'm trying to persuade myself we can all do stupid things and we've no idea of the consequences while we're doing them. You take a peek at your phone when you're driving and the next moment you've run over a . . . And then your life is ruined."

"I know, I know," Rebecka said rocking her. "He's still Tommy. He hasn't turned into someone else."

"Right, though I was talking about myself. I could see how he was feeling, you know? And I was his boss."

"Oh no, Anna-Maria. No, no."

"And I feel so sad about the girl we haven't identified," Anna-Maria went on. "I think about her a lot. Where's her mother? I'll be at home hoovering and find myself wondering if she had any children. Or if she was alone in the world. How are you ever supposed to bear it, doing this job?"

Anna-Maria broke off and wiped her nose with the back of her hand.

"They're saying you've left," she said then. "Won't you be coming back to the prosecution service?"

"I'm working half-time; I haven't left completely, not yet. I'm helping sorting out the tangles. But I'm not sure. I don't think I can stay. Or want to, I mean."

"I plan on fighting you on that," Anna-Maria mumbled. "You know that, don't you?"

Then they gently released one another. And everything felt that little bit better.

One week later, the birches were unfurling their catkins and Pohjanen was buried. That was less painful. No floods of tears. His colleagues spoke about his professionalism. His son gave a prepared speech and sounded composed.

That was the evening Krister turned up at Rebecka's house.

She was down by the riverbank burning brushwood. A warm drizzle hung almost motionless in the air. He inhaled the scent of fresh deciduous wood burning: the acidity of birch leaves, something akin to burnt sugar.

She was feeding more wood to the fire and before she caught sight of him he was able to watch her as though she were alone with herself and the fire. Her gaze lost in the flames. Her face dirty, sweat-marked from all the work clearing the brush, and rosy from the heat of the fire. Her hair swung free, she had the rubber band around her wrist. She looked peculiarly happy.

He had to look away for a moment. Push away the desire to place his fingertips on her lips. Lick her salty skin.

Just for an instant he thought he should turn around, leave her in peace, but that was when she caught sight of him.

"Hello," she said simply.

"Hello," he said back.

They were both very still, as though they had seen an animal in the woods they didn't want to scare.

There was so much inside him that just gave way and vanished. She was all he could see. That whole business with Måns felt infinitely remote.

His sister had said to him: "I don't think she slept with him because you didn't mean anything, you know. I think it was the other way round."

He had closed himself off then. Grimacing with displeasure because she sounded like a pop psychology book.

And his sister had said: "That's not an excuse, I didn't mean it like that. She shouldn't have done it."

They had changed the subject but what she had said stayed with him. It had kept working slowly away. He wasn't sure whether what he was feeling now was understanding or a vain and childish hope. Only here he was in any case. A bit short of breath. He was throwing in the towel, confronted with the realisation that she was it. She was the only one.

He searched inside himself for the pain. Warily feeling his way, like when you have a blister on the ball of one foot, and you test your full weight on it to see if going on would be unbearable.

"Isn't Sivving out here to check you're doing it properly?" he asked.
She grinned.

"He was so convinced I'd cut my leg off with the strimmer he had to go indoors. I'll text him that the danger has passed. Where have you got the dogs?"

"In the car."

"Let them out," she said. "I'll let the Brat out; I didn't want him round my feet while I was clearing this stuff."

She nodded proudly towards the area which now had an unobstructed view of the river.

"Lovely," he said.

He had a lot of words inside him. But they felt too dry, like pieces of paper in his mouth, so he did nothing with them.

They were in a hurry as they went up to the house. He let Tintin and Roy out. She opened the front door. The Brat came flying out like a rocket.

The dogs chased one another around, tearing up ground that had gone soggy with the early summer damp.

She just laughed at the sight.

"We can plant potatoes there later."

They looked at one another. Clutching at the look in one another's eyes like free climbers on a rock wall, they turned to watch the dogs and then back to look at each other again.

"I promised Sivving to turn the sauna on when I was finished," she said. "Would you like to join us?"

"Yes," he said.

And it felt simple. Not easy, it would never be easy, would it?

But simple, certain, and the only thing possible.

Rebecka Martinsson ended up spending a lot of time at the cemetery in

Kiruna. It had become a habit for her to walk there and spend a while at her father's and grandmother's graves every Tuesday, after she had been to see the therapist.

She cleared away microscopic weeds and planted marigolds, one of her grandmother's favourite flowers.

The cemetery was a place to entertain thoughts of a different kind. She always made the time to walk slowly along the raked-gravel paths and read the gravestones of people who had lived before her. There were losses that could never be recovered resting here. The dates told brief tales of lives that had been too short, of parents losing their children and the other way round. Every now and then she would be surprised to see the dates of spouses who had passed on very shortly after one another. Did the living one just let go when the other had died?

It was a cool summer's day, just thirteen degrees in the shade. No need to be reminded they were living in the heart of the mountains.

The noise from the construction site of the new town hall and the surrounding area could be clearly heard. But she could also hear little noises that were all the cemetery's own, a squirrel moving on sharp claws between the nearby pines, the distracted hand of the wind in the trees.

Rebecka wiped the soil off her hands onto her jeans; they were due to go into the washing machine that evening in any case. She had switched her phone to silent, but when she looked at the screen she saw she had missed a call from Maria Taube. She called her back.

"I've sent you some photos of our new bookshelves," Maria yelled. "They're utterly gorgeous. It makes you want to live in our office, almost."

"Do you ever do any work, or is it all just interior design?"

"We're fitting the place out and drinking wine."

Sofi's voice could be heard in the background: "I'm working. Say hi from me."

"I just wanted to check in," Maria said. "How's it going?"

"Slowly," Rebecka said. "But good. We've identified all the companies that did any kind of business with Frans Mäki or with Olle and Anders Pekkari's firm. We're applying Chapter 29 paragraph 5 of the Criminal Code."

"Plea bargaining. I didn't think that was used in Sweden."

"It rarely is. But it gets those involved to talk. You just have to promise them community service and that we won't apply to disqualify them. So they keep coming up with new evidence. How they were threatened into signing contracts with subcontractors they were unable to verify and forced not to argue about invoices that were double the sum agreed, or the supply of substandard materials, poor-quality cement, girders that were too thin, inadequate damp courses, things like that. Now and then you do wonder if they were actually threatened or only too happy to make a quick buck. We landed a really big catch yesterday, though. A newly established municipal joint-stock company the local authority had lent thirty million to. The money was spent on consultants' fees. Examining those consultancy services in more detail is going to be fun."

"Consultants – that's what we should have been, obviously. So are you going to be in a position to put a major villain away? Prison? Bread and water?"

"That would have been nice, but we'll have to be satisfied that the principals are gone. We're turning off the taps."

"And word is getting round that the Prosecution Service is swooping down on companies like hawks."

"Like woodpeckers anyway."

"You're not going back to working full-time though, are you? I'm not going to go on nagging you about working for us."

"Keep nagging. It makes me feel wanted. I've got to stop now, Krister and Sivving are just arriving."

"Krister," Maria said, and her voice became a large airy room the sun was streaming into through high windows. "So how's it going with him?"

"Slowly," Rebecka said, "but good."

They had been spending a lot of time together, Krister and her. Ever since the evening after Pohjanen's funeral. They had not slept together. Sometimes, when it was just the two of them, they would stroke each other's hands. Stroking the back of the other's hand. Squeezing the fingers. Or they would just hold hands and look into each other's eyes for long periods that would finally be broken by their starting to laugh. That felt extraordinarily intimate. And very private. She would never tell anyone about it. Apart from her therapist, of course. She told Agnes Stoor everything.

She ended the call. Her two men were coming through the gravestones. It was slow going for Sivving. She could see that Krister's hand was open and held fairly close to the other man, ready to grab him if his friend were to stumble.

"Have you finished?" Sivving called over. He couldn't wait until they had reached her to start talking. "The dogs are in the car. Not because it's warm. They've said we're going to have some night frosts. Makes you wonder what's going to happen to the cloudberry flowers."

Krister and Sivving took an appreciative look at the marigolds and then they all strolled back to the car at a leisurely pace.

Halfway there Rebecka caught sight of a man two rows away. She recognised him immediately from the photos of the current investigation. Spike Mäki, son of the Lingonberry King. He was standing beside one of the graves and looked up briefly. She realised he had recognised her too, though he swiftly turned his head away and started walking towards the other gate in the wall that surrounded the cemetery.

When they reached the car, Rebecka said: "I just need a minute. There's something I've got to check."

They had nothing on Spike Mäki. He was just one of the employees in his father's company. He hadn't signed any papers. He had no knowledge of the company's finances. He had barely spent any time with his father or the latter's wife. Didn't know a thing, he said.

She could see Spike's broad back, his feet turned sharply out as his huge body waddled towards the gate. He chucked some withered flowers in the waste bin.

She moved briskly over to the grave he had been standing beside. Who was he visiting? His mother, maybe. Why was she so keen to know? Just a feeling. The way he had immediately stalked off.

You and your feelings, Pohjanen was saying in her head.

The gravestone was unremarkable. Grey, no frills. She came to a stop and stared at it. A fresh bunch in the small vase that had been inserted into the soil. Flowers that looked like they'd been bought at a petrol station. Something unnatural about the colour, as though they had absorbed food colouring.

The words on the gravestone read:

INGER STRÖM

*1931 †2001

REST IN PEACE

Inger Ström? Rebecka was thinking. Börje Ström's mother. Why?

But that question went nowhere, it stayed stuck where it was.

She turned back to the car. Sivving was talking about berry picking and about her having to re-dig the drainage ditch around the yard.

*

Spike Mäki threw the withered flowers in the bin just inside the entrance and squeezed into his car. The ache in his knees followed by the relief of finally being able to sit on his bum. He ought to buy a new car. One with more space. The wheel poked him in the belly even though he had the driver's seat pushed back as far as it would go with him still reaching the pedals.

That prosecutor had seen him. But it didn't matter. Nothing really mattered anymore. He never felt happy. Or sad, either. He hadn't been afraid during the police interviews. He had always been scared when he was young, to the point it was something he almost missed.

When he looked back at his life – he was sixty-eight – it seemed to him like an old fishing net that had got all tangled up. Identical grey strands, impossible to distinguish one from another.

All of a sudden the car was parked in front of the block of flats he lived in. Spike had to take a look around to check he had actually parked in the right spot. How could he have driven all the way home from the cemetery with no memory of the journey? How had he not had an accident?

There was one spot of colour in the grey mesh of the fishing net. When he was fourteen. It could have been yesterday. The time that had passed since then was like the car trip from the cemetery: grizzled, worn away, gone.

MAY–JUNE 1962

Spike is fourteen, in a month's time he'll be fifteen. He is alone in the boxing club late one evening at the end of May. Punching the bag so hard that sweat is pouring off him. He will finish year eight in a week's time, he's going to fail a whole load of subjects. Like he cares, it wasn't as if he was planning on being a swot in any case.

He's already well known as one of the town villains. Dad gives him minor jobs like smashing windows, sledging cars, that kind of thing. He doesn't ask why, that's not allowed, ever. They must be people who need warning or punishing. On two occasions he has set fire to buildings. One burned down to the ground, it was in the paper the following day. Spike never says no and even so Dad keeps calling him *knapsu*, a coward and a cunt. Though not in front of just anybody. When it comes to school, the town, the boxing club, Spike is his lad and no other bastard gets to pick on him. But when it's just his closest mates, the scorn comes hissing out of him like a punctured tyre.

He is disappointed Spike isn't much of a boxer. He thinks he's a weakling and keeps saying he's his mother's little boy. Half-joking to his mates: "Can't be sure he's mine." There's always a blow in the offing.

Mum's new bloke is completely different, but Spike despises him as much as his dad does. The new one works at the swimming baths as a caretaker and Dad refers to him as "that edge-swimmer", the kind of person who hugs the side because he's afraid of deep water.

Spike is drawn to his father, wants to be his father, longs to feel he's good enough but keeps getting smacked in the face.

He pretends to be tough, no-one messes with him. Most people hardly dare look in his direction. But the truth is he's always scared. Mostly of his dad. But of other stuff as well. He is terrified of the dark and hospitals and spiders. He can't bear to sit with his back to an open door. He's scared of boxing matches. Only no-one can ever know that. He will mock anyone who shows the slightest weakness in front of other people.

Because it is important to Dad, Spike trains hard. He has given up any hope of amounting to anything in the ring. To his mates he says he's not one for rules. He keeps getting into fights though, when they're at a dance or on the rare occasions he attends school. So at least he's had

575

some benefit from the training. He's got so much clout now he can't hit them on the jaw. A face is hard and without gloves on you could easily break the bones in your hand. He focuses on the soft parts of the body and finishes with kicks once they're on the ground.

Just as he is pummelling the bag with a series of punches, there's a knock on the door to the club.

A woman is standing outside. At first Spike thinks it is some old lady, but once he has wiped the sweat out of his eyes he can see how pretty she is. Tight-fitting sweater and skirt. Like in a film almost.

"I'm looking for Raimo Koskela," she says. "Is he here?"

"Uh, no," Spike replies, forcing himself to look away from her breasts; his training shorts may be baggy, but they're not that baggy.

"He does train here, though, doesn't he?" she asks and tries to look over his shoulder into the club.

He nods.

"Only there's no-one here," he says. "Well, I'm here. Obviously. No-one else, that's what I meant."

He falls silent, feeling stupid.

But she doesn't look at him as if he were stupid. Her chin is trembling and he realises she is about to start crying.

"Raimo's my ex," she says. "We've got a little boy . . . Börje . . . and Raimo hasn't paid. He hasn't got a phone, so I can't even get hold of him."

Then suddenly the tears start flowing. Spike has no idea how to behave towards her. He's never had a girlfriend. He lies about that fact to his mates, of course, but the truth is he's never had a girlfriend, never even kissed a girl. He has no idea how to talk to women and absolutely none about what to do when they cry.

He wishes he had a handkerchief or a bit of tissue to give her to wipe her tears. His hand rises and fumbles at the air as if hoping for a handkerchief to magically appear.

All of a sudden she is looking at him with something akin to – he's not sure what – something like rage. And hunger. As though she wants to devour him. He would be feeling scared almost, but doesn't have the time. Because she grabs his half-raised hand and pulls him closer. The air between them becomes so electric there's a buzzing sound in his ears like you get under a high voltage line. He can feel his heart pumping blood in great gouts, forcing it into his arteries. And the next second her lips are on his and her hand has wrapped itself around his neck.

Later on that particular memory will change: he will remember it as though he were the one who reached out a hand to wipe away her tears. As though he were the one who made the first move.

His cock instantly goes hard. And he kisses her clumsily back.

She manoeuvres him backwards into the boxing club and the door shuts behind them.

She grabs his cock inside his shorts, rubbing the underside so hard he almost faints. Her breasts are swinging under her jumper and he gets hold of them and squeezes. He feels so incredibly randy.

She shoves him onto one of the training benches they use when lifting heavy weights; she pulls off his shorts and pushes up her skirt while stepping out of her tights. He manages to catch a glimpse of her knickers as they land on the floor but then she is straddling him.

It is over in no time at all. All of a sudden he is feeling sated and indolent, his heart has stopped pounding.

By the time he sits up she has already put her pants and tights back on.

She hadn't even taken off her coat.

She steps into her high heels. Before she leaves she strokes his cheek with the back of her hand. She smiles sadly and blinks both eyes. A slow blink like closing your eyes, those black doll's eyelashes of hers still wet with tears. Then she leaves without a word.

*

He thinks about her all the time in the weeks that follow. He tells no-one what happened. His mates would never believe him. And if they did, they would take the piss and ask him if he wanted to bang his mum as well, or some of the teachers at school. He can just see them shoving him as they walk past the old people's home and asking if he fancied going inside for a bit of pussy.

The memory of her body, though, is warming a place inside him that had been completely desolate. He manages to find out her name by asking some vague questions about Raimo; he works for his dad, after all. Inger Ström. He fantasises about seeing Inger again, at a dance, in a shop. Their eyes meet and they just know. Bodies intertwined in her bed, only this time it doesn't happen as quickly, he is the young lover with the staying power she has always desired.

He masturbates so much during the following weeks that the skin of his cock becomes sore. His imagination keeps painting larger and larger canvases. On which he and Inger Ström meet, they make love, she whispers he is the only one, he moves in, he is like a father to her small child.

In the cold and dark of his life of burglary, drunkenness and violence, thinking of her is the only thing that makes him feel warm.

But how is he going to pay their way? What does he have to offer? He's about to start year nine, there isn't even a summer job waiting for him. He gets some pocket money off Dad every now and then but it's enough for booze and petrol for the moped and not much else.

Which is when the opportunity presents itself.

One Saturday evening he is walking to his dad's house because his mother and the edge-swimmer are having the neighbours round for dinner and they don't want him there. The accelerator cable on his moped has snapped. Right next to the carburettor, of course, otherwise he could have chucked the sheath and pulled on the remainder of the cable with his hand. Now he has to make his way on foot all the way to Tuolla.

Dad's pick-up truck, a red Ford Taunus Transit, is parked in the yard. There are four other cars beside it. Music and low voices can be heard from inside. Dad and his mates will be in there drinking. They usually make something simple, ready-made meatballs and baked macaroni, sausages and bread. They'll be playing cards. His stomach is in knots, from both fear and hunger. A few sausages would be nice, only Dad gets extra disciplinarian when he's been drinking and Spike has learned to keep away. He is tired of being subjected to trials of strength, of being forced to arm-wrestle only then to get jeered at.

The truck is there in any case. He walks up to it and tries the handle. Locked. That means there's money inside. He peers through the side window. A pile of plastic bags is on the floor. Loads of money.

He creeps up the stairs and opens the front door. No-one hears him enter. Dad's jacket is hanging there on a hook. He gets the keys out of the right pocket. Quickly and without a sound he runs hunched over towards the pick-up but then changes his mind and heads for the privy instead.

There is a large pack of toilet rolls on a shelf inside. He grabs two of them and goes back to the truck. He unlocks it. The tied-off plastic bags cover the entire floor in front of the passenger seat. He grabs the one on top. Undoes it and then stuffs bundles of notes under his sweater and in his pockets before putting the toilet rolls in the bag, retying it and chucking it back in the car.

Just as he has shut the door of the truck, the front door of the house opens. He feels so terrified he has to stop himself screaming. Instead he throws himself onto the ground and rolls under the pick-up. A man makes his way unsteadily down the steps from the porch and heads for the privy. Spike can't make out who it is, it could be Toivo. No-one else is that big in any case. Toivo lets off a thunder-breaker as he crosses the yard, a real horse's fart. When Toivo disappears into the toilet, Spike locks the truck door and runs quickly towards the house.

Toivo must be having a shit. The guys would take a piss out in the yard. He hopes Toivo isn't a quick shitter. Spike opens the door and puts his father's keys back in the jacket pocket as stealthily as he can.

Then he runs away as if it were a matter of life and death. He keeps his hands on the lower part of his sweater to stop the money falling out as his legs work off the fear. Eventually he's got no energy left and the lactic acid build-up makes him fall to his knees. His lungs are gasping for oxygen.

He can hardly believe what he has just done. But when he gets back on his feet, he doesn't feel afraid. He feels like a man. His sweater is stuffed with sweat-dampened bundles of banknotes, the rubber bands are chafing his skin.

He's going to hide them somewhere safe. He's got a vague notion of looking up Inger Ström. And offering her, well, he's not sure what exactly. He's got to count the money first.

One week later and Dad rings Spike. Spike has wrapped the money inside a wax cloth and buried it in the woods. He regrets his impulsive act. Dad went crazy when the theft was discovered. Spike knows they have beaten the guy they think put the toilet rolls into the bag half to death. He is terrified his father will discover he was the one who took it. He keeps thinking about digging the money up and throwing the notes on the fire, but doesn't dare go anywhere near the spot in the woods he marked with a stone so heavy he could barely even lift it. Just imagine if someone saw him.

When Spike gets the call he is with his mother at the edge-swimmer's parents' house in Piillijärvi.

"Have you fixed the moped?" his father asks brusquely. "Come to the Vittangi crossroads. We'll pick you up there."

"What for?" Spike says, trying to sound calm.

"Don't ask so many questions," Dad says. "If I tell you to be there, you just get on your moped and go, you get it?"

Spike is barely able to replace the receiver. They've found him out. Dad has worked it out somehow. He's going to drive him into the woods and beat him very badly. Let some of his guys give him a real working-over. His stomach hurts so much he has to hunch over for a bit. He's got to turn up, only where's he going to find the courage?

Because the edge-swimmer is fussy about keeping the yard neat and tidy and won't let Spike drive the moped across it, Spike steers at an angle across the neighbour's plot and down to the road. As he passes the neighbour's car he takes a peek through the side window.

There on the seat is a pistol. Without any hesitation at all, he opens the car door, grabs the gun and shoves it into his jacket pocket.

Then he drives to the Vittangi crossroads. He leaves the moped in a ditch. When he gets into his father's Buick, Toivo is sitting in the back, taking up half the space. The crown of his stupid blond head is almost touching the roof.

Pessan-Mauri is doing the driving. He boxed for the North Pole Club back in the day. He's got dark eyes and always talks to you as if you were a dog: "Stop staring" and "Move it".

Dad is in the passenger seat. As soon as Spike shuts the door, Toivo hands him a hip flask.

"We're going to have a chat with Raimo Koskela," Dad says.

"Right," Spike says and can feel the swig of alcohol burning as it goes down and then laying a warm and soothing hand across his troubled stomach.

Raimo, he thinks as the car drives along the river in the brightness of the late summer evening. They think Raimo's the one who stole the money from Dad. He feels so relieved he almost bursts into tears. He has to turn away and look out of the window.

They stop when they get to Kurkkio and Pessan-Mauri goes into a house at the end of the village. He has a look round, no dog starts to bark. He makes his way stealthily back to the car holding a key. It opens a barrier across the road. They drive slowly, slaloming between tree roots and potholes on the sandy forest road; Dad is concerned about his Buick.

When they get to the cottage, Raimo is sitting on the steps leading up to the front door.

"So where's your lad?" Dad asks.

"Börje's sleeping round a mate's," Raimo says. "He's coming tomorrow."

Pessan-Mauri carries out a quick and thorough search of the house and Raimo's belongings. No money. He takes a turn around the house as well, goes down to the shore and checks under the boat.

"We just want a bit of a chat," Dad says and offers Raimo a cigarette. "Only we wanted to talk undisturbed."

Raimo looks worried but goes with them. He squeezes in between Toivo and Spike in the back.

They return to the village where Henry Pekkari picks them up in his boat. He lives on an island in the middle of the river. Spike has met him at the club a few times. He's no boxer. Just hangs around with the other guys. Henry's legs are unsteady as he gets into the boat and sits beside the outboard motor. He has drunk a good deal more than the few words he has uttered would lead you to think. He says hello to Raimo without looking him in the eye.

As Raimo goes with them from the shore up to the house he is beginning to look really nervous. Spike fingers the gun in his jacket pocket.

The talking takes place in Henry's living room. Raimo says he didn't take the money. Dad says it was Raimo who drove the car and no-one has keys to it apart from Dad.

"So I took the money myself, did I?" Dad asks. "Maybe I walked in my sleep and stole my own money?"

Pessan-Mauri holds Raimo's arms and Toivo starts pounding away. Punching Raimo in the face and stomach. But Raimo keeps insisting he didn't take anything. Spike can feel Dad looking at him out of the corner of his eye. He understands why he is here. He's supposed to learn how to stomach this kind of thing. Sissies aren't allowed. Spike maintains a neutral expression, drawing up the corners of his mouth into a slight grin. He can stomach this. He's not leaving Dad in any doubt about that.

Henry Pekkari has collapsed into an armchair and keeps looking away the whole time.

Pessan-Mauri and Toivo take it in turns; it's Toivo who is restraining Raimo now and Pessan-Mauri doing the beating. But Raimo is stubbornly denying any part in the theft.

Raimo's face is beginning to resemble mince. Blood is pouring from his nose and his burst lip and he keeps gasping and grimacing. Pessan-Mauri has probably broken one of his ribs. Spike is thinking it could have been him looking like that. Dad wouldn't have made them pull their punches just because Spike is his flesh and blood. Just the opposite, in fact.

Toivo lets go of Raimo and shakes his arms out. Pessan-Mauri glances over at Dad. What's the next step? that glance is asking.

Spike can see a hint of doubt in Dad's eyes. He is actually considering the possibility it might not be Raimo.

"I can't take any more," Raimo says and spits out a viscous drool of spit mixed with blood. "If you're going to have another go at me, you'll have to reckon on being on the receiving end as well. I didn't take your

583

money, Fransi. How many years have I been working for you? You've got to take me at my word."

If Dad decides it's not Raimo, the step to Spike isn't that far. There's only one key. Dad will start to wonder who could have nicked it from his jacket.

Spike gets the gun out of his pocket.

"Stop lying," he yells and points the pistol at Raimo.

The adults in the room react immediately.

Henry the Drunk leaps out of his armchair as if he'd had a burning lump of coal shoved up his arse. His mouth is wide open but not a sound comes out. Dad is swearing. Toivo and Pessan-Mauri each take a step to the side so they are not in the line of fire between Spike and Raimo.

The force of the feeling running through Spike at that moment could almost lift him off the floor. They are afraid. They are as scared as little kids, the lot of them. Even Dad has gone pale.

"Put the gun down," Raimo says in a hoarse voice. "I didn't—"

He doesn't get any further before the gun fires. Spike is taken by surprise as well. The recoil jerks the gun out of his hand and it falls to the floor.

Raimo topples backwards. A red patch is spreading across the front of his shirt. Everyone apart from Henry and Spike rushes over.

"Bloody hell, boy," Pessan-Mauri exclaims.

Raimo's breath comes in snatches accompanied by the sound of something rattling. After a while pinkish bubbles start forcing their way out of his mouth, but he keeps on breathing.

Spike can't bear that horrible noise.

"Sit down," Dad says to Spike as he picks up the gun. "Where the hell did you get this from?"

Obediently Spike sits down and tells him. Pessan-Mauri and Toivo sit as well.

584

Henry is whining that the bullet went straight through Raimo and into the wall above the sofa. Dad is mocking Henry complaining about the furnishings like a housewife. All you've got to do is hang that picture a bit lower. He orders Henry to get them something they can drink and there's a bottle of moonshine along with five glasses on the table in next to no time.

They drink in silence while Raimo is dying slowly on the floor. Spike downs the alcohol in huge gulps and then gets more poured into his glass. He can feel his father's eyes on him. The sense of power he so recently felt has melted away. Once again he is a useless brat who needs toughening up. Made into a man by those gurgling breaths that never stop. Spike is wondering whether it is going to go on all night. Can't Raimo just die?

It doesn't take all night. After barely thirty minutes Raimo breathes his last.

"You fucking idiot," Dad says to Spike and gets to his feet. "How am I supposed to find out where he hid the money now?"

Spike cannot come up with an answer. Those rattling breaths were horrifying but the current silence fills him with a kind of terror he has never felt before.

Then Dad starts giving orders. Everyone has to keep their traps shut, that is number one. Anyone who blabs will meet the same fate as Raimo. And that applies to Spike as well. No going home and whining to Mum or spilling the truth in the arms of some girl. Henry will have to get rid of the body.

"No, I can't!" Henry tries to protest. "Why should I—"

But Dad just tells Henry to shut up.

"There's nothing we can do about the body now, is there? It's light twenty-four hours a day. Anyone could see us carrying a body out to the boat and sinking it in the river. We'll put the body in the freezer for now and in the autumn when it's dark you can wind a chain around him and chuck him overboard somewhere deep."

"Bloody hell, that freezer's brand new," Henry moans.

But Dad isn't going to listen to any objections. Either Henry does what he is told or there are four people here who will testify it was Henry who put a bullet into Raimo.

Toivo and Pessan-Mauri empty the freezer and tip the body into it.

It occurs to Spike that it takes the combined strength of two powerful men to lift Raimo and put him inside. So how is Henry going to manage to get a corpse that will have frozen solid out of it, drag it down to the shore and into the boat and then tip it into the river in chains? He will have to butcher Raimo, carve him up like an animal.

Spike is feeling so sick from the alcohol and fear he can barely get to his feet. They have to stop twice on the way home so he can vomit beside the road. Dad laughs at him.

They leave him at the crossroads and he drives his moped home. When he gets there he has to wipe dead mosquitoes off his face; they're all over his hair and clothes.

He steals over to the neighbour's car and puts the gun back on the front seat. Just like Dad told him.

Then he pads into the cottage. Mum and her bloke are fast asleep. You can hear snoring from the bedroom. There's the smell of fresh baking. There are two trays of cinnamon buns in the kitchen. He devours one of them. Then a second. And a third. He eats ten cinnamon buns. They settle to form a soft calming lump in his belly.

That is the only thing that helps. Eating. In the years that follow when he wakes at night in a cold sweat, terrified by dreams of blood and rattling breaths. When loneliness squashes him like a night frost in summer.

Not being able to tell anyone, that alone. He is by himself and terrified. He has always kept well out of the way of the police, but now just the sight of a police car parked outside a restaurant and he starts trembling. Alcohol doesn't help.

What does help is eating. When he wakes at night he slices a whole loaf and eats it with butter. He eats buns, cakes and sweets until he feels calm inside.

One Friday at the end of July he has been out drinking the whole night. At six in the morning he is walking on his own and should be heading home. Instead he suddenly finds himself in front of Inger Ström's apartment on Föraregatan. He looked her address up in the phone book and has driven past the building a few times on the moped, but has never seen her. She works as a hairdresser in a salon not far from her home. He has caught a glimpse of her in there, but has never gone in of course.

The front door to the building is open. The letters on the name plates appear doubled, he has to close one eye as he tries to read the surnames. She lives on the second floor.

He hauls himself up the stairs using the banister. Her name is on the letterbox of one of the doors. He only intended to knock lightly, but he gives the door a proper thumping which echoes around the stairwell.

It is only a few seconds before she opens, dressed in a nightie and a quilted pale-blue dressing gown.

He hasn't planned what he is going to say. He doesn't really have any idea what he wants.

"Who are you?" she asks, only then he can see from her face that she recognises him.

Everything he has on his mind only gets halfway out.

"Do you want . . ." he says, slurring more than he'd like. "I've been thinking about . . . I've got money . . ."

Oh no, he realises it sounds like he wants to pay for her services.

"No, not that," he says. "Your husband, your ex, I . . ."

His hand wants to shape a gun but his finger is pointing in the air instead.

Maybe she doesn't understand a thing. Maybe she gets it all.

"Who are you?" she yells loud enough to wake all the neighbours this early on a Saturday morning. "Get out before I call the police!"

She shoves him in the chest so hard he stumbles backwards.

"Get out of here!" she yells again. "Get out and don't you dare show your ugly mug here again, you revolting little shit."

His brain may be slow, but she manages to yell loud enough for her message to be received.

He staggers down the steps and out onto the street. One of the neighbours opens a window to watch him leave as he sticks his hands in his pockets and heads for Hjalmar Lundbohmsvägen. It is a brilliantly sunny summer morning, lovely and quiet. No cars, but the birds are in full song. He doesn't notice any of that. He is hungry. He wants to eat chips and hot dogs. Biscuits with butter on, cheese sandwiches with fish roe spread on top as well.

One August evening Börje Ström comes into the club. He is not the little baby Spike imagined. Nyrkin-Jussi and Sisu-Sikke take him under their wing. When they spar, Spike beats him up as much as he dares. Börje improves quickly but he doesn't have much clout. And when he does and starts to be good at boxing, that's when Spike stops.

The money remains where he buried it in the woods. Spike never goes back to the spot. He often thinks about Inger Ström. But the rest of it feels more like a recurring dream. Sometimes a horribly vivid one, like when he was in Dad's bedroom with Sven-Erik Stålnacke and Börje Ström and had no idea what Dad was going to say. For the most part, though, it feels like it never happened.

588

"You're going to have fine weather," Krister said as he got out of the car and moved round to the other side to open the door for Sivving.

"Fine as wine," Börje Ström said, squinting across the river.

Rebecka got out and had a look round. They were standing at the Jukkasjärvi site of the winter ice hotel. The chalets and the new barn are open all year round, offering rooms made of ice along with a trendy ice-bar. The place looked really appealing.

A group of Japanese visitors strolled past. She guessed they had been in the workshop making ice sculptures. There was a sleepy feel to the spot during the low season. As if even the ground had to recover from the sheer intensity of the tourist period.

The blue water of the Torne river. Her home river. Her house lay some ten kilometres upstream. The sun was sprinkling glitter across the water and a soft breeze was keeping the mosquitoes away. Poikkijärvi, where Nalle was buried alongside his father, and now Tommy, was on the opposite shore.

This is OK, she thought, not looking away from the village opposite. It's a good thing that spot has become part of my story. So I don't forget. Forgetting wouldn't mean it just vanished.

Ragnhild was lashing luggage to the rubber boat. She stopped and went to her car, letting Villa out.

"I don't think she'll run away," Ragnhild said. "She's one of us now."

The dogs in the back of Rebecka's car started barking and whining immediately.

"So let's get them to say hello," Rebecka said.

She let Tintin, Roy, Bella and the Brat out.

The two-legs spent a while observing the greeting ritual that followed, play combined with rigid postures and pulled-back lips. The dogs were finished with it soon enough: once the order of precedence had been established.

"And you're the lowest, as usual," Rebecka said to the Brat.

"It'll be fine," Sivving said to Ragnhild. "Bella's the boss."

"I'm not worried," Ragnhild said. "It'll be good for Villa to be part of a pack for a bit."

"And it'll be good for her to be back on the island," Rebecka said. "We'll bring her with us in two days' time. You can survive that long with us, little one."

She said the last bit to Villa, who was tussling with the Brat.

"If you survive," Sivving said, looking downstream. "That's a mug's game, trust me."

Briefly Ragnhild's eyes met those of Rebecka. She had started praying for her. For her and Paula. It had brought her closer to them than either knew.

She wasn't convinced that there really was some higher power who heard her. The praying served a purpose nonetheless.

She had sold her flat and used the money to buy Olle Pekkari out of the island. They had their hands full with the ongoing investigation into their company. Her brother and his son Anders were going to get off easy. They had acted in good faith to begin with, when the company took on its new shareholders. And when the illegal activities occurred, they had been acting under duress. She was more than happy not to have to have anything to do with them in the future. Olle had let her have the island without making the process difficult or setting the price too high. It was all of a piece somehow. In his spider form, God was spinning a net of goodness across the dark thorns life puts in our way.

She saw Krister's hand give Rebecka's a quick caress.

She and Börje clambered aboard the boat. Krister and Rebecka pushed them off from the jetty.

Villa barked anxiously after them.

"Are you sure you remember how to do this?" Börje Ström asked. He grinned and put the helmet under the sitting board, it would be needed later.

"I'm hoping it will come back to me." She grinned back at him.

She took the oars and rowed them with even steady strokes towards the deep channel in the middle of the river.

Börje Ström shifted from side to side, paddling on Ragnhild's command. Their friends were waving from the shore.

He felt young and alive. Pleased at the strength in his body as he paddled them forwards. Ragnhild standing by the steering oars at his back.

After the match in Hamburg he had thought that it was all over. And that he would never feel his blood bubbling like carbon dioxide again.

JULY 1977

The Volkspark stadium in Hamburg is reaching boiling point. When Börje arrives with Paris and his cutman, the second of the warm-up matches is already being fought. There's a howl from the audience in the vast sports arena. Someone has just been knocked out.

"Everything OK, son?," Paris asks while wrapping Börje's hands in the changing room.

Paris is good at this; he knows exactly how to do the wrappings to protect the delicate bones in the hand while not pulling them so tight you lose all feeling. He only has Paris and their German cutman with him. That's enough. Börje doesn't want a crowd of people babbling away and yelling advice at him.

Although Börje replies that he feels fine, his voice comes out of part of him he is only vaguely conscious of. He has gone deep inside himself.

He is afraid. But being afraid is part of it. Just as long as that feeling doesn't tip over and stop him being able to think.

He's excited as well. Longing to get into the ring. It really is the best place in the world. Better than a woman's bed. Better than a drunken binge that wraps the real world in cotton wool. The ring is a planet in another galaxy only a very few are allowed to visit. No-one else can even come close to understanding that feeling.

He has been training incredibly hard these last few months. He has been doing his runs as though his balls were being squeezed, running ten kilometres in less than forty minutes despite how much he weighs, up and down long staircases, along with sudden bursts of speed. Paris has conjured up a small army of left-handed boxers to spar with. They have managed to keep that under wraps by sparring at the crack of dawn and late at night. The boxers may have been doing it as a favour to Paris, but none of them wanted Big Ben to find out. They did the training at a small gym in the Bronx. "It's like you really do know everyone," Börje said to Paris. Paris shrugged and said: "I'm a nice guy. I've been a nice guy in this business for thirty years. It pays off."

The referee comes into the changing room to go through the rules. This is just a formality; no-one listens to what he says. There will be only ten rounds because this isn't a title fight.

Someone checks the wrapping and approves it with a cross on each hand. Paris ties his gloves on and then tapes them and this gets approved as well. Someone hangs a boxer's blue dressing gown around his shoulders.

Börje skips about, aiming a few punches at the air. He lets out some of the carbon dioxide bubbling inside him. Ice in your head, fire in your heart. Not the other way round.

José Luis Pérez, who beat him in the Catskills, had been expecting to fight a Brazilian boxer.

Paris happened to know that the Brazilian's wife was expecting their first child and the baby was due when the match in Hamburg was supposed to take place. The guy didn't want to travel. So Paris did a deal with the Brazilian and his manager. Then he pulled some strings and a week before the match, there was a message from Brazil that their boxer had torn a calf muscle during a training session and would be unable to attend. The match would not be cancelled though. There was a provision in the small print of the contract that the arranger had the right to replace the challenger with another boxer in the event of illness or death, his own or that of a family member. Three days before the match it was announced that the Brazilian's replacement would be Börje Ström.

On the other side of the Atlantic Big Ben O'Shaughnessy hit the roof. The suits had to work hard to earn their pay but the agreement stipulated a huge fine in the event of breach of contract and the West German promoter was unshakeable. Big Ben had to give in.

The papers leaped on the story. They wrote that the Swede was bound to be out for revenge, even though he obviously didn't have a chance. Börje didn't read any of them. There wasn't a single ticket left for the match.

Nancy bet half her savings on him, which made Börje ask her if she was mad. "You're going over there to win, aren't you?" she said. When he told Paris, the coach agreed: Börje was going to win.

"Just go into the ring and do your job, boy," Paris says. "You're ready."

Any nerves vanish the moment he enters the ring. This is war.

He performs his ritual. Presses his back against the ropes on all four sides and raises his fist in the air. Here I am.

Then he goes over to his corner and sits on the stool. Some boxers rest their arms on the ropes in that position, but Paris says that stops the blood circulating through them so Börje's hands remain in his lap.

José Luis Pérez comes in. Does his thing. Walks over to his corner.

Börje gives Paris a hug. The ref calls the boxers into the centre. Everyone else gets out of the ring. The stools are lifted out. Above them the floodlights shine down like the noonday sun. The audience, looming like mountains in shadow on all four sides, is hushed now.

"Touch gloves," the ref says and Börje taps his gloves against those of Pérez.

Then the gong sounds.

Pérez is taking things easier than Börje had been expecting. Presumably everyone around him has been saying you can beat the Swede easily: he hasn't fought a match since the Catskills, has he.

Though Pérez knows that it won't be any of those loudmouths fighting against Börje in the ring. It will be him and only him. And now he needs to find out what kind of opposition he is facing.

They test one another out over the first two rounds. Thanks to all that sparring with southpaws, blocking Pérez's long left arm comes completely naturally to Börje. He is fast about it and can then counter with his left and land a few dusters of his own. He feels calm when he goes back to his corner. He is breathing without any strain.

Pérez comes into the ring for the third round looking like Börje is a building he plans to raze to the ground. He plants his feet and pummels away with that horrendous left of his. But Börje has no intention of allowing him to stay where he is. He meets the jab straight on with his glove and sidesteps so Pérez has to move to the left, back foot first. Pérez is starting to look worried now. As though the building he had been planning to raze to the ground is about to collapse on top of him. Börje is forcing him to move his feet and keeps deflecting his jabs.

During the break before the fourth round the old-timers in the other corner start yelling advice. Presumably they are telling Pérez he needs to step to the right, front foot first. None of them can tell him how though.

The fourth and fifth rounds come and go. Pérez manages to make that right step from time to time and then his long left arm lashes out like a bolt gun, but he fails to put any combinations together because Börje is quick to jab his way out. And keep his eyebrows out of harm's way. Börje gets in several punches of his own. He peppers his opponent with combinations when Pérez opens up, he is often able to hit the other man's body with his right before landing two hooks to his head. Pérez has no idea how to break this pattern. He is taking punches and being forced to move away. It is making him tired.

In the sixth round Pérez's face is beginning to look like jam that hasn't set properly. He is losing control of his breathing and starts bearhugging Börje. The ref has to separate them but takes a bit too long about it. The public boos. Börje gets in a few hard blows to his body.

"Why doesn't he give him a warning?" Börje asks when he's sitting on his stool before the seventh round. "Has he been bought off?"

"You mustn't think like that, boy," Paris says and rinses Börje's mouth guard.

But that is what Börje is thinking about anyway. Big Ben would have been incredibly angry. Who knows what he might have come up with? Time's up for Sunday school, he decides.

Paris is telling him to breathe but his mind can't help getting in the way.

Not all matches are fought fair and square. It's not that uncommon for referees to award points to boxers from the same country as themselves. The refs are also dependent on powerful people in the business. Sometimes they take money from them. Match doctors will sometimes end a match over a ridiculous little cut in order to give the win to the opponent. The idea that Big Ben's tentacles reach as far as Europe comes as a shock to Börje. Though it's really not that unlikely.

In the other corner Pérez's coach has dropped his water bottle. The break gets extended by the time it takes to wipe the floor. It was obviously deliberate, to give Pérez a bit more time to recover. The audience is booing again.

"Don't leave your head in the corner of the ring," Paris says, pressing Börje's mouth guard in place.

Börje moves into round seven intending to have a go at Pérez's already badly bruised left eye. He is going to sink him. But Pérez is more alert after that little extra break. Fifteen seconds into the round Börje throws a right hook, it fails to connect, he steps backwards, Pérez tracking him like a dance partner. Börje throws a jab but Pérez left-dives in from above, shoving Börje's fist aside and now with Börje's head exposed, his right hand strikes like lightning. Börje's body just topples to the side and encounters Pérez's deadly left hook on its way to the canvas.

The next moment Börje finds himself blinking up at the suspended floodlights. But he can see the referee approaching from the side. The ref has to bend over Börje because the audience have got to their feet and are yelling as if they're in the Colosseum. The ref is counting; Börje can see fingers moving above him.

He gets to his feet on nine.

"Can you continue?" the ref asks.

Börje says yes in reply.

Pérez is waiting a couple of metres away to be allowed to charge at him; his corner is shrieking for the match to continue. But the ref waves a hand dismissively.

"Walk three paces forward and three paces back," he says.

Börje does it. And the match is on again.

Intent on tearing him to pieces, Pérez is all over him like a tornado. Börje ends up on the defensive. He's feeling a bit punch-drunk besides and twice he makes the same mistake of keeping his guard too close to his face, so when Pérez punches with all his might at his gloves Börje gets his own mitts in his mouth. But he survives, ducking very low and backing away, holding the tornado off. When the gong sounds he escapes back to his corner.

Börje takes his head with him into round eight. He keeps himself close to the ropes, parrying the rain of blows and letting Pérez wear himself out. A cannonball launched from Pérez's left misses completely and Börje can see his opponent grimacing. He realises the other man has hurt his shoulder.

Börje moves in. Pérez clinches with him and then has to take several short punches to his body which only tire him out further.

Börje is forcing Pérez onto the back foot and lands several really good combinations. Pérez's eyebrows begin to resemble two mountain chains in the red light of the setting sun.

When there are thirty seconds left of the round Börje can see coagulant running into Pérez's eyes. Pérez is blinking. Fatigue is making him drop his guard.

Börje lands a left hook on Pérez's jaw, his own feet are so firmly planted it is a miracle roots haven't burst through the cement foundation of the stadium. The blows come whirling out of the underworld. He follows up with a right to the solar plexus and then launches the decisive cannonball at Pérez's chin. His opponent's entire left side is paralysed and he collapses, his body twisting and bouncing off the ropes before hitting the canvas.

He doesn't get up. And the ref is quick to start the count.

Börje has won.

The audience are on their feet yelling their heads off. The ref raises Börje's hand. Paris and their cutman throw their arms around his sweaty body. Though Börje's heart doesn't start beating again until Pérez is back on his feet.

The two boxers embrace.

"Good match," Pérez says in Börje's ear. "Big Ben won't let me into the ring unless he knows I'm going to win. Title fights are what I want. This one, though. Great match."

Paris pats Pérez appreciatively on the shoulder. He may have tried to lock his boy during the first few rounds, but who remembers any of that now? And Pérez didn't try anything really dirty, like butting or rabbit-punching.

The ref comes into the changing room while Börje is on the bench getting a massage. He is talking to a few journalists who have been let into the inner sanctum.

"I saw he could follow me with his eyes while he was down," the ref says to the hacks who are frantically taking notes while flashes are going off. "One of his legs was raised. When someone's completely out of it their legs are flat to the floor. And he was able to move back and forth. They're going to give me hell for those extra seconds. But I wouldn't let a guy back into the fight if he's been on the floor unless he is physically and mentally capable of defending himself."

"And you must have been incredibly happy he didn't stop the fight?" one journalist asks Börje.

Börje laughs and says all he wanted was to get back up and maybe get hit some more.

The referee, the other officials and the journalists look at Börje as if he were a work of art in a museum.

Then they all congratulate him on his victory one more time before leaving. They snap a few last pictures from the doorway.

While Börje is getting dressed, Paris is on the phone to his wife. Even from the bench he is sitting on pulling on his socks, Börje can hear crying on the other end.

"What's the matter with her?" he asks when Paris has hung up.

"Eh," Paris grunts. "She was just relieved. I took out a loan on the house and bet the money on you. Don't look at me like that. You won, didn't you!"

The morning after the match Börje is doing a gentle run around the Volkspark before breakfast. The park is pretty big, and it would be easy to get lost because the paths turn into a maze among the birches and the fir trees. There is a graveyard inside, but no castle or imposing residences built for noblemen. This is a park created for the people.

It's a nice place to run. It smells better, almost like the forest. The air outside, in the city, is awful. The inside of your shirt collar turns black and you keep having to blow filth out of your nose. The canal is full of dead rats, and there's a terrible stench from the city's industries and the dye factory.

While his sore muscles are slowly warming up, he becomes aware of how much his body needs a period of recovery after all the hardcore training and the match itself.

He runs past a tennis court where a father, at least Börje got the feeling he was the father, is yelling at his son. The boy is eleven or thereabouts, his shoulders are hunched and his eyes are fixed on the ground. Börje is watching the scene from the path that runs alongside the court.

The father is red in the face. On the other side of the net is another father who is yelling as well, though he appears to be angry with the red-faced man. The second boy is standing beside him, his racket hanging from his hand like a plant that has been chopped. The ball has been abandoned on the court.

A bit further on he passes a group of children playing football. They are all ages and mostly boys. There are no adults present. Most of them are running like mad dogs in the direction the ball is currently headed. Hardly any of them are taking up strategic positions on the pitch. They are laughing and don't seem to care about things like corners or off-side; now and then the match and the fight for possession of the ball continue way outside the lines.

Börje comes to a stop and does his stretching against a large tree.

Two weeks ago he was nobody. Now the whole world is welcoming him with open arms.

He thinks about yesterday's match; it still feels like a golden ball of happiness inside him.

And yet he can't get rid of the feeling that this was it. He has to sit on a bench and have a think.

He has always loved boxing, he's never loved anything else. The feeling when you punch the bag in the gym. When the sweat pours down your body. When you're learning new things, drilling them over and over again until they are in your marrow. That feeling as you climb up into the ring and the ping-pong balls in your head stop bouncing around.

But there's just so much bullshit in the sport. Money rules. Bribes and match-fixing up to your eyeballs.

He is thinking about all the new guys who turn up at the gym with their heads full of dreams of success, or just for the money for food and lodging. Most of them will end up with nothing. Making a miserable living as punching bags.

When they are finally forced to retire from the ring they end up sweeping floors somewhere, shaking, trembling, stammering and having difficulty keeping a single thought in their heads. Börje has met his share of ex-boxers, both those who could have been someone and those who never would.

A few boxers can earn a great deal of money. They have no power all the same. Even Ali had to deal with all the crap. When he refused to be drafted into the Vietnam War, all of a sudden there wasn't a single arena in the whole of the United States he was allowed to fight in.

The sun climbs higher in the morning sky and its light filters through the leaves on the trees.

He cannot be part of this any longer. His love for boxing has gone. It actually died during the night while he was sleeping in his badly bruised body. He is grieving as though he were staring at a gravestone; he gets up from the bench and heads back to the hotel. It feels completely incomprehensible that none of what he is feeling can be seen. The guys who work at the hotel carrying bags and lifting them in and out of taxis are standing outside in their ill-fitting uniforms and hailing him as a winner. The girls at the reception desk do the same. "Great match!" they call.

He waves. Even though almost all of him feels dead.

After his shower he eats breakfast with Paris. In the dining room there is the usual mixture of men in suits, middle-aged couples and a few families with children eating piles of pancakes with cream and jam.

Paris listens to him without interrupting.

"Maybe you should think about this for a bit," he says when Börje has finished.

"You're right," Börje says.

But the decision has become a great weight inside him, like an anchor he will never have the strength to haul back up from the bottom.

The newspapers are open on the table. Börje with his fist in the air and the headlines. The hacks seem to have forgotten all the scorn they heaped on him as well as the stuff they wrote about the match in the Catskills being fixed.

He books a flight to Sweden. The money he earned from the match is enough for the down payment on a small block of flats in Älvsbyn. He gets courted, of course, by the local boxing club who can barely believe their good fortune. And with a bit of help from the guys in the village he learns how to fix the plumbing and repair the roof. A bit of everything. He ends up staying there.

The Torne river has its source in the area around Unna Allakas and Sjangeli, southwest of its seventy-kilometre-long mother lake: the Torneträsk. Our lords and masters have long desired to control it. There are blueprints and plans biding their time in the archives of the power companies. But the river still runs wild and free.

Börje and Ragnhild slid into Talvimaselet, heading for Pauranki. The rapids were hidden behind a bend. They couldn't see them yet. But Ragnhild told him it was time to double-check the cords on his life jacket and the fit of his helmet.

Börje could feel a tingle inside, but still had no idea what he had to be nervous about.

Then they rounded the bend and the rapids were in front of them.

At first Börje couldn't grasp what was staring back at him. Straight ahead at eye level he could see the tops of fir trees.

That's the height of the drop, he realised a moment later. Christ Almighty, we're going over a precipice.

He was gripping the paddle so hard his knuckles turned white.

Ragnhild told him to paddle hard. They had to move faster than the river or they would lose any ability to steer in the rapids.

Ragnhild was rowing one oar forwards and the other one back. She was doing her utmost to keep the prow to the right of centre, her eyes scanning the water to find the clear channel, the course they had to stick to.

The river's too high, Börje thought. Too much meltwater from the mountains.

The drag against the base of the rubber boat was increasing. Foaming white water was rising in front of him. There was no going back now. There was no way out of the current that led straight into the rapids.

The next moment they were in Niskapauranki, the neck of the rapids. And they were headed straight into their frothing jaws.

"Backwards!" Ragnhild yelled.

He could barely hear her over the roar of the cascading water. He was sitting right on the edge of the boat, paddling so hard his muscles were on fire.

They fought to keep left and on track with the correct fall line. The water was whipped into white spray all around them.

They had the whirlpool, the Japanese eddy, on their right now. A powerful eddy that got its name from a tourist who had stood up to take a photo then and there.

"This whirlpool is dangerous," Ragnhild had explained. "We have to keep away from it while threading a way through this narrow passage." And then she had told him about a rafting friend of hers who had drowned in an eddy much like this one. He had been forced down to the bottom. There wasn't enough buoyancy in the life jacket to keep him afloat. His father had stayed by the rapids for ten days until the body was finally flung out and up to the surface.

It was touch and go. Fear felt like an iron band around his ribs. At the very last moment, just as they were passing the whirlpool, Ragnhild yanked up the oars to stop the right one being snapped like a twig. They were holding on to the handles along the side of the boat like grim death.

The prow lifted, the boat reared. They had lashed the luggage to the very front to weigh it down. Börje had time to imagine being hurled off the raft as it tipped onto its right edge and flipped, ending up on top of him while he was trapped beneath it.

The water from the bottom of the eddy was jetting into the air. Foaming waves were crashing over them and the boat felt like a toothpick.

And then they were past the whirlpool. Time to get paddling again. Ragnhild screamed "Päälle vain!" over the thunder, urging them on. They did a ferry glide, fending off the sharp rocks that threatened to tear the raft to pieces as they slalomed between them.

Everything was happening so quickly but then the current weakened. The rapids were behind them.

A stretch of smooth water spread out before them.

Börje looked back: he knew the rapids were two kilometres long. How was that possible? Surely only a few seconds had elapsed?

He looked at Ragnhild, a soaking-wet queen on the oars.

They broke into exhilarated laughter. Let the boat drift. Their arms and legs were shaking with exhaustion. They barely had the strength to wipe the sweat from their eyes. She pointed out the chalet of the bait-casting club on the southern bank.

Börje was amazed by what he could sense in his body. Once the beating of his heart had calmed down. Stillness and joy. Not unlike after a match.

He had never been a man who thought about things to any great extent. Though every now and then he had imagined what his life would have been like if he had returned to the US. Continued to box.

All the lives you hadn't lived because of choices great and small.

But here he is with her. On the way to her island.

Ragnhild's eyes roam along the riverbank. Osiers, silvery green along the shore. The yellow noses of marsh marigolds turned towards the sun. There is mixed forest on the northern bank, the dull green coat-tails of the fir trees trailing in the water. The rigid columns of pines and their secret alliance with the mushrooms beneath the soil.

They pass the pole that marks the limit of cultivation. They will be in Pirtilahti soon, where she is going to row them ashore. They need to light a fire and put on dry clothes.

In two days they will be on the island. This summer she is going to repair the roof with Börje's help. He said he was good with his hands. To which she replied with a grin that the truth of that remained to be seen, though she was pretty sure she could find some use for them.

The snow bridge has melted but it will always remain an option among all the other possibilities.

But if I get to live like this, she thinks. And to row like my life depends on it in white water every now and then. Letting Villa run free on the island. Working with my body to restore the farm. Then I'd like to stay on for a bit.

Börje gets out his phone, carefully wrapped inside a freezer bag wrapped inside another. He takes pictures and sends them to Nyrkin-Jussi and Sisu-Sikke. To his daughter as well, she guesses.

Somewhere else entirely Paula is getting on with her life. With her husband and the children Ragnhild has never met. She can see Paula in her mind's eye: shopping, paying bills and picking up toys off the floor.

That loss is a dark and bottomless pit in her heart. She doesn't know if she can live with the neverness of it. Before long though spicy bog myrtle will be flowering in the forest. Followed by the sweet bells of twinflower like whispers among the moss. The bilberries will ripen and she will pick them straight from the twig and stuff them in her mouth.

I am going to do that at least one more time, she thinks.

She is longing for the scent of resin the sun-warmed old pines on the island give off. They were gangly youths when Queen Christina abdicated. She is looking forward to meeting them again.

She is going to wash *Äiti*'s rag rugs. If she can find any that can be saved, any that haven't been worn down to the warp, she is going to scrub them on the jetty until the muscles of her back are burning.

Then the first thin layer of ice will form like glass across the river. Snow will start to fall. Though far below the river will go on flowing.

And then I will have to see, she thinks. One moment at a time.

She smiles at Börje. There's nothing certain about him either. They are still in the falling in love stage. What happens when the everyday world returns, when the dopamine, noradrenaline and serotonin leave the body? They're going to find out, aren't they.

He is smiling at her now though. Carefree. The sun on his face.

She smiles back and asks:

"Coffee and a sandwich?"

ACKNOWLEDGEMENTS

So goodbye, Rebecka Martinsson. I created you and in the process you created me. You provided a livelihood for the children and me. You led to friendships and new experiences I could never have dreamed of when I started writing about you.

I find it difficult to believe how sad I feel now we are saying goodbye. Thank you for our time together, Rebecka. Thank you for your stubbornness. For refusing to let go even when I made things so hard for you. Your pigheadedness has been both your strength and weakness and I really like your awkwardness and how abrasive you are, your conscientiousness, the way you care for dogs and old men and your ability to have profound relationships and a pretty good life even though you felt so broken. Life entails loss. But it can still work out.

My thanks go to Maria Ernestam and Nina Skårpa, who read the manuscript at an early stage. I also thank everyone with whom I have discussed petechial haemorrhages, the nursing profession, elks and pussy willows, boxing, the policing profession, sex workers, mopeds, guns, mining, grief and loss, love and sex, being a tall woman, God, avalanches . . . and whatever else. You know who you are.

All mistakes are my own. I misunderstand things and putting lies together to make stories is my profession. A lot of it is true though: like the fact that corruption in the construction industry costs Swedish society between 83 and 111 billion kronor a year. That bears thinking about.

Thank you to my Swedish publisher Eva Bonnier, my editor Rachel Åkerstedt and everyone else at Albert Bonniers förlag. Thank you to public relations and communications consultant Anna Tillgren. Thank you to everyone at the Ahlander Agency.

A very deeply felt thank you to my English translator Frank Perry, meticulous and devoted, like the best older brother this novel could have had. Thanks to Katharina Bielenberg and everyone at MacLehose Press.

And a thank you to Lena Callne. Many years ago I was interviewed by her on the radio. There was a boxer in the recording studio as well: Pasi Haapala. He had a lot of tattoos. "If you were going to write a book about Pasi," Lena Callne asked, "What would it be about?"

Thanks to my family (dogs included). I am making my way home now on these tired old legs.

ÅSA LARSSON was born and grew up in Kiruna, Sweden, and qualified as a lawyer. She made her debut in 2003 with *The Savage Altar*, which was awarded the Swedish Crime Writers' Association prize for best debut novel. Its sequel, *The Blood Spilt*, was chosen as Best Swedish Crime Novel of 2004, as was *The Second Deadly Sin* in 2011. Her novels were adapted for television and shown on More 4. The sixth and final book in the Rebecka Martinsson series, *The Sins of Our Fathers*, was named Best Crime Novel of the Year by the Swedish Crime Writers' Academy and was the winner of the Adlibris Award and the Storytel Award for Best Suspense Novel of 2021.

FRANK PERRY's translations have won the Swedish Academy Prize for the introduction of Swedish literature abroad and the prize of the Writers' Guild of Sweden for drama translation. His recent work includes novels by Caterina Pascual Söderbaum and Lina Wolff, for whose novel *Bret Easton Ellis and the Other Dogs* he was the 2017 winner of the Oxford-Weidenfeld Prize, and was awarded the triennial Bernard Shaw Prize for best literary translation from Swedish.